Vimy Ridge   A Box Full o

Vimy Ridge   A Box Full of Tears is a work of fiction. Any reference to historical events, real people, living, or dead, or to real towns, places, and organizations are intended only to give fiction a setting in historical reality. Other names, characters, and incidents are either the product of the author's imagination or are used fictionally, their resemblance, if any, to real-life counterparts is entirely coincidental.

   I chose Lac La Biche and Saddle Lake as the geographical centres for this novel because it was in these warm and accepting communities that I first became fascinated with the Canadian indigenous nations that were so much of our country even before Canada was formed. I make no claim to be an expert on First Nations cultures, tribal traditions, or family practices; neither do I hide my aspirations that future generations of Canadians will work hard to bring them in from the cold.

I sincerely trust that my First Nations readers, hopefully from all across this great land of ours, will forgive any errors or misconceptions that came from my hand as I was writing this book. I want to leave you with the sense that my support, my heart, and my hopes are with you as you continue your struggles to achieve the goals and aspirations of the Truth and Reconciliation Commission. Please consider this novel to be a tribute to your resilience and patience. In my heart of hearts, I truly hope that in some small way this book can help non First Nations citizens understand the depth of the darkness in which our Residential School systems placed your culture and all families and children that lived with it and were part of it

I would be remiss not to mention and remind all of my readers to remember and hold near to you in your memories each and every soldier that served with the 49th Battalion, (Edmonton Regiment), CEF; 51st Battalion, (Edmonton), CEF and the 63rd Battalion, (Edmonton), CEF. Brave men from the Edmonton area that gave their all that we might have so much. Askuwheteau would have been proud to serve with such fine men.

My twin brother Robert and I wish to remember Lawrence, Eleanor, and Russell, three beautiful, young, full blood Cree children that shared our home and hearts as wards of the Alberta Child Welfare system for three years on our farm at Sandholm, Alberta. Wonderful memories linger.

Dedication

This novel is dedicated to two almost diametrically opposed forces of energy, one imagined and one very real. The first is a nostalgic optimism, which allows me to believe there is a place for the idea of Askuwheteau somewhere in our society.

For every hour and every day I spent writing this novel I doggedly stuck to the premise that every culture, every free and intelligent mind, every living room library, should have room for a mythical and even magical thunderbird. As you will see, the Askuwheteau of my legend had the obligation of keeping watch, with compassion and diligence, over our shared earth. I sincerely hope, although his eyes and spirit were filled with tears from his experience at Vimy Ridge, that your imagination and my words will leave you with hopefulness that Askuwheteau managed to return to his commitment.

And last but not least, I dedicate this work of fiction to my friend and editor, Major General (Ret'd) Dave Wightman, CMM, CD.

So then, first a toast to Askuwheteau wherever he may be today. I wish him peace and tranquillity, as these were the original aspirations Manitou had imagined for him.

To Dave Wightman, you have remained true to the Test Pilot's creed, "Knowledge is Power". Nothing I can say or do will ever repay you for your hard work, instruction, and craft. Knowing you are on my team has kept me airborne through the journey of writing and publishing this and my other two novels.

A Historical Reminder:

You would know, in 1763 in the vast territory which over a hundred years later was to become Canada, agents and officers representing the Imperial Crown of Great Britain entered into a bilateral treaty with signatories from the First Nations. This treaty and those that followed obliged the Imperial Crown to deal directly with the First Nations, each as their own governing entity, in respect and recognition of the political structures and authorities of each of the First Nations governments.

The original treaty pledged no discussions on changing or introducing new treaties could proceed which deviated from or diminished the bilateral nation-to-nation relationship established and agreed to within the spirit of the first treaty.

This act, by our then Crown representatives, was to obligate and commit the future nation of Canada to a lasting and significant recognition of their responsibilities and relationships with the people of our First Nations.

It may be said; they who forget the place from which they started may follow a path of great sorrow as they journey forward through the seasons of this earth. So how did we get to where we are today in matters of state as they pertain to our First Nations? Well, frankly, many of the actions taken by Canadian authorities on behalf of the Government of Canada as they relate to our First Nations, have been, over the intervening years, introduced piece meal, haphazardly and often biased towards providing better governmental administration rather than better lives and amenities for the First Nations. The end result is that years of opportunity have slipped by without Canada realizing the incredible possibilities the First Nations are capable of achieving.

It is a sad but honest fact that many of our First Nations governments or tribes are even less well off today then they were when only Manitou smiled down on them. Frankly, I find it incredible that this wonderful, resource-wealthy and socially advanced country called Canada could have come so far over the past one hundred and fifty years and not have had the foresight and political consciousness to reach out, take our First Nations brothers and sisters by the hand, and invite them to play their rightful part in our historical journey as we became one of the leading G7 nations. Our failure to listen and act on our First Nations' call for movement towards sovereignty, reconciliation, and acceptance by and in Canadian society is not a problem that can be allocated solely to successive political governments and agencies. Although governments have ruled our House and Senate since Confederation and must therefore share fair measure of blame for their accumulative inaction, political expedience, and precipitous neglect, we, the Canadian public should also have demanded more from our political representatives and from ourselves in order to reach out to the First Peoples of Canada. Surely our political masters and we as citizens of this beautiful nation can do better in the next one hundred and fifty years.

The Legend of Askuwheteau

"Our legends speak to us of when everything we know today was not yet created. In our language we say this was 'mayes' or 'pamayes', you might say it was 'before time began'. We also know that even before time began there was Manitou.

The Great Spirit Manitou is not known as being either male or female; perhaps it is both and like a boundless marriage between a husband and a wife they live in peace inside the Creator's greatness. We, the First Nations, do not pretend to know what form The Spirit takes on our earth. Instead we believe Manitou is so strong and wise 'He and She' can appear to be and do whatever it wishes.

When our people speak of Manitou we admit there are many powers and qualities we do not know and cannot understand. What we do believe though is that one of the very first things Manitou did on this earth was to put in place a sense of time. From the very beginning of our earth there has been time. It is time that records the seasons, every day's events, the births, and deaths of each of us. And so it is said for everything there is a time; a time for everything that has a need to begin or end.

Then, first amongst the many countless things Manitou created, were the moon and the stars to fill the sky. We say this was done so when mankind looks up into the sky at night we are filled with wonder. For as long as we the First Nations have had legends, we have believed that of all the things Manitou created, we his people are the only living things given the gift of wonder.

Of all the stars, the Creator made the Sun the most beautiful. To the Sun was given light that there might be day; to the Moon, the night was given. After all the sky and everything in it were created and light was separated from the dark, Manitou reached out to shape the earth and put everything alive upon it. In the waters Manitou created wonders to serve our curiosity and on the land a million animals and crawling things were placed so our hunger and earthly needs might be met.

Next, the Great One fashioned the seasons so there might be time and beauty for everything on earth. First came the season we know as spring. To spring was given a warming sun. Manitou gave us spring so there would be a time for new growth in the silent forests. Manitou made spring to be a time when young women's eyes would see love as the way to fill their hearts with children yet unborn.

Summer follows spring. Summer is a time for the soft, bee filled days, when a fawn might grow strong and stand proudly beside its mother. Summer offers the sultry scents of sun filled forests. Summer nights are for sleeping beneath the canopy of the sky so our people could marvel at the size of Manitou's imagination.

Autumn follows summer. Autumn is a time of change; autumn is a cooling and refreshing pause. Autumn is when the trees might wear the reds and yellows of fire in their leaves and yet have no fear of being consumed. Autumn is the time for gathering wood, furs, and food into our lodges so our families can sleep warmly and happily through the long nights that bring the lights, which dance, across our skies.

Lastly Manitou imagined wintertime. This is the season when the fox can walk upon frozen rivers and snow covered lakes. Winter allows the children of our villages to share the gift of their laughter. It is a time when the weak and the old return to Manitou and the earth can rest before the blushing face of spring makes water flow again into the rivers.

For many cycles of seasons, the Creator smiled over earth and its waters and was delighted.

One day, when the sun was in the highest part of the sky, Manitou looked hard upon the earth and knew something was missing. The earth required a living thing that could recognize the Creators achievements and find happiness with them. It was on that day the great and mighty Manitou made the Cree people.

The Ojibwa, whose ancestors are called the Anishinabeg, or First People, refer to the Cree as Kinistenoog, 'They Who Were First'. Manitou gave the Cree, the first of his people, the wisdom to grow and live in peace with nature. Using this wisdom, we learned to take from the earth only those things we needed so that we might continue to live.

Only then, after we had shown that our peoples respected and cherished the earth, Manitou created many other races of people in the hope they might also exist in peace with what the Great Creator had given them.

For many thousands of earth cycles, our people prospered. Our language was heard across the prairie flat lands filled with buffalo.

_____
_____

The laughter of our children was heard in the mountain forests and as far to the east as the land of many lakes where our sun rises every morning. Manitou continued to approve of and was happy when our peoples lived with and remembered their traditions. Manitou saw through our eyes as rivers grew from the ice fields and their waters carved their paths as they learned to spill into the oceans.

Content with the earth and our people, the Abundant Creator turned to make other worlds in other skies. But for the time that Manitou's eyes would be elsewhere, a powerful and mighty eagle was summoned to be the eyes of the Great One. Manitou named this eagle Askuwheteau, *'He Keeps Watch'*.

Every day, as he had been requested, Askuwheteau flew from the first sign of light until the last colour of the sun had fled the sky. He witnessed our peoples as they multiplied and prospered. He kept watch as our Nations grew and moved through the forests into the plains. He observed and was pleased when our fathers' fathers learned from the muskrats and toiling beavers; they taught our elders and our elder's children how to build strong homes. We learned to weave with wood so our lodges stood against the weight of winter's snow and summer's winds. Askuwheteau watched Cree women birth our children and he showed us how to fish in the deep waters of our lakes. The earth was pleased and Manitou remained content with the Cree peoples for winters into winters beyond our memories' measure.

As our numbers grew and our tribes flourished our hunting and our laughter took us west as we followed the richness given to us by the buffalo. The buffalo, in their millions fed us and gave us warmth in our winters. We became more than we could be because the buffalo prospered on the richness Manitou provided.

Our people, taking their language and their customs with them, followed the buffalo west. On reaching the purple rocks with snow upon their heads our people looked up at them from foothills and were happy. It is there we ceased our searching for new lands. For as long as the buffalo and Wapiti have lived, the beautiful eyes of our children have watched the faces of the mountains change in every season. Our tongue was heard from the eastern edge of the mist where the sun first starts its daily journey and it was our words you would hear in the land where the sun sleeps. We were known from the mountains to the farthest seas as the 'Algonquian' and everywhere we lived our tongue was spoken. In Cree and in Algonquian we shared the stories of our people's life on this earth. We lived in peace with the land and Manitou was in peace with us.

After many seasons, Manitou spoke again to Askuwheteau and told him he could rest. In thankfulness, the Creator prepared a box of the hardest and sweetest woods and filled it with marvellous things to see and eat. In the box was placed a great nest where Askuwheteau might rest until some future time when he might be asked to fly again. Askuwheteau went into the box and for ten thousand seasons he dreamed soft dreams, listened for the call of Manitou, and rested. These were the silent years when moccasins and the villages of my people left no marks upon the face of the earth.

But things began to change on our silent land. The White Man came; he came slowly at first. Word of his being amongst us spread from one village to the next until many fears were born from the wind of our wagging tongues. White Man came without his women so we shared ours.

He arrived from the sea and he carried iron sticks. Sticks that were filled with fire that made thunder and killed animals and people without touching them. He came with long knives and iron pots. He appeared with his horse and his strange cloth. He spoke with a strange tongue, which we learned to speak.

In the beginning of those days White Man dwelled with us and learned to live the way we lived. But soon more of his people came to us from where they lived across the great salt water that does not rest. They came in the bellies of boats piled high with wings; wings of cloth that caught and held the wind. Slowly but surely they made our tongues wag with envy. Rifles and leather, wool and axes made from iron. They had pictures drawn on paper and the mysteries of making things from wood and stone. Later they brought their steel rails and iron horses. They brought their women and their children. They left our villages of deer skin and built houses made of wood. Where we had carved paths through forests they built the roads and streets filled with mud that held their villages together.

We shook our heads in wonder as they planted fields of corn; everywhere there was the smell of wood and coal fires. They burnt our forests and made fields of wheat grow where our Buffalo had raised their calves. The fires of their villages made our brown eyes red with the smoke of burning trees and the hard black coal they dug from our earth. If we quarrelled with them then they killed our warriors and took our land and our lakes. Their long knives and fire sticks were so powerful our warriors were like mosquitoes before them.

But it was neither their swords nor their rifles that changed the custom and direction of our ways. White Man brought into our circles a powerful new poison he called whiskey.

They gave us this strange new water that tasted like fire. Whiskey made our people senseless. They offered us blankets that covered us with new and horrible infections. Our people sickening from their desire for more and more whiskey and our women and our children died from infections we had never seen. Neither Manitou nor our medicine men could protect us from the kindness of the white man's gifts.

In our lands, entire communities were overcome with bad health; our people died in their tents. When our elders turned to Manitou to seek help white men and women dressed in black robes told us there was a more powerful Great One. They told us to turn our backs on the only Spirit we knew. They said there was only one true God and that He burned in bushes. They called us heathens, said we must turn to their God or we would be consumed by fire, and have no peace for as long as the sun did shine.

It was then Manitou reopened the box and summoned Askuwheteau once again. Askuwheteau was asked to fly and watch over our lands and return to speak of what he had seen. For many days, the great Thunderbird flew over all of the beautiful and different parts of the world we shared and lived in. When Askuwheteau returned, tears blinded his eyes, it is said that he could not speak. It was thought the changes Askuwheteau had seen had broken his strong heart.   Legend tells us Askuwheteau never spoke again. When he perished Manitou gently lifted 'He Keeps Watch' and returned him once again into the great wooden box so that he might rest there forever.

Now, it is said, although the box remains, it is only filled with tears. It is "A box full of tears".

* * *

Author's note: *I imagined and wrote this so called 'Legend' in order for me to develop the story line, and hopefully, allow you the reader to live within the world of Askuwheteau. There are many amazing true Cree Legends that have been passed down through the ages from one wise elder to the waiting ears and minds of those that followed. This Legend is not one of them.*

Beginning Near the End

I could feel waiting eyes following me as I obeyed signs pointing to 'Walking Wounded Report Here'. A man, deeply sheathed in an expensive looking wool coat, had pushed his way forward and stood in my way. There was something in his manner and dress that set him apart from the others in the railway station waiting room. He wore a dark, stylish homburg hat, which had acquired of late, considerable admiration amongst the well heeled of Europe. His skin was pale and shallow like someone who spent little time outdoors. In his hands he carried a large camera and a notebook; a nameplate pinned on his collar said, 'Edmonton Bulletin'.

"You look like an Indian", he said, suddenly realizing I might not be one of the white soldiers he had been waiting for. "Are you an Indian? Where are you from? What unit are you from"?

He was aggressively standing in my way, blocking my advance; I could feel my own bile mounting to the occasion.

I turned slightly, pushing out a little with my right hand in an attempt to go around him.

"Wait"! He exclaimed, almost as an order. He turned as I had turned; there was no way through or around him without being equally rude and assertive.

The crowd began slowly to push forward; some of the stretchers were being unloaded. These were ordinary people, mothers and fathers, sisters and brothers, and maybe friends awaiting the arrival of a loved one.

Their clothes and manner reflected what Edmonton was, a working city with a widely mixed cultural base of recently arrived immigrants from Europe and Great Britain. The curious struggled for a look; waiting families pushed to find the heart they had been waiting for.

I ended my attempt to continue and turned to face him. My initial impulse had been to simply melt away into the stream of returning wounded, to remain hidden by the sameness of our uniforms and medical dressings. This was stopped by his persistence; I reasoned, he has a job to do; I was resolved to stay polite and accommodating. He might have the very best of intentions.

We soldiers were a news item, not one that happened every day I supposed. I sought his eyes, trying to establish contact, a rapport. He was scanning the crowd, his attention drawn towards bigger game than the one he had trapped behind his bulky frame and aggressive stance. He had cold, ice blue eyes that instantly expressed the surging energy of a man with a short time frame to capture what he wanted and then to move on to some other part he had to play.

"Do you really care who I am or are you just here for a story"?

It had taken only a few seconds before I finally realized he did not care who we were or why we were on that train; to him wounded soldiers only represented an opportunity for a headline, a few lines in tomorrow's paper, nothing more. I was having difficulty keeping my tone unemotional and frank.

"I am from here; I was born in Edmonton". His eyes never even wavered from the task he had assigned them which was to locate someone with a face that might better match his intended article. After all, an interview with a white man would appeal to more of his readership.

Undaunted I continued,

"I enlisted in Edmonton and if I have any real family left they are here in Edmonton. What do you want to know? How was the war? Where was I wounded? How long did it take the ship to cross the Atlantic? What do you want to know"?

The other walking wounded were starting to push past us, medical staffs that had awaited our arrival assisted some. A few soldiers had joined hearts with families who had found them from amongst the many. The journalist's eyes were busy as he followed the line searching faces for a story he could get past the editor.

"No", he said, without even looking at me,
"I was looking for someone else, an Englishman or at least a white man".

He made no effort whatsoever to hide or disguise the cultural contempt in his voice. Now it was his turn to attempt to push away from me, to find a new vantage point not soiled by my presence.

I had tried hard to anticipate my coming home. The home I was coming to had changed but then again, so had I. The army provided me with an arena in which I had learned a lot about myself and even more about the world I lived in. I had come home with a sort of confidence; I had paid my dues; I anticipated the world would accept me for who I was. I was convinced that on arrival Edmonton would look deeper than my ethnic origin.

I understood completely that no one would be there to meet me and yet I held a strong hope that everyone would show a general acceptance for what we all, as a group, represented.

We were Canadians. All of us were returning wounded from one of the greatest battlefields of the war. Surely, I thought, our being together in one place, all wearing the same uniform, some still shielded by their bandages, would mark us as equals amongst equals.

I could no longer swallow the resentment I felt. I pushed my chin into his face with a firmness and resolve he could not ignore.

"My grandfather was an English man who called himself a gentleman".

Contempt had crept into my voice as I struggled to contain my rush of anger.

"Some gentleman! He got my grandmother pregnant and abandoned her and his new borne child in Lac La Biche. My father was a white man from this very city. He wasn't a gentleman either, he abandoned my mother when she was pregnant and carrying me".

My raising voice was starting to push on his arrogance. He was taking carefully measured, short steps, reversing towards the gathered crowd.

My words continued to flow. I was not yet ready to let him slip away from a history lesson about my ancestral past.

"He left my mother without money or hope. I am told he bragged about selling my mother to his white man friends before he drank himself to death. I am a half-breed soldier returning home wounded from the battle of Vimy Ridge. I may be the first man from my family that did not abandon anybody, not even Canada, when they needed my help. Why don't you write a story about that"?

The journalist was a big man with the soft hands of a lady and the hard eyes of a cynic. There was arrogance in his manner that reached out like an unprovoked slap in the face.

Roughly, he put his hand on my hand pulling it away from his coat front. He leaned forward so that his hiss and hatred could be close enough to scar my memory.

"Listen", he derided, spitting his words back at me,

"No one wants to read a story about a fucking wounded Indian no matter where you are from or what your grandfather might have done".

I stepped back in utter revulsion; he pulled his camera closer to his body and turned into the crowd. I stood in shock staring at his disappearing back. It took a moment for my anger to ebb away. The anger was quickly replaced by a crushing realization of just how alone and isolated I was.

I was not a returning soldier like all the rest of the soldiers here were. I stood surrounded by fellow wounded Canadian soldiers and the faces of their Canadian families but I had returned as a wounded Indian. These fellow passengers were strangers now that we were here on the railroad station platform. My service to and for Canada had changed nothing. They were white Canadian soldiers I was just a half-breed.

Like a sailboat I once watched as it had lost its way on the River Thames, I lost the wind that had driven my hopes. I had lost the energy of purpose, which had lain sheltered in my soul. My eyes filled with tears; my heart swam in the panic of despair. I could no longer see clearly enough to read the signs I had been following. It was then, as if the Mighty One had touched me, I saw the truth.

* * *

I departed England as I had arrived, on a ship without sails. In my going to and my coming from England, both ships had been filled, in part, by hundreds of Canadian soldiers. On the voyage over, from Quebec City to Portsmouth, the soldiers had been young, whole, and filled with the wonder youth imparts to those who cannot know the future.

The returning ship had been filled with passageways of red crosses and broken soldiers with damaged bodies and shattered spirits. Many of them had been washed in and stained by the despair and anguish brought about by the intimate knowledge one acquires when introduced to hell incarnate. So powerful had been the pain experienced in our recent past that many of us struggled to face what we might find in the future. A few had hope; a few had family support and the resources through which one could imagine returning to some sense of normalcy. But on the other end of the scale, some of us were so shattered that even medicine and a loving family could not offer licence to hold such hope.

Yet, in the middle of the scale, a number of soldiers, myself included, had nothing else to cling to except our strength of imagination and courage. Almost two years before I had travelled by train from Edmonton to Valcartier and then to Quebec City. Those had been soldier filled trains spreading hot coals and steamy expectations of adventure all along the steel ribbon that bound Canada together as a nation. Now, in late December of 1917, I was returning to Edmonton in a train filled with wounded and damaged men. The lucky ones were those in bandages and dressings. The most tragic of the travellers were those with shattered minds. But who was I to rank the severity of physical or mental wounds; all of us had suffered more than we had even imagined could befall us.

Edmonton would not greet this train with banners or bands. The Mayor had not written, nor would he deliver a speech with words about the glory of victory. There would be no flags on poles or the happy feet of children running to meet the brother or father long missed in households filled with fearful hearts. No, none of that for this train. This train was a hospital train from Halifax. Nurses, doctors, and families with heavy hearts met hospital trains, waiting to learn how the wounds we soldiers bore would change their lives.

Nearly all of the joy that one can expect to feel on returning to the waiting arms of family had already been crushed, shredded, and drowned in the ink and paper exchanged many months before. The Army had long since sent telegrams to advise family members of the imminent arrival of their son or husband or loved one. Mothers and fathers, sisters and wives, knew it was a hospital train; some would have even known the extent of injuries that their soldier had experienced. Some of these soldiers, not unlike myself, had been in the medical chain for some time. In many cases months had passed since the soldier had been wounded on some far away battlefield. Human bodies cannot be repaired like a leaking roof or a broken wheel on a Model A.

Letters had been exchanged but the truth of the physical or mental damage had to wait to be discovered at this meeting. Those that waited were much like the soldiers arriving; both sides knew only the edges of future reality. A slim few of those arriving could continue to hope and pray for a chance to return to the societies and families they had left behind when they first committed their lives in the service of Canada.

The majority of those waiting for the train were respectfully and quietly anticipating their loved one to be carried or assisted from the hospital cars. Both those on the train and those that waited were gripped by a silent, fearful, and powerful anticipation.

Meeting us, there had been a sizeable crowd of people at the Canadian National Railroad station as our train pulled in. The train stopped; the engine sat lifting her skirts of steam to show the power and beauty of her design. A voice said we could disembark. I had stepped into a commotion of words from the crowd. Silent eddies of steam from the engine and the gathering darkness of an early Alberta winter were two of my accompanying headless horsemen.

I felt somewhat alone amongst hundreds of other soldiers and unassisted, as I had been on my departure. I was returning to the place I had departed from almost two years before. It seemed that everything I knew then, everything I had been then, had changed. The man who was returning was not the same man who had departed. The war had changed not only who I was but also what I was. I had left Canada believing there was a heaven and on my return I knew, beyond question, there was only a hell. And even at the very beginning of this story, I must confess that it is so because I have no proof of the former but I had unquestionably been a witness of the latter.

The truth was grandmother had been right all along. My grandmother knew when she told me I was the 'Askuwheteau'. Grandmother's words reminded me Manitou had given her a sign, a sign which had retold I would go out into the world again. I would go out and see with my own eyes; I would see the world as it was and only then, through my eyes, could the Creator know the way the world had changed.

I had gone out alone just as the Askuwheteau had gone out. I had walked from Saddle Lake to Edmonton. I had seen, first hand, the way the white man lived. I had seen the troubles my people subsisted with in Whiteman's villages. I had seen how the residential schools had taken away our native cultures and how alcohol had changed the way our people respected themselves and their families. I had joined the Canadian Expeditionary Force as a soldier and I had worked hard to become like all of the hundreds of thousands of serving white men.

I had learned that becoming a soldier does not change who you were before you enlisted nor does it make you special when you take off your uniform. I learned that my service was something that I could be proud of, a feeling that would never end. I was beginning to see that service to your country feels a little like the feeling a man might have for a woman he loves and honours. I also learned my past and my aboriginal heritage had left its indelible brand upon my very soul. These were things that would remain with me forever just as my fear of a sniper's bullet would also remain. I had ridden on the great steel rail across Canada and had seen a thousand villages and rivers that did not have Cree names. My journey as a soldier had made me understand that neither Lac La Biche nor Saddle Lake were the center of the universe. It had, however, made me better understand that the Nation of Cree People was one of the many great nations, which Manitou had created.   It was then, as the journalist disappeared into the crowd that I started to feel the entirety of what I lived through over the two years I had been away. I had lived with and watched the white soldiers in their army camps. I had become one of them. I had eaten what they ate and I had dressed as they dressed. I had trained with them and had become a soldier with them.

Together with the white soldiers, we had laughed and sung and shouldered our way into Quebec City. The sounds of our heels marching together up long streets and into the waiting dockyards made large crowds cheer our youth; so sure we were of victory. Together as brothers in uniform we had sailed on ships without sails. Ships that carried us to England where we learned to live with death. From army camps in England filled to overflowing, we Canadians had sailed again, across the English Channel. There, for days and days my mind was driven to watch a kind of hell that only Manitou could understand. I watched hundreds of my new friends die in the agony they called The Somme. And like Askuwheteau had flown before me, I had flown above the fields of Europe. I saw the battlefields as Askuwheteau had seen them; battlefields that were being twisted, broken, smashed and tossed by nations of white men, some now buried in those self same fields.

I had seen with my own eyes the death and destruction war had brought to European people and their villages. Indescribable muddle and confusion, individual bravery and self sacrifice, all of these things had marched past my eyes and while watching I had learned to thank God that the life that I was living was still better than that of the local people. I was free to slink my way to some other kind of hell, which with luck, I would be able, in some small way, to control. The local families, most without any men to protect them, were forced to flee or hide in their smashed cellars until the rage of war had passed over them.

I had witnessed countless acts of unspeakable cruelty. Not just the inhumanity unleashed by man against his white brothers but also to all other types of animals and birds which Manitou had put upon our earth.

Beasts of burden so overworked by constant hauling and pulling that when their drivers stopped beating them they simply sank into the mud and grime that surrounded them where they slept without even a hint of the fear of death.

    I had been wounded, lost a wing and could never fly again. But even after all of that I felt I had a purpose unfulfilled. Because I needed time to heal, Manitou had given me time to know the land and villages where my English Grandfather and his families had built their nests. Manitou made me face ghosts from my past so I could learn how much pain, hate, and misbelief filled the hearts of my English family who had lived before me.

    Now I was nearly home; home in Alberta. Again, the Great Mystery had reached out and provided a lasting and knowing lesson. This journalist, this self centered Canadian had no interest whatsoever in who we were as a Cree Nation. The journalist served to remind me of a great mistake I had made; a mistake that only I was responsible for. I had thought my decision to travel into the crucible of war, to reach out and hold a weapon in the name of the British civilization, would make a difference to who and what I was. Who and what I was had suddenly become very clear to me.

    I heard the very word of Manitou, the word 'NO' resounded loudly on that rail station platform. Then softly, like my Grandmother Cold Dawn would speak to me when I was still a restless child, I heard in my heart the truth as it was spoken.
    "You still have not learned what I, the Great One, would have you do. Yes, Askuwheteau, you have learned much in your few short years but your heart has not listened to what I would have you do"!

No one, no one except the Spirit would ever hear the story of my travels unless I told it. As I stood there on the Edmonton station platform my soul filled with the knowledge that Manitou already knew everything I now carried in my heart and in my words. The Great One knew the pain that comes from knowledge. Where there had been hope there now existed a bitter truth. It was the truth of who I was today compared to what I had been when I left my grandmother, Cold Dawn, in Saddle Lake. That final piece of truth came crashing down on me like a firestone falling to earth from a night darkened sky.

Tears blinded me until I could not see. Words were ripped from my tongue. My flight may have ended but there remained a task that only I could fulfill. Manitou, the Great Mystery had not yet finished with me. I may have become the Askuwheteau but I had not yet cried enough to live inside the 'Box Full of Tears'. Manitou was telling me as clearly as the light is different from the dark, before I too could go back into that box I must find my voice and learn how best to tell my story. The first Askuwheteau had returned blinded by tears and unable to speak. The Great Mystery would no longer accept silence. My story must be told.

* * *

I stood on the railway platform until a fellow soldier from my train reached out with the only good hand he had. Taking my arm without a word being spoken he led me down the platform. At the far end of the station building there was a small group of Army Staff, some medical nurses, onlookers; all gathered around a short line of tables filled with containers marked with various signs. We soldiers stood together, in silence, until the hospital and military staff asked us to line up and present our medical papers and identifications.

Every soldier carried a file; in those files were words recording where they had been and what they had done. Every soldier had a different file; some files were handed to doctors or nurses standing waiting. My records, the records of my travels, were quickly examined and put into a wooden chest. The box was labelled, "No further treatment required". My file was the only one I saw to go into that box. Someone at the next desk was speaking.

"You are a veteran now; as a wounded veteran you are entitled to receive a monthly pension for the rest of your life. Canada will give you money every month. Here are instructions on how to apply for your pension".

And so it was, desk after desk, until we reached the end of the line. When the people at each desk were finished saying everything that needed saying they would turn to the next soldier in line and repeated the things they thought he needed to know. As I stood in the line, shuffling forward, one desk after the other, I already knew all the information and questions the person at the next stop would ask. The same shuffle forward, the same listen to the words being spoken, soldier after soldier.

A few of the wounded were led away or carried away to waiting medical ambulances. Some others, a few others, the walking wounded like myself, were told to go away to their homes or local hotels; we were told we should be filled with hope during our weeks of recovery or release. Some were given schedules of when and where to report for further medical treatment and training.

Someone said to me, "Your amputation has healed well; there is nothing more we can do for you. You are free to go home". The papers they handed to me said I was cured and would not need to go into the hospital again. I was told I should report back early in the New Year and the Army would arrange for me to sign my release papers. They gave me the address of an office in Edmonton where I should report. They said I could wear civilian clothes. They gave me some of the money I had earned and said do not forget to pick up my kit bag. Their job was done for the day or the night, it depends I suppose on what you think their job was. Mine, my job, my new job was to become a civilian again, a Canadian again, a half-breed again. Who I had been was now just a part of who I must become. So now, becoming the man I was, like a circle, was just beginning. Prior to becoming a soldier, I had been someone. My time as a soldier had been spent becoming and being someone else. Now becoming who I would be was a process that only I could control and manage.

Someone came to me, a younger lady with auburn hair. She took my hand and led me down a long corridor into a room filled with the smells of coffee and real beef. A man said I could have as much food as I wanted. An older lady with a little hand written tag pinned to her sweater smiled at me and said I should try to relax and enjoy my family.

Some women walked amongst us carrying more of the drinks and food that were piled high on the tables. A few waiting families were gathered around their soldiers; many were smiling now; the fear of what they would find in their soldier had now been faced. I could see the pain they felt for the man they loved but I could also see the anxiety washing away in the soap of hope and the future. Here and there the smallest sounds of laughter escaped from the room.

My eyes told me that of all the others I was different; I alone was different from all the rest. Only I was the Askuwheteau, only I was lost and in pain with no clear way forward from the agony which surrounded me. I was a half-breed Indian without any family and nowhere to go. The others were white men with homes and families with soft hearts waiting to hold them until they were well again. No one came and talked to me, no one smiled and said, "Welcome home soldier".

* * *

I had never felt so utterly alone; even in the deepest forests of Alberta where I spent my youth I had wolves to watch over me. Now I had no one, not even myself, who had any love or kind thoughts for me at all. I stood up from the table where I had sat not knowing where to go or what to do. My mind was a fog of pain; somewhere deep inside my head there was a presence, a hand, a pressure, reaching out and taking all the light and breath away. I remember stumbling out of that reception room. I found and shouldered my kit bag, which had been piled in a heap of hundreds of kit bags just like it. Without knowing I had a plan at all I realized I had made my way across the station platform and out through the wide-open doorways.

The area of the station was just as I had remembered it. A wide road and large parking lot stood out as I exited. I could see the grain elevators standing along side of the tracks on the west and behind the station a large chimney continued to spew cinders and smoke unto the surrounding neighbourhood. The uneven sidewalk presented the streets of Edmonton and life, as it was on that day. I could not focus. I only knew I needed a place to camp, a quiet corner where I could awake tomorrow and find the time to push the edges of where to begin the days ahead of me.

Nothing seemed to make any sense. I had been away and everything in my life had changed but nothing here had changed. I had left from here as a healthy half-breed man and I had returned as a white man in an empty shell. It was here that I had stepped onto a train that took me to Valcartier. I had left here as man with clear eyes, two strong arms and I had returned home a broken man with a mind filled with the horrors of what I had seen and done.

No one even offered to talk to me; I was just a number with a file. No one asked me how I felt; could no one see I was in pain? They did not ask me if I had somewhere to go; I no longer had a home. Not one single person, military or civilian, took the time to say thank you.

When I had departed Edmonton there was not anything I could not do. Now, it seemed as if there was very little I could do. I had departed as a complete man and now I was a man with one arm and one hand. What would Alberta do with a half-white man without any skills or white friends? What would a half-breed Indian do with a mind filled with tears and only one arm with which to hold a rifle or a knife? I had stepped off the train that brought me back as a man with no sense of purpose, with no understanding of who I would be in the future.

A gloomy and downward wind pressed hard upon my every fibre. In my present state it seemed clear that the first and original Askuwheteau had returned to a wondrous box over-filled with youth and unimagined pleasures. The box that lay before me was empty, dark, and careless. I had the feeling my body would slowly become a torrent of tears. But tears alone were not enough. I understood there would be tears enough to fill a box but there was something else that I must do before my life would be allowed to end.

I became possessed by the need to get out of that station. I had to leave this place behind me and find some abode where I could cleanse myself, become myself, put some frame around what my life would mean in the future. First, above many things, before I flowed away in self pity and sorrow, I had to write my story and put it into a box. It was the box I intended to leave behind when I left this life to join my grandmother, Cold Dawn.

Alone in the uniform of a Canadian soldier, unaided and unique amongst every other Canadian citizen walking the streets of Edmonton that night, I turned away from the railway station and walked into the darkness.

Barely aware of why or where I was I stumbled, under the awkward weight of my worldly possessions, without sense of direction, through a large stretch of concrete parking lot. On my left, a grain elevator stood lording its heights over the streets below, casting a long shadow through the streetlights. Cars and trucks fiddled and farted, this way and that; nothing beckoned or pointed a way to turn. A nearby hotel with a small dirty sign above some broken steps leading to double doors that needed painting offered a refuge. My mind cried out for silence; my body cried out for rest. I lurched, like a crab with only one claw, carrying my heavy kit bag into the hotel lobby. I had over a hundred dollars in my jacket pocket. No one would decline a room to a soldier with money.

The man behind the desk only asked that I sign my name in the Hotel register. He looked and smelled like someone that had worn the same clothes, day after day, without pressing or the benefit of laundry. His vacant eyes watched without even casual interest as I wrote my name; once my job was done he closed the register with a nod of satisfaction, his purpose in life had been fulfilled.

Repossessing a smoldering cigarette butt from a nearby ashtray, he pointed the way to a hallway leading to my room. He had taken my ten-dollar bill more interested in the crispness of the bill then the fact that I only had one hand; in a nasal rush of words he informing me that ten dollars would secure five nights lodgings; clean linen every second day, and no room guests.

He did not offer any information about breakfast, dinning room, or other services they pretended to provide. I remember nodding my head and turning to seek the sleep I so desperately needed. I did not tell him I was Métis. I did not tell him I was so lost in a forest containing completely unrecognizable trees that I knew not which way to turn.

My room was just down the hall from the main lobby. A small light bulb in a broken light fixture centered the hallway. The stale smells of tobacco and unwashed bodies were nailed to the walls of the hallways and the lobby. Thick doors of Quebec maple stood in silent vigil over the entrances to the other rooms that paraded in regimental order down the sullen hallway leading to my ground floor room. Not a single sound of life emitted from any corner that might have given clue to other guests sharing the shabby condition of the hotel.

Since nothing of friendship or courtesy had been offered or extended, neither did I offer that I still had my beautiful German pistol in my kit bag.

* * *

What's in a Name

I have seen and done a lot in the twenty-two years Manitou has permitted my spirit to be free. I will tell you some of those stories. I believe the first thing you should know is that I have had a lot of different names. I have had a different name for almost for every phase of my life. When I was just a child, before I lived with my grandmother, my mother, when she was drunk, which I think was most of the time, called me 'Pikwatosan', or 'Little Bastard'. Sometimes mother was said to have called me 'Howard'; she might have called me Howard because she thought my father's name could have been Howard. She had told her friends she was too drunk to remember if the white man she had slept with in a flophouse in Edmonton even had a name. If he did have a name, then I suppose it might have been Howard.

My Grandmother called me *Askuwheteau*, 'He Keeps Watch'. She called me Askuwheteau because she believed with all of her heart that there really had been a great eagle whose exploits were part of a wonderful Cree legend. Cold Dawn's grandmother had learned this legend from the tongue of her Grandmother. In Cold Dawn's mind, legends came from truth, and if the storytellers did not change them they ended in truth.

When I became a man Askuwheteau was the name that I became. It is the name I still call myself even though there is no one left alive except myself who would know why I carry this title.

When I enlisted in the army I used the name Giorgio Costello. I had seen that name written on the side of a building near the Army Recruiting Office and I thought the Army might prefer to enlist a fellow with an Italian sounding name rather than someone with an Indian sounding one. No matter how ridiculous it may sound now, I stole and used the name Giorgio Costello from whomever it was that owned the store it was written on. From the moment that I enlisted the Canadian Army called me Private Costello, Corporal Costello, or just Costello. If I had died at Vimy Ridge, then I suppose Giorgio Costello would have been in my grave.

In England, I tried once to use the name Giorgio Harrington. My grandfather was born and raised in England. He told my Grandmother that he came from an old and established family with a large house made of stone in a city called Lincoln. He had come to Canada on a ship with wings of canvas and then by train and wagon to Lac La Biche. He told Cold Dawn he had come to Lac La Biche because he was a young man seeking adventure. His voyage to see Canada and the native people of our area was a quest, not a commitment, for him. He was not lying when he told my grandmother those things. I say this because in my opinion my grandmother was a quest as well since he certainly did not consider their relationship to have been a commitment.

My grandmother may not have believed all of the stories he told her but she certainly believed that his last name was Harrington. Grandmother believed him enough to use that name on my mother's certificate of birth. What she could not believe then and still did not believe, years later when I was living with her, was that he had abandoned her when their girl child was born.

And neither did Grandmother understand why he never came back or even wrote to tell her why he had left her without a word or so much as a penny of support. She remembered he was beautiful and that she was young. She told me once that Jerome Harrington had taken so much of her heart that she never had any room left for another man to fill her imagination.

Nursing Sister Grace called me Sniper for a little while. And now, now that I am what I am and how I am, some people just call me Fucking Indian. That name is often said quickly, the words run together, it may sound like it is just one word. No mater how it is said, in anger or in jest, it always hurts, no matter who says it or why it is said. So now, when someone asks me my name, I always tell him or her, my name is Askuwheteau. I say Askuwheteau is my Indian name because I no longer need a white man's name. When I stopped being a soldier I became an Indian again.

So this will be my story, the story of Askuwheteau. It will be a story about a half breed boy from Lac La Biche and Saddle Lake. I have never tried to write anything longer than a letter. I am not even sure what a story looks like after you have written it. I am sure it should look like a book and I have read a lot of books. I read a lot now because a one armed man has some limits in what he can do. I am the same man I was when I went to Vimy Ridge but I cannot do the same things nor can Askuwheteau fly the same skies.

I suppose the first question is 'where to start' this story? I could begin by telling you about the two years I wore an army uniform and fought with the First Canadian Corps in Europe. Or, I could begin with tales I remember from my youth when I was just a child like every other child I played with. Perhaps it would be better to commence with why I am the Askuwheteau.

39

I am sure you will agree there will be time for all of those things to be told and since my narrative began before I was born my story must also start before I began.

* * *

My grandmother, Cold Dawn, was full blood Cree. She was born in the time when my people lived as they had lived since time began and not as my people do now. Many things changed in her lifetime but she refused to change with them; she never changed, not even one little bit in my mind. I never met another woman who was as strong and proud as my grandmother. Neither have I ever loved anyone as much as I loved her.

When she was born there were only a few white men living in the area. Everyone in our community except for the white men spoke Cree and Chipewyan languages. Grandmother's parents or the ones before them had moved from the north or the north east to fish and hunt on the lake. There were lots of beaver and muskrats but mostly they lived on buffalo, deer, and white fish. It was said the early peoples had also spoken the Beaver or Sarcee tongues. Others may have been Sekani or Blackfoot; sometimes we would find things other people before us had made and left behind.

As a child, Grandmother had gone to the Oblate Mission Catholic School in Lac La Biche. Everyone knew she was a wise one. She spoke Cree, Chipewyan, French, and English and she taught me to speak them too. It was odd, she thought, that English people spoke only one language. They used to say, "Speak English", to everyone. The Cree and Chipewyan, the Métis and the French, the Ukrainians and the Lebanese all spoke more than one language. The English only spoke English. I suppose that English people considered not having to learn more than one language was justice for having been born English. If you were English, you had everything you needed. If you were an Indian, you needed everything.

Grandmother learned the white man's language from the Sisters. She spoke English almost as well as French and read the white man's paper language. It was through her and from her I learned the way to write. My grandmother told me I was very powerful because I was almost a white man and if I learned what they had learned I could become as powerful as they were.

The Cree have long memories of who were their friends and those that were not. Around their fires they would remember things that had happened in their life times and in the life times of their elders. All that to say long before David Thompson and George Simpson came to our lake the 'Nahathaway' peoples, that is the name we call ourselves, were living in peace according to our ways. White men that have looked into the ground we have lived on have found a few of our early things, our cooking pits, and arrow points. They say we have been in 'Kanata' for nearly nine thousand years. Grandmother said only Manitou would know for sure.

No matter how hard I try I can never begin to tell you what an incredible human being Cold Dawn was. I believe if she had set her mind upon it, she would have walked on the same lake that Jesus walked on.

Jesus must have known he had to prove he was the Son of God and he knew that by walking on the water of the lake his disciples would see and experience his power. It was not the same for Cold Dawn. She realized she could not walk upon the waters of a lake. However, I believe that if she thought the only way she had to provide her people or me with life was to walk on water then she would have found a way to make it happen.

If Jesus and the Great and Mighty Manitou are spirits, then Cold Dawn most certainly was not a spirit. She was as genuine, loving and understanding as spirits are supposed to be, but she was not just a person found in books like the Bible or in the legends we discover on the tongues of storytellers. Cold Dawn was authentic; her heart bled for what the Cree nation had become in her lifetime and her hands were hard and calloused from work she constantly performed both for me and for our people.

If I were to say nothing else about her I would say she had the remarkable ability to discover the dignity of human spirit in every person she encountered. She never, not even once, stopped looking for a person's soul. She never thought or said that the clothes people wore or the way fortune had shaped the way they looked made them different from the rest.

She did think, she told me, if Manitou had placed a person on this earth and he or she happened to cross into the path that she had chosen, then who was she to question the wisdom or the plan the Great Spirit had imagined for that moment of meeting.

* * *

One of the very first memories I have of Grandmother was when I was just a very young child; maybe it was the winter I turned six. I was born in April 1895 so that would give this memory a year date of 1901 or 1902. It was deep in the winter and we two spent most of that winter, when there was enough daylight in our lodge, slate writing and drawing the letters of the alphabet.

"Someday Askuwheteau you will be able to take these letters we are learning now and you will put them all together and you will be able to write and tell great stories that might even live after you are gone".

I had not tried to think about why we were making marks on slate boards with pieces of white chalk. Every day, day after day, we would hold those pieces of slate and I would attempt to make marks that looked like those she had made. When Ma was satisfied with what I had done we would rub the slate clean with a piece of cloth and start all over again drawing different kinds of marks.
I asked her,
"How will you keep the letters that we make Ma when they just become dust after we clean them off our boards"?
She leaned back in her chair, one hand on her back as if it hurt her when she sat straight; her eyes were burning a hole in my face.
She said,
"When you are older I will teach you how to write on paper and we will keep those letters that we make together. A smart man does not keep words on slate Askuwheteau, he keeps them on paper. The things that Whiteman writes on paper are very important to him. It is the pages from many books that allow the white man to know where he has been and who he is".

She took my face between her hands and looked deep into my eyes. She used to do this often when she wanted to make sure that I was listening to her and it was a signal to me that I should try to remember what she told me.

"White men can remember where they have been and the things that happened before their fathers because they have pieces of paper with words to tell them what occurred in the days before they came to live with us on this earth of ours".

"But", I said, "Does their paper talk about our people and do they say who we are and where we have been"?

"Yes Askuwheteau, their words tell them that they found us here and we owned everything we saw and touched. Their paper says we lived on this earth without leaving our mark on it".

"Why", I wondered, "is it important that Whiteman should know who he is and where he came from? You and I Ma, we only have a small pile of white chalk dust to help us remember who we are"!

Grandmother stood up, took me by the hand, and led me gently to the small door standing between the warmth of our fire and the deep cold and grey day that hung like a blanket over the place we lived. She moved the big moose hide that hung in front of our wooden door. The door swung in and out on wide thick strips of moose hide instead of the metal hinges Whiteman used for his doors. We pushed together on the door, the snow had settled all around and left its depth leaning against our now opened portal. We exited on to our front path. Our lodges did not have steps, our floors were earth floors, and our 'outside' started right where our door opened and closed.

We stood there, our two breaths mixing in their clouds of steam, the winter's cold stuck its fingers through our house clothes, some seconds passed as we stood there. She stood beside me, her wide and comfortable hip pressing into my shoulder, her right hand, warm and gentle, still holding mine.

"Askuwheteau, you must never forget where you came from. This is where your heart arrived when you came to me. This is where your heart must remain no matter where your life may take you! A man whose heart does not have a happy home somewhere in their mind is never a man that knows where he has been nor where is he going".

Her left hand described a large arc, which described one side of our snow covered village to the farthest side where it disappeared into the trees covered with crowns of deep snow.

"You come from here Askuwheteau, you are a Cree child and wherever you go you must always know where you came from and who stood with you as you were growing into a man".

She reached down and took a small amount of the soft, top layer of the snow that clung to and covered our deer hide covered feet. For a moment the snow held its shape in the palm of her hand but slowly it changed and became wet with the water that the warmth of her hand imparted to it.

"This handful of snow is like our people are now Askuwheteau. Whiteman can pick us up and hold us in his villages or in his schools and we will begin to change into something that we were not before he came. You, Askuwheteau, you must remember who you were and when you change into water like this snow you must read what you have written and remember who you were. This is the way you can change back to who you were before life changed you".

She just looked at me for a minute and then she took me by the hand again; we returned into the warmth and gathered darkness of our small lodge with its insignificant but constant fire. I knew even then that it was Cold Dawn that kept our lives together through the long and heavy days of winter.

I am very thankful that my mind chose to hold this memory and bring it back to me after I returned from the battlefields of Europe. It was one of the many memories that Cold Dawn left with me that helped me find myself again when I was lost.

* * *

In 1853 an Oblate Mission was built on tribal lands very near the shores of Lac La Biche. It is still there today. The Mission brought us a new God and a new school. Our people were told to embrace Jesus and education and like a child with a new shiny toy we Cree embraced them until we lost, not only ourselves but also the memory of who we had been.

I went to a Catholic Residential school, the Blue Quills Sacred Heart Indian Residential School or as people living there knew it, the Saddle Lake Boarding School. It was there I was taught about your Jesus and how he tried so hard to do good things and help people.

My grandmother, Tahki Wapan, 'Cold Dawn', was my very own Jesus. She was my personal saviour; she not only taught me but she showed me right from wrong and forgave me when I lapsed. I was clay on the potter's wheel; she turned me and shaped me into a living thing that she could be proud of. Then, like Jesus did for the countless generations that have worshiped him, she filled me with the knowledge of others and the wisdom to succeed. She lived for me and tried to help me become more than just a bastard child, more than just a half-breed boy from Edmonton and Lac La Biche and later, Saddle Lake.

The Cree Nation is blessed by having been given strong and hard working women; amongst themselves Cree women spoke of Cold Dawn as a 'wise one'. She was a storyteller; the plains people have a name for individuals who they respect as storytellers. They call such people 'Saa-gay-wayn'. As a child, Cold Dawn had been told many stories about her people and she re-told them to me. She said I should hear and remember those legends and be proud, not just of the accounts themselves, but also of the people who had memorized them and had told and retold them to each new generation.

The most gifted of the storytellers were those who could change their voices and speak in the tongues and in the spirit of animals and birds. Cold Dawn's mother had been such a person. Her name was Kanti or in English, 'Sings', she lived before the church came to Lac La Biche. I know and I believe this because Ma said it was so. Ma said Sings told our stories to many of our people and she had spoken to the first white men when they came to be among us carrying large packs in their canoes.

Now, if you listen very carefully, I will tell you one of the stories Sings told to her daughter, Cold Dawn. Cold Dawn told this story to me but I am not there with you now so I must tell you how to hear this story.

When Ma told this story she would speak with many accents. Sometimes she would speak as the storyteller and sometimes she would pretend to be one of the people listening to her so they could feel like they were part of her story. I used to be amazed at the way she could speak and everyone felt as if she was speaking only to him or her. She would lean forward and look right into your eyes and whisper:

"Do you know the beaver named Long Tooth? The fox asked of me one day. We were not together but we had been hiding together in the long grass by the lake waiting for a deer to come down and drink".

Grandmother would become every animal and every person who spoke in her stories. She would move the way they moved and she would seem to become each of them as they spoke right in front of you so you could almost believe she was the voice they might have used. She would go on:

"The fox would not help me slay the deer nor would he assist me to remove its hide so I could roll it into a bundle and carry it home to my mother. My great grandfather had told my father the fox would only watch and wait until I had left with the meat I could carry; only then would the fox help himself to everything that remained".

If there were room enough, Cold Dawn would stand and walk around all those that were her audience. She would look at them and speak just to them as if she really was the person who had been by a lake waiting for a deer to come and drink. She would continue:

"I know him very well, I said in a very soft voice so that it would not carry over the water to the waiting ears of the muskrats. The muskrats were also friends of mine but they did not live happily amongst the beavers".

She would hold the eyes of every person within sound of her voice, as she would say,

"I whispered into the wind, Long Tooth has promised to keep the water high within his dam and he has kept his promise for all the years that he has lived. I wondered why the fox had asked me such a question because I knew he had seen me on many sunny days speaking with Long Tooth. I had watched the fox and his family looking out of the bulrushes as I had helped Long Tooth move logs so he and his mate could keep the water within his walls of trees and branches. The fox was always watching so he must have known of our friendship".

Cold Dawn would sit and act as if she was the warrior looking out through the long grass that was hiding her hunter from the deer.
"I did not see him this day as I walked past his lodge". Then she would pretend to be looking to where the fox lay hidden. She would search all of our faces until she spoke again.

"I wonder why Long Tooth did not come out to greet me and pass the time of day"?

Now her voice would change again, now she was the fox himself. Her voice would become every different character in the stories she told.
"Long Tooth is dead now", the fox said pointing his nose directly at me.
"I ate him and I took some of him to feed my babies just last night".
Then the hunter spoke again,
"The fox slowly and carefully lifted his head above the ever-moving grass and smiled in my direction licking his lips as he did so".
Then she would become the hunter as if he was searching through the grass tops.

"How did he die then Fox"? I said, "Did he die in his bed surrounded by his children and his mate of seven years"?

The fox moved slightly lower into the soft, sun filled grass, licking his front left shoulder before he glared at me, growling softly.

"He died because he had become lazy and inattentive. Anyone who does not know where I am deserves to die. That is the law of our land; you know the law as well as I".

Then the hunter speaks again,

"The fox turned his head to the right showing me where the deer were slowly, timidly, approaching the edge of the lake. Fox did not see me notch the arrow intended for the deer. Fox did not see me aim and pull the bow back until the red oak was tight and taunt".

Grandmother would walk directly to someone who was paying particularly close attention to her words and speak directly to that person.

"He only felt the arrow as it entered low and straight behind his freshly cleaned left shoulder. I wonder if he heard the words I said as I threw his skinned body into the waiting depths of the lake".

She would end that story speaking again as the fox had spoken;

"Anyone who does not know where I am deserves to die. That is the law of our land and you know the law as well as I".

That was a story my great grandmother Sings told to me through my grandmother Cold Dawn. That is how we learned and that is why we remember.

We did not write in Cree in those days. We did not have a written language until the white man gave it to us. My people had to say their stories and remember them. Then their children would tell these stories to their children so our stories lived, not on the pages of a book but on the tongues of our elders. Only Whiteman needed words on paper.

Whiteman needed everything on paper. When they came to our lake they had a God on paper. Their God had a paper face and they showed that paper to us. They said their God had created all of their elders and he had created his own son and his son's mother and they were there in a book for us to look at as well. But strangest of all for us to understand was why this son of God had been killed and nailed to a piece of wood and they even had a wooden carving of him in the front of their church for us to look at if we dared.

We did not understand how they could draw and crave such Gods if they had never seen them.

Whiteman had lists of things, on paper, which, they would trade for skins but the strangest thing they did was to give each of us a new name. They gave us new names and wrote them on paper. We used to laugh out loud at the names we were called. They did not know our tongue so one man might be called Johnny or Billy while another one was called Henry Moose Hide when his real name was Yellow Hide.

One day they gave us some of our own land on paper and told us that we had to live there. They told us that these pieces of land would be called Reserves and that they would be ours for as long as the sun would shine upon them.

They said we had to share everything we had and they wrote it on paper in a language we could not understand. They took our land and gave us back Reserves and paper money so we could buy things we did not need. Some of my people even bought paper because they thought it would talk to them.

So this will be my story. I will write it as if I were the Askuwheteau himself because my Grandmother thought I was a blessed child that Manitou had touched and told to go out into the world the Spirit had created.

You will walk with me as I grow from child into man. I also want to say things about those days when I tried so hard to be a white man.
I am half white but I have learned that a whole white man cannot see in halves. I learned to believe white men only welcome you when you are a whole man, they do not seem to understand you when you are only half white man. I believe that it so because they can only see us as being half Indian and therefore we are not their equals.

You will be with me as I tried to change the colour of my skin and I will tell you what I learned and saw when I was a white man. Come fly with me when I was in love with life. Come live the hell that life became at Vimy Ridge. Stare through my eyes at the darkness that befalls a fallen eagle; try as I have tried to see through eyes blinded by the tears of reality.

Like the legend of Askuwheteau my story has many tears.

***

A Cold Dawn at Lac La Biche

In my first days, those early days, which I cannot remember, I am told I lived with my birth mother and often many other Métis and Indigenous people in a house in Edmonton. I know where that house was although it is no longer standing. I suppose some hunter or trapper might have built it in the years before Edmonton was a city. When we lived there it was the people in the house that were trapped. Trapped by alcohol and hunted by desperate people for whom life meant what they could remember from the night before.

Cold Dawn told me my mother had run an away from home and followed Métis hunters as they hunted and drank their way almost a hundred miles to Edmonton. Mother would have been about fifteen years old then and her head was filled with being different than everyone else in our village. Grandmother once said my birth mother was too smart to listen and too drunk to know better. Cold Dawn often spoke of Mother. It was as if she could only remember her when she was a child and they were in love with one another.

The only story that the story teller told of her daughter as an adult was,
"And when she died they buried her in an unmarked grave somewhere in Edmonton. And everyday I try to remember to tell her that I loved her for every day that she loved me".

There were no leafy boulevards or fine houses along ramshackle streets where I was born. The tarpaper shack where I first drew breath was part of a squatter's row, below the heights of the old fort and very near to the river that flowed in and around my early memories. My grandmother said it was not a house that was happy. It was an old house even when it was new. That was because it had been made from parts of other houses. Sometimes people living there would take pieces from it and burn them to cook or to keep warm. It was also said my mother only lived there sometimes, perhaps only on those days when she had not found another bed to sleep in. Of all the faces passing through that house when I was a small child, I include her face as one I do not recall. I have no pictures or memories of my own to bind our hearts together.

You will also know it is love's binding that mothers give to their children which forms the structure known as family. Family is a strong word for me. I have searched my whole life through for echoes and fleeting glimpses of the ghosts that I know were from or some part of my family. Of those ghosts that I hold, none are from the woman that bore me.

I suppose my mother gave me her breasts at first, I do not know for certain. I was told she became very sick; sick from the poison called whiskey, sick because she, like so many others of my people, had an illness in her lungs. When I was not yet five, White men took her away and put her in a hospital and sometime later a white man came and told the people I lived with that my mother had died of the wasting disease.

It was common for Indian people to die of tuberculosis in those days. The white man also told everyone to leave the house my mother had lived in because they might get ill and share her sickness and her death.

A friend of my grandmother carried me all the way from Edmonton to live with her in Lac La Biche. He is the one that told me everything that I know about my mother as an adult. I remember that friend very well, his name was Johnny Snake Eye; I grew up loving him. Maybe, because I did not have nor did I ever know my real mother, my heart learned Grandmother was the only Mother who loved me.

When Johnny Snake Eye first brought me to Lac La Biche my grandmother lived in small strong house made from logs. It filled a corner of a large garden that was very close to the Oblate Mission near the Hudson Bay trading post and the little village.

Growing up with priests and nuns was as familiar to me as my cradle. I must have been a happy boy from the moment I arrived because I have no bad memories that hold tight to my heart from those days. For you to take this journey with me you should come equipped as they say in the army. There will be things that you need to know and there will be things that you must accept as being true. They will be true; I promise you the things I tell you will be from my heart and not just words from a tongue that means to deceive and paint in colours that did not exist on the days that I have lived.

* * *

The lake called Lac La Biche was just one of the thousands of lakes that the Nahathaway people, the Cree people, were given by the Great Spirit Manitou. During Alberta winters the lake is a frozen sheet of ice that covers everything from one of its shorelines to the opposite pine topped beach. The wind plays with the snow; the days may pile sunshine or storm and bitterly cold nights upon it's heaved ice and its splintered surface. On those days of the year when the sun takes away the ice the lake smiles at you as it catches and holds the sun's face on the surface of its waters. The lake is never blue. It is grey in the morning and black at night. It never rests as other lakes may rest; a constant coming and going of the wind makes it move and every movement brings another colour, another edge of glass to reflect back the light of day. My people say that many warriors have wasted their entire lives watching the lake change colour and moods. Maybe those that watched the lake change as the skies might change were the wisest ones.

My people have lived near and on this lake since the time that Manitou heard the first baby cry on those shores. They are shores that provided whitefish and beaver skins for any and all that would catch them. We Cree had lived there for thousands of years until the Whiteman came. Whiteman came with names like David Thompson and George Simpson and Edward and Thomas and William. Some of them came and passed through. Some of them stayed, like David Thompson stayed. He lived one entire winter in a house he built from logs. It is said that the Cree people had never seen a lodge like that before. It had doors of wood and an iron stove.

My Grandmother Cold Dawn had only known fires built on stones. They placed those stones for fires in the center of their lodges. Their lodges were made from pine poles covered with the warm skins of buffalo, deer, and moose. They were filled with the cries of babies and the laughter of my people.

Thompson called our lake, Red Deers Lake, and he asked our people to bring him furs. There were lots of furs to take and in exchange he gave the warriors whiskey and rifles. To the women he gave mirrors and iron pots. Later we asked for axes and rope, paper and blankets, knives and cloth; Thompson and the white men who followed only asked for one thing, furs. It was the white man's hunger for furs that changed the way we lived.

Before Whiteman, we Cree lived by killing only those animals that we needed to feed our lodges and ourselves. From the arrival of Whiteman, we skinned what we killed, threw away the meat, and gave the furs to Whiteman for things we did not need. Whiteman killed our Buffalo for their bones and for their hides. That senseless killing took away most of the food our people of 'the plains' needed for life. We, the Indians killed and kept on killing every other animal with beautiful fur, not so that we could eat its flesh and live from its meat but so that we could trade furs with Whiteman. Over a very short period of time, Whiteman grew in numbers and grew rich from the furs we the Cree brought him. In an even shorter period of time, we Cree grew sick from Whiteman's diseases; we grew thin and died because we drank his whiskey and had nothing left to eat. The laughter left our lodges and Whiteman traded whiskey for our future.

We, the Cree only had one language and we spoke it when we made love and when we lived. Whiteman came with two languages, French and English; they used their own languages all the time and we Cree soon learned to speak both of their tongues but only a few ever learned ours.

I recall many things that happened, to me and around me, in Lac La Biche and Blue Quill. They were good communities, small villages with many different tongues and people from many nations. In its earliest days Lac La Biche was not a Whiteman settlement it was a village of peoples. Some were my people, some were white people, and many strangers came that were from somewhere going somewhere else. More or less, except for the drinking and the troubles Whiteman's poison caused, we all got along well in that town.

Grandmother was born in February of 1859; she did not know the day of her birth but the day of your birth is not important in our culture. The month of birth is significant because we call February 'Mikisiwi-pisim', eagle month in Cree. Her parents called her Cold Dawn; there were many cold dawns in the month of February in Lac La Biche. Eagle month reminded Cold Dawn of the story of Askuwheteau and that is why Grandmother called me that name when I came to live with her.

When I came to her we became a family again. She was no longer alone in her house in Lac La Biche; I became the reason she took a breath and followed it with another and another until she could close her eyes in sleep and dream of me. It was because of who she was that I became who I am. I came to her as a blank book with many clean and unruled pages. In my life with her she wrote on those pages until I became something she had created and I was someone who filled her heart with joy.

Almost as soon as I arrived at her house she decided she and I would move to Saddle Lake. Johnny Snake Eye and the men of the Saddle Lake helped her to build a fine small cabin near the residential school. It had a strong door with hinges and a fireplace made from stone. The windows were tight and the roof held back the rain of spring and the deep and madding snow of winter. The walls were made of thick, axe-hewn logs of pine. For all the years we lived there those walls kept out the storms and they kept in the love that we shared for one another.

* * *

Cold Dawn often reminded me of the differences that exist between our Great Mystery and the Spirit of the white man. She told me she had considered these differences and concluded they would rest forever at the divide; by that I believe she meant the divide that exists between First Nations and the other Nations of people Manitou created.

Our people have a name for the one Spirit who created our earth. We call this Spirit 'Kitchi-Manitou'; in our language a name that means the 'Great Mystery'. This name is shared by all of our people across the rivers and miles we have between us. Although some Nations of our people may have different legends all of our people share a common understanding of our creation.

We believe Manitou began to envision life because only Manitou was strong enough and wise enough to see the possibility of creation. As creation began, to each species, there were given special powers or abilities so the earth could be filled with an endless array of life. Manitou created life in harmony with the thought and process of creation and so all things were part of the spirit and the spirit was part of them. Some of these creations were given the ability to walk upon the surface of the earth. Others were given wings that they could fly and feel the wonder of the winds and clouds and see things from above the surface of the earth. Other creatures and living things were given the capability to swim and live within the deepest lakes and take breath from the waters that filled the oceans. To his first people, the Cree people, the Kitchi-Manitou gave a very special ability. To us, The Great Mystery gave the power of wonder.

"Before I was born", Cold Dawn would say, "our people shared the work that had to be done in order to live. Living was the only reason our people worked. They did not work for money; we had no need for such a thing as money. Our people did not work so we could have greater lands or better winter quarters because we owned all that our eyes fell upon and all we could touch. Our people worked to find food; they hunted and they fished in the rivers and the lakes. If they did not hunt and fish, they did not eat. If they did not eat they did not live. But we were lucky then, the waters were filled with fish and the buffalo were so plentiful they came into our forests and they covered our grasslands. In fact, they were so bountiful they covered our paths with their droppings. There was so much, sun hardened buffalo shit that we could stack it by our lodges and burn it in our winter fires.

Our people worked so their children could live and sometimes they fought and made war amongst our own peoples so that people of their own tribes could live. If living meant you took the land of others, stole their women, and then lived in their lodges, they did so in order that their own people would continue to prosper. This was the way of our people in the old days, the days before the white man".

Cold Dawn knew about the old ways. She knew the ways women worked and the effort the men would do so that everyone within their village could experience living. The men would hunt and trap. The women would clean and tan hides in order to make strong shoes and clothes from them. The men would trap beaver and muskrat and the women would clean and make their skins into coats and warm coverings for their babies. The women would take fish from the lakes and they would smoke and cook the flesh so everyone would have something to eat when the snow covered the land as high as the middle of their dwellings.

Women and children would gather wild rice; the rice made children's cheeks round and happy through the winter days. Lac La Biche was good to the people living there. Our forests provided soft ground for our women to press their backs into when they loved with their men. The forests were filled with life and love and when you died there was a quiet place for your spirit to rest.

Cold Dawn would tell me, "The moose and deer, the caribou and bison were plentiful. There were ample fox and rabbit in the woods for young hunters to train their eyes. The fish were abundant and the trees were full of berries and bees."

She said, "Our people did not worry when the first white man came and ate with us and traded their iron axes and cooking pots for food. In the early days white men living amongst us did not cause trouble. It was their whiskey that brought our troubles. Our people had no memory of drinking water that makes you crazy and this became the first problem of many we had when we first shared our land with the white man".

Cold Dawn almost worked herself to death so I could stay alive. She was up before the sun and she did not rest until it slept in the land of the white-capped rocks. She could do a thousand things with her hands to make our living easier and more comfortable. In the evenings, summer through winter, she would tell me and other children memories of her early days. Her elders had remembered and spoken the best of their legends and she remembered how to tell them. She knew many folk tales. When she told stories she would make her voice sound as she thought the animals might sound if they could speak. When a village leader had to be heard in her story she would make her voice sound like his voice might have been.

She told us, "When Whiteman came into our lands our cultures did not try to mix. There was no need for the Cree to become a white man and the white man could be himself amongst us. We traded with each other. They had blankets and cloth. They had things we had never seen which were made in iron and clay. We had furs and food. We had the softness a woman brings into a house. Sometimes a white man would take a Cree woman into his tent and they would live together. White men and our women had families together and we accepted them and their children, they were our people too. In the beginning our two cultures were together but separate; our lives went on because both cultures went on living".

"But then it started to change. More white men came into our lands and soon they took away our food and traded their food that came in bags and cans for our skins. What Whiteman wanted was the richness of the furs of our animals. If we trapped the animals of our land Whiteman bought the skins until very soon we were dependent on the food he sold us. We were no longer equals then, he was whole and we were not. He was whole because he had not changed his culture. We were no longer whole because our lives depended on what the white man would give us in return for what we trapped.

Soon another kind of white man came amongst us. They were missionary people. They were Christian white men; they not only tried to change the life that we were living and the food we were eating, they even changed the way we thought about death.

White men and white women who called themselves missionaries came and built schools. They told us and they wrote into our treaties that all of our children, boys and girls, had to attend their schools.

Going to their schools meant our children no longer had the time and experience to learn our Cree way of life and culture at their mother's knee. In the white man's schools, they talked to us about the life that would follow after our spirit had gone away from our bodies. They sermonized to us about a place their God called heaven; they said we must change our ways before their God would call us into his house. These missionaries may have called their churches by different names but all of them told us we were heathens and if we did not change our beliefs we would not go to happy rest after our spirit had passed.

Slowly at first and then with a rush of passing years we First Nations people lost ourselves. We were lost within our culture because we no longer understood the way we had been and who we had been before the white man came.

With every child that went to white man's schools their wooden Jesus took away our peoples' understanding of the Spirit Manitou and the great legends of our story tellers. We began to depend on things the white men could give to us and we lost most of the memories of how we had survived for thousands of years on our own.

Slowly we, the First Nations, became more like white men and less like ourselves. Gradually we learned to count and write on paper, we learned the history of England and houses, which the Great Queen of London had built. With each passing generation we forgot how to hunt and fish. Because our children were taken from us to live in the Residential Schools we also forgot how to be parents. And even more sadly, our children grew into adults without knowing the ways and love of their parents".

Sometimes Ma would remember who we had been and she would cry. Long stains of tears would trace tiny wet paths on her face. She would ask for me to understand the pain she felt. She cried because she remembered the ways her Cree people used to approach the understanding of creation and why the Cree people held a special place amongst every thing else that lived upon the earth.

She told all of us who knew her that her people had respected the Sisters who came to live amongst them and those men that built the first church. They only spoke French in their school and in their church. They said their language was a beautiful language so they taught our children to speak French. At first we did not think it strange they did not learn to speak our tongues. The Sisters had come from far away and they told us of the difficult times our people had in a place they called the Red River. Many Cree people moved their homes to live near the Sisters so their children could learn their ways. They had cloth and paper. They had things we had never seen.

Grandmother told us the early days with Whiteman were happy days. The First Nations people were used to living in mixed villages; the people were close. In the beginning Whiteman respected our elders and our people learned from Whiteman. Whiteman built fine houses and our warriors watched and learned to cut down the forest and how to build roads. Our people learned to speak English and French. The French people and English people only used their own languages. Our people would laugh and say, "Speak English", or "Speak French" to one another in Cree before we would talk to them.

Cold Dawn had gone to the school the Sisters built. Sometimes she did not like the way she was treated but she enjoyed the learning. If she did not learn about their God and his people, the Sisters would punish her and she was not given food. She told everyone that would listen:

"The missionaries were like the sun and the moon. They brought both light and darkness to the Cree people. In the daytime they brought the darkness of discipline and punishment; at night they brought the laughter out of the children with food and games that everyone could share and play.

They taught us we had souls. They said our souls belonged to their God. They said we would burn forever in a place called hell if we did not live the way they told us to live. First they took our food and then our land and finally they took away the wonder Manitou had given us. The loss of our food, and our land and our Spirits changed everything about who we were and why we were the First Peoples. They took away our Manitou and brought us their light. They grew stronger and we plunged, like a falling eagle, into a kind of darkness where we could not remember who we were".

Within the lifetime of Cold Dawn, we forgot how to survive and live by the work of our own hands. Within the lifetime of my elders we became a people without knowledge of who we had been.

* * *

Not Everything Was Rosy at Blue Quill

Life and living in my village had changed completely since grandmother was a little girl. The people of Saddle Lake wanted a school of their own so the Catholic Church moved their teachers who were at the Lac La Biche Mission to Saddle Lake and built a new one there in 1898. The priest from the Mission asked Grandmother if she would move to Saddle Lake and work with both the white people and the First Nations families to bring peace and religion to the Reserve. When Grandmother moved she moved me, so I grew into manhood as a student, a warrior, and hunter from Saddle Lake.

What I know about Saddle Lake is really the story of my grandmother's life. Grandmother said our village was very like the one she or her mother had grown up in. The difference, she thought, was that we the people had changed. In her day, before Whiteman came, we lived the way we had always lived. We did not understand that there was something called work. We the First Nations people did not work for a living we survived; everything we did was aimed at that one overriding and fundamental need. We lived, loved, killed, hunted, moved, and created what we needed in order to survive.

And we, the First Nations people had survived for thousands of years. Long enough for Manitou to be happy with us as we were. Then Whiteman came.

Whiteman did not change when he came to live amongst us. He came from a nation of peoples that worked. They worked so that they could prosper and accumulate wealth. We, the First Nations, had no common knowledge of that sort of life and I believe, to this very day, that is the major difference between our people and white people. To Whiteman, work meant that the effort of one person could be paid for by the effort of one or more other people. Effort, paid for by the giving of a token or a coin or an object that the receiver could use to buy the things he and his family needed in order to live. It may seem like a small difference but we, the First Nations, were from a world apart. We had no concept of tokens. We could not eat tokens or money nor could we exchange things for our survival. We hunted and we survived.

Whiteman worked and prospered and his prosperity provided for his people to take or buy the lands and livelihood or entire nations of people, which Whiteman then claimed as his own. They had, I found out by going to their schools, a lot of experience in taking and losing land that was not theirs. They had learned from the French and the Vikings how to lose land. Then they learned a lot about how to take land through their dealings with the Irish and the Scots and the Welsh. Now, here in Canada and far away in Africa, India, China, and half of the rest of the known world, what they did to and how they treated indigenous peoples has filled libraries full of books.

The British Crown, and the British paper treaties, which they gave in exchange for land, and power, has proven not to keep the fireplaces of my people burning nor native peoples' stomachs filled throughout the long Alberta winters.

Whiteman came and gave us a paper Treaty. The paper said Whiteman would provide for us and in return we would let him use our land so he could build and prosper. The Treaty said Whiteman would provide head money, blankets, rifles, and a medicine man. We thought that these provisions would mean that we would continue to survive; we could just take the provisions promised on paper and survive. Whiteman criticized us for not working and we never once understood why we lost ourselves as they found our land and our lakes.

At first, there were no roads in our village of Blue Quill. No lampposts or street signs marked the way from one huddling family plot to another. There were no places where footsteps could not fall or voices could not be used. There was a sprawling jumble of rutted tracks and footpaths. Weeds, trees, and nature's face poked up here and there and everywhere. There were only two wells for water so most of the people just carried it in from the nearby creek or from the lake if they lived close enough. The problem with the wells was that they were deep holes in the ground and most of the time there was a skunk or a dog or some other animal that was swimming without breathing on the scummy surface.

The Blue Quill Residential School had a well but it was not shared with the people of my village. The school had many rules about who could enter and even more about who could leave. The main rule was only white people could enter and Indian children could not leave.

Even before you were in the village you could smell it. Our warriors hunted and killed large animals in order to feed their families. When the hunters were not skinning or butchering deer or moose the women were cleaning and smoking fish for the winter. At almost all times of the year there would be piles of bones and old hides rotting away, fly blown in the summer, and the favourite fighting place for the village dogs all year round.

The Indian Agent and the Priests all insisted on personal cleanliness and that every family have an outdoor toilet somewhere close to the houses. Our culture had never seen the requirement for toilets. For thousands of years the men would go to the woods on one side of the village and the women would find comfort in a place of their own.

In our own times the Chief would decide when the entire village would pack up and move to a newer and cleaner site. Now that white man had built the school and his church we pretty much used the same woods and bushes for our toilets. The difference was that we now had to wait until the rain or the snow would wash away the human dirt that clung to sides of each and every family plot.

From the door of every lodge it was never more than an arrow shot to reach the wilderness; the forest and nature could be seen from almost every lodge doorstep. It was never more than a shout to attract a neighbour. The people of our village were close; they knew every person who shared their village space. Every child knew they were safe within the boundaries of their playgrounds.

I remember wise men saying that years were short but the seasons were long. I think they said that because their lives were short and every season brought with it a requirement to toil hard in order to ensure survival. Men and women alike were young from birth until thirty and then suddenly they were old. Hands grew stiff from hauling and cutting and killing. Knees filled with pain from falling, climbing, and long hard treks to find water, food, skins, and lovers. Faces went from glowing youth to sunburnt wrinkles and the scars that living on the razor sharp edge of life can bring. Very old people were fifty years old. The rumour of a seventieth birthday was a legend from another village.

Our medicine men could not bring comfort to those whose bodies failed them. The white men that came to us calling themselves Doctors most often just looked at us and told us to go talk to the Priest about final salvation in the arms of a benevolent Jesus Christ.

In my village and in all Cree villages, young men worked with their women to keep their families alive. In my village young girls became pregnant before they were women. Young children had less than a fifty-fifty chance of seeing their tenth birthday. Treaty money was given once a year and most of it went to pay for things that had already been bought and used, broken or eaten long before the Agent gave out the Treaty money. Treaty people were given one blanket every year. Most often that blanket would be quickly sewn into a jacket or a coat for a hunter that ventured out in freezing weather to provide life for his hungry family of seven or ten.

In the spring, melting ice and snow, heavy rains and long cold nights, turned our village into a quagmire of foul smelling potholes and mud. The heat of summer changed the face the village wore from one of tumbled down, rotting log huts into lumps of stinking tarps and canvas tents. Lodges made from logs were thrown open to the wind and everyone moved outdoors into the freedom of living under the roof of the sky and beauty of the stars.

The food we ate changed too; our diet changed with every season. Winter food was mostly dried fish that had been skinned and cut into strips and dried on long poles set into the smoke from smoldering limbs and special bushes that gave the meat a deep smoky flavour. Winter provided those families with hunters in their lodges with the frozen bodies of animals. Deer, bison, moose, horse, coyote and wolf, and all of the small bodies from fur bearing animals were frozen, cut into large pieces, and roasted on the open fires of family fireplaces.

Spring opened the lake for women and young children to fish and the woods and surrounding hills became a garden of green things. No one grew fat from what we ate; no one ever said no when they were offered food. Later, in the summer, bountiful birch bark baskets filled with berries from the trees and ground would leave smeared smiles across the faces of children not going to school. Only in summer did the children not go to school. When school started children went from ragamuffin, nomadic, screaming, berry eating little warriors into sullen, serious, and neatly dressed little copies of what Whiteman expected Indian children to be.

Only the Blue Quill Residence, the school, and the big Whiteman house stood out in the village that my people used to call home. And it was home to many of us; there were a lot of families that lived there year round, now that the school had been built. The Residence provided room and board for all of the other children who had been taken from their families to come to our village to live with the sisters and priests. The school was the very heart of our village.

Every treaty child had to go to school or else their families were not part of the treaty money and provisions. The Sisters lived their lives surrounded by the words of their God and bars of homemade soap. Everything they did and touched was done in the name of their God and everyone they taught or lived with had to be clean. The Sisters were very strict; every child quickly came to know well the heavy straps and long rulers they carried and used to encourage children to listen, behave, pray, and keep clean.

The hallways of the residence and the school were filled to overflowing with the silence of children too afraid to laugh but clean beyond anything they had ever seen before.

I was eight years old the autumn I went to school at Blue Quill. Whiteman called it Blue Quill Indian Reserve 127 but we knew it as Saddle Lake. I should have gone earlier but Grandmother said I was too 'loose' to go to school; she said my spirit was too free to learn when I was only six or seven winters old. So Cold Dawn became my teacher and I remember passing those years with her in laughter and learning. Springs went by smelling blossoms and breaking pencils; the summers fled the skies while we were fishing and speaking different tongues. We spent every day of our autumns together skinning fish so we could live through the next winter. Winter was when I learned how to write on a slate board with a piece of chalk.

She spent part of every single day, 365 days of those years, pounding Cree, French and English into my little brain. She never once raised a hand to me, not even when I was bad. She had a way of showing me how much she loved me when she held me in her arms. Her eyes would speak a thousand words when I was being bad or not paying attention. But it was her smile, a smile that often hide the heavy marks that time had pressed into her face. It was her smile that was my reward for having met the expectations that she held in front of me for every day I knew her.

When I could write, from memory, the Lord's Prayer in all three languages she went to speak to her friends the Sisters and she won a desk for me to go to school with them. I started in grade four.

"Ma"? I asked her, surprised when she told me what she had done, "Ma, why do I start in grade four when one and two and three all come before"?

I knew other children from our village that had already gone to school, they were my age, and they would only be in grade three. She took my face between her hands; she had hard hands from working hard. Her hands were never hard on me; her hands were hard for me. She said and I will never forget her words.

"Askuwheteau, I have watched you watching me. When my hands move with a pencil, your lips are already moving with the answer. When I draw in mathematics your hand is counting fingers you do not have. When you read to me in French you use words that are not in the pages".

She sat next to me and held my hands in her hands. And then, as she did so often just before we went into our beds at nighttime, she took me, firmly and lovingly, into her strong, caring arms. She held me away from her for an instant as she said,

"You are the smartest child I have ever seen and I have seen a lot of children".

Her smile was like a rainbow at the end of a day of rain, it filled the very corners of the room with hope and confidence.

"I have always known you are special. You are the Askuwheteau; you are the one that watches. Now you will be one school year in front of all the other children of your age in this village. This is right, and just, and that is what I told the Sisters I wanted for you. You will start school one grade higher than you should. That will mean you will have to work harder than everyone else in you your school year. You will have to work harder than everyone else in the school to pass your grade. Because you will be younger and working harder it will shine a light on you that everyone will be able to see. The better you do the brighter will be your light. I know you can do it Askuwheteau. I would not have spent so many hours with you if I had thought you might fail me".

I did not fail her; not even once did I not pass my grade with the highest marks in my class. I did not find the lessons easy, nor did I enjoy the cold dark days in cold dark classrooms as I stood to read passages of the Bible that spoke of bringing hope to heathens deprived of the spirit of an English God. I learned much about England and the Commonwealth. We could recite the history of France and the order of English kings. We learned to speak English and French. We learned to respect the teachers and the priests who taught us. I did not fail my grandmother and I did not fail myself. I learned the white man's knowledge but I kept Manitou and the culture of the Cree people for myself.

* * *

Becoming a Warrior

I was ten years old when Grandmother gave me a Winchester 30-30 rifle. It was 'shot out'; it had been badly handled, but the hammer still struck the firing pin every time I pulled the trigger. A bullet cost almost as much as a muskrat pelt, there was no room for errors if you wanted to pay your way as a hunter. She also gave me twenty rounds; they were dull, and the wax had worn off the tips from being carried in a pocket for a long time.
"These are for practice", she said. Then she gave me ten shiny new rounds; only the Spirit knew where she had found the money to buy them.
"These are for animals with fine skins. We will use those skins to pay for school clothes and books for you to read. The more pelts you bring home the smarter you will be next year in school".

There was an absolute truth in what she said and even though I was just barely taller than the rifle, I understood how seriously I had to take my first hunting trip with a rifle I had never fired before.

She spent many hours talking to me about going out into the forest alone. She had taught me how to watch the place the sun was in so I would know the time of day and how long it would be before darkness fell across the paths I would follow. She told me to remember every path I followed and everything I had seen her do while we had been together gathering food, fishing, or walking on the silent trails surrounding the village. She told me I would be a hunter when I could remember trails that no one else might ever know.

When I was getting ready to go out for the very first time with my very first rifle I knew she would not sleep until I had returned to her. What I did not know was that I would not sleep very much myself.

I carried a small roll of deerskin around my waist that grandmother had fashioned to carry berries and dried fish. Around my shoulders I carried a blanket wrapped in a hard old piece of canvas. The canvas would act as my ground sheet or help to keep me dry if it rained.

I carried that rifle as proudly as a man would carry the flag of his nation. I left our home without a word and walked a familiar path leading to the deep woods. I walked all day by myself, going further than I had ever gone alone before. Sometimes, I did not know why, I could have sworn that someone was watching me as I hesitated at a brook or at a fork in the trail. Look as I might, I saw no one and I carried on alone. As the light began to fall away I came to a place where the lakeshore was shallow and many trees had fallen in the wind. That night was so cold and I was so alone I cried myself to sleep.

The next morning, at dawn, I found a place to hide; I watched and I waited until something would move, either on the water or on the land nearby. I practiced all day how to hold the rifle, how to aim it and move with it as the rifle moved. I taught myself to move slowly like you do with a bow; with a bow it is best to move without seeming to move. I must have held the rifle to my shoulder a thousand times that day and the next.

I never fired a single round until the third day. Over and over again I practiced how my Grandmother had shown me to aim.

She had said to me in my ear as she stood behind showing me, helping to hold the rifle hard and into the soft part of my shoulder where it met my chest, "A hunter never stops breathing. That is the answer to not missing the target".

She had shown me, holding the rifle to her own shoulder, how to line up the rear sight with the front. She taught me how to breathe and to be slow and gentle with the finger that pulled the trigger.

"A good shot", she told me, "will stop and squeeze when every part of his body is still and completely balanced. A great shot will never stop breathing; he will squeeze the trigger at the exact moment when his lungs stop filling and just before he starts to let the air out again. The rifle must not feel the breath because even just a breath can move the barrel. It is the barrel and the eyes of a hunter that make the difference between good and great. A good shot sees the head of a deer at a hundred yards, a great shot can see the deer's eye".

I can swear to you that even at ten years old I could see the deer's eye. When I returned to my home on the fifth day I had thirty pelts, some were muskrats but most were from beavers. I could hardly carry them all on my back they were so heavy and I was very hungry and very happy to be home.

Johnny Snake Eye waved to me as I approached our lodge. He had been out somewhere himself; he carried a small deer over his shoulder. With just a wave he disappeared into his back yard where he usually skinned and cleaned his catch. Grandmother took the pelts without a word; she started to stretch them and put them out to dry. Not until she was finished with her work did she go and make food. She sat watching as I ate. When I had finished she spoke.

"You were not careful with your breathing on the second largest beaver. The shot was too far back on the neck and it ruined the pelt. You must learn to relax your shoulders as you aim".

That night I learned another truth that good hunters learn from their elders. She told me a story about a hunter that brought home far more pelts than all the rest of the men of his village. He would bring home so many pelts that people in his village would marvel at his strength as he carried them home to his waiting wife and family. Then all the women of the village would laugh behind their hands and feel sorry for his family. The poor man had never learned the skill required to remove the skin from an animal without cutting holes in it. The poor wife tried very hard to use what she could. She was a wonderful tailor but even her skills could not hide the mistakes of her husband's knife. The lesson was, she told me, that shooting an animal is a waste of both time and an animal's life, if its meat and skin are not used in the best possible way so our lives benefit from them.

I remember she smiled and was quiet with me the next morning; I had gone to bed and slept until the sun came up. After that I tried even harder to harvest skins that could be used easily by a woman's hand.

For nine years, from 1903 until 1912 I spent most of my days going to school. I went to two schools at the same time. Five days a week I went to the white man's schools and learned what the Sisters knew about white men. For seven days a week I went to Grandmother's school and learned how to live like my people live.

Grandmother sat at my shoulder every day and every night to watch my fingers work with pens and pencils. If my fingers stopped she would burn me with eyes that did not understand the words "I cannot". I knew from a very early age I was everything to her and my love for her was one of two reasons I did not fail.

The second reason that I learned not to fail was because there was a very wise fool in our village when I was young. I do not remember why the elders said he was a fool but I knew him as such because of the way that others thought of him. He wore clothes he made himself. He had no one to make clothes for him and he was too proud to ask Cold Dawn. He had no money because no one would hire him or trade work for what he could produce.

He was a fool they said so everyone treated him as if he was a fool. I had known him all my life and I knew him as a great and caring friend of my grandmother. I saw him following me one day when I went out hunting. I did not let on I knew he was behind me; he stayed a long distance back but he was still there when the sun had gone into its bed.

I had walked all one day to get to my hunting place; all day as I climbed hills and followed the bottom of a creek bed there was a shadow that followed me as surely as my own. It was autumn and the night was cool. Most of the leaves now covered the ground and the sun had lost its heat. I had a cover, a blanket, and some food Grandmother prepared for me. He carried nothing that I could see.

When the colour of the sun changed from blood red to the fading orange of sunset I stopped and busied myself with the trimming of tree branches, the setting of my night bed and the making of my fire pit. I smiled at his silence knowing how he would suffer in the dampness of night and the emptiness of the morning without a cooking fire. Though he left no sounds to fall upon my ears, on the next morning's breeze I could smell fresh meat on a spit and saw smoke rising from his sleeping camp.

All that day I waited, hidden and hunting from the edges of the tall grass on the verge of the beaver dams. By nightfall I had skinned two large and one small beaver pelt and that evening I ate from what I had killed. That evening, when the moon was smiling and the cold of October had crept across the low land where I slept, I smelt again a fine aroma coming from his fire. I stirred myself and with great stealth I sought to spy on him to see how the fool survived without carrying a pack, or rifle, or bow as I had done.

Slowly, as a fox would stalk a rabbit, I approached his campsite and when I could see it through the trees and branches he was not there. I looked into his camp; there was a fine, small fire, under a spit. On the spit there was a large fish that appeared to be wrapped in weeds and rushes from the lake. There was a strong and wide lean-to made from woven bushes. For a bed he had used pine boughs and soft grass. By the side of his fire there were four large beaver pelts hanging in their stretchers, shining from having been brushed. By his bed there was a bundle of short, straight, tree sticks, cut and ready for drying and making into arrow shafts. I could see many hours of labour and the fruits of his efforts.

After some time, he had not made himself known to me so I turned, silently, to repeat my footfall back to where I had camped.

When I returned to my own small fire pit I found a reasonable piece of still warm fish waiting by my pack. On my bedroll, written on birch bark, was a finely written note in English. It said, "A fool is someone who believes he is a fool".

He did not follow me home the next day but, over time, he and I became like father and son. He taught me many things about the earth and the living things on it. He seldom hunted with me but he often went hunting in the same places that I would hunt. And every so often he would even hunt in places at the same time that I was hunting. He would leave things for me to find or find things I had forgotten.

My Grandmother and I cried when we buried him the year that I was nineteen. His name was "Johnny Snake Eye"; he was one of the finest men I ever knew. My Grandmother used to say, "If Snake Eye shows you life you should try to see through his eyes. If he takes you somewhere that he thinks is special, do not ask him why he thinks that way but try very hard to find out for yourself why he reached that opinion".

And then she said something that I have never forgotten. She said,
"You will be a very smart man Askuwheteau if you can discover the special things that Johnny Snake Eye has always known".

Through his eyes I learned how to be part of the forest. Through his skills my footsteps learned to leave no marks except those that nature made for herself. He made me see myself as he saw himself. He saw himself as a man with many skills and many talents and when something extraordinary needed to be accomplished he would reach down inside his many skills and find a way to succeed.

I suppose now that I have lived the little bit of life Manitou has already given to me I too can say Johnny Snake Eye was a fool.

He was a fool for loving me so much that he spent most of my boyhood years following me around and watching over me. He was a fool because he would do anything that Cold Dawn thought would help me to be a better man and he never once asked anyone to do anything for himself. He was a fool because he spoke three languages and never went to school to show the teachers how smart he really was.

Cold Dawn and I, on the other hand, were very, very smart. We were smart enough to love a fool as much as any two people could ever love a man who gave his everything away so we could know him for what he was and not for what he owned or what others thought of him.

When the time came, Grandmother and I put Johnny's body on long poles and hauled his body to his final rest in the dark forest he loved. We laboured long and hard to take him where I knew he would want to be. When his body was wrapped in deerskin and lying on the platform of poles I had fashioned, I spoke out loud to Manitou about a storybook Grandmother had bought for me to read. I had read it once to Johnny Snake Eye when he came to listen to me read before we ate together in our house. I can not remember why I had decided to read that book, it was already very worn, I had read it many times, I was about twelve or thirteen years old and I was well beyond the child book stage. It was a short story about four animals travelling together in some land far away. They were trying to become musicians.

The book was written by brothers called Grimm; I never read any other books by them but I can still recite that story today because of what Johnny said when I had finished reading it to him.

He had listened to how a donkey, a rooster, a cat, and a dog had grown old and their owners had no further use for them and now they feared for their lives. They had run away from their masters because they had beaten them and would surely kill them, all of them. And so they travelled together for some time until they all grew hungry. As the curtain of night fell across their journey they discovered a fine house, which had been taken over by robbers. They looked in and they saw a fire and food upon a table. The animals worked together, one animal after the other getting on the other's back. Finally, the rooster stood on the cat, the cat stood on the dog, the dog stood with his feet firmly on the back of the donkey. Then, all singing loudly in their own voices, they crashed through a window and scared away the robbers. By working together, they saw they could become stronger than each would be if they had worked alone. They became a fine musical band and lived happily forever in a town called Bremen.

"Askuwheteau", Johnny Snake Eye said, his hand helping me close the covers of the book. He leaned forward until his eyes could see directly into mine before he spoke. When he did speak I will never forget the softness of his words.

"I am all of those animals to you and if you want I always will be. You can become three different people and still you could climb on me and I would help you become or do whatever you need. You are as close to me as any son could ever be. I am the man who carried you and walked with you when you needed to leave your mother's home in Edmonton".

There were tears in his eyes when he spoke again. "I am the man that followed you the very first time you took your old rifle and walked all day to find a place where you could shoot it. I am the man that will follow you any time and any where you need a friend or a defender".

He reached out and took my hands in his hands. There was a deep pool of a tear waiting to escape his eye.

"I am the man that will watch you grow into a strong and wise young man who will read books written by men that live even farther away then across the Great Salt Lake. You are my heart Askuwheteau, all I ever ask is that you never forget the fool that loves you".

I have never forgotten him; it is hard, even on the darkest nights when your heart is heavy with the weight of the world to forget a fool as smart as he was.

* * *

A Tear Gets in My Eyes

Grandmother insisted I do three hours of home study every single day of my school life. School was my life and I was her life. School was easy in comparison to failing to meet the approval of my Grandmother. She spoke in different tongues and made me learn their words. She told me stories that had been told to her by her people and required that I remember them the way that she had. She would close her eyes and words would flow from her as if she had memories of them like one would learn to recite a poem or a verse from the bible.

Always, she would remind me I was Cree. She called us 'Cree people'; she would hold my face between her hands and say we were 'free people'. I remember at least a hundred times she told me how Cree people would make their black eyes red from the smoke of small fires inside skin clad circles. She said this had been so ever since the mountains, the purple stones with their white heads, had pushed up out of the prairies to cut their teeth on the moon. She made me believe that being Cree was something to be proud of. She would take me in her arms while she told me this story and she would say,

"I cry for you now, with your black eyes red from the smoke of many fires inside cement clad boxes. Now it is the white man with his wooden Christ that is pushing you out of our forests as he drives steel rails through the stones".

She had thought a lot about the differences between the ways we Cree people approached and thought about our Great Mystery in comparison to the ways Whiteman thought about his God. She was one of few people who could do this with credibility because she had slept in both of those beds. She had lived within the Cree lodges and had been taught at her mother's knee the ways of Manitou and how our people had learned to understand the harmony of Spirit, creation, and ourselves. She had also spent years going to school with the Catholic Sisters and Priests; from them she had learned, sometimes at the end of a whip, the only correct way to approach the Almighty God and His Son, Jesus.

She told me she had learned from the white man that all mankind live on a world their God created. The priests told her there was only one true God and all the other gods, which other people on this earth believed in, were false. Whiteman said that Manitou was false and not the true God. She had been told that Whiteman's world, and the heaven homes of their God are separate, one from the other. She considered it very odd that Whiteman thought he could understand what their God intended and what he meant when he spoke to them through their paper Bible. For example, she said, when the Bible speaks, it speaks as if the Snake was capable of being understood by those that listened. She told me Cree people can not speak to snakes nor do we understand what it is snakes might have to say to us so instead of reading words which are written on paper we watch the snakes and follow them so we might better know how they live upon the earth we share.

She thought, she said, that Cree people live in a universe filled with the spirit of Manitou.

"Our lives are part of and are an extension of what we see and do. We are together with the Spirit not apart from it. We do not believe we can understand what the Great Mystery intended but we do believe we should spend our lives trying to understand what we do not know. We do not go to a place called Heaven when we die, we return to be part of the Great Spirit. We try, while we are living, to understand what Manitou has done for us; when we die Manitou accepts our efforts and we return to being part of everything that is Manitou".

My people have no custom of bad luck being found in the number thirteen. We do believe there are good spirits and bad spirits. We do not believe people live because of luck; people live because they are smarter than the wolf and faster than the hand that holds a knife. Those of our tribe that cut enough wood for their fires to last through the winter did not suffer from the cold of winter. Those of us that liked the soft sounds snowshoes make on deep drifts smiled at the low moon during the long nights. That was the way it was with us that lived together in a tribe. Those that worked hard enough to live had time to watch their babies grow into parents. Those that spent the summer sitting beside the running water of a river or watching spring pass by, as the waves carved against the shore of the lake would find the winters long and hard. We had to labour in order to live; the lives we lived were short enough without having to worry about dying of hunger in a hut that had no wood to keep a fire burning.

Cree people have a strong tradition of sharing and helping those amongst us that need help. We also have a strong tradition that speaks through the voices of our storytellers. That tradition reminds us life is the only thing we own as an individual and life stays longest with those that work hardest to keep it.

So let me tell you what my very own storyteller said was the greatest difference between our view of life as viewed through the eyes of Manitou and a white man's view as seen through the Bible. Cold Dawn once said to me,

"A white man that is being chased up a tree by a hungry black bear will pray to Jesus to save his life. He will make promises to change his life if he is spared and he will promise to put all of his money in the church collection box".

She would shake her head and smile as she told that story. Then she would change her voice and become a strong and capable Cree warrior as he climbed out to the farthest branch.

"Come a little closer brother bear, when your weight and mine is too much for this branch to carry, I will offer my woman your freshly skinned hide, so that my children will be warm when they thank Manitou for putting this tall tree where I could wait for you to come".

Cold Dawn knew a lot about the differences between the way the Cree people lived and died and the fear that Whiteman had about dying.

* * *

On weekends after three hours of early morning studies I would take my old rifle, dress in my forest cloak, and I would walk to my hunting grounds which were ten or fifteen miles one way. When I arrived at the place I had picked in my mind I would blend into the forest and try to become part of the ground itself. By the age of twelve I was an expert at becoming part of my surroundings; when I was twenty years I was a part of every place I hunted and by far the best rifleman for fifty miles. If anyone wanted or needed extra meat or fish, they would speak of it to Grandmother. She would tell me what was needed and I would carry it home.

The first really hard winter I remember was 1913. The lakes were covered deep by snow; during the long nights I remember the wolves talking about having an easy time killing. The wolves, the fox, and the coyotes, were fat and gave me beautiful furs to take home to Ma. Together we stretched them and brushed them so we could sell them to the Hudson's Bay Company. Rabbits were plentiful; they had deep banks of snow and warm warrens in which to hide their newly born babies. Those animals with bones on the end of their legs fell belly deep into the drifts and had to work all day to find enough food to stay alive. In some places the snow seemed bottomless and covered everything in white. There were long periods of wind from the north and the northwest; the wind carried snow on its back, and the snow was deep even under pines that hugged close to the earth. Deer, moose and our horses, had to struggle to find enough grass under the deep snow, I watched them, as they grew weaker while the winter grew into the lengthening days.

I was young that winter. I was filled with youthful hope and the bounty of my hunting filled my stomach and the stomach of my grandmother.

But what I remember most was that it was a winter of adventure and a winter of great sadness. I have strong memories of falling in love, my first love. My strongest memory is of the days I went from the hunter to being hunted. I will share these memories with you.

The lakeshore of Saddle Lake was heavy with broken ice that had blown up in layers in the early days of December. The long path that meandered along the summer shoreline was tortured and demented. Ma had made me a new pair of moose hide winter hunting boots and they were my pride and joy. Moose hide clad feet failed to leave of an impression as snow fell and deepened between the scattered houses of our village. By the end of January, the priest stopped coming out on his weekly visits. A silence that could hide the voices of the children settled over the lake and the village our people. Even many years later the people that lived through that winter called it the 'silent winter'.

Grandmother and I were very close at that time. It was as if our two hearts beat as one. She spent many hours finishing hides I had caught in traps or shot as the occasion presented itself. While we were waiting for the snow to cover our land I had crafted two new pairs of snowshoes from hand picked willow. Every family had a slightly different way of constructing snowshoes; some were longer, some wider, but the building method was very much alike from one tribe to another.

Snowshoes were hand made from specially selected and dried hard wood. They looked a little like an iron spoon that the white man used to eat his food. The outer frames were bent into a spoon shape in the front and the two ends were tied together in the back like a short handle.

Large moose, especially those in peak condition and working hard to find food in the snowdrifts, have tough and strong tendons in their legs. It is these leg tendons that their bodies use to bind and connect muscle to bone. This sinew can be removed and kept pliable with bear fat or other animal fat. Once in place, it is allowed to dry and it becomes as strong and hard as iron. Then came the hardest part, the weaving of moose or animal sinew through holes drilled in the sides of the outer snowshoe frames until you formed a strong net in the center. It is this net or the bottom web that is the platform the wearer uses to walk over the snow. The snowshoes are then tied to boots with long leather straps. With a good pair of snowshoes, you would not sink into the snow. That made walking in the deep snow of the fields and through the forests in winter much easier.

Our women used moose sinew in many of their crafts and the men used it as white men would use rope or cable. I was young; the power of youth and hard work gave me legs that could carry me for days without complaint. Even the coldest of the days would laugh at my smile as I completed, almost every day, a thirty-mile trek along my trap line.

Before every trip out I would fill my backpack and check every single piece of clothing and equipment I would carry. Dried and cured fish and strips of moose and deer meat were my main diet. Ma would fill bags made from deerskin with berries and fruit we had gathered during the summer and fall. Their sugar and a small supply of salt kept my energy levels high and my health sound. I always carried a Winchester Model 1894 30-30 'deer-rifle' and at least thirty rounds of ammunition. Summer or winter, that rifle never once let me down or did not do what I wanted it to do.

I carried both short and long snowshoes, my hunting cover, and one bottom blanket. Two knives, a flint and a small supply of very dry fire starting material completed my personal checklist. Depending on the catch or purpose of the hunt I added or subtracted leg-hold traps and snares. Twenty feet of store bought, half-inch rope was tied around my pack and around my waist. The rope became essential from time to time to help cross broken ice floes, to act as a roof brace for a night camp site, or as a tow rope for skidding animals or heavy objects.

My main focus was living and by that I mean I knew I had to contribute, and contribute every day, to ensuring there was wood in our lodge for the stove. The wood stove provided us with heat and the ability to cook and prepare our meals. I considered my main concerns were the home fires and the condition of our house. That was so because my grandmother lived her life in that house. Ma stayed home every day of the winter. She filled her time with visits to those who needed her advice or many talents. She was well known in every house in our village; she delivered babies, taught the children, gave instructions to young brides, and held the hands of those whose lives were ending. There was nothing she could not do, there was no one she would not stop and talk to.

Everyone knew if they required something to ensure they lived until they could help themselves again, all they had do to was mention their need to Cold Dawn. If their need was food, then that requirement was added to the second most important 'life-task' I had. Hunting for food and furs was the joy of my young life and it took me out of the house nearly every winter day. When I say out I mean gone from the village, on my own, by foot, for four or five days at a stretch.

The woods and forests surrounding our village for thirty miles or more were like an open book to me. I felt at home on every hillside, I knew every bend the littlest creeks would make as they wandered through the hills to end their journeys into the deep cold-water lake called Lottie Lake.

It must have been sometime near the end of January or maybe a little later, I did not have a calendar, and besides, then, the day of month was not important to me. I was eighteen years old, I no longer spent long hours at school or studying under the ever watchful eye of Grandmother. I was a man now. I had to play well my role of being the head of my family or many others who depended on me would feel the tightening of their stomachs.

The beginning of this memory has blurred in my mind. Memories can be like that. It was winter; it was very cold; very few people in my village stirred outside of their doors except to empty their toilet pails and to bring in frozen food or wood. I went out onto my trap line four or five days every week. Each trip out was much the same as the last so the blurring is a matter of how the mind remembers rather than a mind that cannot remember. Food was very important; it was always important in our village. Everyone in our village needed meat to live. Meat came from many different kinds of animals and every animal killed was eaten. But some hunter, someone from every lodge had to go out into the winter, find and kill and bring home the meat of that animal. If a baby was born the new mother needed extra food, if someone died that house might have extra food to share. If the hunters were lucky everyone would share in the fresh meat. The opposite is also true. If the family had not prepared enough food or did not trap or hunt enough food everyone had to suffer. On hard winters the share was smaller than the demand.

Snowshoes make a steady and reassuring sound. Where the snow is hard the movement is no more difficult than walking in the woodlands of summer. When the snow is deep each step requires a special step where the foot is swung slightly outwards and forward then back to centre again so that the spoon shape of each shoe fits into the pattern of the next step. An experienced hunter on snowshoes can travel as far as or even farther than he could on a summer walk. The snow covers everything so in some ways the surface is flat and easily traversed by someone with an experienced eye. Late in the first day of my journey I had reached the beginning of my trap line. The first snare was one of my oldest and most rewarding trap spots. There was a small springtime brook that carved a step cut between two steeply meeting walls of small hills. Tall birch and willows shaded the face of the brook where I always placed my snare. The exposed roots of willows, where they hungrily reach out for the nourishment of the brook, provided a natural bridge where weasels, rabbits, mink, and martens loved to play and dance their endless games of life and death. It was one of the first times in over four years of use that the snare was empty, not tripped or snarled. There were many fresh tracks leading up to the snare but at a distance of one or two yards on either side of where it lay set, the snow covering was fresh and brushed as if a feather or pine bough, blowing in the wind, erased the history of a hundred little feet which remained clearly on the rest of the animal highway. And so it was at the next leg-hold trap and next one after that.

Night was already dragging the slate grey blanket of darkness over the trail and my mind was forced to turn to survival and rebuilding my night camp beneath one of my favourite huge old pine falls on the side of a hill overlooking a creek bottom.

I remember clearly, before I fell asleep, my mind refused to consider the obvious answer to the missing trophies in my traps. The second day found my pack very light of furs as nearly two out of three of my traps along the line were empty; the signs of re-set were expert and about one day old. I had little choice but to face a deeply concerning and sinking feeling that a line jumper was afoot on my line. The only question was who. I knew of no warrior that was out of his lodge and even so I knew of no other hunter that had ever crossed purposely into my territory. Everyone knew and respected the individual's rights to have exclusive hunting and trapping rights within an area of our land. Never before had anyone violated my trap line.

By mid-afternoon of the second day I had reached the midpoint of my trap line. This mystery person had violated a third or so of all of the traps and I guessed him to be one day ahead of me. With every step taken, with every careful approach to the next trap site, my mind had formulated a plan. It was clear that confrontation, if possible, was the only plausible solution. I carefully calculated how long it would take for an experienced trapper to follow my route and lift, then reset, the majority of my trap sites. I then traced the route followed by my trap line in my mind and came up with a point well forward of the place where I now stood. Even with my eyes closed I could have traced a straight line between where I was to a point in the future where I could wait and watch that person make another raid on my traps. The time and place of confrontation would be late in the morning of the next day.

With much anticipation and some trepidation as well I swung away from the path now being followed by the robber and struck out for a distant hill side overlooking a creek bed where pines and thick wood fall would hide my close and attentive observation. A small smile pushed hard on the back of my exhaustion as I pushed myself to reach the future site of our meeting place. Johnny Snake Eye had once shown me a very particular way to rig a snare for heavier animals such as wolves or even deer. I would need some extra time to set my new trap so that I could better enjoy the twisting and turning of the captured.

I worked well into the gathered gloom of an overcast early winter evening. It took one long tree trunk cut like a pole; the twenty feet of rope that I carried around my waist; the counter weight of another large tree trunk that rested heavily on the back end of the trip pole. The trip pole was balanced, front end down and held down by a trip line cunningly awaiting a foot to discover how lightly it required being touched. I fashioned a well-hidden snare noose, which I covered lightly with fresh snow and placed just immediately in front of a leg hold trap. The trap contained a very nice marten frozen to death after his struggles to escape his end. I was fairly sure the robber would be somewhat careless about his approach to the trap site now that he had already uncovered and robbed over thirty such sites along my route. This was someone that had obviously spent some time following my tracks after I had been along the route in the past few weeks. This was someone with good stamina and snowshoe skills. This was someone I was looking forward to holding down on the ground with my skinning knife pointing in to his throat.

I had even considered the price that he would have to pay and that would include making a complete confession of his activities in front of the Head Man, my grandmother and all other warriors of our village. Early the next morning I took up a position well hidden from view. I had chosen a place that gave me an excellent outlook over the approach to the trap site. With any luck my prey would find very little fighting advantage once one or both of his legs were hanging above his head three or four feet above the trap line floor.

Some part of the early morning had passed before I saw and then heard the approach of my awaited quest. He was shorter and slighter then I had imagined but carried a full pack, on snowshoes; he approached without caution with an expert gait. I was pleased to note my guest was fully distracted searching ahead for the next trap site along my route. What happened next brought out a high-pitched scream from the robber and I must admit a very difficult task for me for regain control of my laughter and waiting hate.

The thief had slowed as he sighted the frozen marten waiting in the trap. He lowered his pack to the ground as his feet reached the spot where the noose lay waiting. The motion of the pack tripped the hold-down line. Until then that line was the only thing holding back the overladen weight of the tree trunk resting on and attached to the snare pole. The snare pole sprung up suddenly with a weight and action that could not be stopped by the prey's weight. The well-placed noose was jerked up and around one snowshoe and over the other upraised leg of the hunter.

The whole scene violently exploded into a great shower of tree held snow. Bits and pieces of furs from his now upside down backpack dripped down from the squirming thief.

Within seconds, my left hand held a Cree cursing, upside down, still screaming from shock and surprise, with the beautiful face of young woman from my village. My other hand held my skinning knife pointed and held within a fraction of an inch from the end of her now runny nose. Our eyes met and held. What the hell was I going to say now I remember thinking?

"So!" I said as unemotionally as possible, "Are you hurt?" There was no immediate response but I could smell the unmistakable scent of urine coming from her and I realized that unless we took some immediate and well planned steps she could very well freeze healthy skin and that would have to be dealt with first and foremost before we could get her back to the safety and ridicule of our village. I quickly removed the straps of the nearly empty and now hanging back pack that she carried. Next I removed the one snowshoe that was hanging uselessly from her captured left leg. I then used the skinning knife to cut the rope right at the joint of the knot so as not to waste any of its precious length. As I did that I held her weight on my arm and shoulder and without ceremony dropped her onto her feet.

I marvelled at how lithe and light she had seemed in my arms as I released her from my grip. She immediately did what all women are experts in doing, she began to cry; her face was filled with shame and pain and the fear of knowing that pissing her pants had introduced an entirely different set of circumstances. There seemed to be no other avenues of approach to follow now; we both understood water freezes very quickly at minus 20 degrees. We had to get her out of her bottoms and pants and then we needed to dry her clothing and prepare to share the night together somewhere near here. We had a lot to do and it had to done quickly, without rancour, or her wellbeing would be at risk.

"If you try to run", I said, "I will catch you and skin you like you are going to skin that marten over there". I pointed at the frozen marten lying dead in my now reclaimed trap.

I hesitated for a second to make sure that she knew I was serious.

"I am going to start to prepare a fire so we can keep you warm while we dry out your clothing. You pick up all of the furs you stole from my trap line and put them in my pack by the fire. Then you skin the marten so we have some fresh food and then we will talk."

The trap line was no longer an issue and neither was I concerned about having to build a fire and a drying area so close to one of my favourite trapping places. Survival was now the most important thing she and I had to consider. Not my survival, her survival. Cold and wet at that temperature meant frozen skin; frozen skin could lead to permanent disability or possibly death. I think that even she was beginning to understand the seriousness of the situation that she faced. She nodded at me, her eyes full of unspoken words; she nodded again in agreement, the words could wait.

* * *

I had a good start on a fire pit and a drying rack by the time she had picked up the furs scattered from her bag, expertly skinned the marten, and laid out her bedroll. We worked together without talking. What had been just a trap site was quickly turning into a sleeping camp.

She was not a stranger to me, I had known her since she was a just a tough little girl killing rabbits near her family lodge. She came from a family that Ma, and Ma's mother and grandmother had known for all of their lives. She was called, *Matowinapiy*, 'A Tear'. I remember being told that she had been given that name because her mother had cried at her birth. It was said her mother had wanted a boy child. The father had drowned the spring she was born just as the ice left Saddle Lake. A boy child would have grown into a man; a man could be a hunter and bring in food for the family. A Tear had grown up preoccupied with trying to be what her mother had cried for.

"Cut wood for the fire," I told her. We would need enough to last through the night and we would have to keep it going until everything she had wet was dry. Neither of us carried any spare clothing; one lived, slept, and returned home in what one wore on the hunt. I will not even begin to talk about how strongly a hunter could smell after a few weeks in the same well-worn clothing. I was still to learn that a World War One soldier was the only human being I had ever met that could exceed the sheer impact of stench a First Nations hunter could accumulate over a period of time. The common belief, often expressed amongst hunters was, "It keeps the mosquitoes away". I believe it did to some extent.

Once the fire had reached a hot coal presence, we moved the drying rack that I had quickly made out of willow and birch limbs and positioned it over the fire pit.

Tear did not even bother to turn her back as she pulled off her wet clothes.

She put them on the rack and sat down wrapping her bed blanket and bottom cover around her lower body, as she did so. I had watched her as she bent and stooped and bared her exposed body from the waist down. She was of a slim build with a small waistline; she took no notice of my stare as her woman parts were exposed both to the weather and my rising interest. We ate in silence, each with our own pre-packed menus. Dried fish seemed to be her staple, mine included meat and some small amounts of dried berries. After some moments of silence I offered to share my still ample store of berries, she readily accepted.

The night slammed close around us while we sat in wordless conversation. No stars or light could penetrate the thickness of the storm that hung above us. The wind picked up just a little and blew ashes and ragged pieces of flame around the fire pit. Neither of us spoke. We both knew the shame she had committed would require an explanation and even then perhaps only the Chief himself could judge the punishment required. If it had been a man, a warrior, he would have had to replace, maybe many fold, the pelts stolen and food and meat for the family of the one insulted. I did not think that any Chief of our Nation had ever had to judge a woman who had committed such a crime.

The silence said it all. Where does one begin to say why they violated an established trap line practice? Where would a woman find the words to explain why she was the one to commit such an act? Where would I find the right words to tell her how I had been prepared to take her life if she would have fought back when she was discovered? It was going to be a long night.

We both sat close to the fire pit, she on one side and me, facing her, on the other. Our eyes were like magnets of opposite polarity, they refused to meet. She had a large number of animals in her pack; all of them had been stolen from my traps. She knew it and I knew it. She pulled her pack close to her and started the expert routine of removing their pelts. Her breath came out in little silver puffs. Slowly, silently, this way and that, her fingers flew from cut to cut; it was clear she had done this task countless time before. The carcasses of the animals were quickly and expertly placed on hastily made stick spits and offered to the flames for cooking. Soon the air around the campsite took on a kitchen smell and both of us took turns removing, with our knives, bits and pieces of meat that looked cooked to our tastes. A marten sizzled next to a fisher and a large mink was more than ready for my tastes.

Somewhere just over the dark cloaked back of the hill on which we sat a pack of wolves gave instructions to one another in shrill and commanding tones. Perhaps the smell of meat had attracted them, or maybe it was the smell of smoke. I nodded involuntarily as the most vocal of the pack sang out again; the fear of fire could be sensed in the tone of their messages. We had nothing to fear from a small pack of wolves as long as we had courage, rifles, and a fire. I stared out across the flicker of the flames, let the wolves say what ever they want I thought, the real problem was finding words to open what we both understood must now be addressed.

Our immediate hunger and thirst sated, we sat staring into the fire; her work was finished with the last red squirrel pelt being stuffed into my pack. I watched her mouth begin work knowing that it was near time for her to start to offer her first attempt to illuminate. I already knew, by custom, that not much truth would be exposed in this first rendition of her speech.

"I am of the lodge of honest and honourable people," she said at last. Her voice was soft with a strong note of confidence. I had expected she would mimic the voice of a man, try to talk to me man to man, and try to approach this situation as two equal hunters. A man would ask for me to understand that a mistake had been made. I did not reply, I just sat watching the fire do magic things in her eyes.

"My father answered Manitou's call just before the days the Christians call spring break-up."

She paused and stared once more into the fire. She seemed deeply occupied by the difficulties of finding the correct words to justify to me why anyone would do what she had done. Not just anyone but a woman. Why would a woman break the unwritten law and practice of not raiding another hunter's territory? For just an instant her bottom lip quivered ever so slightly, her eyes sought mine. I realized she had decided to deal with me woman to man and not man to man. In an instant my heart softened. I was already more than ready to hear her out and forgive her if I could find sufficient room within her story.

"You know very well Askuwheteau I have no brothers. With my Father gone from us we have no one except me that can be a hunter." She sort of squared her chin and looked deep into my eyes. "Cold Dawn knows my Mother always wanted me to be a warrior. I am the only warrior that remained alive in our house. That is why I am here tonight."

She stopped again and for a minute or more she stirred the fire pit and shifted the cooking meat from one spot to another.

"I went to visit Johnny Snake Eye just after my father died and pleaded with him to teach me how to hunt. I told him I needed to become a better hunter. I told him I needed to be a hunter like you are Askuwheteau".

So now she was trying to praise me so I would think better of her. I held up my hand, palm out, and said,
"Soft words and praise will not release you from the responsibility for the dishonest things you have done".
Her eyes became hard and focused like a hawk's eyes do when they see a prey. With a sharper tongue she said,
"You must let me finish before you find fault. I know I have broken many traditions and I also know you are ready to see me punished, maybe even beaten for what I have done. Wait and hear me out, then you can decide what I must do to make things right with you".

The pine forest had grown quiet and still. The wolves were somewhere nearby listening, waiting for my reply. Only the hissing of our fire came between the silence that was mine and her request for my patience.

I nodded my agreement. Her eyes flashed a second's victory before she continued. "Snake Eye told me to hunt when you hunted. He said I should follow you at a distance and if I was very careful not to be seen and if I was very observant I would learn everything I needed to know. He told me you were the best hunter in all of the Nations of our people".

She wiped her nose on the back of her hand and brushed the first few tears away from her cheeks. The shifting light of the flames played with her hair and with the youthful skin of her face. She held her hands out, like a small fan over the blanket covering her naked bottom. All I would see were her eyes; they were already shining like a doe's eyes in the flickering of the flames.

Now she turned her round, full, face directly at me. Her eyes caught and held mine. Smoke from the flames drifted between us but her eyes never wavered. I was now the mouse and she the snake. My manliness and the crushing sense of want stuck in my throat.

"I followed you three times. Three times you went out into this forest and three times I followed you. I stayed behind you and at first I only watched what you did to survive because I did not know how to survive. The second time I watched how you did things, where you set your traps and I studied how and where you hunted and how you lived at night".

A small smile slid across the corners of her mouth and she looked down and deep into the bottom of the fire pit.

"You only looked where you were going Askuwheteau, you never once looked back. You are too sure of yourself; too sure that everyone has enough food for their stomachs." She stopped her words, but not her watching, staring intently at my face to see if my expression had changed.

"The third time I followed you was the easiest of the three. I did not follow you I followed Johnny Snake Eye because he too was following you. Snake Eye left many marks where he had waited when you skinned the animals. It did not snow that week and I knew the trail you would follow. I learned many things from you. I learned to change my snowshoes depending on the type of snow I walk on. I learned to always take great care to learn the paths different animals follow as they move within their lives".

When she spoke again, her voice was softer and her eyes avoided mine.

"I learned from you to be very careful where you go to the toilet or the animals will change their patterns to avoid using the path you have used".

She shifted closer to the fire, took some more meat, and slowly enjoyed the taste and smell before she continued.

"I learned much from you about how to make a bed at night and how to sleep alone when it is very cold. I also saw how you take your penis in your hand and close your eyes on those nights the fire made you warm enough to think about a woman".

The silence hung in the cold air, the firelight played with her eyes. The pine trees moaned with the pressure of the wind way high in their tops. My face burned with the knowledge that she already knew more about me than I had ever shared with anyone else.

"Go on", I said, I am listening". But I was not listening anymore, not really; she had bewitched me. She had my youthful heartstrings hanging out there like the marten was.

Both the marten and I had been skinned and were now being roasted over two fires of different kinds. The marten was on a spit and was slowly being turned until he grew hard and stiff as he sizzled, swollen, and engorged, in his own internal juices. I was burning, like a young man burns, from the fire in her eyes. I sensed that her fire too was building as she spoke to me about how hard it was for a girl to be a hunter like I was.

* * *

Yes, I know what you are thinking and you are right. I was such a fool. But you were not there that evening. You were not eighteen and had never made love to a woman. You were not tired from the constant pressure of the last two days. You were not suddenly aware of the fact there were only two of you present within the fan of flame light and the smell of urine drying on a wooden rack over a fire of your own making. I could suddenly see that A Tear knew a lot more about the passion of young men than she would ever understand about the righteousness and sanctity of hunters' privileges.

Softly, gently, almost without any other bodily motion, she stood up from her position where she had sat hidden by her blanket and her bottom bed cover of canvas. Without a word she seemed to walk straight through the fire pit until she stood before me where I sat, cross-legged on my own bed cover. She reached out and took my hand and gently pulled until I started, almost involuntarily to stand. As I stood she knelt in front of me, without a second being lost between our two motions her hands had found the front of my hunting trousers; with purpose and strength she pulled them down around my ankles. Her eyes were coal black and though her head was turned away from the fire I could swear the deep, dark red glow of burning coals of pine logs were dancing in her pupils. The last thing I remember seeing was when she closed her eyes and lowered her mouth on my now completely shameless manhood. The shock and exotic jolt of her action, the sudden heat of her mouth, the excruciating sexual excitement of what she was doing, what was happening to me, was more than any eighteen-year-old could withstand for than a few precious, uncountable seconds. It was a long, long, delirious night.

That is the memory I wanted to share with you because it is one I have returned to a thousand times. Every time the world grows black and threatening. Every time the world has worn me out with distances too far too travel or carnage too unimaginable to face, it is then I escape within the edges of a memory that only A Tear and I experienced. Our love, for it was love for all the time it happened, was passionate and caring.

I think you will excuse me if I tell you that the next morning was neither hurried nor spent hunting. I watched her every move as she ran quickly, bare foot, into a quiet spot beside a nearby tree. She left a steaming, small yellow hole in the hardened snow beside the path. She dashed back to the fire pit. Quickly, hands moving expertly, she stacked small sticks, large end down, in a tent like circle. Then she surrounded these with larger sticks until a tepee structure was built. A spark from a flint caught, smoke curled, she was back in bed beside me faster then the flame that climbed above the first low hedge of wood.

We spent the morning light exploring. I had only imagined before how soft and smooth, how round and firm, how wet and willing. My need was endless, my ability to contain, hold back, was non-existent.

"Askuwheteau you must know just one thing", her lips were pushed up against the base of my neck, just under my chin, when she finally spoke. I suppose I must have nodded; I do not remember.

"Askuwheteau, I have given you more than even my crime against you has called for". She paused when I stiffened and tried to find her eyes. I was not in any way prepared to blame her now for what she had done to my trap line. "Hear me out Askuwheteau, please let me speak"?

In some small way our bodies pushed apart, the lingering heat of her breasts still clung to me as she traced the smallest line with one finger from somewhere about my mid thigh to just below my navel. "My debt to you as thief and a trap line robber is now paid Askuwheteau but my feelings for you as a women have just begun". As if to emphasise the moment, she lowered her voice, her hand moving quickly down to enclose my scrotum, then with just enough pressure to hold my attention she said,

"You are not the first man that I have been with in a blanket but you will be the last one and that I promise you".

The air hung motionless between our mouths. I stared at her words as they hung in that air between us. Of an instant I knew that she had not only stolen everything in my trap line, she had run away with the trapper as well.

* * *

She came home with me to live within my house with Ma that winter. I worked very hard to ensure her house and her mother and her sisters had enough food but I never let her return to the house where she was expected to be a man. She never once, not for a second, ever let me forget she was my woman and I was her man.

Ma never once let me forget that having a woman that loves you is a large and continuing responsibility. I had to work longer and harder to provide food for one more mouth in our home and three more mouths in the house of Tear's mother. I had to spend many more hours on the forest trails reaping the bounty of my trap line.

I shared the stories of my journeys with A Tear because she knew each and every foot of my trap line almost as well as I. Sometimes she would tell me that she missed going out and once I did soften and I took her with me. It was a complete and utter disaster. Instead of working hard to get around the many miles of the line we wasted most of our energy and time laughing and making bigger beds so we could play our love games until the moon was overhead. At night, in bed, even the wolves mocked us by coming closer than rifle shot. They must have marvelled at us as we found new ways to bring pleasure into a night where exposed skin could freeze in just minutes. I knew so little about the mysteries of being in love and making love with a woman.

A Tear was a woman and she was very willing to show me everything I needed to know. I needed to know that her eyes would tell me things her tongue could not. I needed to know there were words like forever and that they could only be said if you really meant them. She needed to hear that I forgave her for raiding my trap line and stealing my catch. She needed to hear words that I had never said to anyone other than to Cold Dawn and Johnny Snake Eye.

She needed to hear that I would love her and keep her safe from everything and every fear she dreamed. We dreamed a lot on those four days together. Those four days of time wasted making love and falling in love are now a memory that I often return to.

Only five weeks later, in the middle part of February, A Tear complained of sharp hot and growing pain on the lower left side of her abdomen. Grandmother had seen this illness before and she applied cold compresses on her side and told her it would be all right. Ma took me aside and told me to prepare a toboggan that could be used to take the body of A Tear to the Church. I stood, mouth open in shock and fear. I asked Grandmother how she could be so cruel. She replied she had seen this illness two or three times before. She said the Sisters had told her that we all had a small finger on one of their stomach parts that was called an appendix. Grandmother told me she had never known of anyone that lived when it became swollen and infected. Grandmother was right. Five days and nights later I pulled the sleigh with Tear's body wrapped in the deerskin Ma had sewn her into. Others from the village followed us to hear the words the priest would say over her. They, all of them, turned away and left me alone with her at the church.

It took me three days to pull her body to the place where we had first made love. It took me a long while to make a tall platform out of pine and willows and I left her there, as is our custom, all by herself to find her way back to be with Manitou. I had over a day to cry myself back to our village. I remembered the way a fire could dance in her eyes. I remembered how she sat so quietly and listened when I read from a white man's book. I remembered how she and Grandmother would talk about me and hide their laughter behind their hands. I remembered many things about the way we were together but most of all I remembered how she made love with me.

* * *

A Call to Arms

A great war started in 1914. It was England's war; Saddle Lake was far away from England and even farther away from its war. Yet somehow, almost everyone I listened to thought it could be our war because we had signed treaties with the English Crown.

The telegraph spoke to the Indian Agent; he then told the priest who talked to us on Sundays. There were newspapers and some houses had the radio box that talked even though no one was inside of it. There were voices for both sides of the fire; not every one of our people knew and understood it was a white man's conflict not a First Nations war. Even the lodges could be heard with voices raised.

Their Kings and their Generals, their people and their problems came over every First Nation village like a blanket being pulled over a beautiful bride. We, the Cree people, wanted to see the beauty of youth and the fire in a young woman's eyes. The blanket of war brought us only grey thoughts and took from us our laughter and our lust for life and love. Our people talked about how much money a soldier could earn if he enlisted. Our families discussed what would happen if their warriors were not with them to hunt and fish for them so they could live and raise their own families. Many but not all of the elders nodded their heads and said it was not their war.

It was not long until the voices that spoke from Ottawa said they would not ask the warriors to come out from the north woods.

The fishermen on the lake could stay by their fires at night and enjoy nights with their wives and admire the furs our women had made into coats for their babies. The mothers would not have to wring their hands and cry into empty buffalo robes at night because her sons were far away. But even so, the teachers and the priests showed everyone the papers telling stories about the wars in far away lands. Still, some thought, were these not lands that Manitou had made and filled with other people? Were these not lands that now had declared war on the King that we First Nations had signed a treaty with?

Some voice would say, "I heard today that a thousand white men from Edmonton are about to take a train to join their English brothers who are already in Europe".

A voice would answer, "Do those that sit around the bonfires not remember Batoche, or Frog Lake? What memory still remains from Fish Lake or the Cut Knife Creek? And what of the words we spoke in silent counsel about Riel? Does no one remember 'les pendards', "the Hangers"?

And as the stories of the white man's war grew many young First Nations warriors sought the counsel of the women they had married or fancied. Our reserves were filled with men talking about being Canadian and that war was a duty. Almost without exception our women twisted and turned and cried as women always do when their man speaks of leaving home to do something far away.

Some women closed their legs so their men could not enjoy the special love she kept for him alone. Some of our women threatened and cried and told their husbands he would not share the wetness and the closeness of her body if he ever spoke again of such a thing. Others of our women threw their breasts and legs open wide and promised joy beyond measure if her man would only stay with her in her robes of soft new fur.

Still in the end there were, just as among the white men, some warriors who stayed in their lodges while others joined the river of men flowing into the army.

The Chiefs and the 'Onikaniw', Headmen or women, all agreed, it was not their war to fight. Our people from all of the reserves had long and heart felt discussions. Many tears were caught on deerskin dresses as warriors spoke of joining the army for travel and adventure. Many curses followed those that walked away from their circles without a word. Thousands of young warriors listened to their mother's hearts. Others sought the counsel of their father's fire and they talked amongst themselves. They could go away and ride the steel rail to a place in the east of Canada where the sun came up every morning. They imagined how the forests would look from the windows of the iron horse as they crossed over rivers without Cree names. A few went to seek the counsel of the priests and the teachers from their schools. And over the war years, from 1914 to 1918, over three thousand five hundred young warriors joined and fought as Canadian soldiers. And that is a number that comes from the Treaty rolls of my peoples. There were even more men of mixed blood that wore the uniform of Canada and fought and died alongside of our nation's youth. I, for one, was one of them.

Ma listened to my words with cheeks lined with tears. She held her eyes down on twisting hands and whispered the decision was mine to take. She said it was my life and I must live it or lose it in a manner of my own choosing. She told me again the story of Askuwheteau and she said perhaps it was my turn to leave the box and go to see the world Manitou had made.

I asked her to tell me why, after all the years of listening to the Sisters and going to the Sister's church, she still held Manitou before the man called Jesus.

"Askuwheteau", she said. "There are many things I do not know and there are many powers in this world I do not understand". She paused and turned to sit upon her chair as she held me with soft eyes. "I believe with all the power in my body that Manitou exists and I believe a great spirit like he or she is can bring a different sky or a different moon to everyone who lives or has ever lived. I have long past stopped trying to say which one of the peoples of this earth has the correct picture of the Great One in their council lodge. Whiteman calls him God; others I have met, or heard of, have other names and draw a face different from the one the Sisters see. I do not know how to answer you directly but let me tell you this".

She got up from her chair and went to the side of her bed where she kneeled and reached under the wooden frame and searched with her hand, first left and then right. Finally, with a strong tug she brought out a very heavy object wrapped in deerskin and tightly bound with rawhide cord. She handed me the bundle and sat down again watching me. She nodded as I started to open the package. I had lived in that house all of the life I remembered and I had never seen this object nor had we ever discussed it. I pulled the deer skin back and away from what appeared to be a very heavy, blackened and burnt rock about the size of a human hand when it is closed. The rock was very heavy; it surprised me with its weight. I had certainly not held nor seen a rock like that before.

"The night you came to me Askuwheteau, the sky was suddenly filled with great hissing and many, many, long streaks of light. Then there were ten or more very loud thunderclaps but louder than thunder can ever be".

She walked around the room; her mouth making noises like great hisses and thunder; her hands described the path that falling things might take, it was as if I had been there to see the sky as she had seen it.

"You had been walking all day with the man who brought you to me. You were just a small boy and you do not remember the night the sky became fire and thunder but Johnny Snake Eye was here that night and he and I saw and heard the noises".

She took the rock from my hand and held it high above her head. Her hand and voice traced a great arc in our room with the fireplace.

"Suddenly, like a great serpent, a deep furrow appeared right in front of this house and the trees around it started to burn. Both Johnny and I threw our bodies over you. We thought we were going to die right there and then but we did not know why.

Suddenly, as it had started, it was over. The noise of the air and the thunder went away. We left you sleeping and Johnny Snake Eye and I, like two timid deer, snuck our way through the furrows that were engraved and torn so deeply into the field we knew as our land. In the ground I saw this rock, this very rock I now hold in my hand. This rock was burning. The whole rock was burning so hard that it charred a deep hole in the ground around it and two days later it was cold enough for me to lift out of the soil."

When her words had finished she again handed me the stone to hold. I turned it over and over as if looking for some sign or mark, which would prove to me the words I had just heard were true and this stone was from that very story.

She sat watching me as I turned the stone over and over trying to imagine the fear and the lights and fire brought before this very house by this strange black piece of stone.

"That stone was a sign for me from Manitou". She sat silently for a long time after she said that.

I could smell the stone; it had a faint sulphur and foul kind of stench. I had smelled similar unpleasant smells in the school chemistry room when we were working with sulphuric acid and iron or copper. And yet Grandmother had experienced this rock in a totally different way. She had heard it and seen it and watched the fire that came from it.

Grandmother said, "Manitou might be like that rock is to you. He might appear to have a different form when you see him than when I saw him. Because of this stone I have a completely different idea of what the Spirit can be and do. I witnessed Manitou's power in this stone. Johnny Snake Eye and I saw the ground burn and together we felt the entire sky filled with sounds and whispering. Our eyes saw the trees part and fall as if they had been smashed like the wheat is separated from the straw. Everywhere we looked the forest burned and the ground was thrown open wherever it was touched. There were two or three days of small fires all around us in the forests of our area after that night of the stone".

She came to me, stood by my side and together our eyes stared and tried to remember the fear and the fire this stone had appeared with. Then, after some time she said, looking deep into my eyes, "I believed my life had been touched because you had been delivered to me. I believed the Great One sent me a message to tell me of Its interest and concern over what you could be some day. Both Johnny Snake Eye and I felt the same feeling, we spoke of it often when you were just a child".

She took the stone and wrapped it the way it had been before and returned it to the place it had rested for over fifteen years. When she came back and sat down again there was a light in her face I had not seen before.

"I know you are special Askuwheteau. Everyone who knows you talks about how clever, and kind, and helpful, you are. I think you have a purpose on this earth but it is up to you to find what that might be".

Grandmother turned her head and eyes to the window overlooking the field where she and Johnny Snake Eye had once walked with fear in their knees and wonder in their hearts. I sat without a word for several minutes, my mind racing to find a reason that might explain what had been printed on her heart all those many years ago.

And then, with a new deep hurt in her eyes, tears flowing down the checks that I would never, with purpose, make to cry, she said,

"If I say do not go I may be standing in the way of what Manitou wants from you. If I tell you to go my heart will break right here in front of you".

She paused and slowly she leaned forward taking my face between her hands again; looking lovingly and sadly into my eyes she said;

"Only you can decide if you go to see the white man's war".

* * *

Another Reason to Stay - 1914

It was the winter of 1914. It was neither short nor was it a kind winter. I had my trap line and many times I had gone out into air so cold it hurt to breathe in it. The top of my lungs felt like I had dripped whiskey down into them. The snows were deep and dry; my face tingled from the unemotional wind, which pushed against my progress. One day in early winter we had a heavy rain that became a strong crust beneath the newly fallen drifts, which followed. The cold and the ice made it a hard year for animals with hooves. Those with snowshoes or padded feet found the forest had become a banquet. The wolves and coyotes filled their mouths with the weak. There seemed to be no place for many of the animals to hide; nature's hunters followed them and discovered them in places where the snow was layered.

It was a hard year for our people too. It was a long winter for the old and the very young. Women without hunters in their homes, young children without a father, all these were in danger of finding death waiting for them in a friendly place. Some of my people found death in their own lodges because they had no food. They knew a kind of death slower than that delivered by the wolf packs. Many of my people were growing thin and some were already eating from pots of stew made from the leathers of their bed furs. When I returned from my weekly trap line visits I would bring as much meat as I could haul but there were many fires waiting for what I could carry. Sadly, there were some men in our village for which whiskey had made life too easy. Their bodies and their minds had become older than their years and they soon became too old to hunt. These warriors huddled in their cabins and fought with their women; together as a family their houses grew weak and the bones of their faces grew sharp.

I was young and strong of limb. The brightness of the days rubbed joy into the power of my measured pace. The winter with its blizzards had left no marks upon the face of the snow except those the flailing wind had made. Pine tops bent beneath their burden of suspended ice. My trail existed only in my mind, no path, or marks, or blaze, remained for me to follow. Following trails of memories filled every hour of my walking. A fallen tree, which reminded me of an arch, told me where my leg trap waited. A hard edge of rock that I had slept near during the softer days of summer spoke to me of the soft water that ran from the ground it guarded. I knew these endless forests like a pianist knew the difference between this piece of black and that piece of white. Only when the snow blew and changed the shapes expected did I stop my restless pilgrimage to find and reset the two hundred traps along my course. Almost always my eyes and feet remembered the paths I had made during the sweeter days of my boyhood springs and summers. I was proud and sure of my talent to find where each and every trap and wire would be waiting.

I hunted with only the barest of necessities. I had a rifle with a sling. I carried two very sharp knives, one for killing, and one for skinning. I wore strong, light clothing; thick leggings made of moose hide, tied round, and secured by leather thongs. I wore a Hudson's Bay blanket like a coat over my softer deerskin jacket. The blanket became my bottom cover when I slept on the freshly piled pine boughs of my beds. My jacket had a long skirt, which could be folded up when walking or let down to keep the wind off my legs. Grandmother knit all of my underclothing and stockings. Together we designed and crafted light and strong snowshoes, which gave my feet their wings.

I carried two pairs of snowshoes. One pair longer and narrower, these were worn when the snow was firm and fast. The other pair was shorter and wider for walking in the silent brooding, black and endless pines along the ridgelines and the lakes.

I carried a small pack filled with dried meat and fish. I made water from the snow and a small flint started my fires. I did not need much food; I ate what was in my traps. Even a skunk tastes good when your stomach hurts from hunger. Over my head and face I wore a handmade cover, a small blanket really. It was the mask I hid behind, it was the pillow I slept on; Johnny Snake Eye was the master and he taught me how to change from looking like a man into looking like someone who was no longer there. Even wolves would pass their cautious eyes over my hiding place and not see me waiting for their lives to end.

It took me two short hours to reach the silent valley where the first of my traps was set. I approached from the high side, the hillside. Fox and Lynx would follow only the bottom ground. The low ground gave the best cover; the summer rains ran deeper in the bottomlands. The wetness and rot of nature provided for the rats, mice, and squirrels. Rabbits pushed their deep paths into the softest parts of the bottomland. That is where my traps would find the best of the furs.

For four or five days I had seen no tracks except those made by wild things. My traps were full. The weasels and the martens liked my little banquets and now my fur pack was nearly filled with the work of my skinning knife. I only took enough of the meat to fill my hunger. The rest I left as bait where Mister Wolf or Mother Coyote thought they had found an easy breakfast.

As was my normal routine, I turned at the end of my line on the fifth day. I would set and reset my traps on the way home. The short days had brought no warmth and my food pack was nearly empty of dried fish and bannock, the unleavened bread of my Grandmother's kitchen.

The late rising light of the sixth day bore no promise of seeing the sun. My shoulders were already stiff and stabbing accusations of overwork as I fumbled out of my pine bough bed. Last night's fire pit was black and cold. Holding a piece of dried fish in one hand and my penis in the other I lavished a long stream of yesterday's snow unto the side of a scrawny black pine. A silence filled the brim of the valley I had slept in. The long trek that lay ahead was already consuming my mind as I planned my steps towards home.

Then, suddenly, in rapid succession, two things occurred which to this day still paint broad strokes of bright red memories across my youthful mind.

From the left side of my vision, the side that presented the valley floor waiting fifty yards or so beneath me I caught just the slightest movement. Movement meant life and life meant target. My hands sought slowly to fill my mouth with the remnants of food and to put away my cold and early morning manhood that would not have brought much hope to even the most inventive of women. Slowly, purposely, I crouched seeking to find the muzzle of the rifle always waiting for my left hand to seek its frozen throat. My eyes swept the valley floor and revealed an unfolding drama in two parts that had already occurred in those minutes before my bladder had forced me to stand from my bed and ready myself for the trails awaiting my feet.

A huge bull moose had ventured out into the early shadows to scrape his massive front hooves into the snow banks in the search of grass asleep beneath the snow. His movement and timing had caught the attention of a pack of four black wolves returning from the north along the valley floor. To the wolves a large moose was food for thought. The thought of survival; I was witness to a drama about to be revealed. The wolves had spread left and right and were crouched above and below the bull watching for an opening. The bull was slowly swinging his head and massive horns, his eyes filled to overflowing with the terror of the moment. The wolves knew as well as he, a healthy bull moose could kill a wolf with one quickly and correctly timed toss of his head. They all understood just as well that four large wolves free to pick their time and place can tear the rear tendons out of an unguarded rear leg in a heartbeat. Once down and injured in the deep snow a moose so hamstrung was doomed to die while watching parts of his massive body being torn away by his assassins.

The place where I had made my bed of pine boughs and my waking movements had been masked by the pines and until now I remained unnoticed by the actors on the valley floor. Slowly I judged the distance to the place where they would meet. Almost without movement I brought back the action and slid one round into the waiting maw of the rifle barrel. Using the ever willing wall of pines I brought the rifle up to my shoulder, eye to the rear sight, seeking the flesh that would satisfy my Grandmothers hunger and that of the village. There were many in my village without sufficient meat to feed their children. There were many children awaiting my return. Just as I squeezed the trigger the bull swung his head hard to the left to meet the arrival of the first male wolf. My bullet found its target. Its path tore a small but deadly path through hard fur and leather jacket into and out of the other side.

The moose's reaction to the sound and impact was instantaneous and intense. He lunched forward, head down as if in pursuit of the very thing he dreaded. His next few hopeless efforts were aimed at killing or wounding the lead wolf. The other wolves, like clock springs overwound, bolted from the recoil of the rifle shot already filling the valley with the explosive crack of its power. Three wolves turned as one to bolt down and to the left, away from the rifle and the smell of death. The bull, his eyes not recognizing anything but terror, tore through the first and second rows of pines. The wolf that I had shot, life no longer an option, exhaled his last breath into the freezing air and snow that filled his mouth.

Why kill a bull moose when all that I could carry was a skinned and gutted thirty pounds of meat? Besides that, a wolf hide would be admired at the Hudson's Bay store; a moose hide would have had to be left behind. When I made my way through the trees and deep snow to the place where the wolf's still steaming body lay, I silently smiled at the choice I had made.

* * *

When the winter snows of 1914 leaked away into the creeks and the creeks swelled the rivers I began to work with great determination. When the other young men in Blue Quill and in Lac La Biche went hunting fish with bow and arrow I worked hard with axe, saw, and hammer to build a new lodge. I hunted meat and I traded it to other men so they would work with me. I wanted to leave my Grandmother with a new and strong house that would winter well when I was away. I had shot and skinned twice as many beaver as I had ever sold before and I left every cent of money I had in a box for Ma.

I begged the Sisters to hold Grandmother close to them if she was sick and they promised they would guard her from evils. I spent many nights in the lodge of Tears' mother and I found a strong young warrior that agreed to live in their lodge in marriage with her sister. I knew in my heart that my two main responsibilities had now been put to rest. Cold Dawn would have a fine new home and more money than she had ever had to look after her and keep her well throughout the days I would not be with her. Tear's family had become my family too. Now a man from a good lodge, a man from within our Band, had taken on the pleasure of a warm bed and the labour to provide his new family with food and safety.

Finally, when everything I could do had been done I walked to Edmonton. It was about one hundred and twenty miles. It was 4 October 1915; the ground was hard so it only took me three days. That was the same number of days required to enlist in the Army.

* * *

Changing Colours Changing Skins

Edmonton late autumns are mostly seen frowning. When the nights are clear they scare you with their beauty. Northern lights and stars so bright you can almost wash your face in them. Winter days, on the other hand, pout around in the streets and in front of buildings. They pile snow in corners on weekends then break into uncontrollable tears all week long in childish attempts to make amends. It can get so cold the smoke from fires goes straight up and snow comes straight down. City people do not like cold so they respond by hiding behind curtained windows pretending the grey skies don't make them worry about their shrinking coal piles. Hundreds and hundreds of native people and half people like I am sit around bars and hotels watching life go by. The white people do not speak to the Indians. The half people pretend they are whole people. At the end of the day Whiteman's eyes are blind to what we could be because we do not know who we are.

One of my biggest shocks when my eyes became accustomed to seeing a city, as just a large village, was every white man I saw was on his way to somewhere or maybe coming back from somewhere else. Whiteman seemed to know how to live in a city. They dressed for the city and they knew how to move around in it. The women went shopping for food nearly every day and the men rose early from their beds and went to work. Those that worked made money and money bought clothes and food.

My people do not understand the need to work for a living. For them living comes from hunting and fishing. When the white man had taken the buffalo away and introduced the poison called whiskey it was easier to be drunk than it was to work for a living.

My people were not comfortable living in a white man town or city. They were not accustomed to walking on roads and sidewalks. Wagons and horses paid no attention to their footsteps. The lights on poles were brighter than the stars at night and the spirits that dance in the winter sky could not be seen. My people started to lose their sense of wonder and the white man began to treat us as if we were not human. But there was no poison on the reserves so they came to live where they could find it. I know they loathed themselves. But just because they were uncomfortable in the city did not stop them from craving the poison that made them crazy.

Edmonton squats on the river like a women peeing in a small rivulet. She has two feet, one on the north side of the North Saskatchewan River and the other on the south. The high banks on the north provided protection and height for the old Fort Edmonton buildings that were being torn down and replaced by a large hotel that would command all the eyes that searched above the riverbanks. The acrid smells that steam trains leave in their wakes mixed with the sweet scents of burning pine and Cotton Wood that leaked out of the thousand chimneys lining the frozen streets.

On either side of the North Saskatchewan River the main Canadian National and Canadian Pacific Railway lines strung their silver fingers alongside its muddy water. Edmonton did not bother anyone in those days. It had a population of over seventy thousand souls but maybe only twenty names were known in the tents of the chiefs in Ottawa. I am equally certain that almost no one bothered with Edmonton either. It was struggling with what to do with an old fort, a new legislative building and two new railroads that carried immigrants bent on farming on land that once was home to buffalos.

We, the First Nations, did not have our land anymore we just had reserves. Whiteman had passed laws and written words on sheets of paper on how to deal with the First Nations as a tribe of people. They wrote words and gave powers to people they called Indian Agents and these Agents had power to give money and medicine and take away our children from their mothers.

Slowly, year after year, Whiteman built new schools and took more and more of our children from their villages and from the places where they lived. Mothers would cry and hope that their babies would come back to them with all of the skills and knowledge that the white children had. The Catholic and the Anglican and the United Church all built schoolhouses and residential schools. These schools stood as a symbol of the authority that Whiteman had over everyone that was not white. And after fifty years during which Cold Dawn had seen the white schools grow and had watched the children learn how to be almost white she said to me,

"These children know nothing of our ways so our ways will die and we, as a people we die with them".

When I went to Edmonton I saw for the first time that being, talking, acting like or drinking like an Indian no longer made the news. The news coming out of England, on the other hand, seemed to concern everyone everywhere. God we were boring in comparison. The Edmonton Capitol newspapers, even the Winnipeg Free Press, were filled with pages of pictures and editorials about the Empire. For some reason the Kings of Europe had gone to war and grand events were occurring on the battlefields of Europe. The news was bad. Over a thousand men were dying every day.

Anyhow I wasn't there to look for work or at least not the kind of work that the Ukrainian, Russian or German immigrants were looking for. I was there to join the Army.

Edmonton had already manned, trained, and said goodbye to one Infantry Battalion. The 49th Infantry Battalion had been authorized in November of 1914 and had shipped off to England just last June. The papers all said that the 49th and about one thousand young soldiers from the Edmonton area were almost ready to enter the battle in France. Another Edmonton area battalion had been approved to be raised, it was going to be the 51st Battalion, they were actively recruiting men and that is the one I was hoping to join.

Grandmother had spoken with the Sisters in Saddle Lake and they had talked to the priests. They had given me the address of a priest in Edmonton who would let me stay until the army took me. I arrived on a bright, clear, and sunny November day. I got a ride with a farmer for the last few miles into Edmonton. The farmer said I was fucking crazy to volunteer and I agreed with him wholeheartedly but I did not let his words change my mind. There were things I needed to see for myself. There were things I did not understand about being a white man and it was time I went to look for myself instead of reading about these things in newspapers and old books.

I told a conductor of a streetcar I had just joined the army and he let me have a ride over the High Level Bridge to an address near the University of Alberta. When I finally arrived at the lovely old brick building that bore the address Father Boisvert had given me I was surprised to find an Italian speaking priest answer the door. He didn't speak English but in French we reached an understanding. He knew I was coming and he would show me where to enlist and after evening mass he showed me where I could sleep.

He seemed nice enough but I knew right away he preferred the company of other men. In my culture we felt the weakness in men like that. We called them two spirited. They were men but had the spirit of women.

In our culture we considered them too weak to do a warrior's work; they did not hunt so they had to cook. I had no idea what the rest of Canada thought of two spirited men; it seemed in Edmonton they let them look after Indians and half breeds. Later on, in the army, I feared for the life of any man that showed the same weakness.

The Canadian Expeditionary Force had many ways to attract men off the street or off the farms and into their river of recruits. There were pictures in the newspapers, on the sides of buildings, there were large signs on the top of some structures; every picture said I should join and serve my country.

The next morning Father Luciano Capono and I walked the short mile to the Military District Recruiting Centre. We didn't talk; he had seen the skinning knife I carried into the shower room. The knife spoke louder than words. I slept with the door open that night confident I would be alone in the room with four beds. I had seen in his eyes the recognition of where he and I stood on the issue of relationships.

Some short distance before we crossed the street to where the Center stood Father Luciano explained he had a short errand to perform. He turned and disappeared into a small store with Italian writing on the sign above the door. Women in dark long coats came and went through the door. They went in with bags in their hands and came out with small bundles of things wrapped in paper. The young ones smiled at me as they passed by, the older ones talked in loud voices in a language I could not understand. They all had soft, dark eyes like the girls from Saddle Lake.

I stood outside and waited. I recall wondering to myself what lay ahead for me in my pursuit to be a white man. It was then that a completely obvious conclusion slammed into my half Indian, half white man consciousness.

Here I stood, unknown to anyone except myself. Unknown because the only thing I had to prove that I was alive was the fact I was standing there. I carried no papers, I did not have a birth certificate or citizenship papers. I had been born in a room filled with people that drank and lived like every next day might be their last because it was true. My Mother had never registered my birth; it was not necessary to show a piece of paper to prove that you had been born. Anyhow, she would not have known how to do that anyway. I had been taken to my Grandmother's care where she was told I was the son of her daughter whom she had not seen for two years. She was told my name was Bastard or Little Bastard but sometimes my Mother had called me Howard. There had been a man that lived in the same house that my Mother had lived in and his name might have been Howard. And for all the years that had followed I had been known by the only name Grandmother had given me. I was Askuwheteau, 'He keeps watch'.

I was a half man. I was half Cree and half white. I was a half man with only half a name. An Indian could have one given name; a white man would have two names, a first name, and a last name. I was tall, thin, and very fit. I was a hunter and a student and I could speak four tongues. I had gone to a respected school where I had been well known and acknowledged as the best student they had seen for years, maybe even forever. Now I stood alone here on a street in Edmonton wanting to volunteer for the army but who was I? What name should I give as my army name? I knew they would not care what my name was as long as I had a name. Should I use my Indian name or should I use a white man's name?

My eyes turned to a street filled with faces. Every face was of a different shade, a different age, and each face spoke silently of its own background and ethnic origin. I turned and stared into the window of the store Father Luciano had disappeared into just minutes before.

I studied the reflection of my face in the store window. What story did my face tell? I knew I did not look like my brothers on the reserve. They were of a darker skin; their eyes were black pools of impenetrable thoughts. They were as lithe and well formed as I but I was taller, broader in the shoulder and my eyes reflected the browns and hazel of my father and grandfather.

A young man pushed out of the street side door of the Italian Store. As the store door opened and closed I saw a name painted in gold and outlined in black, 'Giorgio Costello, Italian Pasta and Delicacies. The young man turned towards me and silently walked by carrying a small package, something his mother might have sent him for. Our eyes met. He could have been my brother; we were of the same size, our eyes were dark brown, he held himself erect, shoulders back and alert. Our skins were of an olive shade not known to the English or French families but well accepted within the closets of their minds.

My thoughts were racing. Did I want a life of continual explanation of who I was and where I was from? If I wanted to live with the prejudice of fellow soldiers concerning their relationship with a half breed, then I should go forward into that recruiting center as Askuwheteau. I could sit with them, explain, and prove how many languages I could speak and how good I was at mathematics and geography. Or, I could just walk in there and say I was a boy from a family that had arrived from Italy thirty years before; I did not need my father's permission to join because everyone could see I was over eighteen years of age.

Father Luciano exited the store with a flourish. His expression was one of satisfaction and expectation as he handed me a small leather-bound Bible. Later on I found, somewhere on the second inside page, it was called a "travelling edition". It was an Italian edition.

I do not know why he had bought an Italian version. Maybe it was all they had or maybe he had just forgotten to ask for an English version. I opened the Bible, standing there in the street. I realized that the Father, in his heart of hearts was doing something very special. It was a special moment, not only for me but also for him. His gift was a token of friendship and a missionary's hope that through the Bible I would find Christianity. To me the gift was an omen. In that second I became someone I was not.

From that moment on I was Giorgio Costello. I asked him for a pen and asked him to sign and date the inside cover. When he asked me what name he should write in it I took the pen and printed the name, in front me, on the door of the store. That is how I enrolled in the Canadian Expeditionary Force and into the Depot of the 51st Battalion, CEF.

The 51st Battalion was formed in January 1915. By the summer of that year it had managed to dispatch two formed, but not completely trained company sized sub-units to England for further training. Since the unit recruited in Alberta and considered itself to be from the Western Military District some of the soldiers started to call them the Edmonton Regiment.

Almost immediately or at least from the very first moment I put on a uniform I was visually transformed from a half breed boy to a soldier. Amongst the first things I learned to do was 'standing in line'. I became very good at standing in line. I quickly learned I was just a number and it was the person or thing at the end of the line that was important. I needed to be interviewed, stand in line. I needed to have a medical, stand in line. I needed to sign some paper or other, stand in line. If I needed to go to the toilet, stand in line. Even the toilet was more important than I was.

By the time December was about to be birthed, Alberta weather was holding true to form. Edmonton did not have a military training area so other than basic lectures and marching there was no place where soldiers could train. The solution to that problem was simple; send us to the brand new training area in Valcartier, Quebec.

On 10 December, all of us that had recently joined were issued new uniforms, boots, and a long woollen coat called a Great Coat. After stirring words about how we would be the backbone of our brand new battalion that would be reformed in England, we lined up and marched on to a train. A train going east, the very same east where I had been told the sun came up out of the Great Salt Lake that never rested.

Each of us had been issued a large canvas bag called a kit bag. We put our new ranks, names, and numbers on those bags. We were told, 'One man, one bag'. We were told, 'Every man is responsible for his own kit bag'. We were told, 'A fool and his kit are quickly separated'. We were told we were going east where a large army camp was waiting for us so we could become soldiers.

We already knew a lot about being soldiers. We had learned private soldiers are lower than whale shit. We had learned every soldier with something on the sleeve of their battle dress jacket was higher than a Private and therefore they were not whale shit. I had learned it was best to stay very quiet and not say very much to anyone unless they started to talk to you first. If someone had something to say to you and if they had something on their battledress jacket it was best to stand very tall, stand at attention, listen very carefully to all the words that were not curse words and always just reply, 'Yes Sir', or 'No Sir', depending on which response seemed the most appropriate. That was the best way to become a soldier.

My mind holds firmly to the two days and nights I spent riding an iron horse as it ploughed straight ahead on its path through hours of wheat fields long shorn of their bounty. Then there were five days and nights of forests and rocks. There were glimpses of lakes and rivers, all without names, all with people. There were iron bridges that had been flung over deep cuts the water had carved. All of this was just as Cold Dawn had told me in her legends. I spent almost every minute I was awake gaping out of a train car window. For most of the journey the sound that iron wheels made as they rolled over the break between one piece of steel track to the other filled my spirit with a sense of movement and adventure. I swore the beat of my heart often matched the steady staccato of the wheels crossing over the rails.

The train cars became known as 'either cars'. They were either too dark or too lit. They were either too hot or too cold. They were either too loud or too silent. Towns, villages, cities came and went. Sometimes we stopped and white people got on or got off. Only the faces of the soldiers stayed the same. The other faces changed, the faces of the men and women that were not soldiers changed but the land and trees were a constant ribbon moving past my window. I saw signs pass by my window; some were in English, and some in French. There were Cities and towns with name in Cree but no one except me might have known that. I was the only one that said,

"Winnipeg means murky water". The soldier next to me said,

"How do you know that"?

I said, "The conductor told me".

That was more or less the point along our journey I began to understand that what had been my people's country was no longer ours. What had been our villages and our hunting lands no longer belonged to us. This Canada I was travelling through was not a Cree country, it was Whiteman's country and now I was part of them. The Cree country that had been here existed only on the Reserves white man and their papers had given to us. This was no longer a Cree Nation this was a Canadian Nation.

About a day before the train stopped and I got off I realized that the Indian in me that had been Cree was now a Canadian soldier. I learned a lot about being a Canadian soldier by looking out of the windows of that train. I also learned by looking into the eyes of the other soldiers that were part of my journey that the further east we went the sadder their eyes became. Their eyes began to look like the eyes of the children that lived at the residential school at Saddle Lake. Their faces did not change but their eyes became sad and hollow. It was as if the soul that lived behind those eyes had walked away into some quiet forest and would never again return.

My strongest memories are a blur of about eight weeks at Camp Valcartier; rifle ranges, ill-fitting uniforms and poorly made boots that melted off our feet. We lived in tents at first and then the real snow came. By Christmas time we were living, over one thousand of us together, sleeping in long rows of beds, on the floor of one large building. We were told we were waiting for a large convoy of warships and passenger ships to arrive in Quebec City and then we would all go together to a place in England where we would become real soldiers.

Valcartier was cold and there was snow but there was marching in long lines of three abreast; eating food I had never tasted before; sharing toilets with ten or twenty other men at the same time. Then there was the joy of a Ross rifle at eight hundred yards. Faces, everywhere I remember faces; most of all I remember being alone in a sea of young faces just like mine. Slowly but surely I became the man I said I was and not the man I had been before I joined. I became hidden in the timberland I had invented. I became Giorgio Costello from a farm just outside of Edmonton somewhere. I spoke when I was spoken to, I never drank and I never lied but I lived a lie as big and quiet as Giorgio Costello.

When it was cold we marched a lot. We would line up in three rows of men. Rows as long as a hundred yards, each marching man would occupy a yard and together we three hundred men would march as if we were one. Sometimes we would sing songs I had never heard before but I learned to sing them. Sometimes we would march in silence and sometimes we would all silently curse the rain or the snow or the road or the fact that we were marching. Slowly though we all became the same man marching.

Sometimes we did not just march on roads, sometimes we had to march in front of desks, or tables or doctors or officers that needed to tell us how much we still had to learn. One of the marches we all had to do was to march ourselves in front of a Paymaster. The Paymaster was an officer responsible for everything that had to do with how much money the army owed us and how much of that money we, as individuals, had actually received from the army. The Paymaster wrote in our pay books every time we received money and we were responsible to keep and hold and produce our pay book every time we wanted to receive more pay.

The pay book was the most important book or record every soldier had and believe me when I say every soldier took great care to maintain and hold on to that little cardboard covered book. It was always buttoned up inside a battledress pocket and if you watched soldiers closely, as I did, you would often see them consciously or unconsciously, reach out and check the pocket they carried it in to reassure themselves of its safe and continuing presence. We were paid one dollar per day for every day we served in Canada, soon, when we arrived in Europe, our Private's pay would climb to the princely heights of one dollar and twenty-five cents. Even then I remember thinking one dollar and twenty-five cents is not very much money for the pleasure of letting some German soldier shoot at you in Belgium.

Soldiers, I quickly discovered, were expected to learn and to do a lot of things. You learned never to question an order from a superior officer. Everyone was superior to a private soldier. Soldiers were to do everything they were ordered to do being mindful that not only was their personal honour at stake but so was the honour of their battalion. The battalion and every symbol of the battalion were second only to God himself. Soldiers, it seemed, might very well die alone or with others of their platoons or companies but they always died for their battalion.

Another thing every soldier had to do was to sign a military form in front of the Paymaster that allowed the Paymaster to take money out of the monthly pay owed to us so that the Paymaster could send a monthly allocation of moneys to the soldier's mother or wife. The soldier had no choice about how much money was to be taken out, the soldier could only decide to whom the money would go. We were paid thirty dollars a month, our pay allotment was one half of what we earned. If you were married it went to your wife. If you were single, it went to your mother.

I sent money every month to Cold Dawn. I had made a visit to the Indian Agent in Saddle Lake before I had departed on my three-day walk to Edmonton. I had shared with him what my intentions were and he agreed to receive and hold all mail sent by the military or myself in a special box that could only be accessed by Cold Dawn or myself.

I knew the Agent would speak to Cold Dawn after I left and I also knew the money I would send her would keep her safe and provide for her for all the time I was away in the army.

When she wrote to me she would often comment how good the Agent was to her to give her all that money.

* * *

An Ocean Between Dawn and Me

If you have never heard Christmas carols sung by one thousand throats, then you have never heard Christmas carols sang the way they should be sung. Christmas in Valcartier was a soldier's Christmas. There was marching in long rows right up to the day before Christmas. There was marching in long rows on the 28th and 29th of December but on the four days of Christmas there was a soldier's Christmas.

It seemed as if some incredibly large hand had come between what we were and what He was. The silliness of getting up to the urgency of bugles sounding did not stop. The absurdity of having a thousand men line up for one hundred toilets could not and did not change. If your name started with 'A' you were still first in line. If your name started with 'Z' you could pee in a pail outside while you were waiting for your turn to pee inside when it was you turn because your turn came last. That was the way the army was in Valcartier. But it was Christmas.

Voices changed from shouts to civility. No one shouted for four days. The officers walked around through the kitchens and the messes and training buildings and they became who they had been before they had become officers. They spoke about their families and we talked about ours. Tables groaned piled high with ham and turkey. Soldiers wrote letters home to loved ones and some of the lucky ones who had received Christmas mail read them to those who had not. Some guys, two I got to know from Leduc, even shared their Christmas cards.

It cost a soldier nothing to mail a letter home; some soldiers spent their nothings writing tens of letters, some like me wrote only one. In my mind I wrote a letter to A Tear as well but of course only Manitou would read it.

And every day, two times a day, there were voices singing. Five hundred voices here, three hundred over there. Hundreds of voices, each in their own groups called church parades. There were 'Catholic Church Parades' and 'Protestant Church Parades', even if you didn't call yourself one or the other you were ordered to get in line and march to one or the other. The Padres would preach; the Priests would do their magic of converting wine into blood and crackers into bread. But the real magic came from the voices. At the end of each service, someone had figured out that if every voice, in every church, could sing Silent Night and Oh Come All Ye Faithful and if it were done at the same time, the camp would fill with heavenly sound. If you have not heard those carols sung by one thousand throats you have not heard those songs the way they should be heard.

Then New Years came and went; I suppose what I remember most was the amount of snow that fell. Snow and French voices singing songs that could have come from Normandy or Brittany. This was an entirely different culture; New Years was different from anything I had ever seen before. Men got drunk; oh nothing new about that but in their drunkenness there was a new kind of melancholy. Primarily everyone was held firmly in the grip of an entirely new level of loneliness. Everyone seemed to be held in an unrelenting longing to be home with family. Christmas had been tables groaning under loads of food and freshly cooked pie made from fruit. All that was new to me I admit but no one seemed too sad about Christmas, no one stayed in their shell and pretended they were not here. New Years though was different.

First, there was the drinking and then the voices started in song. Songs soon led to men instinctively gathering together in the small bands of individuals that shared the same accents. At some point of the evening, most of us had gathered in the mess hall, which was the largest standing wooden structure on the Camp. I came to realize I really had almost nothing in common with anyone else in the entire group. I spoke many languages; most of these men only spoke one, either English or French but not both. I came from a geographical area in northern Alberta that no one else came from. Although I did not discuss my childhood experiences with any of them I was certain that not one other single soldier in that mess hall that New Year's night had ever run a trap line or slept on pine boughs while waiting for the wolves to finish their nightly chorus to the moon.

Everybody knew there was a convoy of troop ships and naval escorts forming on the east coast. Large numbers of the men currently at the Camp had already been warned that they would soon begin a two-hour train trip to Quebec City to begin the loading for departure to England. By midnight the joy of a New Year had been sucked out of the Mess Hall. The men here were not yet close friends, faces were recognized, but they were not yet brothers in arms. We had not faced the scale of stress and survival it takes to weld companies and battalions together. A sloppy silence of individual loneliness covered the floor and everyone on it.

By the time midnight tolled and some voices reached out and carried Auld Lang Syne across the floor, there was a sadness Christmas had not known. Even men too drunk to make their own way back to their beds must have wondered what the hell had made them join this fucking army in the first place.

I think that during Christmas most of the soldiers honestly missed being with their families and friends. At New Years, I believe, most of the soldiers missed everything that had been important to them in their lives.

During the first week of January 1916, I was part of a draft of forty-two soldiers from the 51st Battalion that marched out of our Valcartier barracks and onto a train going to Quebec City. We were a fine and proud looking body of men that knew a lot about shovelling snow and cutting down trees on a rifle range that would be a rifle range only when spring arrived. In the meantime, since we had been trained to be soldiers in the snow we had to go to England to be trained to be soldiers that could live in the mud. A few more hours of steel rails and waiting in shunting stations made little difference about who we were as soldiers. At the end of our journey we were marched off the train and onto the dockyards of Quebec. Two days later our ships weighed anchor and sailed off into a fog bank filled with foghorns and blinking lights. Those two days made one hell of a difference on who we were as soldiers.

* * *

We no longer were Canadian soldiers under training in Canada. Now, every man jack of us was a Canadian soldier on his way to a war in Europe. Straightaway we were real men with our hearts in our mouths. A new kind of adventure was about to start. The shouting may have sounded pretty much the same but the listening part had changed. Now men were wondering how long it would be until the man standing next to them would be a casualty. Canadian newspapers were filled with daily reports of the hundreds, and on some days, thousands of Empire and other Allied soldiers that had been killed in battles somewhere called Ypres or somewhere else on the Somme. Now the bullshit about training to be a soldier would soon be over. Very soon all of us would be training in England. Soon all of us would be learning how to live in the continually harsh and desperate conditions presented by trench warfare. It would not be long before our lives would go from days spent training and nights spent in the relative comfort of barracks into one where everyone had to face the unmentionable terror of being a target.

Portsmouth. I had never even heard of Portsmouth before I boarded the ship in Canada. Everyone seemed to have some dreamy, far away look in their eye when they said the word Portsmouth. I had no idea what an English city would look like so I only remember the long wait getting into the harbour. Small tugs and some navy ships were busy moving submarine nets to let us pass. The harbour was filled with the vomit of soldiers standing at the rails.

Rain soaked everything I was wearing and all of our new Canadian woollen uniforms smelt like dead sheep and mothballs.

I remember longing to get off the ship. It was old; it belonged to a British shipping company that specialized in transporting immigrants to Canada before the war. It was a patchwork of chipped paint and rust that covered every inch of clothing unfortunate enough to touch it. The decks had been out of bounds for most of the six days of sailing. Gale force winds and the fear that German submarines were in the area had created havoc amongst our own officers. No one seemed to know if it was safer to be below the water line or above the water line. What did it matter I remember thinking? If a torpedo hits us we will all either drown or die in the freezing winter ocean anyway. What matter if death finds you below or above the bloody deck? Anyway, we never did see a submarine. The food nearly killed all of us and most of us were so sick we would have chosen to die from drowning rather than having to go back down to deck four for another slimy meal of oatmeal and sour milk.

It was no longer raining when we started to disembark instead it had long since become a fairly serious hail and snowstorm. Long lines of soldiers shuffling through passageways, into deck lines, onto gangways and out onto the dock. It was amazingly orderly except for the occasional chasing of a service hat tossed asunder by the cold wet sea wind that was crashing into everything and anything not tied down. The wind was howling at well into thirty miles an hour and driving hard sleet and hail sized snow into the backs of the lorries lined up waiting to carry us to the Salisbury Plains.

The roads from Portsmouth were lined with small villages. Stone houses surrounded by brick walls covered by moss looked out at us as we bumped and clattered the forty miles of back roads leading to our rain soaked tents. The town we were suppose to be going to was called Aldershot but it looked like a rabbit warren filled with tents being held down by wet looking soldiers.

We were quickly lined up, marched into eight-man tent groups and then spent the next many hours resetting tents and kitchen lines that had been blown down in the storm we had arrived in. All I remember was being wet all day long and freezing in our soaked tents the entire night as well. This is how our European training started and that is how it ended. Nearly everyone was sick. Everyone cursed and marched, marched and threw Mills grenades, marched to and back from rifle ranges. It was like that for the whole of January through to March when three others and I where picked to go on a sniper course.

* * *

Everyone, every single soldier was introduced to trench warfare. The trenches dug on the Salisbury Plain were nowhere near like those on the Somme that we later learned to die in. They were wider, straighter, never shelled, and relatively clean. In France they conformed to the battle lines that indicated which side had won or lost; no line of battle is ever a straight line but they were in Salisbury. Still we did learn to live in the mud. Our Canadian boots melted off our feet and we waited for English boots to replace them. Our horse harnesses rotted on the backs of our horses and no one could replace the bits and pieces that they were made up from because the British harnesses were different. Not better just different. The made in Canada Ross rifle was a complete disaster. It would not, could not, work in the mud and we were mud soldiers. We could not mark our maps in the rain because no one had ink or crayons that would not run in the wet. The paper used in our message pads and in our maps simple rotted away in minutes after becoming wet. It was always wet it seemed.

And then there was the food. English food and food in England were two separate stories. I did hear tell from soldiers that had actually been granted leave to go to London or Portsmouth or other nearby centers that there was such a thing as English food. They were told that before the war English dinning rooms and restaurants actually cooked, produced, and served very acceptable and rather tasty meals. Now there was a war on and over two million hungry and restless men and women had come to fight a war in Europe. They were getting ready to fight that war while living in England. Everyone who came to fight the English war had invaded England from the hulls of their ships and all of them required feeding.

England, the English and British farmers, simply could not cope with the demand for beef, chicken, bacon, pork, and grain foods. All of that had to be slaughtered, packed, crated, salted, cured and shipped across the Atlantic Ocean from the America's, Canada included, or from Australia and New Zealand, and into the mouths of the waiting. First of all, pork and beef do not remain fresh when carried on trains, ships, and trucks for very long. The vast majority of meat and for that matter all food types were cured, salted, smoked, and packed in boxes long before being shipped to feed the waiting armies billeted in England. The end result was that army food in Salisbury was just plain awful and in France, we were told to expect it would be ten times worse. They were right.

The 22nd of March 1916 was a Wednesday. My training company had been assigned what I called a 'run-up rifle range' all day. A run-up range was one on which there were no fixed or installed target lines or points. Instead, the ranges were made to feel like the soldiers were actually advancing forward, their fire and movement up the range was controlled by the various levels of officers and non-commissioned officers in accordance with a previously agreed scenario and time sequence. All this was rather novel and sometimes even fun; most of our days on the rifle range were just spent doing target practice at different ranges.

A day on a run-up range was conducted in the following manner. It would start with a lot of shouting and yelling; the first line of soldiers would depart from firing point in long lines stretching across the ground to be covered. More yelling and shouting as some targets would appear in front of the advancing soldiers. Some of these targets were made to pop up after the range crew pulled some ropes or they appeared out of trenches in the ground, which contained them. That line of soldiers would fire, either standing up or lying down depending on who was yelling, at the targets as they appeared. The position, which the soldiers took to fire at the targets, was decided by whoever was doing the yelling. That line would then depart the firing line, have some tea standing in the freezing snow or rain, and the next line of soldiers would go through the same exercise. And so on, and so on until lunch was brought out to the range.

Lunch would consist of three or four steel boxes of food on the back of a horse drawn wagon. Some cooks and their helpers would line up the food on folding tables. Soldiers would use their own eating containers and implements, which were always carried by every soldier. These eating utensils were just part of the nearly one hundred pounds of personal kit and gear that every soldier had to carry, learn to march with, and be accountable for every single day of their days as soldiers. One man, one kit, was the watchword and if you lost your kit it was replaced and the cost to replace it was subtracted from your pay sheet. Only soldiers that were killed in battle were not charged if their bodies did not have all of their kit. Some severely wounded soldiers were also excused from payment but we were expected to have a pretty good excuse such as, 'I lost my left arm and could no longer carry my kit'.

Soldiers tend to have very dark and strange senses of humour and missing kit stories made for good soldier stories, some of these jokes continued to make the rounds and were told countless times by soldiers as if they were their very own experiences.

"So Private Jones, you lost your rifle I see".

"Yes Captain I lost it last night during our raid into no mans land".

"Well, Jones, I will have to deduct it from your pay. Let me see, ah yes, one Ross Rifle, with cleaning kit and bayonet, 22 dollars and fifty cents. That will be all Jones, report to Company Stores and get a new rifle, you are dismissed Jones".

"But Sir I can not go to Company Stores to get a new rifle Sir"!

"Why not for the name of God Jones? Why can you not go to Company Stores"?

"Well Sir, don't mean to be a bother or anything but I lost my left leg below the knee last night Sir. A machine gun bullet I do believe hit me. Took my leg completely off Sir, but it was all right, my mate Bill helped me hobble back to our lines".

"Lost your leg below the knee you say, so did you lose your boot at the same time as you lost your left leg Jones"?

"Yes Sir. Lost my boot and sock and my left leg below the knee Sir. I am terribly sorry about all the fuss Sir".

"Oh damn it all Jones, let me see then, sock 12 cents, boot 1 dollar, Ross Rifle and cleaning kit, 22 dollars and 50 cents, that will be a total of 23 dollars and 62 cents deducted from your pay Jones; any further questions Jones'?

"Thank you Sir and yes Sir, I did bring back the Captain's pistol Sir after he was shot and killed on the way back. Can I get a reduction on my recovery of lost items if I return the Captain's pistol Sir"?

"Don't be stupid Jones, one man, one kit. Captain Smith's pay book will now be credited with the return of his pistol. Damn unthoughtful of Captain Smith to get killed like that; how on earth did he think we were going to recover the pair of binoculars that he was carrying. Now off you go Jones, you should see the doctor about that lost leg I would suppose".

The 23rd of March started like any other day at Aldershot. We lined up for the toilets, we lined up for the shaving stands, we lined up for breakfast, and then I was told to report to the Company Commander at his Company Headquarters' tent.

A Corporal glared at me from behind a table with a lot of files on it. He barked and growled and sounded liked someone that had slept in a wet tent and had to line up for the toilet and the shaving stands and the cold oatmeal that was called breakfast. I had learned never to take my eyes off anyone that thought they were important, somehow watching them made them think that you might be important too and it normally meant less yelling and barking. I told him that I had been ordered to report to the Company Commander and gave him my name. He told me to sit down on a bench in another nearby tent. After some time, six other soldiers from the 51st Battalion joined me, none of us knew why we were there, but we sat, six wide, on a bench for four. We had been told to sit and wait after all.

A Sergeant appeared about an hour later, by that time the six of us were warm and well acquainted. We all seemed to have one thing in common; we knew that we were better shots then everybody else in our training companies. The Sergeant did not bother to introduce himself. He read off our names, we nodded our heads, he said we were better shots then everyone else in the training battalion and therefore we had been selected to go on a special sniper training course. He then gave each of us a piece of paper, duly signed and stamped which contained all of our names. The typed instruction included a time and place to report for sniper training, the start time for the course was clearly underlined and included notice that each candidate was immediately granted four days leave. The Sergeant draw himself up, stiff and ramrod like in front of us and announced the course would commence in four days and until the course started he had decided to grant us all leave from the unit until the time that we were required to report.

You could have heard a pin fall. Imagine that, in spite of the fact that the Officer Commanding had signed the paper, the Sergeant had decided to grant us four days of leave. Four days to do whatever we wanted to do but we had to do to it somewhere else and could not do it here.

I reported back to the Corporal in the Company Commander's tent. He handed me a leave pass and transportation warrant which allowed free travel by train to just about anywhere in England. I then was ushered in to the paymaster's tent and given a lot of English money.

My next stop was the YMCA tent where a lovely English lady of about seventy years gave me a rail map, a map of London, a small printed booklet explaining the locations of the major English Cathedrals and a picture of London Bridge. Another gentleman at a desk selling tea and cigarettes gave me a lecture about over indulging in alcoholic beverages and provided me with a brochure on Syphilis and other transmittable diseases.

John Edward Martin came from Edmonton; he was the fellow I had sat next to on the bench in the briefing tent. The short period of time we had shared, hip-to-hip, on the wooden bench had been enough to form a skeletal framework of friendship. On being informed of our good luck of having been granted four days leave we two had agreed and did meet at the rail station and made a beeline to London. We were both pretty much country bumpkins. London was certainly the largest city either of us had ever been in.

Troop cars were generally speaking the oldest rolling stock on the rail line. The seats were plucked and torn, paint was scraped and missing and most of the sliding windows had stopped functioning years before. It really didn't matter much to John and me though, we had about an hour and twenty minutes to make up an outline plan. Using the piece of paper the lady from the YMCA had provided with addresses and names of recommended hotels and guesthouses near Victoria Station, we traced possible routes and picked an area where we would try to find accommodations. In our original conversation we had discussed staying together at least long enough to get settled into a room before we both struck off on different courses for different reasons.

I think John was completely overcome by the universal urge that young men suffer from when separated from young women for an extended period of time. I was mostly but not entirely consumed by the urge to discovered how incredibly large London was. Arriving at Victoria Station for the first time certainly did not disappoint either of us. For the morning and then part of the afternoon we stayed together. It was almost immediately obvious we did not share a lot of common interests. He was a farm boy with an overwhelming desire to find a place where he could plant some seeds. I wanted to test the water's depth and feel the good earth beneath my feet before I choose whether to fish or cut bait.

For a time we concentrated on getting lost, that was pretty easy. Discovering where we were didn't really help either because we were just two of many soldiers wandering aimlessly round waiting for the pubs to open. I did manage to convince John to walk through the timeless Cathedral of Westminster before silver strains of laughter and women's voices hauled him off in pursuit of younger underpinnings.

We had agreed to share a hotel room and both of us had our own keys. I went my way and he hotfooted off to a pub we had discovered near Victoria Station. Damned if I know how he managed it but he found another bed to sleep in and I did not see him again until we got back to Aldershot.

Although John would not admit it he was found by a lady who spent a lot of time searching for men just like John. She was playing the love game; she was looking for love without attachment and had learned the hard way, some would say the only way that some men were more then willing to pay the price to play the game.

John should have paid a bit more attention to all those lectures we all had about the risks associated with unprotected sex with previously unprotected women. At any rate, not that it is here or there really, John did return to Aldershot, he did start the course with me but he ended up in a military field hospital and did not finish the sniper course.

London was just sitting there waiting to be explored. I must have looked like a star struck goose looking down on Lac La Bitch on a clear night in August. It just seemed to me that every house, office, shop, and workplace was immense. Buildings seemed to grow right up out of the streets. Wide steps and stairways beckoned feet to follow. Windows were filled with models of women and men dressed in suits and dresses.

Everywhere, just everywhere, a bustle of crowds wove their way in one direction or the other. Horses pulled carts and wagons across streets that intersected and led to even more streets and intersections. Lorries and automobiles hooted and clanked as they competed for space and running room. Some houses had windows all along their rooflines where people lived. Other tall buildings had windows framed in stone that must have been more than eighty feet above the streets. Streets were paved with small stones or bricks. An army of men with buckets and shovels walked the streets tipping horseshit into wagons. Automobiles wove through the walkers and pedestrians seemed mindless of the constant rattle and prattle of a thousand lips. What, I wondered, would Cold Dawn think of this if I could let her see through my eyes?

My feet and map carried me down to the Thames. The river had banks completely closed in by cement. Hundreds of boats and ships sailed right through the middle of the city. I stopped and watched in amazement as a lovely little sail boat, all painted white with its name in gold paint, zigged and zagged from one side of the crowded river's surface to the other. Of a sudden, a barge cut it off; the two respective Captains exchanged comments concerning the ancestral linage of the other with frequent invitations to visit Hades or some other nearby part of the underworld. The lovely little sailboat lost way, bumped alongside of some other high piled barge, and was last seen with sail asunder and being towed by another craft that appeared to be piled high with pigs and crates filled with fowl.

Even after all this time I still feel sorry for the brave little Captain of that sailboat. There he was trying so hard to make way against tide and wind yet in the end he lost his way and I expect much of his pride. As I followed my map along towards the grandest cathedral in the English world I thought maybe I had seen a small play on how the British Army must have felt in those first few months that they faced the massive German war machine in 1914.

Westminster almost crushed me with its size and splendour. Everywhere I walked there were beautiful men and women in wonderful clothes and boots. Everywhere I looked these beautiful men and women were hurrying here and there as if the war rested on their shoulders alone. Pubs on every corner were filled with laughter and drunken soldiers shouting for more beer. Shops along the streets cried out for you to enter and buy a new hat or a baby carriage. And then I found the Palace where lived the King of all the Englanders and all the people of the Commonwealth and all the other places that England ruled. It was even bigger than that fancy new hotel being built in Edmonton.

I went back twice on two separate days just to stand and stare at Buckingham Palace. I had to rubberneck through the gate or across the places in the fences that permitted a view. There were soldiers on horses and soldiers in boxes that paraded all day long. It was wonderful to see the power and majesty of the building in which the King and all of his family resided and controlled. But, I must tell you, one of the biggest shocks I had during my holiday in London did not result from the buildings or the river or the palace. The shock came when I looked at the map of London and saw all the Parks. But it was not the parks themselves that shocked me it was what had happened to the parks that were supposed to be there.

War had changed man and man had changed the parks. This war had London by the throat; the German submarines were sinking tens of ships every month and sometimes even every week. Millions of men and some women had come to Britain to form armies and navies and air forces. Millions of men and women needed food to eat; hospitals to get well in, and the military needed every inch of space that it could get to build temporary buildings.

I walked for miles in London following the roads and paths that lead to, into, and around the major city parks. With few exceptions all the paths and roads were filled with people; some even seemed to be enjoying the memories of when the parks had been filled with flowers and trees and lakes filled with water.

Now, people worked in the parks. On the days that I made my trips down The Mall and along Horse Guard Road and from there along Birdcage I was greeted by thousands of small gardens getting ready to grow vegetables. The entire lake at Saint James Park was being drained down to the very bottom so that a temporary military building to house the Shipping Office could be built. Hyde Park was filled with parading soldiers and anti-aircraft guns.

Only the Serpentine remained as a body of water and its banks were filled with nannies and children with boats. In Regent's Park, a place where my little guide book advised I must visit I found that the Army Postal Service had erected one of the largest wooden structures ever built in order to provide the Army Postal Services with enough space to handle all the incoming and outgoing mail from soldiers of every part of the Commonwealth.

Alexandra Park, once a beautiful place to walk and enjoy the flowers throughout the year was now an accommodation center for thousands of families from Belgium that had fled the ravages of the German invasion.

* * *

John Edward Martin did not go with me to Buckingham Palace. He said he had seen enough parks and palaces filled with vegetable gardens and refugees. I thought he was crazy to miss the chance to see the King or the Queen coming and going on their daily routine of visiting military camps and hospitals. I know it may sound a little cruel to just come right out and say it but I believe that it served him right when instead of seeing the Palace he found a lady who had a gift that kept on giving. Had he gone with me to walk through some of the parks that had been designated for soldiers on leave he may have met a pretty girl like I did.

Her name was Sarah Ruth Middleton. She was a Private in the Women's Army Auxiliary Corps and she drove a Rolls Royce staff car for a Major General. We met in Hyde Park where she was parked waiting to pick up her General. He, a British Lord by birth and a gentleman by nature was having lunch nearby with some friends, also generals, with whom he had gone to university.

Sarah was completely fine with just waiting for the general to have lunch with his friends. She told me later that her routine was pretty much always the same everyday around lunchtime. The General would call up a few friends and they would go a quiet little Officers Mess just around the corner from Hyde Park. She would drop him off and he would walk back to their parking spot a couple of hours later. She would sit and read in the auto on inclement days or sit around on a park bench, feed the pigeons, and naturally become the center of considerable attention with the passing by of many soldiers. And what red blooded man would not want to make small talk with a pretty girl in uniform trying to keep the pigeons from shitting on the deep British Racing Green Rolls Royce that she was driving.

I liked Sarah at first sight. She had steel blue eyes and a completely peaches and cream complexion. She was tall, over five foot six with a willowy figure that stood out even under her long uniform jacket and ankle length skirt. Honestly, she was beautiful and she knew it. I had stopped to stare at her; I was only doing what every other soldier must have done. Odds on that occurred about a hundred times a day so she was certainly used to soldiers stopping to stare at her and her car.

I just didn't know what to say so I said,
"I don't think that I have ever seen a women as beautiful as you are".
She said,
"Where are you from that you are so rude as to say something like that"?
I said,
"I am from Edmonton Alberta which is in Canada and neither have I ever seen a Rolls Royce before today either".
And from there on forward we just sort of stood there talking about all sorts of things.

She said she had never met a Canadian before. I said I had never talked to a lady who wore a uniform and drove a car. She said that she didn't always wear a uniform and she might have some free time after her general returned from his lunch. I said that I had not eaten since having cold oatmeal at the Other Ranks Mess in Aldershot at around six o'clock that morning. She said she was genuinely sorry that the food was so bad in all of the army messes. We then talked about English food and food in England. That led to her picking me up in her motorcar at my Hotel later on that evening.

She took me to a little pub she knew; it had a secluded parking lot where she could park the Rolls where no one could see it from the main road. Not seeing where the car was parked there was important because no one would need to know it was not the general that was her passenger.

The pub was filled with people that seemed to know a lot about hospitals. Sarah said her father ran a hospital and that everyone she knew came here because the food was good. I do not remember what either of us had to eat. I remember drinking very warm beer and pinching myself that a pretty girl like Sarah had risked driving a military vehicle on a non authorized trip.

She talked about wanting to do something on her own, without her mother and father telling her what to do. She told me they had picked the schools she went to, they picked the university she attended. Her mother ensured that her friends were from the same schools and she thought that her mother had even decided whom she would marry.

Sarah was very proud that she had just marched off and joined the Women's Army Auxiliary Corps. Her parents wanted her to be a doctor and she thought she might do that when the war was over. I told her about how hard it had been to leave my grandmother in a house that I had built for her. I told her about how cold it was in Camp Valcartier and how deep the snow had been on the rifle ranges that we were still building when I left.

Sarah told me that she felt very sorry for all of the soldiers because they had to work so hard and live in such misery in the battlefields of France and Belgium. I told her that she was beautiful when her eyes were wet with tears.

Sarah asked me if I would like to see London Bridge at night. It seemed the bridge was just near to the pub because as soon as we departed the dinning room she led me up a long and narrow set of stairs leading to a room with windows that overlooked the bridge. The room could also be used for guests of the pub if they wanted to spend the night; it had a large bed, a bathroom, and a closet.

The room was dark but the shutters opened on to a street that had a nice view. There were no lights on in London because the German Airships had been using them to find the city on their bombing runs over London. A lot of civilians had been killed by German bombs and had made the city feel closer to the soldiers in the trenches she said.

Sarah was absolutely correct when she had said she did not always wear a uniform. In fact, she was out of hers before I was out of mine. I remember, afterwards, I said that I was very sorry I was so fast but it had been a very long time since I was with a woman. She had placed her lips right at the bottom of my jaw where it becomes the soft part of your throat. She told me that she thought my heart would explode because it beat so fast. She said that was all right to be fast and that we had lots of time until the car had to be returned to motor transport garage.

I was a lot slower on the second and the third time. By the time we stood and dressed together she had completely stolen every thought that my silly mind had held. As we walked out through the darkened halls and into the parking lot the only thing that I could think were things that included her. When she drove away, without lights, in the silently ticking Rolls Royce, I was already counting the hours until she had promised to meet me again at Victoria Station.

Other than that I had an interesting time visiting places which the London City Guide said were 'must sees". For the rest of my nearly two remaining days I pretty much just walked and waited until Sarah was parked somewhere waiting for her General. I saw a lot of buildings and a lot of parks that were being turned into gardens. Oh, and I got to see London Bridge from the window of the same pub the next night too.

On the morning of the fourth day of my leave I said good-bye to Sarah and took a train from Waterloo Station Aldershot. We stood, pressed close together just before I stepped up into the train car. Her hands were strangely cold as I held them. Her cheeks were wet and salty. She kept saying,
"You can write me any time; I promise to write back".

I told her I really did not know what love was like but if what we felt for one another was love than maybe that was the way I felt about her. Her eyes were red and very sad when she said goodbye. She promised that she would write often. I had already given her my military address and we both promised we would meet again in London just as soon as I could get another leave. She left me a phone number at her family's home. She said if I called and asked for her mother and told her that the hat Sarah had order was ready for pick up she would know I was coming to London.

It was a short train trip really; the train ride took about an hour. I sat by a window, staring out as little English villages and railroad stations came and went. We only stopped a few times; my car was close to the engine and I remember marvelling at the banging and clanking as we shuddered to a stop to let more soldiers on.

I think that nearly everyone on the train that day was a soldier. Almost all of them were very quiet; some were desperately trying to hide their emotions behind their greatcoat collars. The one emotion I do not recall seeing was someone physically demonstrate a desire to be returning to Camp Aldershot, or West Down South Camp, or Larkhill Camp or any of tens of other army camps that made up the Salisbury Training Area. With every wheel that turned a revolution on that stop and go trip back to the army I kicked my ass, over and over again, for not having just said what my heart had felt. My heart said, on every click and every clack,

"Damn, I think I really love that girl".

John Edward Martin missed that train and the one that followed that one. He did make it back though; later, while we were on the sniper course. He told me all about a lovely lady he had met in a pub while Sarah and I were out looking at lights that floated on the Serpentine. This woman, 'his' woman he called her, and about ten other ladies shared a two room flat and worked at a kitchen that provided food for the South African Military Hospital in Richmond Park. He said she was very lonely because her husband had joined the army in 1914 and she had not seen him except for one time when he came home from France on leave.

John was very proud of the fact that Eleanor, her name was Eleanor, thought he was a wonderful lover. She told him she never took money from the men she slept with but she did need some money to send to her poor old mother who was feeling poorly in some town called Petersfield. John told me his entire stay in London had only cost a few pounds. Eleanor had provided all the food because she could take a bag of it home everyday when she left the hospital.

You seemed very pleased with himself that all they had needed was beer money and he had paid for all of that. He felt so sorry to hear about how much Eleanor loved her dear old mother in Petersfield that he gave her all of the rest of money the army paymaster had given him when we first came to London. She had been so happy to get so much money she hauled him off to a large store on Regent Street where she had bought a brand new dress. They had made love in the change room. He thought it quite funny that their love making had upset a couple of the ladies who worked at the store. Eleanor just laughed at them he said.

About two weeks later though John wasn't laughing and I would guess in retrospect, neither was Eleanor. John went to see the doctor because he was having great difficulty hitting targets at eight hundred yards and also because he could no longer take a pee without crying. Snipers have to hit targets at eight hundred yards and snipers do not live very long in the front lines if they have to cry every time they take a pee.

John went back to being an infantryman shortly after the doctors cured him of the syphilis Eleanor gave him. The last time I saw him I reminded him that syphilis might have been the only thing Eleanor ever gave to anyone for free.

* * *

Going to War

When they said, "You have been selected to attend a Sniper Course", I just supposed, without any further consideration, I would be packed up and sent to some other group of tents somewhere on the Salisbury Plain. Well that was a bit of a miscalculation so allow me to tell you how that all unfolded.

Five days before, a small group of five other soldiers and myself had been ordered to report to the Company Headquarters ready to commence a one month course at the Third Army Scouting, Observation and Sniping School. Each of us had been given that all important signed and stamped piece of paper which gave our individual number, rank and name, unit, and a description of the course we were about to report to. Not one of us had any indication that the place of instruction, the Third Army, was in action in France at that very moment and that the School was located just behind the main defensive line very near to St Eloi, on the Ypres front.

As our small group of 'sharpshooters' reassembled on Monday morning at the Company Headquarters the exposure of where the course was to be held and the fact that it meant we were now being assigned to an entirely new and different unit was like stepping out of a safe tent and being assaulted by a bucket of cold water. Mouths dropped, eyes sought out confidence while theirs held none but disbelief. I thought the safety and security of the rain and cold of England was about to be supplanted by the mud and terror of trenches in Belgium and the grinding war of attrition in France.

The 'hurry up and wait' was over. It was back to the tent lines to pack up all of my personal kit according to battle order. Everything that I needed to carry into battle went into a large back pack and a small pack; the remainder went into a kit bag. The kit bag was then carried over and given to the Company Stores for forwarding to my new unit destination. The Company Orderly Room changed my records to show my new mailing address; they issued a posting instruction to a new unit, written in three copies; one for my old unit, one for my new unit and one which would be forwarded to Canada for permanent records.

My orders said that I was now an Infantryman in B Company of the 49th Battalion. I was certainly pleased to hear that because the 49th, just as was the 51st, had been raised almost entirely from soldiers from the Western Military District and most of the recruits and officers were from Edmonton and the local area. I had certainly been reminded many times that the 49th was often referred to as the Edmonton Regiment and some even called it the Loyal Edmonton Regiment. I was very sure that I would feel right at home and that I might even run into someone from the Lac La Biche area if I were lucky. The 49th had been raised before I had joined. It had been officially formed in November of 1914; it had sailed as a unit to England in June of 1915 and had been deployed in France since October of 1915. The piece of paper I was given confirmed they were part of the newly formed Third Canadian Division and they were in action on the Ypres front.

At about the point in time where I had packed and cleared out of the Orderly Room a very large, mean and efficient Sergeant by the name of Edward Prudholm appeared and using very few words he made it extremely clear that I belonged to him, body and soul. Further, he said, I would do exactly what he told me to do just as quickly as I physically could perform that order 'or else'.

Prudholm was proud of his Swedish heritage. He had come to Canada with his parents, he had no formal education, but his size, loud voice and physical strength were impressive. His deep blue eyes could fix you in place as if he himself had issued a physical threat. He didn't talk very much and he shared stories about his lifetime even less. We did find out that he was from ranching country out near Nanton. He did say once that his father used to bite the balls off young bulls and then he would look at us as if he might find us in that same category.

"I'll never ask you boys to do anything I cannot do myself", was his favourite opening line, which was frequently followed by, "There ain't nothing I cannot do". I should mention, I suppose, just for general interest; Prudholm was the first and only man I ever met that could swear, cuss, and use the Lord's name in vain and never once, for five long minutes, use the same foul word twice.

I had lots of time, on the train ride to Portsmouth, the voyage by ship across the English Chanel to Calais and later the train, truck, and horse drawn wagon rides, to contemplate exactly what 'or else' could mean. I learned that 'or else' meant Sergeant Prudholm had made this trip before so he knew what to expect along the way. Since he was a Sergeant and a very big, mean and loud one at that, he normally got just about everything he asked for as we passed along through the steady chain of moving soldiers going somewhere to do something. He had the task of getting six of us from the 51st Battalion to the Third Army Sniping School. Clearly, it did not matter one red rat's ass if we liked what he was doing or how he was doing it, he was going to get us to the Third Army Sniping School. The problem was no one, or very few people in the Third Army at least, had any idea as to where the school was on any particular day. It took us three days of walking or catching rides on horse drawn wagons and sometimes just waiting, for the school to find us.

We each carried about seventy pounds of personal kit, a rifle, and ammunition as well as gas cape and hood. It had been raining in France since November. Not a single road or trench or indentation in the ground remained empty of the greenish sludge that owned the surface of the soil. Never in my life had I seen men living in such conditions. My mind circled and played with the memories of the two nights spent in an Inn that overlooked London Bridge.

Everything that was real here was as strange and charged with emotion as had been those nights without sleep.

Somewhere far away, far away to the east, a constant insult of sound, sometimes just a rumble and at other times more pronounced, crashed and collided with the clouds. It was as if a curtain had been drawn across the land. On one side of the curtain there were thousands of animals, vehicles, rail tracks and the constant movement of men bent beneath their packs. On the other side, the side on which the war was being fought, there was a ravaging thunder and constant spewing of the voice of the guns. Even from far away I could hear the air tearing as if a great piece of it had been removed. There seemed to be hardly a minute when there were only the sounds that we made walking in the mud. Everywhere I walked I seemed to be only looking down. Looking down at my boots as they played and sprayed the muck and mud of the fields and roads we walked on. Now and then the ground trembled, shock waves passed along from trenches hidden from my eye because my mind refused to accept that for over two years now, white men had been killing their fellow white men at a rate never before imagined.

As I watched my feet move forward I wondered where I was pushing them and why? The mean and ever present Sergeant Prudholm was the only source of direction I knew. Only he knew and only he gave instructions as to where our next steps would take us. I found myself wondering when Askuwheteau would start to see things that only his eyes would choose.

On the fourth morning of our rambling from field to village, from ruined barn to a military police checkpoint and then off again to another village ten kilometers further to the south we were finally found. We had gone from English miles to European Kilometers. It took some time for my feet to recognize the difference.

The Sniper School wasn't really a school at all in the normal sense. The last group of eight or ten sharpshooters had been returned to their respective units two days before. The school was really just a small group of soldiers that called themselves a school and found accommodation and purpose because of the overwhelming necessity to match what the German Army had already put in place. The Sniper School consisted of two Sergeants, one Staff Sergeant, and a very old and tired looking British Cavalry Major. They and we new arrivals were billeted in what had been a hotel. The building now lay largely in ruin. Most of the hotel's roof had been the victim of a large artillery shell. Roof tiles and beams lay scattered across what might have been a tidy outdoor garden before the war. There were no intact windows; the remaining holes had been sacked over with canvas but the massive front door that greeted the street still swung gently on its large iron hinges.

The resourceful owners of the old hotel had patched up what they could and moved the kitchen into a couple of rooms in the large old vaulted cellar. They now offered rooms in what had been the wine cellar. The food and baths were excellent in spite of the fact that no one ever asked what or where the meat came from. Two younger women acted as waitresses, washed dishes, did laundry and slyly offered comfort in the wine cellar for what most of the soldiers considered a reasonable price. Seven members of the Sniper School were lined up there the first night of our arrival. Sergeant Prudholm made it very clear he would be first, third and if he wanted to try again later, he would qualify for a discount.

"Remember Giorgio", he said as he disappeared down the broad stone steps leading to the second basement level that had been home to local wines for over three hundred years, "I never ask anyone to do anything I cannot do myself and I can do just about anything". His deep, rumbling laughter seemed to excite the wide assed waitress he had his arm around as they matched steps into the candlelit bedroom that must have existed below.

I got to know the Cavalry Major fairly well that night as we shared a small bottle of Armagnac. We sat near a centuries old fireplace. It was just a large, smoke and fire blackened huddle of fieldstone but it was immense. Its mouth was six yards wide and it rose twelve feet above its hearth. A series of iron rods and posts were fastened to the inner sides of the firewall; it was difficult to make out the functions each of the individual cranks and handles must have performed back in the times when it had been used to heat water for the laundry.

The laundry, now done in another part of the basement cellars, had been part of this level before it had been converted into what was now the hotel's main sitting room. It was more like being in a bunker than sitting in a hotel main lounge but it was warm and safe from the ravages of war that had already and could very well again sweep across this little village anytime soon.

Major Penberthy, I guess you would say, was the 'father' of British Snipers and Sharpshooters. He had been born into a family and class of people that had enjoyed countless days and generations of game hunting and competition shooting on their privately owned estates in England. He told me when the war first started the number of British soldiers and Officers killed on a daily basis by German and Austrian snipers appalled him. The German Army had gone to great lengths to acquire and later to design and build special rifles with special telescopic sights offering far better accuracy and range than their normal service rifles. He had a soft and articulate manner and in spite of his rank he did not seem at all over impressed with his position. While sipping slowly on a small but warming glass of the vintage Armagnac he said,
"We British considered it very unsporting to shoot Germans with a hunting rifle. We were months into the war before our very own soldiers started to write home to their fathers to send them a favourite rifle they might have had at home or had seen used at a local competition. Slowly our units started to arm a very few specialist shooters to go out and try their hand at killing German snipers. Now I run this school, for men just like you that have special skills and abilities, so that we can dominate no mans land in just the same way as the Germans have been doing for the last two years".

None of us really knew what to expect as we started off just after dawn the first morning. We walked as a gaggle down the old village main street that led, after about a kilometer or so, into a large field. It was hard to tell what this might have been, perhaps a pasture for cattle? Now the signs of war had erased much of its field-like appearance. Shell craters pockmarked the entire area. The feeble scrapings made by soldiers as they attempted to survive the shrapnel still bore witness to the ugliness that had seeped from the thrones of Kings into the farmers' fields of France. A previous battle had swirled and cratered nearly every few yards; some old earthen trenches still drew lines across hedges and into shattered wood lots. Into and around this field the Major and his small band of brothers had mounted targets, figures of soldiers in German, French, Austrian, Canadian, and Belgian uniforms. The distances from firing points were anywhere between three hundred to twelve hundred yards. The idea, the School instructors said, over and over, was to see how well we could find, identify, and hit targets at various ranges. We spent two days doing that, just that. I had a great time I must tell you with the Ross Rifle that someone in the Canadian Corps must have provided the school Intelligence Officer for Canadian soldiers to train on. In fact, I liked it so much that I took it with me when I left. It really wasn't theft, it had been and still was Canadian property, and all I did was return it to the Battalion for its original purpose. However, during the course, we only had that one Ross rifle. We were six Canadians until my friend John Edward Martin started to complain about his burning bladder, so we had to share. The British used a few different weapons with various modifications to their Lee Enfield service rifles. We had a chance to zero and to shoot them all. By the end of the second day I started to feel a little uneasy about how our training was being conducted, what we were doing and how we were doing it. We had just spent two days shooting on a range. That is not at all what I had imagined sniping would be.

After most of the early winter light had marched off the field and left us standing discussing how far we could see and which targets were still visible because of the various colours that they were made up from, we all trooped back to our sorry little ruined hotel and the comfort of a hot meal.

Speaking of food, the difference between the foods I had become reluctantly used to in Canada and Aldershot and the French cooking at the Sniper School was unbelievable. Canadian army cooking consisted of throwing everything available into one or two big pots where it was stirred until unrecognizable in its original form and served with a large spoon as a ball of mush on an enamelled plate. The English Army cooks started with the mush that Canadian cooks ended up with, then they added water and green peas and called it food. French cooking employed the skills and effort required to remove the skin from a weasel. The proper knife would be used for the required cut. Every stroke was done precisely and with meaning and intent. Meat was prepared not cooked. Seasoning was an art not a handful of salt and pepper flung into the pot.

In Canada, breakfasts in Valcartier had been the best meals of the day. Real bacon and eggs and huge pancakes served with maple syrup. The constant routine of serving that wonderful breakfast allowed more time for the army cooks to turn lunch and supper meals into mush that no one could recognize.

"Hey, what do you think this is? Could it be beef"?
"Nah, no one could make beef taste like this, it must be pork".
"Pork? Are you kidding, pork is white meat, this is dark and stringy".

"Ah, now we know why the piano disappeared from the theatre last night"!

On the second evening, following a wonderfully prepared and served dinner with red wine from the cellar, we rose as a group from the table and, somewhat like a small flock of seagulls, settled under a sputtering candle in what was now the main lounge of the Hotel. The lounge had been just a part of the massive first floor of the Hotel basement before the entire roof and top two stories of the building had fallen victim to the explosive force of a German heavy artillery shell.

Discussion and protocol were slowly becoming relaxed somewhat, students and instructors were becoming more acquainted, the liberal availability of brandy and Armagnac certainly helped. No one seemed to notice when I slipped away to seek the assistance of one the women on the hotel staff. I do admit that I had noticed she was extremely resourceful in all of her assigned duties.

She did not seem surprised as I approached her; neither did she show any alarm or wonder as I explained in my Canadian accented French what I hoped she would assist me with. She listened attentively for a while, nodded her head at the payment I offered and motioned me to accompany her quietly down into the bowels of the third floor of the labyrinth of the basement, which had many rooms for many purposes.

Two hours later, both exhausted from our consultations and labours we smiled politely and went our separate ways. She did remark, on parting, that she had never received such a strange request from a man before but that she had found it extremely exciting; she had enjoyed the entire event tremendously and that if I ever wished to repeat such an affair she would be a willing participant.

I, on the other hand, in just two hours of explanation and encouragement, had played the dominant role in the design and watched the skilful hands of a seamstress construct and sew a wonderful sniper's top cover and bottom cover made from all sorts of cloth and materials that had been used over the years in the curtains and table clothes of the Hotel. It was a richly blended combination of earth tones and durable linens. We invented and made a complete hood and long flowing over-jacket, which reached down to my boots. We overstitched both the hood and the jacket with a web of netting that had been part of a covering from the vineyards used to keep the birds away from the grapes. Into the net we had strung countless stripes of greys, browns, blues and green cloth until the cover seemed to be part of the fields that I intended to lay in. The undercover was a fine piece of canvas that had been an awning over a window now long since missing from what had been the front of the Hotel. To it we had added some pockets and secure fasteners so they could be used to hold and carry the bits and pieces that a sniper might need and use in his work. Again we had added an over webbing so that we could attach pieces of earth toned materials to change and modify its outline and shape.

In a very formal way, Madeleina and I nodded and shook hands at the end of our efforts. Both of us knew we had established a relationship deeper than just the casual guest, hotel worker acquaintanceship. Both of us were proud of the fruits of our labours. She assured me that she would not share our secret liaison with anyone. I paid well for what I had received.

I re-joined the group in the makeshift bar briefly and after some time, followed the flow of bodies retiring to their rooms. I, in turn, had a lot to do to prepare for the morning. At four AM I rose, dressed and left a short message on the Staff Sergeant's door in which I explained that I had gone, in advance of the others, to the rifle range in order to zero the Ross Rifle for the day's training. And then, frankly, using my initiative and my new sniper's smock, I just disappeared.

During the second day of our range training I had been careful to notice the lay of the land, the way it approached the targets and how it appeared from each approach as we had progressed down the range and had deployed and fired from each of the distance markers along the way. My objective was to remain undetectable by the group for the greatest possible amount of time as they made their way from the hotel to the range. The perfect spot, I thought, was in the middle of a low lying mud hole located just at the very beginning of the range boundary. No one had fired from there because it was wet, smelly and filled with a few inches of green looking, putrid rain, and runoff. It was an excellent position for a sniper driven by the intent to live through his mission.

As the first crack of sparrow fart appeared downrange to the east, along the far edges of the rifle range, I sighted and zeroed the Ross rifle. I watched carefully to see how the muzzle blast would disturb the water in which I was now immersed. I was in a long flat depression filled with two inches of cold, green looking pasture water. A large wagon or perhaps a vehicle of some sort had made a sharp turn in that spot some time before. Its movement through the low lying and soft ground had thrown up a deep rut, which in part acted as a long shielding ridge that covered most of my shape and length.

Lying in the rut, I shaped and folded my smock and bottom cover to provide the maximum cover from approaching eyes. Eyes that would be able to observe my location from the direction from which I knew the class would approach. At about eight o'clock, just as what would pass for first light emerged, the entire School shuffled in line down the edge of the field and onto the area known loosely as the first sniper position. They were gathered in a tight little group about two hundred yards from where I lay. There was some consternation in the voices about the fact that they had expected to find me waiting for them on the range. A drumming chatter ensued between the Major and the Sergeant Major regarding whether or not they should commence without me. That was the point at which I fired my first round at a German figure target situated at one thousand yards, the maximum range for all of the targets. The sharp crack of my rifle had them throwing themselves on the ground, most seeking some sort of cover. A minute or more passed which allowed me plenty of time to re-sight and assign my attention to what would be my next target.

By switching quickly between observing their reaction to the crack of my rifle and sighting for the next target, I could be pretty certain that no one, not one single one of them had any exact idea as to my general location let alone my exact position. My next round was fired about thirty seconds later at another German head figure situated well on the right of the range at eight hundred yards. This target could be seen through their glasses and a few of them had now cottoned on to the fact that I was putting them through a fire and observe exercise. The Major and the Staff Sergeant were now getting their glasses up to their eyes to try to discover my location.

Now I had only to concentrate on who was trying to discover my location and when I saw that their attention was somewhat away from my actual position.

I engaged the next target of my choice, which was directly in front of them at six hundred yards. The Major reacted first, giving instruction to observe the ground in the area of my rifle report and as the remainder of the class fumbled for glasses or tried to ascertain where I might be located I loosed the fourth round of my demonstration at a target only one hundred yards from their position. It was a large garden cabbage, one that I had picked up on the way out that morning and placed on the top of a Canadian figure in the exact middle of the range. It made a very pleasant shower of contents as the .303 round entered and exited. At that point I became very still and quiet. I was content their attention had been acquired. This is what sniping was all about and I had hoped my demonstration would have some effect on course content.

My silence and inactivity must have clearly signalled my demonstration of stealth and firing from a concealed position had ended. Now began the waiting game. How long would it take for the class to discover my hiding spot? At first they proceeded without any real plan. They struck out, each with their own idea of where the sound of the shots had come from and they rushed around without strategy or real direction. After some time, the Major called a halt to the hunting fiasco and in a loud and demanding voice called my rank and name and in no uncertain terms demanded that I make an appearance. Luckily for me I was lying only about thirty feet from where he stood at that moment and he was looking downrange while I was lying almost directly behind him.

No one had even imagined I would have selected a sniping position in the depths of the cold and uninviting slough they had all so strenuously avoided walking into.

With some drama, I reached into the folds of my ground cover and extracted the only flag I had been able to find within the ruins of the old hotel. The French tri colour, wet and muddy, as were all of the items that I had carried that morning, made a sorry little attempt to mark my position as it clung, damp and spiritless from the end of my Ross rifle bayonet. Perkins, one of the soldiers from our group was the first to notice it. He shouted some meaningless string of cuss words that ended with "in the fucking little lake". After I was assured that everyone was looking in my direction I stood, in my sniper hood and jacket, looking like a creature that had been born in a swamp. Their silence said it all. I, the way I stood before them, was a sniper. They were soldiers that knew how to shoot straight. If this was going to be a sniper course or a course for snipers, then they would have to change the way we were going to school.

I spent the next three days and nights giving instructions on how to plan, sew, construct and employ the very simple, shapeless, and effective camouflage over covers that were to become standard fare for everyone that followed as students at the Third Army Sniper School. I made no effort to pretend I had any experience in this new skill we were all trying to develop. I was completely truthful when I told them that ever since I was just a boy my grandmother and I had worked hard to sew and make jackets and covers that would let me live in the forest as if I were a part of the forest and not as just a hunter with a rifle. We all knew what we were doing at this school, a school that had no buildings or classrooms, was something brand new to everyone in the British Army and in all of the Commonwealth armies as well. We had no previous frame on which any of us could build a real sniper course. Our army had depended on what had been learned from watching the Germans and the Austrians.

They were way out in front of what we were doing to command and control the areas between our opposing lines, which we called 'no man's land'. It was only our experiences, the things we had seen and done as individuals, which we could then modify and make to work to our advantage. In the first instance, everyone selected to be a sniper had to be a better than average shot. That was a given and many hours on rifle ranges was one sure way to weed out those soldiers who could shoot well from those who were truly exceptional. At least we had that right when we started the course. The Major had said over and over again he also wanted to build into the course a sense of teamwork. Team work where two men would work together, one as the shooter and the other as an observer. The observer had to bring with him great eyes and an even better memory. The sniper team required a memory, which could record and memorize what they had seen and what had changed since they last saw it. It was often the case that when something within their vision changed that the sniper realized he had a target.

Over the next few days all of us worked to improve our sniper's hoods and covers. We discussed how important it was and we practiced how to make and keep maps of where we had been, what we had seen and how many, the time and the kind uniforms that were on the other side of our sights. Slowly, and with great care we acquired and passed on our experiences and skills on scouting, observation, and sniping. Our course was together as a group for just over two weeks. In the very beginning we were just standing around watching each member demonstrate his ability to identify targets at longer and longer ranges and then sight and engage the target with skill and accuracy.

By the end of the course we had learned and practiced how to plan a route out from our own battalion lines into the area we wished to occupy to accomplish our mission. Then we learned how to draw maps and accurately record trench lines, wire obstacles and other defensive features such as cement or defensive positions. We visited a nearby French salvage depot which held a large collection of German guns, howitzers, machine guns, uniforms, trenching tools, wagons and in fact just about every piece of war machinery that the German Army had in the field. From those two days we learned a lot about what to look for in and around the enemy lines that would help us to identify the kinds of targets and the types of uniforms their officers would wear and how they might be different from their ordinary soldiers. As the Major said time and again,

"Kill a soldier you eliminate one rifle in a trench; kill an officer and the trench is without a leader".

The course ended in a storm in a wet and rain filled field. All of us had been tasked to build a sniper position within a tightly described area and the School staff would then seek us out and locate us. The idea, they said was to improve our standard of camouflage and give us a better idea on where and how to develop sniper positions to their best advantage. Each of us by now had become either a sniper or an observer, and for the first time we were working together as a team. The area the School staff assigned to the other two teams were rather loosely described by bounds within the rifle range, "You locate with the south west corner of the second sniper position", or "You develop your position close to the main pathway leading to the eight-hundred-yard marker".

As for me, I was the only member of my team because by then we were down to just five remaining sniper students, John Edward Martin having departed for medical attention from the nearest General Hospital.

They provided me with a map and on the map they had marked an exact location where I would establish my nest.

The plan was simple; each team would retire to their allocated area on the training range. Each team would then choose and build a snipers' nest and occupy it as if they were on an actual mission. The School team would start with sniper position number one, they would critique that position, learn as much as they could from that experience, then the entire group would move forward to sniper position number two. Eventually they would all end up at my selected sniper site. The place they had given me was on the one-thousand-yard target location. It was a flat, bare, target area almost without natural cover and at the end of the rifle range. There were just a few trees and shattered tree trunks remaining behind the target itself. The trees were meant to act as a bit of a backstop for any rifle rounds that were fired long. The area itself provided almost no possibility to establish a really professional hide. I cheated of course.

I dove immediately into the little bit of the remaining poplar forest and skinned the bark off as many trees as I needed. I carried a couple of shattered tree trunks forward of my intended site so that the eye would be fooled into assuming that devastated trees were part of the range area. I then stuck a large piece of a smashed tree, severed and shell broken, into a standing position near the billboard kind of target that had been erected on the spot.
Next, I dug a small hole directly under the center of the target stand and filled it with tree parts using pieces of bark and fragments of bark from shattered tree limbs.

Then, using the frayed bits and portions from the various targets that had been shot through, crushed, and scattered over the immediate circle around the standing target I covered the newly dug hole and the tree parts with as much of the target paper as I could reach and manage.

Finally, I placed a manikin figure, one I had stolen from the four-hundred-yard target area, into a sniper position within the hole in the ground as if the figure was me and it was the sniper they were suppose to find.

With the decoy position in place, I wove long pieces of tree bark, which I had taken from the standing poplars, into the webbing of my top cover. I laced them close together in long strips so that at a casual glance they would appear to be just part of a badly damaged native polar tree that was growing within full view of the target billboard. Soon my sniper cover matched my natural background looking as near as possible to be just part of the log I had moved and erected near the path they would follow as they approached my lair. I then became the standing and shattered tree that they walked right by. They were so sure they had immediately found where I had dug my lair they had all stopped looking for the sniper. The entire train of them, all the students and the instructors walked within two yards of my tree stand. Immediately that they trooped by I stepped out behind them, cocked my rifle, and stood very still until they realized their error. My Ross Rifle was pointed down at the ground but they certainly understood the implication.

The Major regained his composure first. He asked that I brief the group as to how I had managed to become a tree near a target where no tree should have been.

I very carefully explained how I approached the problem. I told them a story about how a wolf would walk right past a hunter hidden in a tree if you could convince it that there was dinner waiting by the side of a trail. People and animals will see what they want to see, the trick is to let them see what you want them to see. I described how Canadian hunters in the forests try to disappear into and become part of the forest they live and hunt in.

"The best way to hide in any place you might find yourself", I said, "is not to be yourself when a wolf comes looking for you".

I became a qualified sniper from the Third Army Sniper Course on that late, wet, and very peaceful, afternoon. It took a few hours before individual members of the course could concede they had walked right past me on their way to laugh out loud at how they thought I had made it easy for them to find me. Later after more than one fine bottle of local red wine the Major admitted his heart had nearly jumped out of his tunic when he had turned to see me, rifle in hand, after he had clearly been deceived into thinking I was somewhere else.

I remember making a mental note that Askuwheteau would live a long life if he could just remember what the Major had learned that day.

* * *

Fighting to Live Dying to Fight

It was on the 24th of April 1916 that I actually located, cleared into, and became part of the 49th Battalion. At that period of time the First Canadian Corps was three Divisions strong with about 50,000 Canadian soldiers living, if you could call it that, in the killing fields of Flanders. The Corps was part of the Second British Army and we were deployed in the south sector of the Ypres Salient. The Canadian Corps covered about six miles of ground between a completely destroyed town called Kemmel and another completely destroyed town that had been Ploegsteert. The conditions were so bad that it was said some senior officers wept when they saw where they had sent the men to fight.

Imagine the surface of the moon. Now imagine that the moon was flooded with water and the earth you lived in, perished in, dug in or struggled to kill the enemy in, was so thick and impassable that you had use your hands to move your boots one step at a time. Now, into that flood of putrid muck pour two or three million artillery shell craters, trenches, ruined equipment, unburied bodies, dead animals, ruined forests, and villages. Now add to that the fact that just before I arrived, at the end of March, British engineers had blown up not one but six enormous underground mines in a very small area called St Eloi. The entire surface of the countryside had been transformed.

Canadian soldiers were perched on one side of these ugly holes in the ground and German soldiers were hanging by their fingertips on the other side of the rim. Everyone shot at everything that moved and those not actively shooting were watching those huge craters fill with water. There was lots of water; it was one of the wettest springs in the recorded history of Europe. It was there, in Flanders fields, that I learned the truth about killing and war. It was there that I became a soldier and learned how to live as a sniper. It is still so painful to remember that my mind refuses to let me forget.

I dare say, anyone who was at Ypres, Festubert, St. Eloi Craters, the Somme, Vimy Ridge, or any of the many other battlefields the Canadian Corps and my 49th Battalion fought, will forever be able to close their eyes and see the incredible and hideous toll that white men inflicted on the opposing tribes and nations of his brothers. You who were not there to see what Askuwheteau saw with his eyes, those of you who did not suffer in the rain filled trenches, can not begin to understand the maelstrom and confusion of emotions which attack the mind when witnessing your brothers hanging from barbed wire. There are no words, which can describe the horrors of what I saw, but I will try. I will try to take you there the way my mind takes me back whenever I close my eyes and Manitou asks me to show the way it was.

We lived together as a tribe of men that all belonged to the same battalion. Within the Corps there were many tribes and many battalions but those men that called themselves the 49th Battalion were as close together as anyone I knew in my village of Saddle Lake.

Each and every Canadian battalion had four infantry companies. A company contained about two hundred and fifty men when it was up to strength. The companies were given names that were from the English alphabet, A Company, B Company, and so on. The men of these companies were even closer than men from the same battalion. These men saw, fought along side of, and lived with each of the men from their company for all the time they were alive. They were their lodge; they were part of their small tribal group.

When I first joined B Company of the 49th Battalion I thought I would be in the front lines for as long as I could manage to live. But that was not so. I, and nearly every member of the fighting 49th were continually shuffled, like a deck of cards, between being deployed forward at the very front or being behind the front lines in a sort of reserve area or at a rest area. So, you see, every soldier went backwards and forwards from trenches where the Germans had their opportunity to kill you just a few yards from their lines or you were trying to kill lice in a reserve position a few miles behind the firing line. It provided for a mental state that permitted you to be scared shitless about being the furthest forward or being bored to death waiting to go forward again.

When a battalion was assigned part of the line it would normally only have one or at a maximum two of its four companies forward in the 'main fire trench'. The other two companies would be "in reserve" behind the forward or main trench line in the 'support line'. Battalions and their companies would move forward into the main fire trench, stay there for three or four days and then rotate back into support or even further back into a rest area behind the main fighting area. That way soldiers did not have to face the constant stress of sniping, patrolling, repairing trenches, and being shelled by the enemy on a continuous basis. In their turn, mortar crews, machine gun crews, infantry riflemen, engineers and artillery observers also continuously rotated between manning the main trench lines and being in reserve. Those forward were the 'front line' soldiers and the remainder were held in reserve close to but not on the immediate front. It was the constant going forward to the front and the relief of going back into reserve that both saved the vast majority of us from going mad and also caused the greatest stress for those who were confused, muddled and weary from the seemingly never ending horror of standing their turn in the war within the trenches.

And then there were the snipers. We were part of the constant rotation of companies and battalions. All of the snipers from the battalion worked for one man or at least for only one headquarters and they took their orders and they did their patrols on a schedule the Brigade and the Division had approved. My observer and I did not form part of the sections and platoons of B Company manning the front trench during their turn forward but we did go forward with them and we lived with them in their trench line when we, ourselves, were not forward in a sniping position. Snipers worked together to give maximum coverage to their part of the line and they would usually go over the wall for two or three day patrols every time their company rotated into the main firing trench line.

From the time that I joined B Company I worked with only one man as my observer. He was a good man; I learned to love him like a brother. It is strange to say it but although we shared everything on a minute-to-minute basis we never really did share very much about our pasts. We both had pasts that were bottled up inside our hearts and heads. Hearts cannot talk and heads can be too thick to know when to share. Arthur and I both had very thick heads. Thick heads or not Arthur and I learned and sharpened our skills during the endless grind that was the Somme. By the time our Canadian Corps was rotated out of that hellhole we, as a team, were survivors who could kill.

In October of 1916 our Division along with the entire Canadian structure of the First Canadian Corps were moved, or I should say, marched and shuffled along by train, tram way, and sometimes by horse drawn wagons, to take up a long, narrow, defensive position along the eastern edge of a prominent whale backed and visually dominating ridge line called Vimy Ridge.

Vimy Ridge; you have to say those words as if you are starting a prayer. Vimy Ridge; it controlled our every thought, our every minute, our very lives and all too often, our deaths, for all the time that we stood on guard behind her. Now that I look back on the nearly seven months I lived and nearly died on Vimy Ridge I still cannot describe the living, changing, dominating symbol, the very point of the needle of death, that it became to me. A symbol of dread, a symbol of what lay ahead, a symbol of what we could do as Canadians. It was not just my symbol; I believe that Vimy Ridge became the same expectant symbol of the future to every Canadian that served in her shadow.

Vimy Ridge may not have been the biggest war effort during the war, in fact our attack on Vimy was just one small part of the British Army spring of 1917 overall attack plan to crush and push the Germans out of their dominating defensive lines. The Canadian effort to attack and capture Vimy Ridge was not even the first such attempt on Vimy Ridge by our allies. Our causalities were nowhere near as horrendous as the losses of the French Army and the British Army Corps that had attempted to capture the ridge before it was assigned to the Canadian Corps. The thing was, every other allied assault and attack on that impregnable catastrophe called Vimy Ridge had failed; ours would not.

When Canadian soldiers marched out of the horrors of the Somme to have their first look at Vimy most were completely underwhelmed. As we approached the low lying escarpment, battalion after battalion marched along and through torn and mashed roads and villages until we were about 5 miles northeast of the French town of Arras. Arras stands on the western side of the ridge on the Douai Plains.

The highest part of the Vimy ridge, which itself is just over four miles long, has a total elevation of only 476 feet. That means at its very highest point it only rises about 200 feet above the floor of the Plains. But it wasn't a matter of how high it rose; it was the fact that those 200 feet had given the German Army a physical presence and an unhindered view for tens of miles in all directions. From the heights of Vimy Ridge the German Army occupying the heights could reach out with their eyes, their rifles, their machine guns and their artillery and kill anything that their weapons could reach. Now you are starting to see what Askuwheteau saw the first time he saw it.

Just imagine for a minute what those first few weeks and months of this war in Europe were like. In 1914 the German Army was marching, almost unstoppable, on their way to the Atlantic Ocean. Huge parts of France and Belgium were falling under their relentless attacks. The French and the British Armies were hard pressed to find foothold as each of the opposing armies manoeuvred and tried to outflank the other. By the time the German push had been stopped the Germans held the vast majority of the dominating ground. Part of that dominating ground was this now completely ruined, insignificant ridgeline that was the home to a now demolished village with the name of Vimy.

It took a couple of weeks, if I remember correctly, for our battalion, our brigade, division and the entire Canadian Corps to relieve and replace the British IV Corps that had held the ground below Vimy Ridge since February of 1916. The Brits had been very busy during their time here. They had discovered that the Germans had been mining into the deep chalky soil of the entire front.

Tunnelling became not just a tactic; to those soldiers that built the thousands of yards of underground shafts it was more of a preoccupation. It became a game to see which side could tunnel better, deeper, faster, and plant more explosives and kill more soldiers that were unfortunate enough to be on the "front line rotation" the day the mine was exploded. Along with the surface war our troops also took over the underground, which included all of the tunnels and the mines. It did not take very long until Canadian tunnelling companies proved to be amongst the very best in the world at working underground.

Finally, about the end of October, the Vimy line was Canada's line and my job as a battalion sniper started all over again in a new area. But being a sniper in a new area does not make the work we do new. Nothing can make killing another human being make sense. Nothing can ever make watching your bullet strike home through a telescopic sight make sense. It never did make sense to me no matter how many times Arthur and I went out to do what we did so well.

* * *

A Letter from Home.

Vimy was different to all of us and there was a lot of buzz in the air about how we were really going to show everyone how the Canadians could do things right. Visibly, the battlefield around Vimy didn't seem much different from everything else I had seen since I had arrived in France. The ground was torn and mutilated; every part of the countryside that had been built on was flattened into tossed piles of rubble. Here and there, alongside erased streets and roads, soldiers from unit headquarters or unit aid posts occupied basements and cement foundations. Most of the soldiers had colds and fever; everyone was wet all the time. It rained and rained and rained and then it froze. That was pretty much what every day I had spent with the 49th had been like up to now.

But there was something other than the usual smell of death and shit mixed into the mud. There was a new sense of being a nation creeping into the voices that I talked to. The Fourth Canadian Division was finally joining us. All four of the Canadian Divisions were being put together under our own Corps. No longer would our units be part of British Formations. We could stand proudly and point to the differences and nod our heads as we saw other Canadian units with their bronze maple leafs pinned to their hats. There was a significant feeling of pride in all the Canadian soldiers over this move. It was a sign we would now be recognized as being Canadians and not just British citizens.

I saw the pride in soldiers' eyes, hands slapping backs as units passed in trenches. Now, I thought, the tribe is all together; the warriors will sit together around their own fires and tell stories about their own lands. It was something I could feel, a feeling that was as real to me as it was to everyone I spoke to about this new Corps from Canada. Even though the majority of our soldiers had been born in Britain or as a minimum had parents born in England, there was now a wider held sense that we were all from the same country, a country called Canada. I, being a Cree, smiled when I realised that a ground swell of change was coming over our formation. We Cree already had that feeling, the feeling of being a nation. We, the First People of Canada, had known for thousands of years about being part of something larger than just a lodge, or a village or a tribe. But all of us, all of the First Canadian Corps were Canadians now, not just soldiers from Canada.

And behind our unit lines there seemed to be thousands of additional Canadian soldiers. There were all kinds of army units that I had never seen or heard of before. There were special units building tunnels and mines. Some of the units were made up entirely from black men that were from the east coast of Canada. I never saw them but the officers were talking about them as labour battalions. They were building wonderful little rail lines that carried very small cars, which in turn, carried all sorts of ammunition, wire, wood planking, causalities and sometimes even food and new equipment and clothing.

It was just after the day the officers went around telling everyone the Vimy line was now officially ours to hold as a Canadian Corps that we started to receive mail from home again. For at least two or three weeks our mail had been lost or delayed because of our move from the Somme. So for most of us, we considered the rail lines special because they carried the mail.

Mail was one of the most important morale boosters that existed for every man, friend or foe. And one cold and awful day one of those trains and one of our battalion orderlies delivered a letter addressed to me as Private Askuwheteau Costello. It was a letter from the Catholic Church in Blue Quill.

I did not call her Tahki Wapan but some did. I did not call her Cold Dawn but most did. It seemed that everyone in Lac La Biche knew her or knew about her. It was certainly true that everyone, even the new born babies knew my grandmother. That was particularly true when she died. Everyone remembered her then. Some people even remembered that she was my grandmother and some were sorry I had left her alone and had gone off to war. Everyone for miles around went to her funeral service, or so her priest and good friend Father LeBreton informed me. Father LeBreton was a priest from the Sacred Heart Indian Residential School.

The Father was the only person who wrote to tell me of her death. In fact he was the only person other than Cold Dawn that ever wrote to me during all the time I was overseas. The Father wrote in his letter that Cold Dawn had not been seen outside of her house for a couple of weeks. Someone from the village had gone over to check on her. They had found her in her bed. She had been dead for some time.

For every day I was in Europe I was alone amongst soldiers because I would not let them see my fear of dying. She was alone amongst her people of the village who had never known a moment when she did not live for them. That is how she was and how I remember her. She always lived outside of herself. She lived for all the others that were around her and never once asked for anything in return.

The letter also said that hers was the biggest funeral the priest had ever seen. In fact, he said, up until then, it might have been the largest funeral service ever held at Blue Quill. All the teachers and all of the students from the Residential School were allowed to go to the church service. Almost all of the local village people, First Nations and White had gone to pay their respects to a woman who had gently and resolutely represented our people, in four different tongues, for all of her adult life.

He also remembered that Ma could repeat every word of Treaty Six between the Crown and our Nation. She could speak with great recall about stories passed between our leaders and how and what Whiteman had promised in return for our lands and support following the great uprisings at Cut Knife Creek, Batoche and Lac La Biche. She could remember every name of every family that had been helped by the Indian Agents through the years. She told everyone it was a very short list and therefore it was easier to remember than the other one, which contained the names of individuals and families, wronged by the same august men.

She was an unpublished encyclopaedia of knowledge concerning local customs and medicines. She knew without fail what illnesses were cured by eating or drinking medicines that could be made from plants, roots or other things available within our forests and our animals. Grandmother was a master with a needle and a pail of tannery salt. She could take a deer hide in the autumn and by spring it would be a deerskin jacket worth ten dollars or more at the Hudson's Bay Company store in Edmonton.

Father LeBreton's letter also wrote that Cold Dawn's house and home, the lovely weather proof and snug log cabin I had worked so hard and long to build during one whole summer and well into the fall was no more. Just like Cold Dawn it had passed into flames within a few short days of her death.

No one came forward to say they knew Cold Dawn was dying. No one apparently knew when or why she had died. No one came forward to say the names of the village men who had moved into her house as soon as her body had been taken from it. No one claimed to know who or how the fire started but the Father said unfortunately the only thing saved from the fire was one very old 30.30 rifle that might have belonged to me. Every other sign of my work and all of the memories of Cold Dawn were scattered, by the winter winds, onto the ice and snow, which surrounded and covered our village in the winter of 1916. I know that if her ashes could speak to me they would say "Kasinamatowin" 'I should forgive'.

I have tried to forgive the men that burned her house because they were too drunk to care. I have tried to forgive my entire village for hiding the names of those men from me so I could face them with my anger. I have tried to forgive all of them for erasing every single book, paper, note, and memory Ma had guarded over until Askuwheteau could return. I have tried to forgive all these things Grandmother, please forgive me, and ask Manitou to forgive me as well. I have tried for weeks and months but I cannot and I suppose I will not.

So, after I received the letter I was truly alone, utterly alone. I was alone with a million men all of whom were part of the same undertaking and part of the same Army. Yet as of that day, the day I opened the letter, I was completely alone in the world I lived in. I say lived in because I firmly believe that there are two completely different worlds. There is the one that I live in and the one that you live in. My world contains everything that I know and do and have done. Your world, like mine, belongs only to you. Only Manitou can know all of the worlds for all of the people that have been created. This is why the Great Spirit is great and why we, as he has made us, will never be able to completely understand the good and evil that lives together, side by side, in the hearts of mankind.

Cold Dawn had been my closest and only living relative. She had been the heart and the soul I talked to when I was afraid. She was the spirit I imagined that watched over me as I hunted and trapped and now she was no longer there when my need for her seemed indescribable. There was no one else in my direct family line that I knew of and neither had I ever heard Ma speak of anyone still alive in our line. My mother had died when I was just a child. No one knew for sure who my father was and therefore I had no idea if he was alive or dead.

Within my own village I had no one I would say I was close to and the church was nothing more than a cold place that proudly displayed a hand carved wooden statue of Jesus nailed to a cross. Never, not even once, could I ever get my mind around why they prayed to and about a man that had been crucified and killed on a cross of wood. Why, I wondered out loud a few times until I got sick of being cuffed on the head, did a God not fight back and fill the earth with the powers that Manitou had shown?

I did not have a place or true friend within the schools that I had attended. The schools we went to were filled with old nuns that smelled like mould and soap. Their habits were layered thick with symbols and cloth until they were so stiff they could not run and play with the children they taught. I had no Indian or white man that I could call brother, not even one. Johnny Snake Eye was the only hero I had lived with and his spirit was now sitting by a fireside somewhere laughing and sharing stories with Ma. It was not that I had expected Ma to live forever. Forever is a very short time for most of my people living on an Indian Reserve. Doctors would not move to our reserves and build hospitals like they did in Edmonton or in other large cities. Nurses were not available to help our children that died from fevers which white children would have been treated for. Our old people did not receive the care they needed when their backs were too stiff or too sore to carry fish from the shoreline into their homes for the winter. Whiteman was ever ready to share his God with us. The Indian Agent and the Priest were always there to remind us of the majesty of their King and Queen. But, when it came time to really matter, Whiteman slept peacefully in his house with a stone fireplace. Cold Dawn died alone in the house that I had built for her because in the end, neither her people nor their people cared enough to care.

All of my experiences with white men had been fearful. If I saw one on the street their eyes were filled with scorn because I did not dress or act like they did. If I went to church the white men sat in the front, closest to fire and the wooden Jesus. We Indians sat in the back, one whole row would be left empty between our people and their people so that the sweet scent of smoke filled clothing would not offend the white ladies praying for forgiveness in the front of the church.

If I met or was taught by a white man in school every minute was filled with more fear. Fear that they would throw something at us or me because we did not answer some question about who discovered Canada. I always said the Cree people had discovered Canada but I said it under my breath. Many Cree children said things in Cree under their breaths. They had to be careful what they said about their own culture and their life styles at home because they feared and knew what a heavy classroom book felt like when an old man in a black robe who sometimes did terrible things to young boys in his room threw it.

Many unanswered questions and often physical pain and abuse were part of the school we went to. It was the distance that remained between our culture and their culture that was part of the reason Ma had questioned why I wanted to go and fight the white man's war. Every Indian ear had heard it said that Whiteman's God saw every person as an equal when you kneeled before Him at His altar. Every Indian eye had seen that was a lie when we tried to speak out loud about the history and strength and endurance of our Cree culture.

I told Cold Dawn that we should not just feel the anger and the pain that some of the teachers had inflicted upon some of us. I said we must also recognize that many of the people that wore black robes amongst us were loving, warm, and truly cared for each and every one of the students under their care. I had seen the tears of children that did not understand but I had also seen the tears of priest and nuns that did understand and tried for every minute of their lives to show Indian children the way to learn and way to understand what their God would want from us. When I had told Cold Dawn my inner feelings she reached out as she had done when I was child and took my face into her hands. She looked deep and long into my eyes and she asked me:

"And what will you learn from your travels Askuwheteau? What will you tell our Mighty Spirit about all of the things that you have seen"?

"I will have to learn from what I will see Ma. Only the future can speak to you with answers that you want".

And now she was gone I had no one that I could give my answer to, no one except Manitou.

For some time even I had questioned myself why I had felt driven to walk to Edmonton and join the army. Now, with this letter in my hand I knew the answer to my own question. I had joined the army in order to start my journey. It was the journey of Askuwheteau. I had gone to this war because Ma had thought I was Askuwheteau. She had believed in me and therefore I must believe in myself. If she thought Manitou had called me to see the world, then I knew I still had much to see and many tears to cry before I would go back to the Canada that did not want me.

Since I did not have a box in which to place the tears that I cried that day, the letter on which the message was written became a stained testimony to my loss. For a long time afterwards I carried that letter in an inside pocket of my battledress jacket. I carried it next to my pay book, which was, until then, the most important document in my possession. But over the weeks and months, the letter slowly melted away in the water, dirt, and sweat of a soldier's toil.

So, from the moment I opened and read that letter, I knew I would never again be able to walk into a normal home and feel comfortable. Comfortable in the way that one feels at "home", at peace with one surroundings.

With Cold Dawn's passing I no longer had a home. For many months, for days after days, my home had been trenches and shell holes. The war and constant fear of death sat like a vomit stain on a deerskin jacket. Very few soldiers could wear their fear right out in the open without being ashamed of the stain. My real home in Blue Quill seemed so far away; now that Ma was dead there seemed no sense to call it home at all.

The life I had lived before was now completely disconnected from the reality of trench life and sniper patrols. My home was something dug into a trench wall. For most of us life at the front was a hole with a corrugated tin ceiling, walls of wooden beams and roughly hewn lumber. The ceilings of dugouts were always just above one's head and there was a constant necessity to duck under or dodge food and parcels hanging in rat proof bundles from the cross beams and corner supports. From that point of time forward my old life in my home at Saddle Lake was a place I could only touch when my eyes were closed. There was not even anyone that I could write to in Blue Quill. Letters, even if I wanted to write them, would contain the truth about the hell I lived in now; who in Saddle Lake would want to share that with me. From that moment forward I never wrote or received another personal letter while I was at the front.

* * *

Arthur and I Together

We were a team, Arthur and I, we were a good team, but we did not get to sit on the duckboards at the 49th Battalion forward trenches because it was some idea that we had concocted. Arthur and I did what we were told to do. That is the way an army works; someone decides what to do, the rest do it.

I think I learned how the army works. It is a big machine that has two parts. The first part starts way up in the sky somewhere with the King or someone like that. Also in this part of the Army there are wise men in Ottawa and in many big cities and it is their responsibility to tell the Generals when to go into the field and where to go. Then there is another kind of army, the second part. This part of the same army does not live in barracks or camps. This is an army filled with young men with tired eyes, their faces filled with mud and the dirt of the ground they fight and sleep in. This was the army that Arthur and I were in.

In this second part there were no baths or bathtubs, no clean kitchens filled with steaming pots of meat and potatoes. There were no beds pulled tight for inspections, nor were there clean sheets and boots polished until they shone. No this was a different army than the one in Canada or England or anywhere else that I had been. This was the First Canadian Corps; a man named Byng commanded this part of our army and we were all called Byng's Boys. It was not unusual to hear soldiers call themselves Byng's Boys. We were proud to be Canadians in France; we might have been dirty but we were proud.

The next thing you must know it that except for a few nurses and people that worked in hospitals there were no women in this army. Everyone in this army was a man except for those men that were officers and they were called officers and not men. I know that sounds funny but it was the officers that told the men what to do and when to do it and we, the men, did what we were told.

Captain Johnson was an officer. He was my officer and he commanded the Third Division sniper teams. During the Ides of March, he came looking for me. Arthur and I had been over the wall but we were back in our battalion area. The men called the 49th Battalion the Edmonton Regiment; the Officers called it the 49th Battalion. We had been out forward of our lines for over twenty-four hours and it had seemed like an eternity. It had been a very long eternity, not because our task was different but because the continual artillery barrages, both from the Germans and from our own guns, had made living in a hole between their front lines and ours a certain kind of hell that cannot even begin to be described.

We had lain, covered by our cloth and nets for the whole time. Sniper camouflage is a thin and fragile shield from the steel that whizzed, hissed, and grumbled over and around us. We lived with gunshots and shrapnel, if it would have found us we would have died. That was pretty much the equation we had to accept. Neither Arthur nor I were heroes. We were shit scared just about all the time we were out and the fact we didn't have to act brave was because we understood how the other felt. Knowing what fear was made it somewhat easier to be a coward and just get on with what had to be done.

When Captain Johnson found us we were asleep, huddled in a water logged hole just big enough for a machine gun and two people. It was a crew pit that happened to be empty just then. The machine gun and its crew had been blown right off the step of the trench during the night. Parts of the crew were still visible in the mud beyond the front lip but with the rain and rats that would disappear within the next day or two. Those killed would be recorded as killed, letters would be written to their next of kin, replacements would be sent in from a reinforcement battalion. What was left of the machine gun had been gathered up and given to the armourer who would scavenge what he could for spare parts. There were no spare parts that could be scavenged from the dead. The rule was, if your body ended up in no man's land it might mean someone's life trying to get it out of there so it could be buried. Well, since that body was already dead it was best to just leave it where it was until it slowly disappeared into the mud and destruction that was the front line.

Johnson had kicked the bottom of our boots, the universal sign to inform a sleeping man that he was now on duty. Cold, wet chalky soil stuck to our battle dress and ground cover. Johnson waited while we peed into the side of the trench before we followed him back down the trench line in the direction from which he had come. It was raining so we were invited into the Company Commander's command post bunker. It had been dug into the front of the forward trench about half way between the company boundaries. A command post took constant labour to maintain. There were wooden steps down into the underground excavated space. The space was then filled by a table, a couple of map boards and sleeping benches dug out of the chalky ground. There was room for a lantern and a small stove. A pot sat boiling away a witch's brew of a black and foul smelling mixture of liquid said to be coffee.

The duckboards at the bottom of the bunker were under water. Even in the best and warmest place in the company lines life was no better than a hovel where man smells and fear filled your every breath. I had seen my people living on reserves during spring flooding of the lake living in conditions better than this. At least on the reserves no one was trying to kill you when you went into the woods to go to the toilet.

Every man on the battlefield, German, French, Englishman alike, generated nearly a pound and a half of shit every day. There were no toilets with toilet seats and paper nearby. There were only toilet trenches in areas that had been marked and designated as latrines. Sometimes holes were dug. Most of the time the toilet area was only a piece of ground in a toilet trench. After some period of time that trench would be covered in and a new trench and a new toilet area would be designated. The forward areas were always under the threat of artillery fire. Every now and then, an artillery round, theirs, or ours, would land and explode in the old or the new toilet area. Anyone in the area died instantly from the shrapnel or the blast; the remainder of men still living in the area were subjected to a towering shower of body parts, water, mud and liquid human excrement. That was not something soldiers wrote about in their letters to their loved ones but it was a common occurrence in Flanders Fields.

The Company Commander was sitting in the corner of the bunker discussing with the Company Sergeant Major the future location of trench toilet areas. Captain Johnson and I found a place near the table corner to conduct our debriefing about the sniping patrol Arthur and I had just completed.

Captain Robert James Johnson was from Edmonton. He was businesslike but friendly. He had been raised on a farm near Camrose; he had no airs, made no favourites or exceptions. We talked openly and frankly about sniping, where our lair had been, what we had seen for the two days that we had been out. I drew him a map that showed our route in and out. He asked me what procedures we had used to get safely over the wall and back in again. He laughed when I said, "Prayer".

He made notes about how many shots we had taken, how many confirmed hits. He did that because our Corps kept records of that sort of thing. We talked about camouflage and equipment, we showed him what we made by hand, and the modifications we had made to army issued equipment. He seemed very interested.

"How far out can you identify a target with the scope on your rifle"? I thought about that for a second or two.

"Just eyes alone, on a good view, about two hundred yards. With binoculars in daylight, out to four hundred and with the Warner Swasey about six hundred. If it is more than just the top of helmet exposed, like maybe someone standing shoulders up, it could be a little further I suppose".

He seemed satisfied; "There is a rumour that you have the best eyes in the Battalion, is that true"?

I looked at him, his face was serious; dirt and water tracked down his young face and ran into the seam between his skin and his scarf. He must be fishing for something I thought.

"I only know that when I was hunting I could see further and better than any other person I went out with. At Sniper school I recorded the longest hits and had the best scores. Maybe I was just lucky, I do not really know".

We were quiet for a minute before Arthur said;

"On a rifle range in Salisbury I saw him hit any target within an inch of bull's-eye out to four hundred yards with a standard Ross Rifle. With a Mark III sniper rifle and a good sight he can hit anything he aims at out to four hundred yards and most of the targets out to six hundred yards. In my opinion he is the best shot in the Division".

I stared with amazement that a silent man like Arthur could say so much.

We huddled together in that little corner of the company bunker for a half hour or so. We silently drank coffee from the black iron pot, the Company Commander asked us personal questions about our families, and, "What have you heard from home"?
All of us had lice; there was a constant scratching and moving amongst us, that was a common trench phenomenon that no one noticed but we all shared. After a while we all ran out of words so we sat taking the heat from the tin cups of coffee into our hands. We listened to the water dripping off the burlap bags that almost covered the entrance into the bunker.

Captain Johnson fumbled inside his field coat, undoing buttons until his hand reappeared with a small silver brandy flask. He took a small pull on the contents and without any emotion or acknowledgement returned the flask to its customary place of hiding and safety. No offer had been made to share; no expectation of offer was felt. Men in the field had only a few private luxuries, that flask was his.

Mine was a little leather jacketed Bible written in Italian. In silent moments, in the company of myself, I would read parts of it try to translate those words I knew into French and then, using a fragmented memory of my bible classes at school, try to remember how the passage sounded in English. It did not make me feel closer to a God I did not understand but it kept my mind from wondering how Grandmother felt when she died all alone in the house I had built for her on a site that she had chosen on 127 Blue Quill Indian Reserve.

With a deep sigh Captain Johnson sat up a little straighter, reached into his small canvas backpack that he always wore slung over his shoulder. Most of the Field Officers, men with ranks of Major or higher carried something similar. The packs provided a dry place to transport maps, written orders, field notebooks, extra paper, pens and a cigarette or two. Captains such as Johnson would also have a list containing the vital information of the men under their command, trench maps, and changes to daily routine. For the leaders, the Officers, since the trenches were constantly changing, moving or being modified by work or the destructive force of the enemy, it was important to keep a good record of where you were and where you thought the enemy was. All that plus the God Damned rain, the mud, the stink, death and toilets that were not toilets also had to be kept track of. Sometimes men got so lost and wandered so far from their unit lines that they would be listed as missing; letters might even have been written to their next of kin before they showed up, embarrassed and contrite, on a midnight resupply column.

Johnson spread a small-scale map on the tabletop gently moving the extra ammunition boxes and the coffee cups off to one side to make room.
"This is a pretty up-to-date map of Divisional lines, trenches and defensive lines".

He paused and made sure that I was following his finger as he continued to trace a line on the map.

"These symbols and trenches marked in red are what we think about the German line across from us".

He handed me the map and I spent a few minutes studying it and mentally comparing his paper map to what I had in my head. Arthur looked over my shoulder in silence, grunting now and then he agreed with what he saw.

"I have not been east of this line here".

I pointed my finger at the Third Division boundary between the Fourth Canadian Division and us on our left flank.

"This is where Arthur and I spent the last two nights being shot at by every gunner in the country. This German machine gun post is no longer there, it has been moved at least one hundred yards to the north and it should have coverage over to about this part of your line".

I traced and stabbed with my finger as I showed Johnson the topographical areas in question.

"Between the two of us", I pointed a thumb at Arthur,

"We know every trench and hidey-hole within four hundred yards of these trenches".

Again I pointed out the area that I was talking about. To no one in particular I added,

"We have been damn lucky so far to see so much and still find our way back".

Captain Johnson stood in silence as he fumbled with his buttons and had another small pull on his comfort flask. He just nodded as he put it away.

"If you were above this area like say looking down from an airplane do you think that you could identify where you are now and the area that I have just shown you on the map"?

He looked very serious as he folded the map and returned it to his small pack. He sat down and turned to look at me through narrowed eyes. I had to listen to his question again in my mind before I completely understood what I thought he had asked of me.

"If I was in an airplane? You mean if I was an eagle and I could fly over this shit-hole would I know where my nest was and would I recognize all the things we have here"?

I sat down and closed my eyes trying to let the question and what it meant in terms of what I would be doing sink into my understanding.

"I have never been off the ground Sir", was about all that I could think to say.

At that moment our eyes met and held.

"I have never flown in an airplane but I think I have an idea what the ground would look like from up there. I imagine everything looks different from the top down and the airplane is moving so there is not much time to see and recognize what you are looked at".

Without another word he stood and shook some water off the outside of the coverings on the entranceway. Some of the rain had managed to find its way from the sulking burlap through his scarf and down his neckline. He gave a little shiver as he pressed the front of his neck covering to absorb the cold intrusion. His eyes never left mine as he reopened his coat button and extracted a long thin envelope. With one hand he handed me the letter and with the other he dug out the flask and for a second or two held it to his lips.

"Well", he said, "the Major and I think that you and Arthur need a bit of break for a few days. Arthur, I am giving you seven days leave. I suggest you go to Paris and get drunk but don't forget to come back".

I noticed Major Winser smiling slightly. Up until then he pretended not to be listening to our conversation.

Winser stood up and turned to us taking a couple of short steps around the table as he picked up a small package off the jumbled table and opened it. There was a softer, more fatherly tone to his voice as he said,
"Well Costello, you are going to get a chance to see how the earth looks from an airplane or an eagle or whatever you use to get up there and over our area. I believe a man like you with eyes like yours may be able to see more than a pilot can see because you will know what we are looking for and what you are looking at".

He fumbled for a few seconds with the small package he held in his hands.
"I cannot send you off to the Royal Flying Corps as a Private so as of this moment I am promoting you to the rank of Corporal".
He handed a piece of cloth, shaped like a shallow V, which is the Canadian and British rank badge of a Corporal, to Captain Johnson. Johnson shook my hand with his right and handed me the stripes with his left. My smiling friend Arthur exploded,
"Jesus Christ, he gets promoted and I get to go to Paris. I think I got the best deal".

As for me I still do not know which was the biggest surprise, the promise of an airplane ride or being called Corporal.

Arthur and I stiffly and silently backed out of the 'officer's dugout'. It was still minutes away from full dawn and some light but not heat was pushing its fingers into the roughly hewn edges of the dirt that was our home. The sky of Flanders was covered with thick leaky clouds. Every minute or so one or two guns would spit a large hunk of death into the low hanging clouds and somewhere over on the German side or along our line a filthy pillar of earth and its contents would spring up and cascade misery and steel shards along its path. All along the east side, the German side, the horizon was being drawn by the dawn in a broad stroke.

We turned together towards our little hidey-hole. Side by side we stood for a moment, shoulder to shoulder, each taking comfort and thinking of the other. I remembered an 'outing' we had made just a couple of weeks before. We had been scheduled within the Division patrolling plan for a four-day 'out'. Fate had stepped in during the late afternoon of day four. We had four days' rations, ammunition, water, and after four days on a sniper patrol we always ran out of 'give a shit'.

It had gone slowly at first. We were too close to the German lines; our muzzle noise had created interest from a German sniper team. The next three days had turned into a duet for four that only two could win. The Krauts had tipped their hand first; a long-range shot had passed just an inch in front of Arthur's glasses. It struck my backpack, which he was using for support under elbows. The round had dug a long path through our water bag and into the ground near my knee. Unfortunately for them Arthur had seen their top cover move slightly in reaction to the muzzle blast and my replying round killed the shooter.

For the remainder of the daylight on day four and for the next night and day we were at a complete standoff. We did not know if we had killed the sniper and neither did the surviving observer from their team know if we were wounded. The end result was that for hours into day five we remained as motionless as possible, not moving in case we would tip our position into a kill shot. The range between us was only four hundred yards, an easy kill if the target could be confirmed. We, for our part did not know that only the observer remained alive and common sense drove us to avoid instantaneous response.

During the long hours of day five, running out of food and water, we discussed our options and agreed to a plan. As soon as darkness drew her cloak around us we slowly and methodically packed and moved forward a hundred yards or so. It was tiring work. Every movement had to be deliberate and under our top covers so as to mask as best as we could our intentions and our positions. We had constructed and left behind two rough, crude head figures stuck up on short sticks that might just be convincing in the uncertain light of dawn.

Dawn and then full light brought us no reaction. From the improved cover of our new position we strained in search of the elusive German team. Mid-day brought us nothing but growling stomachs and a growing thirst. At two o'clock a British airplane drifted slowly up and down the line using a safe distance behind our lines as a safety margin. From the German side there appeared a German squadron of fighters, at low level at first but suddenly climbing into Canadian airspace. The single Brit pilot must have been used to this tactic as he immediately turned and dove hard for the security of a Brit squadron that was wasting fuel flying formations over the green and still producing farmlands around Ablain-St. Nazaire, a small town north and behind our Canadian left flank.

The appearance of the German squadron attracted the attention of Canadian machine gunners and for a short few minutes we could clearly hear and sometimes even see Canadian machine gunners shooting and pointing at the German fighters and even more interesting to us was the German machine gunners shooting at the Canadians. The German sniper observer took this hubbub to try and make his move back to his own trenches. He made a fatal mistake. Once he had broken ground cover and had started to run through the tangle of wire, broken ground and shell holes he was as dead as any fly on my grandmother's only kitchen window. I remember wondering if I had taken enough lead as I completed the trigger pull at the end of my breathing cycle. His body was thrown forward and for an instant his legs continued in a comical dance as he disappeared in a horizontal dive ending in a shell hole. It was the only time that I can remember Arthur saying more than four words together in one sentence when we were out on patrol.

He said,

"Well I will be damned! That was a stupid thing to do".

He was a man of few words but I really loved that guy.

But here we were together again in a strange and unpredictable situation. A scratchy piece of music was playing on a worn out record and record player hidden now by the covering on the Company Command Post entrance. The Major and Captain Johnson must have completed their meeting with the Company Sergeant Major and thought to bring some comfort to all those within listening distance.

Without words at all Arthur and I looked back along the trench line that led to the front. There were plumes of steam from men's breath and wherever there were men there were small clouds of smoke from their cigarettes. More steam was visible from the early morning tea ration that was being pooled between sections and platoons of men on the daily, early morning, stand-to alert.

We shared a small smile with nearby soldiers that were trying to wring some heat from their tin cups into their cold, dirty hands. As we stood deeply breathing in the wet and stench of the lines our eyes met and we both suddenly broke into giggles like two playground brats. Arthur was now officially on seven days leave. I was going to have a complete change of clothes at the Divisional bath unit and get my Corporals stripes sewn on. Then, like Askuwheteau himself, I was going to see Whiteman's world from the heavens above us. Unconsciously my hand had found my pocket and I was squeezing those new stripes until I found that my hand hurt.

"Damn", we both said together, like we always did when we had come through a night, a scrape, or a patrol where the odds were iffy, "Life is good".

* * *

Wings of Askuwheteau

Arthur had not wasted a minute of his seven days' leave. As soon as we shook hands and grinned about how much fun we were going to have he packed his large pack, turned in his other kit to the company stores and walked out towards Battalion Headquarters. From there he followed trenches that took him through Brigade Movement Control and finally to the Third Division rear area and the bath unit. There he was issued a clean uniform and a transportation warrant for travel by train to Paris. He had a pay book, which showed how much money he was owed. The paymaster nodded wisely and made sure he advised him not to spend it all on one night but he was a big boy now, a soldier now, no one could tell him how to enjoy himself. That was left entirely in his own hands.

And as for me, after months of going between duty on the line and time in the Battalion rest area my life was about to take an amazing turn towards normalcy, or so I thought. Almost all soldiers in the forward areas were hungry, cold, and wet, frequently filthy dirty, lice ridden and when not scared to death they were horny. A week of duty with 16 Squadron RFC was like closing a book by Dante and waking up living in Lewis Carroll's Alice's Adventures in Wonderland.

The Squadron was flying from a grass strip field at Brauy-la-Buissiere, just a few air miles from the newly established Canadian front near Vimy Ridge.

Somewhere, somehow, in the magic that officers can do, this British squadron had been loaned to the Canadian Corps Headquarters so we could have our very own eyes and camera in the sky over our lines. Captain Johnson had briefed me on how it all worked. I really only paid attention to the stuff that I thought was important to me though. What I took away from all the words he said was the pilots flew the airplanes and took all the risk. When one of our artillery batteries or regiments needed someone to fire guns into places that our observers could not see from their place of observation, then a 16 Sqn pilot and one of their observers would fly over the lines and control how our guns found our targets. More interesting to me was the fact that they had very good cameras which I could learn to use and maybe I could even take pictures of where I thought our sniper patrols should be located for operations including when we made our assault on Vimy. And finally he had been perfectly clear; I would get to fly for a whole week and get to learn how to operate the camera from the airplane. Captain Johnson seemed very confident that if I was very good and worked hard maybe my eyes would make a difference in how we fought the next battle. I was very excited about all that other stuff as well but my heart nearly burst with the thought of being able to fly.

If Ma could only know she had seen the truth of my future. If Manitou was watching, then He or She would soon see me flying and watching over the earth just like his mighty eagle had done a million moons before. I, Askuwheteau, was once again going to fly over the nation called France and see with my own eyes the ruination that Whiteman had made out of the farms, forests, towns and nature Manitou had created and left in man's care.

So, while Arthur was packing and singing some silly little song in French under his breath and busied himself with handing in some of his belongings to Company Stores I was packing my kit bag and getting ready to make my way out of the battalion lines and out of the front area to the grassy field where 16 Squadron lived and flew and sometimes died in the wreckage of their fragile machines. I had to carry a few personal belongings along with me in my great pack and one kit bag. It was an hour walk along familiar trench lines and communication trenches to find the Battalion rear area and administrative headquarters. Following many requests for directions and having been pointed up and down a lot of very unprepared rear "reserve line trenches" I finally found the dugout which processed soldiers that were departing from the unit for other duties or recording new arrivals as they reporting in from their holding or reinforcement units well behind the front lines.

I handed in my hand written orders signed and stamped by my Company Commander. They recorded my time out and informed me to report back to them on my return to unit. A new set of written orders were prepared for my next stop which was to be at Third Division Rear Headquarters; this leg of my journey too would be a long walk carrying my humble kit bag. These orders were slightly different though. They included authorization for Division to issue me a new uniform and new personal kit as well as approval of my new rank and temporary assignment to the RFC. I was standing and walking with a purpose as I left the Battalion for a week of new sights and sounds.

The remnants of roads slowly emerged from the desolate landscape and slowly grew better as I moved further back into the rear area of the Battalion. Better did not mean less crowded through.

They were filled to overflowing with wagonloads of stores and ammunition being moved up into the fighting areas that lay in front of the main transport routes.

Here and there crudely painted signs pointed the way to medical facilities, inter-brigade boundaries and of course, directions to Third Division Headquarters where I would find transport and further orders and papers that would show I had a duty to fulfill with the Royal Flying Corps.

An army runs on orders. There are orders for everything. A signed order meant that I was issued with a new uniform. The order that stated I was promoted was authority to have my Corporal rank chevrons sewn on. They made notes on my official record of service and noted my new rank would increase my monthly pay by nearly three dollars.

Every man in our army had records. Every event, posting, training, medical visit or treatment and every pay issued was recorded and made a permanent part of every individual soldier's service record. Not only were the Canadian units good at killing and brave while being killed but soldiers took pride in knowing that their service pay and records were being professionally kept and administered. Even if a soldier was directly struck by an incoming artillery shell or disappeared, as they frequently did, into a massive mud hole filled with fetid water, soldiers knew that someday, their record of service would make it back to Canada and that their loved ones and families would have the solemn pleasure of knowing where and when they had served and died. Small pleasure perhaps when seen through the eyes of a Canuck soldier fighting for his life in front of German machine guns but still a proud and significant detail that said, "the Canadian Expeditionary Force looks after its soldiers". And in the vast majority of times, it did just that.

The orders given to me by Captain Johnson and signed by my Company Commander were all that I had needed to get me all the way from my hole in the ground in the front lines into the Division rear area.

Those orders had said to 're-kit' and 'promote' so here I was, after another few visits to personnel records, clothing stores and the paymaster, a brand new man so to speak. I was now a smart looking, even if slightly under pressed, Corporal of infantry. I had a new set of field battledress, newly issued underclothing and a new greatcoat and boots as well as gas mask, webbing and great and small pack. In just hours I had gone from the very fire-step of my battalion into the tailor shop where I was transformed from sniper into a field-smart Canadian soldier. I was once again a little like a schoolboy on my way to learn how to use a camera and be a passenger in an airplane.

Nothing on earth I had ever done before made my heart beat so hard. Nothing had ever felt better than looking at myself in the cracked and finger stained mirror that hung, slightly askew, from a wire in the clothing stores at Divisional Rear. Well, now that I look back on that moment, maybe my first night with Tears had been better than that day but my memory of being with her is special for very different reasons.

Division provided a small truck and a driver from the Third Division Motor Transport Company to continue my journey. I sat in the back, under a canvas tarp with two clerks who were transferring records and boxes of paper requisitions for supply items. The clerks were headed for a rear area Service Corps unit further back; they dropped me off at the Royal Flying Corps liaison unit, which was part of the large spread of tents, buildings, and barns that was First Canadian Corps Headquarters.

This was the sprawling and beehive home of the General that commanded all of the Canadians now located in France. I had noted the name of the small village, Camblain-l'Abbé, as we had turned off the main supply route and started to bump and bang through the potholes on the overworked road that led us to a check point and worried looking military police.

Everything seemed peaceful there. Everywhere I looked there were direction signs indicating the direction to various services or units that made up this strange, and new to me, part of my army. The entire area seemed much like a large market area. The streets and large spaces of farm fields were filled with horses and wagons and odd looking motor trucks, some with their boxes open and others being loaded or unloaded. Nothing except a frenzy of activity seemed to link all the effort together.

Soldiers and officers were coming and going, alone or in small groups, from one area to the other. No one kept their heads down. No one seemed to worry about snipers or artillery shells that might take your life at any second. This was a lot like what I remember Camp Valcartier had been like when I was in training. A YMCA structure centered what seemed to be hundreds of clean and well-fed young soldiers.

After weeks of exposure to the constant bath of mud and filth that was provided by life in trenches this appeared to be more on the side of rest and recreation. Here, there would be a lot less worrying about death from German shelling. This, I began to understand, was just part of life behind the lines.

I was soon to learn that here in the rear area everyone considered themselves to be part of the army but not part of the army that was in contact with the enemy. This part of the army went forward, from time to time, in order to find death. It was only that part of the army already forward that waited for death to find them.

I really didn't have time to have more than a very hot cup of tea from a wagon canteen located just outside of the door of the farmhouse which the RFC liaison office occupied.

No sooner had I arrived then a very smart British staff car and driver pulled in and asked for me by name. After loading up a few belongings we were off in a small cloud of mud and softly falling rain along a road looking for the entire world as if war and every memory of war had been erased. I knew we must surely be out of the combat area when all signs of heavy artillery batteries and their fields full of their stacked boxes of ammunition had disappeared.

Instead, our rutted way was burdened with hundreds of soldiers. Not fighting soldiers like the Royal Canadian Regiment or the PPCLI, not even like the 49th Battalion that I came from. These soldiers were from the hard working supply and services units that existed to move and provide the enormous quantity of materials used by the hundreds of thousands of soldiers holding the forward trenches. Some of them, when you got miles back from the lines, were "labour gangs", contracted to carry, haul, lift, and provide but the vast majority were uniformed soldiers.

On the route we followed, large work parties were to be seen moving and stacking ammunition. Some men of Chinese origin were busily laying small gauge railway tracks along the verge of the road we were driving on. The build up for the battle for Vimy Ridge had already begun. I saw miles of light tram track along our route and quickly began to understand that behind our battalions there were hundreds of thousands of soldiers of every profession.

Soldiers were digging tunnels, building and repairing roads from the rear to the forward areas. Men in droves were laying pipes that carried thousands of gallons of water into the forward areas to water both the animals and the soldiers. There were gangs of men wearing Engineer, Ordinance, and Supply badges, mixed with the badges of the Canadian Overseas Railway Construction Corps. They were labouring away in a chain of workers that must have started right at the seaside docks. From the sides of ships reaching forward, thousands of men were repairing or building small rail tracks. It was on these trams and trains that the army carried forward tons of rations, food for the animals, ammunition and stores into the waiting trenches of fighting units all along the hundreds of miles of destruction scribed by the front lines between the German army and those of our allies.

It wasn't until I had seen all this industry with my own eyes that I came to understand the size and immense effort that German white men had put together in France in order to kill other white men from Europe and the Commonwealth. I was nearly struck dumb with what I saw on that short drive along a rutted road that led to Brauy-la-Buissiere. Through my eyes I was beginning to see the size of the man-made machine whose purpose it was to kill other men on this battlefield. I had not yet begun to question what that many men could have done had their efforts been aimed at building up the nation instead of tearing it down.

All this was as new to me as trench warfare would have been to my English driver. He only knew and understood life as he lived it on this side of the line. He had never "been to the front" he confessed. His face was deeply lined by forty some odd years of being in the service of an unnamed Lord from London.

He was dressed in a clean uniform with a very warm and dry looking Great Coat. His uniform was made of wool like mine, more or less of the same quality and cut, but his was of the light blue shade of the Royal Flying Corps. We Canadians did not have such a service though men talked of such a possibility. I knew that if you wanted to fly you had to apply and be accepted in the RFC.

He told me his name was Edward and that he had been a chauffeur, and carriage man, before the war. His Lord had joined the flying service because he had bought and owned an early model of a flying machine. When the Lord joined the Flying Service he took his driver with him. The Lord had died in a plane crash long before the squadron had gone overseas to France. Nevertheless, Edward was doing his duty the way the Lord's family would have wanted had they known he was there and if they had thought for even a minute about his fate.

Edward never asked a single, solitary question about who I was or why I was on my way to 16 Squadron Royal Flying Corps. I supposed that he had been raised in an environment where one does not seek personal information from strangers. He was from a culture much like the one I had been raised in. Our aboriginal culture treats men as equals and it is only through deeds and actions that opinions would be formed. Edward babbled the entire trip about what a jolly fine fellow had been the Lord. And after we got through all of that he banged on about some matinee he had watched last night in the other ranks drinking mess. A matinee I thought, a matinee? What the hell is a matinee?

For a few minutes of driving we had been getting deeper into the scarred and smashed city of Brauy-la-Buissiere. The city had been a major coal-mining center and commercial area for the surrounding farming area for hundreds of years.

Major transportation links connected the city to the sea and other surrounding cities and regions. At least that had been the case before the Germans had arrived with thousands of cannons and soldiers with the intention of advancing until they washed their feet in the ocean.

The French Army had stopped the German advance in 1914. Now Brauy-la-Buissiere was a ruin, a shadow of its former self. The beautiful cathedral lay in ruins; hundreds if not thousands of families had been cast out of their war ruined homes and farms to make way for the largest defended trench system in the history of the world. Manitou must have cried a river of tears for Belgium and France since the lines had formed between our armies and the Germans.

Many smaller communities surrounded the immediate old city center; some groups of building bore the names given to small farming villages. Some groupings of farms just clustered together nameless as they had for hundreds of years. These little hamlets bore only the street names that connected them to a village or the city. Small roads, streets and lanes crossed; here and there a farm would still look like a farm.

The houses were constructed of stone and rust red brick. The windows I could see were largely shuttered closed. No one would chance exposing glass to the possible intrusion by either eye or random artillery fire. Every window, large or small, lay hidden behind its individual hefty, wooden, shutter; each in turn hanging from heavy iron hinges. There were low, plastered, stonewalls along every street. Tall gates made of thick wooden planks hanging from heavy hinges allowed entrance to the farms and the orchards that lay behind. Every gate we had passed was firmly closed, shutting the house off from access from the street.

Suddenly we emerged from the village that we had been driving through and almost without announcement we had arrived at the grass strip airfield that 16 Squadron, Royal Flying Corps (RFC), called home. A sorry looking sentry standing by a small, sand-bagged, sentry post, did not even acknowledge our approach. Not much defensive effort had gone into the construction of this first line of defence. The walls were thinly built; no trench existed beneath or alongside. I only saw one rifle poking out from the large opening in the front that served as a window on the main road and provided visibility to the entire field.

My head turned in disbelief as we advanced. Clearly no one expected to be attacked by the Germans way out here in the countryside. The private waved us through after having stopped us to ask for a cigarette. Neither the driver nor I smoked and his last motion was one of disgust for our purity.

We didn't have to worry about rising dust as we swayed our way down the rain-soaked gravel-patched lane leading to a farmyard. Most of the original farmyard had been completely taken over by vehicles and tents. There were some newly erected Nissan huts. A small collection of tenders and fuel tanks clustered around the original farm buildings. Most of the original farm buildings had been covered with tarps and canvas lean-tos. The original buildings must have been found to be too small for their new purposes; the addition of canvas tarps gave air and space for the squadron to grow. That space now seemed to be filled with stacks of boxes and strange looking parts of machinery that must have been for airplanes. I was surprised that not one single airplane was visible on the field.

It was early afternoon and no one I saw was what I would call 'completely dressed'. Some men were gathered around a large table, they appeared to be folding paper maps. Others were sitting around in front of what could have been the original barn building watching a few other airmen kick a football. There had been an orchard behind the main farmhouse. Hedges at some point might have surrounded it. The apple trees now supported tents that appeared to be a workshop of some sort and someone had built a raised platform, which gave height and presence to a very large old wooden water barrel or water tank. Towels of all colour implied that it might be a communal bath of some sort.

We stopped in front of a large, recently whitewashed farmhouse that I soon found out had been converted into the Squadron Headquarters, a small officers mess and quarters for the Squadron Commander and the Adjutant. After I had dismounted, Edward waved me through its front door and said he would deliver my kit to the field tent that would be my home for the next week. He had already explained that he would also report in to the Adjutant to inform the Squadron I had arrived. The Adjutant would take my number, rank, and name and then amend the squadron strength by one. I found out that 16 Squadron was very good at adding and subtracting by ones. The average life of a new pilot after having been cleared for duty was less than twelve flying hours that month. That statistic wasn't based on combat air hours; that was just flying hours in general.

As Edward disappeared with my kit a youthful looking private, in army battledress emblazoned with RFC badges, took his place at the narrow doorway servicing as entrance to the Squadron Headquarters.

"My name is Ward", he said, in an accent so thick that at first I could barely make out the language he was speaking let alone the words he had spoken.
"My first name is Liam; I am the Squadron runner which means I get to do everything that anyone else does not want to do". He paused there and without blushing added,
"That's not to say that no one else wanted to meet you it is just that meeting new arrivals is one of my jobs and the Squadron Sergeant Major said I should meet you first and then I will get to introduce you to the Squadron Sergeant Major".
(By the way the army writes the rank Sergeant Major as Sgt Maj).

"I am very pleased to meet you Liam, my name is Giorgio". I extended my hand and was surprised by the strength of his returned handshake.

Liam had a broad and open face. Even with the amount of time that he must be spending out of doors, his skin was so pale that I had to look twice to make sure that he was not sick or feeling poorly. A long patch of freckles spread across a generous nose; a mop of bright, copper coloured hair stuck out from both sides of his field cap.

I let his hand drop, deciding immediately that I was going to like this fellow soldier. His face and eyes were friendly and understanding. I just started right off to tell him all about myself and he responded by listening attentively, nodded his head from time to time as I went on.

"I am a Canadian from a small, little village near Edmonton, Alberta. I am a sniper with B Company of the 49 Battalion; we call ourselves the Edmonton Regiment though when we are amongst friends. My battalion is one of the four infantry battalions that make up the Seventh Canadian Infantry Brigade. There are four brigades in every Division and we have four Divisions in our First Canadian Corps. You may already know that our Corps has been ordered to attack and capture a very prominent hill feature along our front lines that is called Vimy Ridge. I have been sent here by my Battalion Commander to learn how to take air photographs and to make sure that I bring back the best possible air photos of the area that we are going attack over. Can you help me do that Liam"?

Liam looked at me through friendly, ice coloured blue eyes; he had a small smile that seemed to be a permanent feature on his pale but handsome, inquisitive face.

"Well now", he said, "I am Newfoundlander. People here just call me English but we are closer in miles to Canada then we are to England. We are a British colony where most of us are proud to call ourselves Newfoundlanders though our citizenship papers calls us of English descent".

He seemed amused that he had finally found someone to tell his story to.

"Do ya know where I'm from then? Do you know of Newfoundland at all"?

He shrugged when I nodded my head and under his breath he added as if he not seen my acknowledgement,

"We're not really very many folks all told anyhow so not to feel bad if you never seen nor heard of us"!

"Anyhow", he said in a loud voice as he gestured for me to follow him over to a part of the office wall where a big hand-painted map of the airfield and surrounding area hung as sort of pride of place.

"This here is a map of our air field and all the buildings and things in our immediate area. I painted it, that is what I was before I joined the British Army. I was a painter, an oil painter; I was attending the University of Arts, London, as a member of the Camberwell College. The Royal Governor of Newfoundland, a fellow by the name of Sir Walter Davidson arranged a scholarship for me in England for three years. Anyways, the war broke out and by now I and just about everyone at the college had joined the army. Since I was from Newfoundland I tried, without success, to join the Royal Newfoundland Regiment. By the time I tried to join they had already been wiped out, or nearly so, at a place not far from here called Beaumont Hamel. The Dean of Arts was worried that too many Newfoundlanders had already died in this bloody war so the college worked some deal for me to get into the Royal Flying Corps and here I am painting signs, airplanes, and maps for the Squadron Commander".

It was just about then that the Squadron Sergeant Major walked into the outer office. He was a towering giant of a man with a soft voice and a big cane that had been hand cut and carved from an apple tree branch. His very first words were,

"No need to be concerned Corporal, I will not eat you as long as you learn and follow the rules of the Flying Corps".

I thought to myself, after what I have seen in the hellholes of the Somme and Ypres and in front of Vimy, I could learn to like anything that did not come with being shot at. That didn't work out too well, as I was to learn soon enough.

***

The Sergeant Major started off by apologizing for having put me up in a field tent out in the apple orchard.

"My name is Wilcox, William Wilcox. Just like you do in your outfit you can call me Sergeant Major to my face and what ever you want when I am not listening. I would prefer if you consider me to be your friend while you are here Giorgio, you are my guest. I will take a very particular interest in everything that you want to do while you are here. We, that is, 16 Squadron are very proud of the work that we have been doing with and for the Canadian Corps. We get along very well with all of their staff. I am sure that we, you and I, can get along a great clip as long as you do as I say and not as I do".

That little joke had him laughing even if Liam and I did not immediately respond. All I could do was to do nod my head. He was a very impressive fellow, wide shoulders, and spit and polished from hat to toe. I could see immediately that he was not a man to be fooled or fondled.

'We don't have nice clean underground accommodations like you soldiers from the front line have Corporal", he said with a hint of sarcasm in his voice.

"I suppose you will miss not having the rats keeping you company when you go to sleep and I just know the quiet and solitude of an operational airfield will keep you awake".

He walked over and poured three cups of tea from a pot sitting on the side of a small stove in a cubbyhole not far from the clerk's desk. The desk was huge, neat, and clean and occupied almost the entire front section of the office, closest to the entrance door. I quickly learned the desk was sort of a dividing line. Everyone and anyone could enter the Squadron office but only those that were invited or worked behind the desk were welcome to go behind the desk.

"A little late for tea maybe but I missed mine today attending a funeral for one of our pilots killed yesterday near the Vimy line".

Without asking, he splashed an ample dash of milk in all three heavy clay cups and handed them out without ceremony.

"I want you to feel right at home here Giorgio, I have a pretty good knowledge of what you have been going through out there with the Canadian Corps".

He casually walked over and picked up a hand full of medals that were sitting on a side board near the window. With those in his hand he came over and stood beside me, talking in a matter of fact tone.

"I was a Company Sergeant Major with the 2nd Battalion of the Dorsetshire Regiment. I served in India in 1914 as part of the 16th Indian Brigade. We fought in Mesopotamia where I was wounded and captured. Later, I made it back to England on a lot of different hospital ships and when I was well enough to put my uniform back on I joined the RFC. You see Son, I know a little bit about being shot at and shooting back".

I nodded my head and met his steady gaze. He just wanted to make sure that we were on the same page. He was a soldier and so was I.

He went on to explain that the adjutant had written up a training plan and flying schedule, a week long routine that required staying close to flying operations. He took me over and quickly pointed out a board that looked like a very large calendar. Closer investigation showed days of the month broken down into hourly slots and lines across the hourly square which included the number of the aircraft, the pilot's name, the observer's name, mission number, and a small block for comments. My name had already been penciled into almost every day's activities at least once. It seemed like they had a plan to keep me busy for the time that I was going to be here.

I remember following him around as he pointed out the major working and operational areas of the squadron as it was situated on the ground. The beauty of the trees was completely hidden by the muddle and mess of tent canvas. Still, the large L shaped farm house had been whitewashed and though the entire area stunk to high heaven of horse shit and cow dung, the farm house had a friendly and pleasant look. When I compared the squadron area to what field soldiers of the Canadian Corps were used to this air field looked inviting and park-like.

The three of us walked in a large circle through the tented accommodation area and over to the flight briefing area and the pilots' ready area. From there I was introduced to the three levels of dining facilities, one for the officers, one for the senior non-commissioned officers and one larger tented area which held the main kitchen and the Other Ranks dining area. Everything was neat, clean, and well drained. Where it was possible, stones had been painted; ropes marked the paths so that they could be followed at night. With some pride the Sgt Maj snorted,
"Bit better than what you have been used to I'll bet"?
I assured him this looked a lot like heaven after what I had come from. He stopped and stared down at me from his six foot four height,
"Don't you worry Corporal", he said in a lowered voice so that only he and I could hear, "We will make sure you get a sleep-in and have a run into the village while you are here. It won't be all work and no play".
He gave me a little wink as he turned on his heel and led me into the kitchen. After a few quiet words with the cook, and a nod of agreement between the two of them, I was treated to the first real bacon and eggs with pancakes that I had eaten since I left Camp Valcartier in Quebec. My God they were good.

The remainder of that first day was a mad kaleidoscope of memories, some good, and some of the kind you only allow to sneak up when you have been drinking too much and your head is filled with dark thoughts.

* * *

There was a warm welcome by the Adjutant and a visit to the quartermaster stores for issue of flight coat, helmet, goggles, gloves, neck scarf, flying boots, and bedding. There was an amazing introduction to flying safety, which included detailed instructions on how not to vomit into the airstream and how to urinate into a small bottle if that needed to be accomplished during a flight.

One of the Air Observers, a Sergeant by the name of Randal, gave me a short hour course on the duties of an Air Observer. Most of it concentrated on map reading from the air and how to prepare and not expose the frames, which contained the film from the air observer's camera. The camera was mounted like a big clumsy looking box on the right side of rear cockpit compartment. It took a lot of fumbling, cursing and holding tightly on to the negative frames. They had to be manually inserted and correctly removed from the camera box in flight, in the slipstream or else the pictures taken would be just black sheets of film.

The Squadron Commander was an old man of about thirty. His name, engraved on a brass plate was prominently displayed on a triangular place card holder that fronted his desk. It said Major Hugh Mills and following his name there were the initials of a lot of medals and decorations. I made no pretence that I understood what any of them stood for. He was ramrod straight when he stood and walked. He had a large scar that came out of his hairline, down his broad forehead and ended almost at the corner of his upper left lip. I heard later that he had crashed an airplane early in his pilot training; he told other pilots that it helped him to remember to watch his altitude on approaches to the field. He had incredibly blue eyes; they were as cold as ice but surrounded by laugh lines at each corner.

His uniform was a complete disgrace. It was spotted and patched with blobs of castor oil, maybe blood but certainly, spilt tea or coffee. His boots were polished to an incredible shine but the Adjutant admitted it was the only thing he let his batman do for him. His pockets were pregnant with supplies; one carried his flight book, another held a pen or two and yet another had a very large wooden pipe and an equally large tobacco pouch sticking out of it in an untidy lump. All of his pocket buttons were undone, his hair had not seen a barber for months, and he seemed to carry his helmet everywhere he went. Everyone called him "the Old Man". He knew the name of every single person on his field; he knew their wives' names and the names of their kids. He knew who was flying next and who was not. He drank too much and he flew every single day that it was possible to get a plane in the air come rain or shine. Everyone on the squadron loved him like I have never seen before or since in a military unit.

Almost as soon as we had met and exchanged the courtesies common to such an event the Major waved the Sgt Maj and me into his office. It was spotless, not a thing was out of place. Air photographs and maps covered a huge area of the walls. On a large board in front of the Commander's desk was another board on which was written all the names of all the pilots that had flown with 16 Squadron and the dates the pilots and observers had joined or departed or were killed. It was a long and detailed list.

"I am very interested to learn a little about you Corporal and what you think we can do for you"!

The Major had swung himself lightly into his chair behind his desk. His eyes were boring a hole in my face as he leaned forward to hold court.

I glanced over at the Sgt Maj, his face was relaxed, there was a small smile pulling at the corners of his mouth. With just that one look I knew I was in a safe place and I could pour out everything I hoped to achieve and everything I had kept hidden, some of it even from myself.

"Well Sir", I said as I leaned back into a chair, which had been strategically placed centered in front of the Major's desk, "I will start with the truth and end with what I hope to do while I am here".

I still do not know why I told them just about everything about being an aboriginal boy from Saddle Lake. I told them how Cold Dawn had raised me and how I had learned to hunt and fish by watching the examples left for me by Johnny Snake Eye. I told them about how I had joined the army, how I had picked my name and all about becoming a sniper and working with Arthur in the 49th Battalion of the Seventh Brigade, Third Canadian Division, First Canadian Corps. As I was speaking I realized just how much I had done since I had become a soldier. How far away from home I really was. What shocked me was, as I spoke, I realized how little I understood about why I had joined.

At the end of all that, about 30 minutes later I suppose, I said:
"Being a sniper means that in order to stay alive once you are over the wall you have to be faster, better and smarter than everyone in front of you and usually it helps if everyone behind you knows exactly where you are and for how long".

I got up and walked over to the air photographs that were displayed on the wall of the Major's office. I had already seen they were laid out in a mosaic presenting a fairly current coverage of the Canadian line as it existed at that time. The photo coverage started somewhere on the left side of our positions. That would mean the photos started at the right edge of the British First Corps because they held the left side of our area. One of the air photos clearly showed the small village of Souchez which was one of our inter-Corps boundary points and Arthur and I had already been there on a previous patrol just a few weeks before.

"My mission on the day of the Canadian assault on Vimy Ridge will be to establish a sniper position on the far left of the existing Canadian front, just left of the 10th Canadian Infantry Battalion which is occupying the trenches your picture shows right here".

As I spoke I pointed my finger roughly along the trench line and ended up with my finger pointing to a small feature just forward of the Canadian trenches that still belonged to the Germans.

"You may know this feature as 'the Pimple'. It is high ground and heavily defended by the Germans and has a number of artillery observers and machine gunners all along its edge facing the approach our soldiers will take on the morning of their attack".

I went back, sat down in my chair, and moved it just slightly forward towards the desk.

"I know all this because for the first time in our history, all four Canadian Divisions have been put together as a Corps and our officers have insisted that every rank right down to the lowest member must be briefed and rehearsed on the entire days' work that they are expected to do. I have seen maps just like these on numerous times over the last two weeks".

I hesitated there for a moment; I could see that my introduction was failing to impress either of them.

"My partner Arthur and I have been tasked and we went forward to see and get approval from the Canadian battalion now holding the left side of our line so that they include us in their plans and have us marked on their maps".

I paused there for a few seconds before I continued.

"My Platoon Commander trusts Arthur and me to do our job and he was the one that asked for permission for me to come and spend time with you so I could have a better understanding of how the ground looks not only from ground level but also from the air. I do not know if you can take better pictures than you already have. But I do know that if I can use your air photos to find and kill the Germans holding all the cards on the top of The Pimple than maybe, just maybe, some Canadian soldiers will live to see the sunset on the day we all stand up and start our walk across that piece of ground. I also know for certain that none of us wants to take that walk but we all will have to do it."

Then I sort of added under my breath;

"In fact a lot of soldiers may be dying to take that walk".

A long moment of silence reached out and smothered the moment we were in, suspending everything except the fact that we were staring at one another.

"Tell me something Corporal Giorgio Costello, do you think your eyes are better than my eyes or the eyes of all of my pilots and all of my observers"?

I didn't hesitate for a second,

"No Sir, I know, not just think, my eyes are better than yours. I know for a fact my eyes are better than anyone else's in this squadron. If my eyes were not the very best eyes in the world than my Great Creator would have picked a different man to fly over these lines and do what I have been asked to do".

The Major sat there glowering at me for what seemed like a long time. Then he slowly reached into the bulging pocket holding his pipe and without taking his eyes off mine he slowly crammed some tobacco into the bowl. After another visit to the same pocket he retrieved a match, struck it on the side of his desk and held the flaring flame to the bowl as sounds of gurgling air found their way through the stem and into the room around us.

Just then the unmistakeable sound of an airplane motor flying in the area of the field reached all of our ears. The Major jumped from his chair and was two steps in front of us before he said,
"Come with me Corporal, come quick".

The three of us broke out of the front door and skidded to a halt facing the field in the direction of the aircraft sound. Down low, out about a half a mile, was the grey outline of an airplane turning in on the approach as if to land or fly low level over the length of the field. As it turned, for just a second, its side view was exposed, and then wing down it continued to line up with the track intended.
"There", the Major cried, "There! Did you see that Costello? Did you see that? What was the number on the side of that British aircraft"?
He stood straight, tall, and turned to challenge me to see something that I supposed he must already know.

"I have no idea whatsoever Major", I said without taking by eyes off the airplane that was continuing to turn in on the line straight towards the landing strip.

"I certainly did not see any number on the side of that aircraft but I can assure you that it is not British. It is painted in German colours and there is a black and white streamer on the left wing and none on the right".

"Jesus Christ get down, get down, get down", the Major cried just before machine gun tracers cut all across the right edge of the field; some rounds found resting places in the walls of the building we had just exited. I had pushed the Major just hard enough to make sure his frame was behind a small, stone wall, which formed the original walkway into the farmhouse. The Sgt Maj and I both dove into the same small slit trench someone had dug weeks before on the unlikely possibility of just such an event occurring. The German pilot gave us all a one-fingered salute as he pulled the nose up of his scout and slowly proceeded to turn back to the east towards his home base and a future beer with sausage.

The three of us emerged at the same moment, each taking some time to brush the wet dirt and sand away from our clothing. A small group of officers had exited their mess and were excitedly discussing the nerve of the German pilot that had been so bold as to pay a visit this far back into the rear area. The Major casually retraced his steps back to the point where we had been standing when we had first exited the squadron office. Without ceremony he reached down and retrieved his still smoking pipe. A quick and thoughtful suck on the stem seemed to confirm that it was still operational. With a sort of satisfied nod and looking at his well used tobacco burner, he fixed me with his eye before saying:

"Well Corporal, nothing wrong with your eyesight I see".

That was the end of that conversation. The Major walked back over to speak to the pilots now excitedly discussing the merits of jumping in an airplane and giving chase to the German plane. The German was still visible as just a small shadow on a darkening cloud cover.

The Sergeant Major cast a somewhat softer look at my uniform and added, "You might want to have a bath before dinner and a few drinks afterwards Giorgio. I do believe the Major liked your story I know I certainly did. Have a good night's sleep if you can, I plan to keep the Squadron hopping to make sure you get what you need while you are with us".

Oh, I can remember a little bit about the first night's dinner and later in the mess with a bunch of rowdy airmen. But other than that I got far too drunk to remember much else. I was the new boy in town; I was different from them and I had different experiences and different stories to tell about what it was like on the hellhole that we called the front. They were a friendly bunch of Brits. They worked hard during their duty hours and they drank hard when the curtain fell across the runway. Oh, and one more thing about me, they all wanted to buy me a drink and who was I to say no.

* * *

Next day, my first real day with 16 Squadron, started before I was really sober. My head hurt, I had a complete memory loss as to where I was supposed to wash and shave. I ended up in the Sergeants' lavatories but everyone was far too polite to tell me to piss off. Breakfast was so big and consequently good that by the time the sun was up I was feeling much more like a Canadian soldier on holiday with the newly minted Royal Flying Corps.

I had a few minutes to myself just after I exited the Other Ranks dining room. The morning air was filled with fog patches and little catches of cold air that seemed to blow around the old farm without direction or purpose. I let my eyes work over the entire area trying to see it as the farmer's wife must have seen it. The farm yard still bore the strong persistent smells of horseshit and farm animals. Here and there were piles of sand and mud and sand-bags that clearly outlined the shell scrapes dug in case an airman needed to dive into cover from some German scout firing into the airfield. All that flashed through my mind and yet, I thought, the farm house and the old yard still had some sort of pleasant and persistently welcoming qualities about them.

The Squadron Sgt Maj came looking for me at six AM, 0600 hours in military time; he ushered me into the old barn. It had suffered some hasty modifications to widen and heighten the door. A little paint had recently been splashed around on some of the plastered walls. Most of the original animal pens and such must have been used to fire the kitchen stove because the barn was now used as the main repair hanger.

A large portion of the interior space was filled with boxes of aircraft parts, used and new motors on stands while a large open area on one side was mainly filled with a large flat table like surface which I later learned was used to cut and paste and paint aircraft fabric needing repair or replacement.

There just wasn't anything that the few hard working aircraft technicians could not do to and for an airplane. Sadly though, the same sort of repair shop did not exist for the soft skinned easily injured pilots and crew members that flew them.

It was then and there that I came face to face with the wings that I would use to fly. There, one alongside of the other were two BE 2c biplanes. They looked even more fragile than they were. They smelled of fuel and oil. Someone had put a sign on one of them saying when the glue and paint would be dry enough to touch. They glowed of wood varnish and paint. The craft sported two cockpits, one behind the other. A very clean camera was hung immediately on the right side of the pilot's position, which was located in the back, closest to the tail. The front cockpit was well forward, right up between the two wings, which was the gun less seating arrangement for the observer. I must have looked and acted like a boy in a candy shop for the rest of the morning. It really was love at first sight. My God, I thought, these are the wings of Askuwheteau. I felt my hands tremble as I touched and ran my fingers over the surfaces of canvas and wood.

* * *

I suppose they just let me gawk at the airplanes for a few minutes. They must have seen similar reactions hundreds of times by other non-flyers when they first confront, face-to-face, one of these marvellous beasts. Nearly everyone had seen them in the sky and had marvelled at their grace. Some, I know, were shocked at the noise they could make and I frequently heard soldiers tell stories of how upset someone was at a church function, a funeral, a wedding or a garden party in England, when one of these infernal things came hopping over the tree tops. Horses had been known to break away from their handlers and trample riders or carriages in their dash to escape these monsters from the sky. The tales about dogs or other animals doing the maddest things in reaction to being overflown are legion. But as for me, I just stood there and stared. My good lord, I remember thinking, how can such a strange looking craft with its shiny motor pushing out of its front and a fragile looking set of wings get off the ground and dance with clouds and birds alike?

I approached the nearest airplane very slowly, my hand out to touch it as if it might bite. A voice at my shoulder softly said:

"My name is Bert to my friends and Bumbles to my two flat-headed fitters".

I turned, somewhat startled, I had not even noticed the very young good looking boy with old eyes and a large angry pink wound on his left cheek. He glanced around with a mischievous smile on his face as he nodded towards the two Sergeants who were casually standing behind the near right wing of the aircraft parked close to us. They recognized me as having been at their washstand that morning.

They nodded in my general direction before they kicked off into an act that obviously had been rehearsed and preformed many times. In unison they hung their heads and in a theatrical voice much in vogue at black minstrel shows, declared:

"We don't call him 'Bumbles'; we call him 'Bloody Bumbles' when he bends the under cart"!

They then bowed curtly to one another and shook hands. That little act brought a few handclaps from the other airmen on the hanger floor and a deep and throaty laugh from Captain Bert. He must have heard that routine many times from those two clowns. Their little comic break gave me a few seconds to assess what kind of man this Bert might be. He was very young, average height at about five foot eight. He was slim in an athletic way but the thing about him, which immediately held your attention, was a smile that just did not know where to land. It sort of started at the corners of his mouth and ended up in a big, toothy grin, mouth open, and full of chuckles and snorting sounds. It was just impossible not to like Bert right from the very start.

The rest of the morning just washed away with the falling rain. Between Captain Bert and the two fitters they took turns helping me through a stiff learning curve of 'how' flight, 'why' flight, 'when' flight and 'getting in and out'.

It really was a damn strange layout, the pilot in the rear compartment, and the observer in the front, closest to the propeller. The only place to put the camera because of the location of the wings on the fuselage was to mount it directly where the pilot sat and therefore he had to climb in, around, and over, the big box camera and the mount holding it in place.

By lunchtime, in the Other Ranks mess, my head was spinning trying to remember things I needed to know if I was going to be allowed to fly in the observer's compartment. Strap in and strap off, how to hang on and what to hang on to. I learned quickly why aircrew wore scarfs and why they dressed so warmly even on warm days. Fire was the greatest fear for aircrew, it meant only one of two things; put the fire out or burn to death trying to put it out and there wasn't much time to do either of those two choices. Bert did not dwell on the things he had to do in order to get the plane into the air and stay in the air but he was assuring and confident that as long as he was in control we would be as safe as the German fighters would let us be. Two or three times during the various demonstrations and training sessions Bert would say:

"Nothing to worry about Giorgio, just tell me where you want to go and I'll be right there behind you".

He always uttered a little laugh whenever he said that. Funny, but I did not even feel a second's fear about death in the air. Maybe that was so because I was Askuwheteau.

The camera followed lunch. The truth about the camera was that it really is surprising that anyone ever got a good, clear picture of the battlefield trench system or anything else for that matter. Most of the cameras used were really just bigger versions of what a store photographer would have used to take your picture if you walked in off the street in Edmonton and asked for a picture of yourself in uniform so that your mother might have something to remember you by.

These box cameras took up a lot of space on the side of the plane and had to be mounted in a spot where it had uninterrupted vision of the ground beneath it. Next, they were clumsy 'plate' cameras; the photographic negative had to be inserted and removed after each picture. This took a lot of effort in the rain and wet; the fact that the flying environment is filled with clouds, cold, and being shot at didn't help either.

The most important and devastating thing about being an observer was that I didn't get to take any pictures with the camera. That was because my seat, the observer's seat, was way up in front of the pilot.

It was explained to me that this position was selected in case the mission called for bombs to be dropped from the plane. The Observers position was well up front so that it would be over the center of gravity. This meant, according to Bert, that the plane was very stable if the observer was taken out and bombs were carried under the wings. However, the position was so far forward that the observer could not really see very well because of all the struts, wires, and the obstructions of vision from the wings themselves. In fact, on this model of airplane the observer had to stand up, hang on and look over the wing to see if any enemy airplane was following behind or under the BE2c

So, they explained, as a team of two, their job was to find and fly over the area they had to observe. Once over their target, the observer would locate and indicate the targets. The pilot would take the pictures. The observer managed and controlled the individual film frames, loading them into the camera, and storing them after they had been exposed. It was a little like two one-armed men, trying to hang paper on a moving wall. Everyone had to do their job or else it just didn't work.

Routinely an escort scout or fighter aircraft would stay with them and provide protection from the German fighters. A standard reconnaissance flight was somewhere around an hour in duration.

"Safe as a house", said pilot Captain Bert.

* * *

It was nearly sundown before my day of lessons and instruction ended. The face of the end of winter sun had not even shone through the sullen wet blanket of cloud that carpeted the aerodrome. Low ceilings and dwindling light meant very little chance of a German Albatross on a hunting trip over the field. Bert and a few of the hanger crew suddenly opened the front clam style doors and "C" for Charlie 19 was pushed out into the front ramp and the prop was being turned before I realized I was going flying.

Someone handed me my leather helmet and goggles; another tugged at my flying coat. An airman named Frank yelled "Just a quick circuit to give you a feel of what to expect tomorrow".

I stepped up and in; hands helped me to remember how to pull on the straps. Bert held his thumb up and I said something stupid about "I have always wanted to do this"; the chocks were pulled out and an airman on each wing provided the steering as we began to roll out towards the edge of the field. There was a lot of tail wagging and some hands to get us pointed into the wind; then, with a soft mist coming back off the prop and wheels we started our run into the air.

The hanger was at the south end of field, we had turned into a northerly breeze, and within just seconds we did a couple of ground bumping hops. The revs were up; everything sounded great and my heart jumped, as we were airborne. The taking away of the earth from beneath the wheels left us with wings hanging only on air and just the sound of a motor pulling. In that moment I was Askuwheteau. For the entire length of that moment, what an incredible moment it was.

I can remember every second of that, my first flight, as if it was yesterday. Like one can remember a first kiss or the first large fish you catch, so were those seconds incised on my memory. I had my eyes fastened to the movement of the ground below and forward where I could see out through the struts and wires. It seemed as if we were still and a ribbon of the earth was being quickly drawn past the side of the cockpit. We were low, not more than twenty feet; the end of the field we called the aerodrome flashed under us and the hedge between the end of the strip and the little road that ran into the village quickly marked our place on the moving strip.

My sight was filled with green and movement; I could focus only on the movement itself, nothing else. Then suddenly, without reason, two wooden spars and some few pieces of cloth from the top of the wing above me were joined by a hailstorm of splinters that quickly disappeared into the slipstream behind my head. The upper wing folded in slow motion; the nose came down aimed to strike the ground just yards ahead. My hands instinctively came up to hold off the expected impact with the front of the compartment. I felt the undercarriage make contact with the hedge line on the far side of the little road. I was aware of a hot, sticky, stream of dark red liquid slashing into the back of my helmet. We did one small bounce off the stone hedge line and struck the field, hard, nose first, at an angle. I can close my eyes and see the wooden prop as it broke into an arc of flailing hardwood shards. The tail swung up violently; we were thrown into a cartwheel until we struck the ground again, wings down. My ears were insulted by a million sounds of splintering, tearing, and an engine, off its blocks, screaming at its own death.

We slid upside down for two or three seconds. Cow shit and horse dung mixed with dirt and grass obscured my upside down view. My body was now only halfway in the compartment; the collision with the ground had thrown me out of the lap straps, I had been hurled like a sack into the bottom of the cockpit. The cartwheel had acted with sufficient strength to toss me up and out again. I was carried forward, sliding along with the breaking wing and wires. I suppose for a second I was part of the bottom skid plate we were moving forward on. For the second or two that we were sliding, though I could not see, my ears were filled with the shredding and breaking and tearing apart of the wings that I had trusted with my very soul. Then everything except my heart stopped moving.

For ten seconds or more I could not move. There was a pressure of weight holding me captive. I was face down in the dirt of the field and something, I knew not what, from whatever remained of the now upside down and smashed airplane, was pressing down and into me. Somehow I managed to push up into the mess above me and succeeded to turn my head to look towards what had been the tail section. The nose was down, the tail well up with everything splintered and broken; fabric hung down in torn shreds like pieces of camouflage strips ready to be sewn into a ground cover. I could look up and into the rear compartment.

Bert hung, glassy eyed, from his lap strap. His legs were inside the compartment but he hung, arms down, head down, just a foot or two from where I squatted. He was motionless, blood streamed from a large open wound somewhere on his neck. The only sign of life that I could see within his body was the steady pulse his heart still managed.

His heart was alone now as everything else about him slipped away; his young and still beating heart was dutifully empting his body of blood, one spurt at a time. His flight bag and map case were still loosely clinging to his shoulder.

* * *

Askuwheteau's First Tears

I had seen a lot of dead men in the trenches. I did not have to ask myself the question that my blurry eyes had already answered. A bullet had struck Bert directly in the back of his neck and had exited where his Adams apple would have been. He did not even know that he was no longer flying. With that one-second of being face to face with him, circumstance, cause, and effect, a full tank of fuel, now upside down and leaking eliminated every other possible thing I could have done.

As so often occurs, when shit happens, things often go from bad to worse. There was a searing flash and a somewhat surprisingly muted "whoosh" as the fuel tank burst into flame. Luckily the first pressure and heat was upwards, towards the now exposed bottom of the wreck.

With nothing else on my mind except survival I started clawing my way out from under my resting place with every ounce of energy and strength that fear provides to men who are about to burn to death. My mind stopped shrieking, "survive" when I was about a hundred yards away from the crash site. At that distance the heat from the fire no longer felt like it would melt my clothing. My goggles were hopelessly smeared; I could barely see through them; my hands were screaming in pain from using them like crab claws to haul myself along the rough county field we had pitched into.

It was only when I could not feel the flames licking behind me that I tore my helmet and goggles off and stole a quick glance at the wreck. It was now a bare bones skeleton of crumbling wooden frame and already consumed fabric.

Bert's blackened body still hung, hands down, head down, from the cockpit that he had died in. For that instant he remained completely part of the inferno and then, like a deck of cards, the top wing, which had been resting on the ground, collapsed. Bert disappeared into the center of the burning mass. A sickening hiss and black smoke issued above the wreck like a weird sort of flag to mark a hero's death. As if to add structure to the macabre performance before me, wires, and cables breaking in the heat, played a short, non-harmonious requiem.

Unconsciously I suppose, I had stood up. It wasn't until I stood that I was even aware of how my body felt or if I had been injured. My first reaction was one of shock and disbelief. I did not appear to have any missing parts or major wounds. My mouth was quickly swelling into near balloon proportions where my upper teeth had cut through my lips when my head hit the front rim of the observer's compartment. The entire front of my flying coat and trousers were completely drenched in the ugly bath of still sticky blood, water, and sludge from the field. Though I would not know it until one the RFC medics arrived from the aerodrome, my back, from the top of my helmet to my waist was awash with Bert's blood. To add to the gore, a bullet, maybe the same one that had killed Bert, had torn a neat, linear piece out the left side of my helmet. Part of my upper ear had gone along for the ride. It is amazing how much blood seemed to flow from that missing piece of ear. Both of my eyes were as black as a blueberry pie within an hour of the incident.

Other than the physical extent of my visible injuries I seemed whole. But in my mind, that soft, hidden, and secret place, where souvenirs are gathered and held, it was there that the ghosts from that first flight would remain.

I could see a small convoy of rescue vehicles and a fire truck on their way from squadron lines. I sank to the ground again in a vomiting huddle of nervous exhaustion. My body was wracked with the horror of what remained in the burning airplane. I had managed to crawl away from it. And furthermore, for some unknown reason which I cannot remember doing, I must have reached up and recovered Bert's map case that was hanging down from his arm or lap. It contained his flight map, some notes on landmarks and air photographs. Bits and pieces he had selected for his own use either as reminders of route markers or for future operations.

I lay there, my mind continuing to scream a completely selfish gratitude for having been spared. On another, unspiritual level, I knew how incredibly lucky I was being here at all instead of hanging in my harness along with the recently departed pilot I had already learned to like.

I know it did not look very manly but I just rolled up into an unimportant little ball and waited until the Crossly 20/25 tender trucks and medics arrived.

They told me later Bert had died instantly. They said no sooner had he pushed hard on the throttle to begin our little circuit of the field than a low flying German fighter was seen to be turning in directly behind our still bouncing BE2. Everyone was so enjoying watching my amazement at being flung into the air for the very first time that no one had remembered to check the airspace around the field for enemy aircraft. Just as our wheels were off the ground they had all rushed forward, arms waving and voices giving warning. All to no avail! Perhaps a trained observer would have been watching for just such an event.

I do not know if someone with more proficiency in the front compartment would have made a difference. The German sunk down until his wheels were almost on the surface of our field. He closed rapidly as we struggled for altitude. He had a straight from behind shot from about 100 yards and he did not miss. Two seconds of machine gun fire directly into the top wing root and the rear compartment and the German pilot was only yards above us as he pulled up to avoid the breaking wreck that we became. He, the German, would be back at his home station within minutes of the engagement. No doubt he would be telling all of his fellow pilots what an easy kill he was awarded on his visit to the aerodrome of 16 Squadron RFC.

A sort of silence settled over the aerodrome that evening. No one laughed or sang songs. The normal ruckus, which I had heard coming from the aircraft repair hanger the night before was completely missing. There were quiet, respectful lines in front of the cooking pots and condiments table. A number of men came over joining me at my table but no one had words to erase the sights, sounds, smells, and tastes that remained in my mouth. The Chaplain came and sat with me for a few minutes after I had gone alone into my tent after dinner. He seemed very nice. He said he was from someplace called Windsor in Ontario. His parents had come from Germany and had settled in Canada. He did not look me in the eye when he talked about how sad it made him when the airmen cursed Germans and Germany. He said that he would write a letter to Bert's mother and tell her as much as he could about how well-liked he had been in the squadron. He wished me goodnight without even asking how I was. Maybe he could see into my soul and knew that Askuwheteau had never, not even once, imagined that he could crash as well as fly.

The Squadron had issued me a new set of flying clothes that evening for my introductory flight scheduled for six o'clock in the morning. I already knew from experience that it would take a lot of washing and time for me to get Bert's blood off my hands and out of my mind. That said, I also knew I had to forget everything about the way Bert had died if I wanted to move on to all the killing that was going to become known as the Battle of Vimy Ridge.

I cannot say that I remember sleeping that night. If I did I certainly did not sleep for very long. The memory of the euphoric moment as Bert and I pulled our wheels out of the low covering of grass kept struggling to overcome the sight of Bert hanging in his harness just before the inferno erupted. I tossed and turned trying to imagine how a real observer might have turned to watch over and behind our flight path. I kept wondering if Bert could have avoided dying if I had been better at doing what I knew I should have done. And just when I knew that any further sleep would be impossible, it became impossible to stay in bed. Four thirty was reveille.

Reveille came without sun. The Squadron's airfield awoke without a sense of humour. The clouds were nearly as wet and low as the spirits of the unit. Bert's death and the fire that followed had occurred in plain view of almost everyone and anyone that could endure it watched it. Flight safety and take off protocols had been broken and everyone knew it. No one had been standing watch to ensure the skies were clear of German hunters. The entire event cast a dark pall over the squadron and crew. Bert's death, right there in front of the entire squadron had struck a chord not often heard by RFC Other Ranks. Certainly flying officers frequently did not come back from missions. Often inexperienced pilots might not even make it back from their first operational flight. It is not that death was unexpected.

The Squadron Commander's board was filled with the names of officers who had lost their lives while flying with the unit. The board was full and the war was far from finished. No, a pilot's death was expected. What was unexpected was that Bert was shot down and killed just a few short yards away from where the squadron lived, worked, and played. I could see a lot of men looking at me as I dressed, washed, and prepared for the day; what I did not see was anyone who could smile as they looked in my direction.

Five o'clock was breakfast. At precisely Five thirty a pilot and I had our pre-flight briefing and an update on the battlefield including some new developments on the German side of the line. At 0700 hours, the very beginning of false dawn, we were airborne; this time I remembered to swivel and watch.

I had only the shortest of time to become acquainted with the pilot. He had some sort of title before his name, a busy little moustache under a long thin nose, and an accent that can only be accomplished when you keep your jaws from moving and your mouth in a small round circle.

"Hamilton-Hewes is the name on my log book", he said as we shook hands.

"Damned nasty thing that incident with Bert and you yesterday".

He stopped there, looking hard at my eyes to see if I would flinch or carried some harboured fear. I did not blame him for wondering if my experience yesterday would come between our mission and my ability to function as an observer.

"Can't promise we won't see another German out hunting today Corporal but I do promise to keep my eyes open".

"Yes Sir, I promise to do the same".

He seemed satisfied with my reply and we both turned to the business of getting our soft and vulnerable bodies, map cases, gloves, helmets, and hopes, into our very bare compartments.

A 'pusher' scout aircraft called a DH 2 accompanied us. It and the pilot came from 24 Squadron. They were stationed on a field nearby and would stay with us for the entire flight. It was called having a fighter escort; most of the reconnaissance flights conducted by 16 Squadron were escorted missions. It was just too damned dangerous for a photographic mission to be flown all on your own. Thirty minutes of climbing west, away from the front lines in the relative safety of nine thousand feet gave me ample opportunity to marvel at the world below. Way out to the east and beneath me the Belgian coastline, what little the Germans did not now own, and the immediate French countryside unravelled around us. Countless fields, nameless villages, and small knots of woods, were knitted together by a web-like linking of tiny roads. Within minutes of being aloft I was hopelessly lost. The constant changing of sky, clouds, sun slants, and countryside confounded my ability to identify them on my open map. The area on both sides of the ugly scar that was the current front line spread out lush, green, and seemingly full of history and life. The scar itself, though miles away to the east, was like a wide brown line that some angry child might have drawn on a flat chalkboard.

We were ten miles away from the line, and nearly two miles above it. Somehow, in those few minutes of my second flight, I just could not for the life of me relate today with the horror of the trenches that I lived in day after day. Here, in this marvellous flying machine I felt detached from the violence that existed below.

Here, with the countryside spreading out like a slightly rumpled blanket of green, with the early morning sun pushing shafts of bright light here and there across the ground below I did not, could not, bring myself to feel like I was part of yesterday. I began to feel suspended on the end of a pin. The pin moved and I moved with it. The pilot behind me was the complete and only master of my movement and my fate. I turned around to find him smiling away at me, a pipe in one hand, which he waved from time to time to give change of direction instructions to the accompanying fighter escort. He leaned slightly forward and shouted above the constant wind and motor noise, "Just turning south-east over St. Omer, we will have a go at the line now if you don't mind"?

I gave a weak little wave with my free left hand and turned quickly to the map on my knee. Cheeky bastard, I thought, he knew all along I was as lost as an arrowhead in the fatty part of the hump of a running buffalo.

Cold trickled and seeped into every part of the compartment and reached with tiny fingers to find exposed parts of faces, hands and uncovered necks. Long streams of layered clouds and patches of high airborne fog provided an icy covering of mist. These mists quickly turned to water; the water into drips and streams that seemed to have no boundaries or dams to stop them. I was quickly learning that even here, in the cleanest of air, being a soldier in the clouds could be almost as miserable and cold as it was hiding behind a canvas covering in a trench filled with dirt, duckboards, and sandbags. Now though, I was found; I had St. Omer under my finger and my eye on the changing ground. Stay awake Askuwheteau, I thought to myself, or you will be landing and have no idea where you have been.

Hamilton-Hewes waved his piped filled hand again at the near-by DH escort and closing together we turned eastward at full revs.

* * *

Take a Picture I am Flying.

The soft, gentle introduction to being an air observer was over. No more turning away from the front line and making lazy turns high over the quiet green farms of France as they spread out towards the coast. There had been no German fighters that far back to come around and ask if we had a spot on our dance card. Now that we had announced our intention would be to conduct an observer mission we were bound to attract some attention from the German side. The escort fighter had closed up considerably; his wing tip was close along side and even my inexperienced eyes could see the intensity of the pilots, both the escort, and mine had gone from Sunday flying to the real thing. With my finger pressing down hard on the spot on the map over which we were making our turn I found myself leaning forward, up to the edge of the compartment, my mind fixed on trying to keep track of where we were and what I could see beneath us. This flying stuff was not as easy as it had first appeared.

In what seemed to be just seconds we started a long downward sloping slant from St. Omer. We were southwest of the line and flying together towards the northern edge of the Canadian front which itself was only a fractional part of the existing front line. As we approached, the first thing that my eyes distinguished from the squalid ruin of earth was the occasional dark, angry, towering shell burst. They would spout up for a second before falling and disappearing again into the mud and destruction they had come from. Unheard from our height above them I knew that each small volcano could very well have meant death or wounding to any unfortunate soldier within close proximity to the burst.

Just then we banked hard, right wing down, turning south to fly over and along the length of the First Canadian Corps Line. I had already handed Hamilton-Hewes the first of the four negative frames that we planned to take on our pass over the line. We had intended to start our almost north to south flight path just north of the German held Pimple. From there we would try to hold steady and overfly the entire nearly eight thousand yards of front. Our photos were intended to update those already existing of the line. We had enough time to take one photo every mile. The first one would start at the Fourth Canadian Division trenches and include the supply routes in to and out of the British Corps that held the left hand, or north, shoulder of our defence line. Our photo plan called for the next, the second photo, to be taken over the ground held by the Third Canadian Infantry Division.

My mind was a complete whirlwind. I knew my immediate concern was one of observing and assisting the pilot to maintain our photo mission trajectory. Next, I was totally responsible to keep track of the time since the last photo was taken and to indicate when the next photo frame was to be exposed. The pilot was flying, navigating, watching out for enemy aircraft and clicking the shutter. If we were working as a team, all of our photos would overlap and we could present a complete composite air photo map of the line we were presented with at that time. I was determined not to lose contact with the ground; I wanted to know, as accurately as possible where we were in relationship with the map. Suddenly, with just the slightest instant of visibility a light grey shadow crossed under our plane, almost involuntarily I started to gesture and point at the ground. My own battalion and all of my army friends were down there just a few thousand feet below us but so was a German Scout and it appeared to be coming up to play.

Without any warning some German anti-aircraft fire came up at us, the first few rounds bursting well above but slowly getting closer to the six-thousand-foot altitude we were at. I swivelled my head to watch the rounds explode and drift away far above us. We quickly lost a few hundred feet to keep the artillery guessing I supposed and we as we covered another mile of trenches that soon became the beginning of the Second Canadian Infantry Division.

From our height it was very easy to see the prominence and outline of Vimy Ridge and the German defences that weighed down the entire landscape. Finally, we droned over the First Division in their confusing trench lines on the right flank of the Canadian Corps line. Captain Hamilton-Hewes, while flying the airplane, was watching for distinctive photo points, keeping an eye on me in the front and one eye on the position of the DH escort aircraft. It amazed me that he managed to get three out of the four photos taken. Not bad work for a new team with an inexperienced observer to point out the photo points and general direction to follow on the flight path. We had been lucky I thought; only one German fighter had come out to see what we were up to. Our photo run was now complete. We were descending very rapidly. For about a minute or so we had come, engine banging and sputtering out of low ragged piece of damp cloud. We continued to glide downwards towards the southwest and away from the front trenches. I could no longer put my finger on my map and know the point that we were above. Damn, I thought, it would sure be easy to get lost up here.

I quickly turned around to give a small wave to the pilot intending to shout something like, 'well done'. My jaw must have nearly hit the edge of the compartment to find that three British aircraft had joined us and were worriedly bouncing up and down on our right side.

Some hand signals were being passed; with a wave of the pipe we turned hard right, nose nearly straight down in a more westerly direction toward greener fields and abundant patches of fog and rain. The fighter escort stayed with us but the other three British fighters turned hard behind us to continue on their mission, whatever that had been.

After a few minutes of rapid descent, we banked hard left again, wing down, close to the ground. A mud filled field of heavy guns, horses and stacks of ammunition appeared and vanished under our wings. A road filled with wagons and marching soldiers followed only to be replaced by the remains of a large ruined church and the shattered shells of walls that must have been a fairly large village. Next, we flew directly over a large body of waving soldiers in a field. They were having a meal; steam could be seen rising from the kitchen wagon.

Then I remember a large group of tents, some with red crosses flying from their flagpoles. We were very low now, lined up with a long straight road filled to capacity with long lines of horse drawn wagons and then, suddenly, without more than the slightest of bumps, we were down, on the ground, rolling along a green field. My swivelling head managed to recognize the old barn 16 Squadron used as a hanger. I never once had made a note. I had not marked the route we had followed on the map I held on my lap. I never saw where the three airplanes had mysteriously joined us at six thousand feet had come from. I had never even reached back to retrieve and store the three photo frames the pilot now calmly handed forward to me as he bumped along trying to steer the plane using only prop wash and rear rudder. Jesus, Askuwheteau, you will have to start doing a better job of being an observer or they will kick your wide-eyed ass back to the battalion.

Two men were running towards us from the hanger. In just seconds they were outboard of the wings helping to push and turn, their efforts were necessary to get us and keep us in the right direction as we returned to the airplane park just in front of the hanger. I could feel the tension staring to drain away from my body. My first flight, God it had been over an hour, was finished. The whole of the time had flashed away; it seemed like only minutes ago we were bouncing out to the field to take off. My head swam with what I had seen. For a few seconds I thought my heart would fly right out of my chest. I had a flood of returning sights, a kaleidoscope of destruction and human effort; a beautiful painting of earth as seen from above; the horrors of trench warfare in the wrenchingly ugly scar that was the front line.

We bounced along the last one hundred yards or so of our odyssey; I remember being pulled apart by a million emotions. How incredibly lucky I was to have this opportunity to fly and see the Manitou's earth from above. How crushing it was to be torn asunder by the length and breadth of anguish and human suffering that had been spread out beneath our flight path. My mind railed at the sheer size of the wickedly churned destruction. Towns, roads, farms, cathedrals, cities, countless family homes and the lives of thousands of farmers had been smashed, stirred, and destroyed by the hate of the guns. Everywhere along the front where my eyes had stabbed, all that I had seen was destruction. If, as my grandmother had said, I was the reincarnation of Askuwheteau, then it was tears of misbelief that blinded my eyes. There were no words I could form with my mouth; there were no thoughts of logic that could express the pain that Whiteman continued inflicting upon his very brothers and their tribes.

With a rush of silence, the prop stopped turning. I could feel Hamilton-Hewes stirring behind me as he turned off fuel stops and electrical switches. Hands reached in from beneath the wing, a face spoke to me asking if I had enjoyed the show, the photo frames disappeared and were quickly whisked away to the photo development tent. I stood up, turned, one hand on the correct strut, and gingerly accepted a helping hand down and out of the cockpit.

"Damn near call with that German fighter what"? A familiar voice from somewhere behind me asked.

I turned to face the sound of the voice and found I was standing face to face with Captain Hamilton-Hewes. A large grin had spread from one corner of his Honourable face to the other. "If you had not pointed down just at that moment I would have missed him climbing up underneath us Corporal. Well done, well done indeed".

German fighter? Was that grey shadow I had seen a German fighter? Good God, I thought, that shadow was a long way away beneath us, why would Hamilton-Hewes be concerned about that? Captain Hamilton-Hewes had strolled off a few yards and was now speaking to the Squadron Commander. He turned and in a loud voice for everyone in the area to hear, "Going to have to keep this one"! He was grinning away like a dog eating shit off a thistle all the time pointing in my general direction.

He continued; "We had just begun out photo run when a damn German scout came up at us directly from below. Our escort could not get a quick shot at him because of our close proximity. I had not seen him sneaking up from below me and if Giorgio had not pointed him out we might very well have been picking ourselves up in no man's land just about now".

After some genuinely hard back slapping, Hamilton-Hewes sauntered off in the general direction of the Squadron Operations tent and I followed the unit Adjutant into his office to report on how little I had actually seen of the air, the ground, or everything else that I suppose must have been going on around us on my first operational flight.

* * *

The Squadron was a four-ringed circus. In the forefront of the show, at least in my opinion, were the aeroplanes themselves. They, like infants in a lodge, demanded the entire attention of almost all of the squadron's non-commissioned ranks. Maintenance of the planes consumed the entire daylight and some of night time hours as well. Like infants they were the very centres of a beehive of activity. Engines were removed, repaired, and replaced. Fabric was stretched, patched, and painted. Wires and rigging pulled, tuned, tightened, or slackened off. The Machine guns were cleaned, oiled, polished, shone, loaded, test fired and remounted. Wings were inspected; struts and spars were checked for strength and stiffness. And it seemed to me that every time I looked someone was oiling, polishing, painting, or realigning one shining part or another. Inside the frames of their fuselages, there were seemingly miles of cable and wire; these wires formed part of the skeleton that held the plane together and gave it shape and structure. I watched with eager eyes as bamboo and spruce were cut, bent, and used to replace broken or shell shot pieces of various planes as they returned from the front. I remember thinking that some of these airmen would be able to make beautiful snow shoes if I could just have a little bit of their time.

The second ring of the circus was the squadron routine. Every man jack, including the officers, had to live by a set routine every day they spent with the squadron. The airfield had a life of its own. It lived to make airplanes fly and every single person had a role in doing just that. I quickly learned that just like the army the Flying Corps had adapted army ranks and trades into specialities and specialists in order to master the new work and equipment that confronted their tasks.

There were still many of exactly the same trades as I was used to seeing and working with in the army. Cooks still cooked and clerks still did the paper work but the Flying Corps devised whole new groupings of men that shared the responsibilities to keep airplanes capable of flight. There were men trained to repair and replace things made from metal and there were men trained to work with wood and glues. Others were specialists in photography and film; still others worked with paint, needles, and fabric. Individually each did his own job; together they formed a team that was the squadron.

That brings me to the third ring of the circus; in the third ring you will find only those that fly the planes, the pilots themselves. Now here is where the circus becomes a stage; a stage on which, at any time of day there was a curiosity show. It is a piece of the whole yet separate from all of the rest. Pilots are a band of brothers and yet they live and die all by themselves. They are solitary heroes who depend on everyone else in the squadron to get them into the air and once in the air all dependency stops. Once they are airborne the dependency that pilots have on every single member of the squadron swings violently and completely into the reliance on and strength of their own skills. During each of their flying missions their lives hang on their individual skills and the readiness of the airplane that they are flying to respond and react to their urgings and directions. Sadly, it is very often the inmates of the third ring that are found at the very center of a funeral service.

And so that brings me to the fourth ring. This is one that needs no explanation. It is a 'some time' ring, a place that only exists when very special circumstances exist, even then the players change, and though the show remains the same the players on the stage can be a different group at any moment of the performance. The fourth ring of the circus is called 'rest and recreation'.

The word 'rest' is common enough. Every human body requires rest as part of life. The 'recreation' begins when a body at rest is driven to the basic urges that each of us follows to find some source of pleasure in the shortest possible time. When I was a boy and Ma gave me time to spend by myself I would almost automatically turn to Johnny Snake Eye for diversion. He would find some string, rope, or wire and we would practice tying knots or making snares. Sometimes we would set up targets; pieces of coloured cloth or the bodies of dead animals. We would practice shooting or firing arrows at them. Sometimes hours would pass and Ma would have to come and push on me so that I would know that recreation time had changed back to normal survival and life. As I grew older, into what the white man calls a 'young man', I would often practice the skills of stalking and hiding. It involved all of the specialties I had learned becoming a hunter. I would dress for the season. My outer clothes would be designed to match the colours and shapes of my surroundings. I would pick just the right moments to establish my watch and I would depart only when the objective of the watch or stalk had been established. As I said, this activity, one that I did in great secrecy, was a practical part of my hunting life but it really was recreation. It was recreation for me because the preys that I was stalking were the elusive and sometimes beautiful young women of my village.

The women of our village did not have the same freedom of movement and time that the men enjoyed. Their lives were filled with work from the very first streak of light in the east until the reds and yellows of the afternoon sun had faded away.

Cooking food, preparing skins, raising babies and keeping fires burning was a full time job. Women would share the watching of children with their sisters and in that way they as individuals could find time to go to the lakeside or the pool of water where the creek turned into the rocks and splashed with sounds of pleasure as it passed through the trees. These were special moments for the women of my village. They could trust their sisters to watch over their growing children and take a short but mind changing moment to cleanse their bodies and their clothes. It was a custom that men allowed their women these moments to themselves. The bathing ritual was a mystery that women all did and most men never attempted to understand. It was the mystery of a woman's cycle and the women knew they had to wash downstream in flowing water on those days. So, for I as a hunter, those women upstream represented the real target and those downstream would be observed only in casual interest. And besides, the fathers and the married men watched closely to see if the other men were watching their wives or daughters. There was sort of an agreement in our village; it was best for men to stay away from the lakeshore and the stream when women went to bathe. But I was a hunter and no one knew where I was at any time. Since no one ever knew where I was on my usual hunting ground, if I wished I could pick the prey to spy upon and when I would spy upon it. As a young man and until I grew out of the period of time when I was satisfied with only watching our women when they were naked, that was one of my favourite recreational activities. It was a recreation that gave me little rest.

In the Squadron, the fourth ring was available every night in some form or the other. Those airmen that had duties requiring them to be on the airfield had the camaraderie of their fellows within their drinking mess and dining tents.

Those that were given time off for a night, which usually meant that they did not have to appear for parade in the early part of the next morning, could walk to or even better catch a ride in the squadron truck that was going into one or more of the local villages. The men on time off provided the money; the cooks and women of the local villages provided the recreation.

Our local city, Brauy-la-Buissiere, had lost most of its identity. Nearly all of the young men, nearly all of the coal miners, had volunteered to join the French Army at the outbreak of war. By early 1917, the time that I was with 16 Squadron, nearly as many French soldiers had joined their forces as had British and Commonwealth soldiers combined. Over seventy percent of those that joined were killed, wounded, or captured. That meant that over one million young French men were never coming back to their villages to marry or farm or raise children with the sweethearts that they had grown up with. That meant that a lot of young, healthy and sometimes starving French girls and women were left as willing prey. They worked in restaurants, bars and night spots in nearly all of the local villages that were hosts to the thousands of allied airmen and soldiers that were part of the fourth ring of the circus called 'rest and recreation'.

Brauy-la-Buissiere, a coal mining and farming community had been nearly five thousand all souls prior to the war. Some mining still went on but it no longer could be called a farming area. The surrounding fields had been tramped by thousands of horses' hooves. The constant movement of wagon wheels and truck tires had destroyed all of the roads in and out of the city and in the small villages surrounding it.

An entirely new light railroad crossed near and through what been the village square and it travelled out to the south-east bearing the thousands of tons of ammunition needed by the hungry artillery guns of the Canadian and British Corps lined up along the route to Ypres. One could never really tell by just walking by a farmhouse if it was still occupied or not. The heavy shutters over the windows were almost always kept closed, day or night. One just never knew when a heavy artillery round would come whining over the smashed and crushed fields and slam into the village breaking windows and sending glass slithering over the centuries old streets. Most of the houses, even if they still contained some of the original occupants, had long since been taken over for use by military units. If not used directly by some headquarters or unit they had been commandeered for use by soldiers, on a formation by formation rotational basis, for a few days' rest and recreation.

Our local village, Halicourt, had three restaurants, five bars, and one old hotel known for some surrounding miles as a 'house of ill repute'. Now you are getting to understand what rest and recreation from the squadron lines really meant to most of the young, healthy, worried, frustrated and lonely young men of 16 Squadron RFC.

The next day of my odyssey with the RFC started all right. I had stopped vomiting by about two in the morning. Shortly afterwards I discovered myself wandering around outside my tent trying to remember where the toilets were in relation to where I had finally regained consciousness. I must have made it to bed for at least three hours. Reveille washed the field from the opening of a bugle as I and about 170 other members of the squadron lined up for the washing tubs and shaving areas.

My head kept reminding me I was scheduled to fly with someone called Lieutenant Appleguard at 0900 but my stomach thought the whole thing was a bit of a joke. Frankly I just could not remember why I thought I should try to outdrink ten or twenty aircraftsmen that had obviously had a lot more practice drinking Armagnac then I had. They at least had tasted the stuff; I had not even heard of the drink until my first glass at the Sniper School had nearly burned a hole through my oesophagus as it made its way down to my stomach. Someone, the barman I think, had told me it was made from apple juice. I remember thinking that real men do not hold competitions that involve seeing who is still standing after a certain number of drinks but what could possibly go wrong with drinking something made from apple juice?

I was sitting in the mess tent, my head hanging over a plate of very good looking fried eggs and toast when my new found friend Liam Ward came and gently sat down beside me. I tried to make eye contact but that made the table start to move around in a bit of a circle and I knew that was not supposed to be happening.

"Squadron Sergeant Major wants to see you". Liam let that hang there for a few seconds before he added,

"At eleven hundred hours on the rifle practice range. It is starting to rain again so flying operations are probably going to be washed out for the entire day".

Liam pushed back his chair and stood up near to my left side and I could feel his eyes boring a hole through my miserable body.

"The Sergeant Major is putting together two rifle teams of ten men each. He said to tell you that they think they are pretty good shots with a service rifle and he has bet a few pounds that you can teach them a lesson or two".

Liam started moving away as if he was afraid that I might make a mess out of his nice shiny boots. He must have turned around just before he stepped out of the tent. His voice had a measure of sympathy when he said,

"That gives you about five hours to remember what you did with the brain you were not using last night".

I got up from the mess tent table and went directly to bed. I was confident Liam would be back to my sleeping tent in plenty of time to wake me up so I could get dressed and get out to the practice range by 1100 hrs.

The Sergeant Major had organized a bit of a different kind of circus using me as the main attraction. First of all, without a single word or mention to me, he and the Squadron Commander had had a few drinks and together they lashed together a bit of a sports day using some excuse wrapped inside a rifle barrel. They then went out and organized three teams of rifle shooters. Each shooter would fire one magazine of .303 calibre, standard service ammunition. Nine rounds each. The first team was under the captaincy of the Sergeant Major with ten riflemen drawn from the non-commissioned ranks. The second team was to be under the leadership of the Squadron Commander also with ten shooters, all of them pilots, and the third team was a team of one. That would be me.

Within the boundaries of the airfield, along and against the longest side, running from south to north, there had been room to construct a very rough rifle practice area. It had been added when the Squadron took over the farmer's field and, such as it was, it became known as The Rifle Range. It was just about one thousand yards long. Liam had even included it in his billboard painting of the Squadron area.

At the very end of the range a small berm, an earthen embankment, had been added later. It had been made from sand bags and put in place to act as a barrier for rounds that might be aimed high and therefore could travel beyond the confines of the range. In fact, there was very little to worry about long rounds because at least another thousand yards of open fields and farmland stretched well out from the last row of targets. The Squadron would post airmen on the road to stop any passers by from wandering into the range area when it was in use. Liam told me he thought the range had been utilized at least twice in the year that he had been in France. I believe, because of the appalling lack of use the range had received, RFC Headquarters, on review of musketry practice might have mentioned that 16 Squadron needed to make an effort to improve. Whatever was the excuse or reason, three rifle teams would be on the firing point at 1100 hours; rain, clouds, winds, notwithstanding, the challenge had been dropped. I had every reason to take the challenge personally if I could just get over my hangover.

At Eleven hundred hours most of the squadron personnel were gathered around the firing point. The event offered a change from daily routine and it had taken on a bit of a carnival atmosphere. Some airmen, if not all, were busily placing bets on the team they thought would win the competition. Just to be clear, not everyone knew that I had some experience in this sort of thing. The majority of the bets were in favour of the non-commissioned team. Being British, most of the officers came from better than average backgrounds. Some might even have been from landowner families. That would make them owners of all the game on their own land and that usually meant most of the officers had at least fired a rifle prior to joining the Service. Had I not known better I would have bet on the Squadron Commander and his team of squires.

The Armament Section had prepared twenty rifles. They had fired and sighted all of them and each rifle was then given a number from one to twenty. Contestants were to reach into a bucket, draw a number, and compete using the rifle that matched the drawn number. On the surface, the selection of teams and weapons sounded pretty fair but of course I cheated. There were twenty rifles for them and another one for me. I had gone out with the Armament Section at nine hundred hours. I picked a rifle that looked fairly well shot in. Together with the section Sergeant, we reset the sights, modified the trigger pressure, polished the firing pin, and reset its position within the breach guide. I then fired a few rounds at four hundred yards to zero the weapon. Before I went out to the range I asked the weather station to give me up to date wind data for the 800-yard marker of the target area.

Shortly after every one had gathered around the firing point I made a formal request to the Squadron Commander to allow each of the first two teams to compete against them selves up to the distance at which they could no longer actually achieve hits on the targets. There was considerable moaning and groaning about my suggestion but since I was the visiting rifleman, after some discussion, I was allowed to shoot last at the last target distance that the winning team had achieved.

It really was a lot of fun watching men with very little experience in rifle drill or target practice struggle to hit a target at two hundred yards. After much laughter and cursing about the condition of the range, the terrible rifle sights on the rifles, and of course, the wind throwing them all off, the officers managed to win the completion. They managed a total of twenty-two hits out of one hundred rounds on an eight foot by eight foot target at four hundred yards. No one had hit the eight by eight target at the six-hundred-yard range.

I asked the range crew to cut the target size down to four feet by four feet and to replace the targets at four, six and eight hundred yards. They drove down the range to the hoots and hollers of disbelief and some wide eyes. It really was a bit of a turkey shoot to be honest. It was a grey day; some rain was still falling making the targets seem further away. Even without a Swasey sight, a standard pattern .303 Lee Enfield Service rifle in good hands, fired at a four-foot by four-foot target at eight hundred yards is like shooting at a barn door from inside the barn.

I searched quickly through the face of the crowd gathered around to cheer or jeer depending on how my first few rounds went. I located Liam standing near the front of the nearest group and closest to my firing position.
"Liam", I shouted, "I need a runner, do you think that you could give me a hand"? His face lit up and a steady grin was more than the answer that I wanted.
"I am your man", he shouted, running over to the firing point like a greyhound with a powered butt.
"Now listen carefully Liam, your safety is at stake here. I want you to run down to the four-hundred-yard target. Take that long fence post with you and tie this white handkerchief on the end of it. Make sure you stop and stand at exactly the same distance as the target but move off to the left side of it by at least twenty feet. Every time I fire a round, you have a look at where the round struck the target and point with the end of the post to where the round hit. Do you understand so far"?
Liam was listening intently; with wide eyes he nodded his head. He had never actually been on a range when men were firing more or less directly at him even if he was some twenty feet away from the target.

"I am going to fire ten rounds at each of the four, the six and the eight hundred yard markers. When I have fired a round I will wait until you mark and show the position of the hit and I will then wait until you return to your safe area on the left before I fire again". I paused to make sure that he was still nodding his head.

"When all ten rounds have been fired, I will stand up and wave you down to the next target distance. Immediately you are there and in your safety position I will start firing the next ten rounds. Are you ok with this"?

The Squadron Commander and the Squadron Sergeant Major had been listening to my instructions to Liam and they both had sly smiles as they nodded their heads in agreement.

"Liam" I said again, a little softer this time. "On your way back after I have put ten rounds into the eight-hundred-yard marker, take the target boards out of the ground and bring them all back here to the firing point so that everyone can see the fall of shot".

Liam turned without another word and started walking at a brisk pace down the range to stand by the first of the three target ranges that I would engage.

Later that afternoon after the bets had been settled and the target boards had been nailed up in the Corporals drinking mess as trophies to be gawked at and stories told and built up, the Squadron Commander asked me to join him in his office.

The Sergeant Major had brought in a small clear glass bottle filled with a light brown liquid called Scotch whisky. With some ceremony he had slowly and deliberately poured three small glasses, each with about one ounce of liquid. To that he had added a small teaspoon of water. All three glasses sat on the Major's desk.

For a few minutes we discussed some generalities like, "Have you had a chance to get back to England on leave"? And, "Does your mail service work all the way from Canada"; that sort of thing. After a few minutes the Major stood up and came around to the front of his desk. Without ceremony he reached out and one after the other, starting with the Sgt Maj, he handed out the small glasses of Scotch.

"Corporal Giorgio", he said, standing almost at attention,   "God damn if that was not the best demonstration of rifle shooting I have ever seen. Not one single miss".

He then raised his glass and gently touched the rim of my glass with his, he turned and repeated the glass touching with the Sgt Maj and without another word they both nodded in my direction and downed the glass in one gulp. I followed their lead, never having been toasted before, and then, having nothing to add I added nothing by saying, "Thank you Sir".

Every man in the Squadron knew me by my first name after that. The memory of squeezing gently on the rifle trigger and seeing Liam point at the bulls eye or target center, round after round, helped to erase at least somewhat, the one that still sticks in my mind, that of watching Bert's body slide, every so slowly, into the inferno of our crash.

We were already airborne by seven the next morning. The sun had not yet peeked through the low ragged clouds that hung like a wet rug over the soggy green fields of our surround. The ceiling was said to be around 4,000 feet but bits and pieces of it floated down like a ragged shirt on a beggar's back. Our escort had landed on our field just as dusk had sputtered over the windsock the night before. He had stayed overnight with the other pilots, drinking and talking about women I would suppose.

It seemed to me that pilots had to be ready to die at least once on every flight so they were entitled to think about firm thighs, hard beds, and long nights, if that helped them through their short flights into the hell that awaited them, suspended in the air.

The escort, a Captain from 24 Sqn, took off with us and stayed very close consumed with bobbing up and down behind us. I had met my pilot yesterday at the rifle range; Captain Ernie Hubbard had been one of ones that at least hit the four-hundred-yard marker. We had shared a few laughs as we did our flight briefing. Hubbard was a thin tall man; energy seeped out of his pores and caused him to appear to be in two places at the same time. All the while he was talking his eyes would range constantly as if they were independent from the conversation. He was one of those kind of infectious personalities that you just cannot help but wonder what the hell he would get up to next. But let me tell you, in his hands an airplane just came to life.

The flight called for a quick dash over the front lines. This would not be a camera morning; it was strictly an eyeball opportunity to see the line at low level. Our flight path would be direct from the airfield to intersect the front lines at Cite de Chaumont. We would turn hard right, flying almost directly south along the front line at low level. Captain Hubbard assured me that this tactic gave us the very best opportunity to get in and out quickly and not be bothered by a German scout. He told me to concentrate on the ground, see and identify as much as I could and then we would come back and compare what I had seen to the new series of air photos that we had taken just two days before. I certainly wanted to get a good look at the Pimple and the inter Corps boundaries between the British Division on the left and the 4th Canadian Division which formed the north most Canadian formation.

I remember the urgency and excitement of the apparent speed of the ground as it passed beneath us in our rush along at tree level. As always, in the few hours that I was actually in flight, I felt steady and secure in my forward compartment, but the ground, the earth, and the sky, combined to dance and twirl at the pilot's wish. In just minutes we had gone from the wet, green, of flattened farmers' fields and small villages lying in ruins just below our wings into a torn cesspool of poisonous scars. Suddenly, as if an ugly wall had fallen over which now lay broken and festering along its length, we were over the front. Our right wing dropped hard following our turn from eastward to southwardly. We picked up a few hundred feet of altitude, Hubbard kicked and swung along the very top of no mans land that lay between good, on the west, and evil on the east. He shouted loudly behind me, "That is the Pimple coming up on your left, half a mile".

I forced myself not to blink; every second of sight was of vital importance. A kaleidoscope of destruction, cement bunkers and long twisted lanes of wire; huge decaying craters filled with decomposing bodies, the fresh scars of heavy artillery rounds overlaying the older abyss of months of constant pounding. This was Vimy Ridge. At this altitude, Vimy Ridge rose up on our left wing. It was a seven-thousand-yard feature dominating the countryside along its length.

The Germans had held it since 1914; every minute, every day, of every month, they had used their engineering skills and tenacity to strengthen and deepen their command of this vital observation point. Control of the ridge gave them miles of unfettered view over the Canadian and British lines to their west.

The French, the Belgians, and the British had suffered hundreds of thousands of causalities trying to capture and wrestle this ridge from German hands. Very soon, I thought, the Canadian Corps was going to stand and stride forward from their firing steps and try to achieve what other armies had not achieved. For nearly six months General Byng and his Corps staff had given every officer and soldier the opportunity to learn and understand what was going to be expected of them. Knowing what was expected was one thing, if they would live and look down with victorious eyes from the heights now held by the heinous Germans was another.

Arthur and I were going to be just two of those over fifty thousand Canadian soldiers standing and stepping into the very mouth of the hell I was now overflying.

Here and there a human face would flash under our wings, long lines of unbroken wire still holding firmly to their stakes passed just beneath our wheels. There, just there, some flash and smoke from a bursting artillery shell fired by a nearby Canadian field battery. And then suddenly, right wing hard down, gaining a few hundred feet from the falling away of the ridge, we flew west, over the long lines of Canadian and British artillery layered back from our forward line. Our scout slid up on our right, the pilot with one thumb up as if he had really enjoyed the trip. We slid in and out of low cloud; cold wet fingers of water tracing paths between my scarf and my skin. I shivered in disbelief of the extraordinary joy of flight. Now what could I remember of all that I had seen?

The remainder of the day and all of the next was spent poring over all of the available air photos taken of the Canadian line.

Pilot after pilot, each briefed by the Squadron Commander, had been arranged to come forward, to spend their time and experience adding to my brief and sketchy three days of flying over Vimy's lines. Their skilled and trained observers accompanied the pilots that came to add to my knowledge. Every pair had something special to add, some detail that maybe others had missed. Each team provided detailed notes and even hand drawn sketches to give further depth and understanding to the German trench and defensive positions. When not being briefed I spent every available free minute crafting notes and writing details concerning German defences and locations. These detailed notes when combined with the new set of air photographs would be hand carried by me to Captain Johnson and from there they would make a journey all the way to the hands of General Byng and his staff. Askuwheteau was alive and well.

* * *

On the fifth late afternoon of my duty with 16 Squadron the Sgt Maj sent Liam to look for me. I had just finished dinner in the dining tent and was seriously considering going back to the map room to spend some more time comparing various photos taken at different times of day to see if I could squeeze even more information out of them.

"The Sgt Maj thinks you should take a bath and put on a clean battle dress Giorgio", said Liam with a bit of a serious look darkening his otherwise white and freckled face.

"What the hell is he up to now"? I said to no one in particular. Liam filled that gap with one sentence.

"He thinks that he is going to accompany you and I to the local brothel and get us both laid".

Slowly, very slowly, Liam's face started to change. The darkness slipped past his now curling bottom lip. His eyes opened ever so slightly like a dog's do when catching the scent of a freshening female. His hands came up and ended in a sound clap as he turned a full circle like a dancer in a dance.

"And", he said, "The best God Damned part of the whole fucking thing is this! Captain Hamilton-Hewes is paying for the both of us, drinks and all. He told the Squadron Commander that he owes you his life for seeing that German Scout before he did and he thinks it is the least he can do".

Damn, I thought, Hamilton-Hewes sure had a lot better memory than I.

The Sergeant Major drove the Crossley. I had been told that every RFC squadron had at least eight or nine of these sturdy tenders. They had a two seat open drivers cab with a small sliding window that allowed rearward viewing into the wooden box area. The cab and the box were covered with canvas tarps to keep out the rain but that never seemed to be achieved. The driver sat in the back with Liam and me. Nobody talked; it was hard to talk when your face is completely full of a grin.

The truck bounced and banged along a road now ruined by the army trying to save France from ruin. There were no lights, sometimes we saw groups of men on the road, they were going away from us as we peered like drunken fools out of the back of the trapped box. We shuddered to a halt somewhere along the route, voices in English asked and responded to "Where the hell do you think you are going"? The loudest voice came from the front of the truck.
"Listen mate, I am the Squadron Sergeant Major from Number 16 Squadron, His Majesty's Royal Flying Corps, if I want any shit from you I will have it on the end of my boot. Now get out of our way we are on the Kings business"!
That seemed to satisfy the Royal Military Police Corporal who had been unfortunate enough to be standing guard at one of the check points along the military supply route.

We lurched off again and soon the left and right of the street were filled with dark and darkened houses. The Sergeant Major had made this trip before; he knew where to turn and where to park. Once stopped with the motor silenced he banged his fist on the cab and yelled; "End of the line girls, this is where you get off". That seemed to amuse him because the air surrounding the truck was filled with loud guffaws and hoots. I had always liked a man that could laugh at his own jokes.

"Corporal Giorgio Costello", boomed the Sergeant Major's voice. "Get around here and bring that runner fellow with you. Liam and I winked in the darkness at the Sergeant Major's attempt to act official and disciplinarian. "Yes Sir, Sergeant Major", we both shouted as we were leaping from the truck to the ground and scampering to the right hand side driver's door.

The Sergeant Major sat in the driver's seat, a wide and happy grin spreading across his handsome, mature face.
"Listen boys", he said as we pressed our faces to the open window. "All of the pilots threw some cash into the kitty yesterday. It was a handsome sum let me tell you. I drove out here yesterday afternoon and made some arrangements with Madame Pompier, the lady that owns and runs this here very reputable home for lost and wayward ladies of the night. The Madame has been paid in full, she assured me that both of you would be very well looked after in every regard".

He paused there for a second scanning each of our faces I suppose to ascertain if either or both just happened to be listening to any words that followed 'ladies of the night'.

His attention drifted away from us for a few seconds as he gave instructions to the unemployed driver of the vehicle. The driver scampered in through the back door of the Inn to announce our arrival. With the departure of the driver the Sgt Maj continued his instructions, this time in a soft and fatherly tone.

"Now listen to this and listen well. Do not give a single additional franc to anyone for anything. That includes drinks, tips for service, food or God forbid, damages. You are both overnight quests of this fine little rooming Inn. I will be back around ten tomorrow morning to pick you up. You two scoundrels be out here at this spot in this parking lot at 10 Hundred hours. I have no intention of entering such an establishment ever in my life".

His face was the picture of serious study for a few seconds and then he could no longer even believe his own story. At that point he again broke down into a few seconds of pure, unadulterated laughter. With a wheeze ending his laughter he added,

"If my wife ever found out that I had been anywhere near such a place let alone that I aided and abetted two young innocence bastards like you to go into it she would have my balls for bookends".

At that moment the driver returned with a bottle of wine in one hand; he slid into the left hand passenger seat leering out at us saying,

"The Ladies await your attendance gentlemen". That caused another outburst of hoots and howls. With a slipping clutch and shrieks of laughter the vehicle restarted and clanged into life.

And with that as his farewell the Sergeant Major let the clutch out, the truck lurched forward; he could be seen struggling hard to get the vehicle to turn sharp enough to miss another parked truck that had taken up most of the back yard parking lot of the darkened and foreboding shape that was called 'l'Auberge de l'Innocence'.

I looked at Liam and he looked at me. We had no idea what exactly lay ahead; it was like walking into a kitchen where you had been told you would enjoy the food. Expectations were running high but questions remained; questions like what to eat first and what might be on the menu that could ruin your appetite.

* * *

Liam reached and found the door handle permitting entrance to the back hallway. The night had been starless, deep piles of cloud hid the moon. The village had shown no sight of itself, except as it lay in shadow. It was as if everything we expected had lain hidden from our sight. That waiting, the element of the unknown, had heightened the expectations.

The words from the Sergeant Major had promised everything we wanted had been arranged. I cannot speak for Liam but at that point I had no idea of what I really wanted. Frankly the prospect of talking to, let alone being with, a fully grown and experienced white woman scared me more than facing a full frontal assault. I was far from feeling like a raging bull as the door swung noiselessly on its hinges; like two little mice we vacuously pushed our feet over the threshold.

The back hallway was dimly lit, an oil lamp with a clean glass hung from a hinged bracket on the wall. The wallpaper was a deep red with patterns of flowers or maybe they were leaves pressed deeply into its surface. A deep cream brown, wall to wall carpet almost encouraged your boots to step into it. At the end of the hallway another heavy door waited, slightly ajar, a small amount of brighter light leaned into the hallway like an invitation. I pushed gently on the dark wood, a flood of warm perfumed air wafted around the edges of the swinging door.

A larger, carpeted hallway led in towards the center; a large square salon with a massive stairway dominating the middle awaited our quickening hearts. Three women, one slightly older, perhaps in her late forties were in close and amused conversation near the stairway.

Sounds of music escaped from a distant room just off the main foyer that could be seen in what must have been the front of the Inn. A large fireplace held a burning fire that added to the warmth and aroma of the moment. Liam and I stopped, both plainly unsure of the next card to play.

Somewhere in a room not visible from the center stairwell a hushed but constant tinkle of conversation emitted. Men's voices and women's laughter broke and fell like crystal from a vase. The eldest of the women standing by the stairwell stopped speaking in French; in an amusing accent she said in English,
 'You must be the heroes that we have been talking about. Your Squadron thinks a lot of you and so do we"!

She paused for a second, her gaze gliding first to me and than to Liam. She held her head at a beautiful angle; a long graceful neck adorned with a large dark stone on a gold chain gave her almost fairy-tale appearance against the background of oil lamps. The other two women, they were at least in their thirties I would say, had turned to look at us two dumb struck pumpkins with our hats in our hands. They seemed amused at the physical power that the sight of them standing there was having on us. They both simultaneously turned towards us; in unison they curtsied, just the smallest step, the lowering of their shoulders exposing ample cleavage behind the deeply cut necks of their dresses.
 I spoke in French, introducing Liam and myself. All three of the women were visibly surprised to hear my Canadian "patois", all three nodded at my effort to address them in their own tongue. No hands were extended, no one moved to show first choice; the cards stayed on the table. I remained unsure of what the game would be.

The Sergeant Major's words to us before he had driven off, his mouth full of laughter at what we were about experience, echoed in my mind. "The Madame has been paid in full, she assured me that both of you would be very well looked after in every regard".

In English I said, "Just to be perfectly clear Madame, we understand, both of us understand", nodding at Liam, "that this lovely Inn is a business for you and for your beautiful young ladies".

Her eyes widened in amusement, her head again turning at an angle that accented the natural beauty she retained from her fleeting youth. It was not often the young English men, nor men of any race, would be thinking of anything except the physical act of love after they had entered such an establishment. Her eyes were steadily on mine as she awaited my next statement.

"Mr. Wilcox, the Squadron Sergeant Major, was here yesterday, he drove Liam and me from our airfield to your Inn tonight. He also told us everything about the financial arrangements he had made with you and how you had made certain commitments that you intended to honour. Am I correct Madame or have I made an error in the matter of our being your guests until tomorrow morning"?

The Madame was quick to reply, "Oui, oui, Monsieur, I assure you that Mr. Wilcox and I have reached a completely agreeable understanding of what you expect, and you are welcome here. Lisette", she nodded at the woman on her right in the light blue dress with a delightful décolleté, "and Bridgette" nodding to the lady in blue and white on her left, "are but two of my ladies; there are others should you wish to be introduced. All of my ladies are, how should I say in English, at your disposable"?

"Madame", I said in mock apologetic tones, "we never doubted, for an instant, you and your beautiful ladies' willingness to fulfill the contract that Mr. Wilcox has paid so handsomely for. It is just, since we have not previously been introduced as a lady may well expect, I, that is Liam and I just wanted to be sure our evening was going to unfold in accordance with your good graces and understanding".

Liam turned to me, his mouth slightly open; his eyes and ears trying to comprehend what the hell was going on. I let my left hand slowly slide over his elbow; a soft reassuring pressure seemed to relieve the doubt and questions, which seemed to be coming between his expectations of instant gratification and my bargaining for position.

It was then that Madame Pompier undertook the unexpected. She moved quickly to my side and put her arm through mine. As she did so she nodded her head slightly but in clear indication to her two ladies in waiting that they should attend to Liam.

"Monsieur" she said throatily and with just the slightest purring sound, "may I say something that you may find slightly unladylike at this moment"?

Her eyes were locked on mine and she was pressing her arm and shoulder into my chest.

"Of course Madame Pompier, please consider me your friend and admirer, you are in your own beautiful home and you may say whatever your lovely heart desires".

"All right then Giorgio", she said, "if I may call you by your first name"?

She had managed to push the two of us slightly towards the fireplace. A large and impressive painting held prominence of position above the glowing grates. It was an erotic scene of men and women together in various stages of dress and undress set against a background that might have been a river side.

In the centre of the picture, clearly the center of the artist's focus and detail was a couple engaged in some activity where the female faces one direction and the male, while lying prone and holding her by the ankles, faces in the other. For an instant I thought I must remember to ask the Madame what the meaning of that painting could be.

"Giorgio, I do not often exercise my own desire in these matters let me assure you of that. I am the owner of this Inn and most of my energies, you understand, are spent with the burdens of keeping a roof over our poor heads".

She pouted very prettily, her face masked by false sadness in order to solicit my sympathy.

"But in this case, I must admit, I find you very handsome and though you may find me far too forward, may I suggest you and I take a walk to my private quarters for a glass of wine or cognac? Perhaps we may find subjects of mutual interest, ehmmm"?

The dawn was not spectacular the next morning. We had indeed spent the night as if it was just a short instant as she had suggested. The sun barely found more than an inch of space between the horizon and the clouds to show some small part of its warming potential. I lay there enthralled again, was it the third time that she had demonstrated what the couple in the picture were doing? I remember being amazed that even after a full day of studying air photographs, the Madame had not even for an instant let me forget that I had energies in reserve for just such an occasion.

* * *

At ten hundred hours I stood alone in the parking lot. I gazed up into the expansive and pleasant windows opening unto the wide but narrow balcony of Madame Pompier's private suite. She had told me she had given up the master bedroom on the front of the house for two very good reasons. First, the windows of that bedroom faced the German lines and therefore stood a greater danger someone or something might shoot into or strike out at that particular side of the Inn. Also, those windows had to be constantly closed and covered by their heavy shutters so as to avoid showing light or offering glimpses into the activities that might be occurring within its walls. Next, she said she enjoyed the view over the back of the property and the parking area, which had been a farmyard in years long since past. Besides, from this bedroom she could see into the west and watch the sunsets over the fields that spread out just behind the street. It had been that street and the joining road, which we had travelled up from the airfield. As I stood there I could see and hear the motor of the squadron truck returning to pick Liam and me up for our return to the airfield. I only had eyes for the window though; the Madame had pushed back the lacy curtains and was standing, outlined by the light from the window. She had promised to wave goodbye, I had no idea she would do so completely nude.

Liam exited through the back door, the same door we had used to enter into the hallway that now seemed so far away. On either arm, he escorted the now identically dressed two lovely women that I had not really had the chance to become acquainted with.

The squadron tender, one of the many Crossley 20/25 trucks that they owned, turned a tight corner in the parking lot and surged to a sputtering halt.

The warm and somewhat amused face of the Sergeant Major was turned, as was mine, to the balcony window. Madame Pompier threw a warm and lingering kiss in our general direction and then, being the lady that she was, stepped out of sight behind the curtains. The Sergeant Major and I, now turned our attention to the grand arrival of Liam and his two escorts, both as nude as the Madame had been just seconds before. The memory I retain from those few fleeting moments certainly added to the glamour and the clamour of our departure ceremony.

No words were exchanged. No additional show of affection performed. Liam hauled himself over the tailgate and into the back of the waiting truck. I followed with as much energy as I could muster after a sleepless night. The Sgt Maj, now assured that we were once again safe and sound within his care and jurisdiction, slipped the clutch; the truck responded with the shortest of jerks and we wheeled out and onto the short drive home. Words cannot do justice to the silence all of us enjoyed, each of us alone with our own recollections, memories both real and imagined.

* * *

If Askuwheteau Could Talk

When our grinding, bumping, bouncing little Crossley had finally pulled to a halt in front of the Squadron Operations building no one, not one of us volunteered to be the first man out and on the ground. The Squadron Sergeant Major had turned to peer at Liam and me sitting in the back of the box. Liam had been wordless for the entire trip. There was a deep and far away look on his face like a big boar pig might have while pissing in a field surrounded by expectant sows.

As for me, the night just past was like a ceremony I had witnessed in the Kensington Gardens of London on the Serpentine. I, and a lady named Sarah, had joined a small group of soldiers; all of us were in London from our army camps in and around the Salisbury Training Area. We were not together but we were all soldiers together, all aimlessly watching people come and go as they watched us walking aimlessly. Some English families had gathered near the waters edge. Night was falling, gathering darkness was being held back only by the fact that so many people did not want to see the end of a rare October day when the sun had shone in London. And then I witnessed something I had never seen before nor have I seen since.

A lady, maybe more than one, I cannot say for sure, had made some circular balls using paper and glue. They looked like round light globes, the kind that you might see on Coal Oil lamps that hang from the ceiling of the Hudson's Bay Store in Edmonton. The base of these lamp shades, there were three of them, were shaped a little like a boat bottom so when they were placed on the water the lamp shades floated, merrily, each with their own bright colour reflecting in the darkening water surrounding it. Then, to my utter surprise, a candle was set alight in each of the globes. The light spread and captured the colour of the shade, and each globe, like a soul with its own life, sailed and shone and captured the evening for an hour or more. I could not bring myself to leave. I could not take my eyes off the floating, flooding, lights that sometime came together on the surface of the Serpentine and sometimes sailed apart to dominate the water in a solitary way. I tried a couple of times to explain the way it made me feel to my companion Sarah but the harder I tried and deeper I dug into my emotions the more difficult it became to find the words that my heart was lost in. Finally, almost in desperation to explain to her the impact this scene was having on me I said,

"Somewhere in this world Sarah, each and every one of us has a family. Some of those people we never met and will never meet but they are still members of our family. For some of those people their light has shone and long ago they faded out just like some of those candles have already done. And for others, maybe even for those others that are or were the closest to us as we were growing up, their light provided safety and illumination for the steps we had to take".

Sarah's eyes were growing softer as I spoke; I had a sudden confidence that I had found a way to express the symbol of what we were watching on the surface of the Serpentine.

"Did you notice Sarah, some of those lights stayed together for the longest time even though other lights were sailing far away to other parts of the Serpentine? Our lives and our own journeys are just like that aren't they? Some people stay at home and stay within their own family groups and others, for reasons that they might not even understand, move on as if driven by some unseen wind or force".

"And which light are you my friend Giorgio Costello? Where will your wind take you on this journey that you are making all the way from that strange sounding place called Canada"

"My light will know when its heart has fulfilled a duty that it has to a great and powerful Spirit that ordered me to see what man is doing to his fellow man". Sarah sort of pushed back a little, her hand on my chest, her eyes hard on my eyes.

"You are a very deep man my Canadian friend. I can see much hurt in your eyes but maybe that is because you are a soldier and understand much better than I how much the world is hurting because of this awful war".

I reached out and took her hand in both of mine. It was a small, soft, and very white little hand. Her parents had given and provided every single thing that her little heart had desired and yet she had joined the British Women's Army Auxiliary Corps so that she could give back something in return.

"Here Sarah is what I understand. You have given me a memory that will continue to float along with me no matter where I go; no matter how long my light will shine, that memory will be part of me. I do not yet know what the Mighty Spirit will ask of me, or what my story might be when I have to tell it in front of the Great Council of the Spirit. But this I know; you have given me three days of great joy; three days of being away from all the training and explaining. You have given an entirely new candle to the ship that my soul sails on at this moment".

Only a few eyes turned to watch a Canadian soldier being kissed long and hard by an English lady in a uniform in Hyde Park.

The evening I spent with Madame Leontine Pompier was somewhat like that evening in London. Just like the ladies at the Serpentine in London these three French ladies had worked behind the scenes using skills that few men will ever understand. The ladies of the Inn had also lit and launched a fire that fascinated and held both Liam and me within their circle of light, a magical sort of fire and light, which only a woman can kindle in the hearts and loins of a man. There was nothing evil or wrong or immoral about what we five humans did in the Auberge. We, all of us, went willingly to the waters edge. The ladies had used their craft and beauty to hold Liam and me within a circle of soft sounds and light and the pleasures of the flesh.

But now the night of magic had flown. Reality and war returned our hearts and heads to where we were and why we were there. My one night in the bed and arms of Leontine was now no more of an extraordinary memory than that which I had of my evening on the Serpentine. I enjoyed and I had participated but I doubted that I would ever again have the opportunity to either build or launch such a magic memory that it could float upon the water.

I had learned much through the eyes of Askuwheteau. The Royal Flying Corps had given me wings. With those wings I had flown above the broken face of Vimy, I had been given to chance to see deep inside the cauldron where lives are cast aside and success measured in yards. Now the question remained, what could I do with everything I had seen?

The notes which each of the pilots and their observers produced offered unique and detailed observations concerning details and locations of German defences, machine gun positions, bunkers and unbroken wire. I would take these back to my Battalion, they in turn would send the details up the various lines of command until they added to the First Canadian Corps battle plans and future artillery lists of targets. All of these would doubtlessly mean that men and limbs would remain attached and alive on the day of our attack on the ridge known as Vimy.

I would return to my Battalion with an entirely new set of air photographs of the Canadian Corps line. All of these would also have been sent up through Flying Corps channels to Corps engineers and Divisional operations planning staffs. But the fact that I had a complete set of photographs would add immeasurably to the intelligence and information my Battalion Commander and his Brigade Commander would have available to them. Vital information as they strived to squeeze every advantage out of what they knew about the ground over which their units would have to fight. Having eyes overhead able to look down and into the defensive lines of both the Canadians and the Germans gave an enormous advantage to all levels of command as they planned their own, individual paths through the attack routes that men would have to follow. The camera and I had been those eyes looking down; I was now a very special messenger with a very special message.

My day of departure started with the opening of the skies. What had started, as a drip was now a raging downpour. Most of the men of the squadron stood at hanger doors and stared out into a sea of rising water that sloshed and rippled over paths that had been trodden by the wheels of planes on better days.

I made my way from tent to mess, from mess to operations and finally stood, sorry to be leaving, in front of the Squadron Commander's desk. Major Mills had pushed back his chair as I walked in. The desktop was piled high with requisition forms and photographs of recent missions over the German lines. Sergeant Major Wilcox, looking relaxed, hung around in the background like a best man at the altar.

I stood at what could best be called 'relaxed attention' waiting for an invitation to sit down or relax. The Major's eyes were squinting; only a small edge of pupil showing from behind heavy eyebrows and lids. For an instant I thought, my heart jumping, I was about to be dressed down for some as yet undisclosed indiscretion I must have committed somewhere along the line.

"So Corporal", a voice finally taking shape from behind the desk, "You had a busy week with us didn't you"? He held his hand up, palm outward as a sign that it was not a question I was required to respond to.

"Your record of duty here shows that you arrived properly dressed and prepared for your duty". He seemed to be reading from a set of prepared notes that were hidden from direct view in a file folder that he held in his large hands.

"The Squadron Sergeant Major was initially very impressed with your level of energy and interest in all things concerning squadron routine, discipline, layout of facilities and the like. He makes a special note of your first impression when coming into contact with one of our airplanes. He also notes you were a willing student and easily achieved passing qualifications on flying safety, instructions concerning camera and film handling, duties of an observer and so on". His eyes were now staring up from his desk as if searching for my reaction to this unexpected formal debriefing routine.

Major Mills turned his eyes and attention to the Sergeant Major who by now had established a position, facing me, at the front edge of the major's desk. He too looked very formal and official.

"I believe this might be the time to call our next witness into the room if you don't mind Corporal Costello". And with that Private Liam Ward marched in, unescorted, with a considerable show of military drill and precision. I was very impressed to see that Liam had mastered any parade square drill as a runner and a painter. I could not help but notice that he carried a large, silver, tray tucked under his left arm and held tightly to his body.

"Private Ward has a few words to say to you Giorgio", then turning to nod at Liam the Major pushed back a bit in his chair with an innocent look of expectation.

Liam made no attempt whatsoever to gain eye contact with me. He obviously was enjoying whatever role he was supposed to be playing as he turned to Major Mills and offered the tray.

"The best silver tray reporting for duty Squadron Commander", he said as he lifted, turned, and placed the sterling silver tray on the corner of the Major's desk. He then reached quickly into his left pants pocket and extracted a pint-sized bottle of a dark brown liquid. Placing the bottle on the tray he, again following some sort of military drill format that he must have practised prior to this performance, removed, one after the other, four shot glasses from his right pants pocket. Then turning to me, his ears turning a deeper red and new color in his cheeks he said, "I want you to know Giorgio that when the Sergeant Major told me that my main duty for all of last week was going to be looking after an army Corporal joining us for duty I really wasn't too happy about the whole thing". He sort of shrugged his shoulders and let one of his goofy grins spread across his face.

"Anyway I just wanted you know that if you want to transfer over to the Royal Flying Corps I will volunteer to be your squadron sponsor any day and any time".

With that little speech out of way he turned towards the doorway into the office and with a true parade square voice he bellowed, "Cook Sergeant Bloudwin, Present the Cod"!

Immediately the doorway was filled with a smartly marching Sergeant in a cook's smock and hat. In his bare hands he carried a fairly large, dead, unscaled fresh fish. The fish was held out, away from his body, pointing out head first as he marched in. He turned, halting directly in front of the desk. With a great stamping of feet the Sergeant offered,

"Sir I have the pleasure of presenting the Cod; it arrived just this morning from Newfoundland. I can certify that this fish was kept on ice throughout its journey and is as fresh as a spanked baby's ass Sir".

With that pronouncement the Major, straight faced and solemn, rose slowly from his chair. He took the Sergeant Major by the arm and turning together they both stood in front of the desk facing me. The Cod, eyes as blank as a nun's sin sheet, was held out at arms length just a foot or two from my face. As amusing as all this was, well rehearsed and reasonably serious, I had no idea what the hell all this was leading to.

The Major nodded at Liam. Liam retrieved the tray with the pint and glasses and held it out in front of the Sergeant Major. With some ceremony, detailed measuring and checking to ensure that each glass, as it was filled, matched the level of the next until four glasses of what smelled like rum had been poured.

With the glasses now topped up we all stood, looking very sombre and expectant. Liam still holding the tray with the drinks now turned to me and said.

"Giorgio, in Newfoundland we have a custom called 'kissing the Cod'. We usually do this when someone from 'away' drops in to visit the Island for the very first time. But on this occasion, by way of respect and friendship and for all the really good times we had together I would like to make you an honorary Newfoundlander. In order to be a Newfoundlander you have to kiss the Cod but don't worry, just like everything else that we did this week, 16 Squadron Royal Flying Corps will show you how it is done".

The tray was now offered in turn to the Major, the Sergeant Major, myself and finally, setting down the tray, Liam held the fourth and final glass.

"Now this drink is a special type of rum that we only have in Newfoundland. It is called 'Screech' down home and everybody drinks it by the gallon. I just happen to have this here small bottle, which my dear old mother sent me all the way from home just before Christmas. Now then this is what we all are going to do and say, it is called 'The Screeching In' ceremony or 'Kissing the Cod'. I will ask each of you this question. 'Is ye a Screecher? And you will reply 'Deed I is me old cock, and long may your big jib draw'! You will then, turn and kiss the Cod and do heel taps with your drink. Everyone got that"? We all nodded, mouths working to try to remember the accent and the phrase.

"Giorgio, Is ye a Screecher"?

With glass in hand and one eye on the goddamned fish I reply, in as full a voice as I could muster without laughing,

"Deed I is me old cock, and long may your big jib draw", then, right on his two stone cold lips, I kissed the Cod.

The rum itself was as hard as any that I had ever tasted but even straight up it did not take away the smell and taste of the cold eyed dead fish.

"I now declare you to be an Honorary Newfoundlander Giorgio and I look forward to repeating this ceremony when you come down home to visit with me anytime that you wish".

We both leaned in together and shook hands. I knew that it had taken a lot of nerve to convince the Squadron Commander to take part in this. There are a lot of moments and events that happened to me and around me during the time that I served with 16 Squadron. My very first flight, the realization of what it must have been like to be the real Askuwheteau and the horrible death of Captain Bert. My day on the rifle range with all of the voices and laughter and Liam running up and down the range pointing out my hits. The incredible night Liam and I had spent at l'Auberge de l'Innocence'. Faces and names of Pilots and observers that had worked and toiled with me as we tried to make the most out of every air photograph available of the Canadian lines around the Vimy Ridge feature. But this was personal; this was special. Liam had really stepped up and made a difference.

The same ceremony followed for Major Mills and the Sgt Maj. By the time it was over I could not refrain from commenting that the Cod was starting to look like he was enjoying it.

I remember a lot of smiles, patting one another on the back, promises of 'lets keep in touch', and then the same gentleman driver with the same lovely old staff car arrived and it was time to return to the mad house that was the real world I had come from.

"Just one further word Corporal if you don't mind", Major Mills had turned suddenly to pick something up off his desk. He pushed some papers aside, stirring the neatness and orderliness of his daily administrative tasks until he located whatever it was that he wanted to show me.

"We in the Royal Flying Corps are very fortunate to be able to pick and appoint soldiers from all of the Commonwealth armies and from all and any of the various units they might come from if we have a need."

The Major sort of leaned back on his heels as he was speaking; I suddenly realized that his eyes were focused hard on mine. I glanced around the room quickly; everyone seemed to be hanging on his next words.

"You came to us from a fine Canadian Battalion; that battalion must think a great deal of you to send you here with the mission that you told me you wanted to achieve. You should be extremely proud of yourself Giorgio for the level of professionalism and the attention to detail that you displayed while you were here."

I swallowed hard, every eye was now on my face, I felt my lips working to find a suitable response; I felt that it was their efforts and hard work that had made the difference and I had intended to say something like that.

The Major lifted one hand, palm outwards, he still had a few more words to add and he held me there, my mind spinning with how to thank him and everyone else that had made my week such a great memory.

"Captain Hamilton-Hewes believed that you saved his life with your quick recognition of immediate danger and you alerted him to what certainly could have resulted in your aircraft being destroyed by a German fighter aircraft, possibly with a loss of life, yours included. Captain Hubbard wrote you a very strong commendation for your extraordinary efforts as an Air Observer and for your subsequent hard work and diligence in preparing a complete set of air photographs for the First Canadian Corps area including the detail of the boundary between the British First Corps and the Canadian Corps".

Mills paused there for a second, letting the paper that he was holding lean gently on his chest. His face had changed, it became softer, his eyes more relaxed as if his formal presentation was now completed.

"Following a strong recommendation from the Squadron Sergeant Major and the two pilot Captains; and I might add, I know that if Captain Bert as you called him, were still alive he too would have stood strongly behind this piece of paper that I am holding. I have recommended you to the Royal Flying Corps Headquarters for the award of the Distinguished Flying Medal for devotion to duty performed whilst flying in active operations against the enemy".

I had no idea whatsoever what he was talking about but I realized that what he had done and said was a great honour not to be taken lightly. My mouth must have been hanging open like that of a winded moose just slightly in front of the wolf pack.

"There is a lot of time between a recommendation and the granting of the award Corporal and you should know that just because you have been so recommended does not necessarily mean that it will actually be awarded. I did, however, want you to know before you return to your unit that I have made the recommendation and that it has been sent to the RFC. Thank you very much for what you brought to my unit and what you have already contributed to the war as a whole. I will be forwarding a letter to your Commanding Officer and your Division asking for you to be transferred to the RFC for further training and employment as an Air Observer". He stopped there, his tone did not sound as if he was offering a choice to say no thank you.

I cannot remember what I said in reply; I remember that my heart was pounding, faces spun as hands were extended in good-bye and congratulations.

Liam damn near broke my ribs with a strong hug; the Sergeant Major slipped me a full and heavy bag to take back to the unit. The Major was standing back grinning like a schoolboy that had just won the one-hundred-yard foot race.

I said something about my first duty being to return to my unit and get on with the plans I had made for my sniper position at the Pimple. I spoke about the amazing experience of flying and working from an airplane; someone pushed me out the door and into the left front seat of the running staff car. I was still waving as we turned by the centuries old barn at the end of the mile-long road that led along the grass covered runway.

* * *

Askuwheteau At Vimy Ridge

I had always looked forward, as every soldier looks forward, to letters from home. All that looking forward had changed but I did have Arthur. Arthur and I had been together as a sniper team for over two months. Although not at the same time, we had both attended and passed the British Army snipers' course conducted by the Third British Army Sniper School in France. We had not met until he had been assigned to the 49th Battalion and then further assigned to my company sniper section in December of 1916. We made a good pair. He was a good shot, just not good enough at long distances. He had a funny little twitch just before he squeezed off the last few hundreds of seconds of trigger pull. That didn't matter all that much for targets out to four hundred yards but beyond that it could mean an error of two to four inches. The difference between a miss and a kill in our business was always measured in inches at five hundred yards. At a distance of over five hundred yards only the very best shots make the grade. This was not a game we were playing; this was literally a matter of life and death. To say it another way, the shooter that kills lives; the shooter that misses does not go on. Arthur had a sniper's eye but not the sure and steady trigger pull. He could remain still, without moving for hours, slowly scanning, and searching.

He had great positional memory, he could remember the ground he had scanned; if something had been moved or changed he could come back to it and wonder why it had changed. That skill made him the best spotter I ever worked with.

Arthur had been bred and buttered in Halifax. The ocean, sea birds, and stinking fishing boats were ground deeply into his psyche. His father was still a fisherman and Arthur had spent most of his growing up years in small boats searching for codfish before he had, "just walked over and joined the army", he said. His mother had been raised in Moncton, New Brunswick; she and her family spoke French at home. His mother had spoken only to him in French and his father had only used English. As a result, though he did not have a way with words, Arthur was completely bilingual. The ability to speak French came in very handy when a soldier was on leave anywhere in France.

The Divisional leave center was in Amiens. Since the Commanding Officer had approved Arthur's transport to Paris, he proceeded there by train. As per nearly every other train in northern France the car he sat in and all those that he saw were filled to overflowing with hundreds of young soldiers going to Paris to become men again. After having listened to their leave aspirations, every man had the same one, it was clear there would not be a prostitute in Paris safe from immediate pillage the instant the train arrived at the station. Arthur had some two hours on that train to reconsider his leave plans and immediately upon arrival in Paris he transferred to another track and paid for and boarded another train heading west to Le Havre.

Le Havre is a large, unwieldy port city with a constant ebb and flow of ships, humanity, commerce, and sailors. Better, he had thought, to compete with a few boat loads of sailors than to line up behind ten thousand soldiers a day.

He fell deeply in lust the night he arrived and had spent most of his entire leave in bed with or in the company of a woman he met while leaving the grand old railway station, Gare du Havre. Not being a fellow of many words, he spoke little of the week he had spent with her. Instead his grin and attitude more than accounted for having been away from the constant hell we lived in.

Leave away from the line was like having your soul handed back to you. It literally was a 'breaking free', breaking free from the filth, the death, the constant sound of artillery with its metallic lullaby. Leave away from the front presented the incredible possibility that death could not find you. It meant that men on the other side of the street did not hate you. It meant that going into the dark night could mean you might meet a woman who would make womanly sounds and surround you with womanly odours and womanly needs. If you were really lucky she might press her fingers into your youth in hope that you found in her the things that she hoped to find in you.

Leave from the operational front was short and infrequent. Leave from the daily routine of death and fatigue was rationed out like caviar at a wedding. Still, when Arthur returned to the Company he had a new bounce; there was a rekindled light that showed through and was part of the dark brown of his eyes.

"Snipe", he said! For some reason known only to him Snipe was the nickname he preferred to call me.

"Snipe, her name was Rhamond".

We were sitting together, huddled really; it was a cold, wet day, and we had been discussing our detailed plans on the route to take, both in and out, for the patrol we were scheduled to make the next day or the day after that. I looked up from the map for an instant to find his eyes locked on my face and a silly grin on his lips.

"She was only seventeen when the war started".

His words were slow and measured; I could tell he felt compelled to tell me some part of his affair in Le Havre. There was no hint of vanity or ego, none of the usual signs of manly bravado that is often associated with men when they take to bragging about women they have paid to love them. His mouth worked a little as if it were full of words, which he had yet to put in order. I set down the map board and pushed back, just a little, to better watch his face as he spoke.

"She was born and raised on a farm near a little village that is not far from here. It is on the German side now and she has nothing to go back to".

He stopped there, his whole face working to find the next point at which to start his story.

"She told me there was nothing left that she could go back to anyway. Too many memories! Too many tears!"

He focused on my eyes, boring a hole in me, trying to judge my reaction to what he had already revealed.

"So she could not go back and now she lives in Le Havre".

There was a sense of finality in the way he said that. At least a minute went by before he spoke again.

"Anyway", he said finally, "her parents and two brothers were killed by an artillery round that hit their house as the French Army was being pushed back. They had hidden in the cellar but they were all killed except for her. She was on the other side of the chimney foundation and it saved her. She said it was awful to see".

He spoke slowly, measuring each sentence as if he was giving a briefing at the end of sniping duty. In all the time I had known him he had never put more than a few words together in a sentence. He was a listener; he was a watcher, and a man of detail. I was starting to see a whole new side of him during this short discussion.

"She took their only farm horse and some coins they had in a cupboard and rode east towards where she knew the French Army was deploying. She said she felt better when she saw some of them in a field. She said the presence of French soldiers made her feel safe".

He paused there for a moment. His hands and shoulders slumped forward as if he was deeply involved in the story he was telling. Emotion filled every word. I could feel the hair starting to stand up on the back of my neck as he spoke.

"She found an empty barn along the road she had followed; it was very near the Chapel of Ablain St Nazaire. She kept the horse with her; she said she had grown up with that horse and there was a sense of trust between them. She cried when she told me the horse was all she had left to remind her of the peace and family that she had known and loved".

His hands had found a piece of old string or torn cloth, something that he had intended to weave into our top cover most likely. It was as if he had no control over what his hands were doing while he struggled with the message he wanted me to understand.

"The next morning three French soldiers heard the sounds that her horse made; it was thirsty and needed water. The soldiers followed the sounds, they found her and raped her".

There was a tear on his cheek; he made no effort to wipe it away. I watched as it ran down his face leaving a slightly cleaner track as it neared the corner of his strong, firm, jaw line.

I could not help myself from reaching out again and putting my hand over his. We sat like that for a few minutes, in silence, until I could feel the tension and hate slowly ebbing out of him.

"She said they all took turns, one did it twice. They told her they would kill her if she made any noise. She said they had been drinking and that their body odour made her sick. She said after they started she sort of stopped feeling human. She just thought about animals that she had seen mating on her farm and then she closed her eyes so that she did not have to watch them watching her".

I said something about how awful it must have been and that I was sorry he had become involved in all this. I remember saying I had hoped just the opposite had happened; I had hoped he had a wonderful time and a great memory from his affair.

The expression on his face changed as I spoke. For the first time I saw anger in his eyes as he looked at me. He brushed my hand away and straightened his shoulders. There was almost a hiss in his voice as he said,

"You have no need to feel sorry for me! I was not the one that was raped. I was not the one who had to watch as they shot her horse right there in the barn and cut pieces of meat off it so that they could carry it back to their dugout or unit or slime hole that they were hiding in. She had already accepted what had happened to her. She was crying because she wished it could have been me that had been the first man to know her as a woman".

I was shocked by his sudden show of anger. I realized then how special the girl must be to him. Somehow, someway, she had opened a door for him and his emotions had poured in on her until some part of her had become himself. I could only hope for his sake that the emotion he was displaying openly and freely to me was being returned by her wherever she was today.

"God damn it Arthur, I am so sorry. I did not want in any way to offend you. I just wanted you to know that this is a powerful story you are sharing with me".

I sort of shrugged my shoulders, I did not know what else to do or say. There was a long silence before he started to speak again.

"She said they were proud of what they had done and they asked her if she had enjoyed being fucked by real men. One of them gave her a train ticket that he had in his pocket. He told her that he wouldn't need it for a while. When they left she cried for her horse and then she used the ticket to make her way to Le Havre and waited until I came along".

He tried to hide a small little earthquake of sorrow and separation that had escaped his control. Then, by way of showing he was finished, in a little murmur, under his breath, he said, "How much of that do you think is true"?

I had the common sense to realize, at that moment, that what was happening there in that dirty, little, dugout in the side of a filthy trench on the First Canadian Corps line was one of most seriously personal things Arthur had ever revealed to anyone. I sat there staring at him, conscious that I was slowly shaking my head in misbelief.

I said, "I think the story about the artillery round, the horse and the three soldiers could very well be true. All of them were horrible nightmares, which no one could ever forget and most likely they are too repulsive for her to just imagine".

I paused, leaning forward just a bit as I said, "I have never met Rhamond so I cannot even begin to be a judge of her character. Honestly Arthur, as your best friend, that is not my place at any rate. In my opinion it is best to judge someone by what they do and not what they say they do or will do".

Just then a small group of soldiers, speaking in lowered voices clambered past our little dugout on their way forward for the night watch on the forward firing step.

We both waited until they had moved out of earshot before I added, "I am not sure what she meant when she said she would wait for you Arthur".

He grew very serious at that; his eyes left mine, his head hung forward a bit as if there was a sudden weight that he could not overcome, and in a voice that I could hardly hear he added, "I gave her some money, about a month's pay I suppose". His eyes sought mine again. "She promised she would take the money and find a job and maybe a small apartment to live in. She promised she would wait for me to come back to her. She gave me the address of a church where she would leave her new address with the priest so I could find her on my next leave. She said she went to the Notre Dame Cathedral almost every day and she would leave a letter there for me".

I reached out and put my hand on his hand again. He did not flinch or try to pull it away. I tried to choose my words carefully, I did not want to lie, nor did I want to hurt his feelings. It was evident his relationship with this woman was real and for him at least it was deep.

"Arthur, you are a great friend and a wonderful soldier. You and I are both under a lot of pressure every day of our lives and you deserve to have a few dreams and a few moments to cherish when we are sitting out there up to our asses in cold mud and water". I removed my hand from his and reached into my battledress pocket where I still had a few sugar cubes from the 16 Squadron dining room stashed away. We both spent a short minute enjoying the sugar rush as the cubes hit our tongues.

"Maybe she will wait for you and maybe she won't. You will not have an answer to that question until you take your next leave in Le Havre my friend".

He just smiled at me and went back to being his quiet, efficient self. My God, I thought, I wish I had gone to Le Havre with him. Just imagine, I thought, leaving the constant horror that was a soldier's life in the line and finding a woman that professed to share a love that could last a lifetime. What a memory to hold close to your heart. That got me to thinking again of my wonderful days with Sarah in London. Soon, a long grey cloak of guilt for not having written to her turned and folded and smothered the rest of the daylight hours we spent huddled in the stinking hole that we called home.

* * *

Suddenly Arthur and I were only a day away from having to start our long and solitary march out from the security and familiarity of the 49th and into the long trek that would lead to our sniper position planned to look up and unto 'The Pimple'. While every other soldier in the 49th had been briefed and told countless times where to be, what to do, and how to do it when the time came, Arthur and I had been left completely to our own devices to fulfill our mission. In the early morning of the 6th of April a battalion orderly gingerly pushed our dugout tarp aside and announced that I was to report to the Company Commander's command post as soon as I could manage.

I slopped and sloshed my way through the communications trench until I turned left into the main north-south part of our battalion front line. The gas curtain that hung from the company commander's dugout was open; a faint light splashed halfway up the mud encrusted steps leading down into the dugout. The sounds of voices droned through the constant sounds of light howitzers and heavy gunfire. Overhead, an unceasing train of artillery projectiles traced their one-way path towards the German lines. Captain Johnson grunted "wait" after I had called his name a couple of times down the sunken shaft leading to the underground hole we called Headquarters.

Someone said, "You shouldn't go up there I haven't finished the bandage".

Johnson came up the stairs slowly and deliberately. His face was a mask of pain etched in white. His cheeks, normally slightly reddened by his constant brandy intake were the colour of washed stones. He held his left hand in his right. The entire end of his left arm was a mass of blood soaked and dirt covered bandages. His eyes sought mine as he said,
"Fucking sniper shot me in the hand".

His voice got caught in his throat for a second as he leaned against the steeply slanting entranceway wall. Clearly he was not yet used to not using both hands to manoeuvre his way through the labyrinth we lived and died in.

"I was checking the sentries and got careless"!

He grunted as if that would make it easier for me to understand. An outbound shell screamed just over our heads and ploughed into the mud immediately over our forward parapet. Clearly one of our own guns was firing short. This round was dud, the next one might not be.

I pushed him slightly down the steps again and pressed my back against the wooden braces holding up the trench wall where it disappeared down and into the stairwell. We stood staring into one another's eyes. I felt a knife edged wave of dread wash over me. I had come to value his quiet and reassuring leadership. We had an understanding, a sort of friendship, a brotherhood that we shared. I knew immediately, all that was about to change. For a few seconds there was a strong bond of disbelief and compassion that held our eyes together.

"I used to play a fucking guitar in a small band in Camrose. Guess I will have to learn how to play drums now".

Just the smallest of movement pulled a corner of his mouth into a shallow and ironic smile. I nodded just to show I appreciated his sense of humour. The quirky smirk rapidly disappeared into a shadow of pain and disbelief as his eyes swept down over the wad of cotton bandage that hid from sight the real truth of the moment. Every few seconds an outgoing shell rushed and grumbled over our heads. The Canadian Corps artillery was getting very serious about their task of cutting wire and preparing for our assault on the tortured ridge known as Vimy.

Slowly, with a gentle touch, I put my hand out and took a firm hold of the cloth of his exposed jacket shoulder. He let himself be tugged up the last step until we stood, side by side, on the trench duckboards. The night was filled by light mist and fitful rain and the sounds of gunners, from both sides, filled and refilled the air with the grinding anonymous sounds of death and uncertainty. A voice from the dugout said, "There isn't anything I can do for him; you should arrange for a party to get his body out of here as soon as possible".

"You should not be here Captain", I said firmly, trying to keep the scolding out of my voice.
"You need to see a doctor, get that hand looked at. A couple of days to get over the shock and pain would stand you well".
I knew I was out of order; it was not my place to tell a Captain what to do but a genuine concern for his welfare pushed rudely on my treatment of military etiquette. Then I added, more to myself than to him, "If you are lucky they will send you back to England until you heal. You could do with some time off just like the rest of us".

With his remaining good right hand, he dug with the familiarity of constant practice into his slightly open battle dress jacket and extracted his flask. He pushed it up into my vision nodding at the firmly closed top. I pushed my rifle behind my shoulder and screwed the cap off. Without hesitation Johnson pulled long and deep at the contents.
"Bastard sniper"!
His voice filled with venom and hate.
"He killed Major Winser with his first shot, took him right in the eye".
The air kind of went out of him suddenly as he slumped against the trench wall. I moved quickly to provide a firm brace for him lean on if he so needed.

We both stood there breathing hard into the foul and stinking air that filled the space around his once cosy little dugout and company headquarters. He reached down and pulled his wounded left hand closer to his body as if he was consciously offering it comfort and protection. His face was grey and lined with dirt but his eyes were hard and determined.

"I guess that I am the Company Commander until the Old Man names someone to replace Winser. I cannot leave until the new Company Commander shows up".

We both unknowingly sort of slumped together, each putting pressure on the other's shoulder. I said more or less under my breath but it came out loud enough for him to respond with a nod, "I suppose that could take some time".

Captain Johnson had another long pull on his brandy; God knows it was the only painkiller that he would get for a while. Out of the side of his mouth he said, "I would like you to go up the line and find Lieutenant Younger in 13 Platoon. He is the tall red headed fellow from Weslock that reported in a couple of weeks ago. As far as I know he is a good lad and had some experience before he was wounded at Ypres".

I shrugged, I knew him to see him, and I certainly knew the part of the line that 13 Platoon was holding.

"Tell Younger that he is the Company 2IC now. He should appoint his Sergeant Major as acting platoon commander".

A few seconds passed with us leaning on the minute and trusting the shared shoulders to provide for something that would have to pass as comfort. Finally, almost reluctantly, in a lowered and failing voice Johnson said beneath his breath,

"And tell him to get his ass down here with his kit as soon as possible".

Without a further word Captain Johnson's knees gave way, his eyes rolled back into his head and he slowly and unceremoniously slid back first down the steps of his dugout.

It only took a few minutes to get Johnson's batman up from the depths of the dugout and attending to his immediate safety. I ordered the first four men that I saw to secure a stretcher; there were a lot of those in every trench system. Most were in use as beds for the soldiers holding the line. Without speaking or questioning my orders they were quickly carrying an unconscious Johnson down the remaining steps and into the relative security of the bunker until a medical orderly could have a look at his hand.

I hurried off in search of Lieutenant Younger. No doubt in my mind he would have one hell of a big job to fill Johnson's shoes who always seemed to be awake, slightly drunk and completely aware of what was going on in the company. As I pushed my way down the traverse and main trench lines in the direction of 13 Platoon I made a very large mental note of the name of the sneaky little bastard of a soldier from 12 Platoon that I detailed to carry Johnson's stretcher. I hadn't said anything as he pulled the last drop of brandy out of Johnson's flask before putting it back into his breast pocket. I would have a moment to spend with that private soldier. I asked Manitou to let me live long enough to get back to the Command Post so I could express my displeasure with his treatment of a man that meant so much to me and every other life that served in this shit hole that we called our defensive line.

* * *

Every soldier on the line, every heart that beat behind the front and especially those that waited for their platoon commander's whistle knew that we were getting close to the day we were 'going over the top'. There was certain suspense in the waiting. There was a certain dread in knowing that the uncertain security of the trench lines was sure and soon to be even worse the instant that a foot was set over the firing steps.

Men of all stripes and ranks caught themselves looking left and right at familiar faces and wondering if they or the man next to them would be alive to see the dawn beyond the rumoured day of the attack. The lead up to these moments had been intense and gruelling to the extreme. Hundreds of thousands of men had been digging, hauling, building, positioning and planning for the moment that soft and vulnerable men would break cover to confront the enemy. The enemy, though no one felt the slightest pity, had been pounded and crushed and mauled and treated as badly as any modern army had ever been treated up to this point.

Every minute of every hour, all day long for over two weeks there had sounded the constant and repetitive voices of the Gunners' Choir. The voices of individual pieces mixed and collided. The pitch and cadence jangled and alarmed. It was a kaleidoscope of terror in two parts. The first part, distant, far away, and reassuring was the sound of guns of every type as they shouted out in the climactic voice of joy. They had been aimed and fed, laid on line and on target and their deadly cargo had been released. A lanyard pulled, a spark struck on the bare and expectant primers. The shock of release hurled the round up and out of the barrel as the action hurtled back in recoil and response. The piece recoils in the opposite direction to the outgoing round. The barrel, on slides, pushes hard against the recoil springs, hydraulic pistons, and recuperative mechanisms.

Gunners sweat and toil to feed the waiting maw of the breech, their ears deafened, near bleeding, from the concussion of repeated overpressure and the resounding discharge of the beloved guns they call their colours.

Guns, howitzers, naval cannons, pieces of all sizes and calibres had been lined up, in depth, behind every yard of the front. Millions of rounds and projectiles had been wrestled, hauled, and prepared for just this crescendo of steel and destruction. Every single round was earmarked, planned, and prepared for one single, solitary purpose. Destroy the defence and will of the Germany army that held the heights beneath which we waited. Once fired, the barrel and the breech slowly returns to the "in-battery" position, ready to fire, awaiting expectantly another filling and explosive release of death into the already shattered air.

The second voice is played together, in harmony, by the passing projectile and the ever resistant surrounding atmosphere. Now the voice is vibrant, moving, a train-like crescendo that traces, with a path of sound or sounds, its flight over and out until it pitches down and hurtles into the waiting earth below. Now, constantly mixing with the first and second voices is the death hooded percussion that the projectile makes as its fuse activates the deadly sequence of ignition and explosion. Ear rending, mind numbing, death dealing sounds that crush the human spirit, destroy the human ear, flatten lungs and objects with their sheer volume of noise as if the door of hell itself has opened in your face. Then, finally, at the very end of every cycle come the more intricate and softer notes. The sounds that life and limb make as they are torn out, thrown away, turned into unrecognizable forms of matter no longer of use to the Army.

Most of the time, we that remained had no occasion to bury those recently living. The difference between living on the battlefield and being on the battlefield was not one of luck, it was simply a matter of time.

Men together in trenches were much like ships that pass in the night. Each of them, as an individual, was on his own journey. Each of them was totally responsible for their own health, cleanliness, and habits. Yet each to the other owed respect and support. They, to a man, understood their lives and future depended in no small way on the greater abilities of the whole to act and fight and survive through the prolonged hell that was the day to day. Individual courage was not discussed; group courage was demanded. A battalion and its component parts was anchored and steered not by the heroes but by those who had lived through the anguish of battle and returned to live in the trenches after the battle was over. Life on the battlefield was a constant and shared struggle. Respect was won and held by those that struggled with the ravages of battle, overcame fear, and survived to fight another day. I knew many, many frightened men in the 49th Battalion but I can honestly say that I never met a coward. It never ceased to amaze me how the human mind can accept such adversity and pain and yet rise again to the occasion of standing, side by side with their comrades, as unimaginable waves of apprehension and the threat of death wash over and around them.

That night the battalion was scheduled to continue the endless cycle of making repairs to the defensive area we occupied. Each platoon held discussions with the Company Second in Command and Company Sergeant Major; they were responsible for discipline and detailed administration of every man on strength.

As soon as night's inky shroud had fallen, selected men from every section would put their rifles up on the fire step, in case they were needed and they would bend their backs to a few hours of hard labour. There was mud to be moved just as always, time and time again the filth from bottom of the trenches was recycled using picks and shovels to move it back to surface level. There was a constant battle against gravity and nature; every day proved that rainwater had a clear advantage. Tonight it was duck board repair and replacement; there would be work on the traverse trenches running between the main and the parallel trenches in each of the section areas. The constant rain had filled the sump holes and the latrines. Additional duckboards were being brought forward and put in place for the 'stepping off areas' in the forward positions used for the attack on Vimy Ridge.

Arthur and I would not see any of the labour being poured forth tonight, nor would we be participating in it. Our next sniping patrol had been ordered and approved.

Our new sniping position was the result of my recommendation made after my flights with 16 Squadron. The Division had approved my recommendation to establish a hidey-hole just forward of the 10th Battalion. They, the 10th, were part of the Fourth Brigade and about as far to the left of the existing Canadian line as you could go. My report had said that many Canadian lives might be saved if we could control and limit German sniper teams that were clearly in place all along The Pimple feature. From their position the German sniper teams would be able to observe and control the ground down onto the very start lines that the Fourth Brigade would be stepping out of as they began their assault on Vimy Ridge. Some Corps Staff Officer must have seen the wisdom of my recommendation. It was going to be a long and tiring route march with all of our equipment.

To add to the labour we had to make it before sunup the next day. Someone had paid attention to my report on how the snipers should be deployed on the ground prior to the attack going in. Now all we had to do was to get there and do our job.

If Ma had been alive I would have probably written a letter and left it behind with the company clerk. The clerk would have put it in a military mailbag and the big overarching administration that existed within each and every level of the army would have managed its homeward journey back to Lac La Biche. Writing a letter home on the day or night before a big push was very much a custom for most Canadian soldiers. It was a bit of a morale booster for soldiers to know their words and thoughts would live on after them.

In the end though, all I did was think for a while about the letter I would have written in the event that I did not make it back from the planned attack on the ridgeline that lay in front of us. It would have been a cheery letter full of things like, "each of us is ready to do his duty", and maybe even, "If you get this letter Ma I want you know that you mean everything to me and I am so proud to be your son". I might even have tried to ensure that the Company Commander or the Platoon Commander had a few good words to say about me in the letter that one of them would send to my home to tell Ma that I was a casualty. Their letter would say that I was wounded or dead and that the Company was very proud of how bravely I had fought on the day of my last battle.

But I didn't write that letter because I just didn't care the way I had before when Ma had been alive. I never had informed anyone, not one single person, that Ma had passed away. I had no doubt whatsoever not one single person on this earth would care enough to read a final letter from me when and if it was delivered. I would not court death, which was not even within the realm of my thought or belief. It was just that I completely understood the daily routine of the village I had lived in and where Cold Dawn now lay buried.

No one, not even the priest who walked the quiet streets of the town on a daily basis, lived, thought, or wore an ounce of concern for the kind of life I lived or died in. Only the soldiers still living here, on both sides of the line, really knew what our world was like at Vimy Ridge.

I had never informed my platoon officer nor did I change my next of kin status as I was supposed to do. That change would have informed the Army that my pension allocation and my monthly allotment of salary should no longer go to Saddle Lake to an address in the name of Cold Dawn. I never really thought long and hard about why I made that decision, it just didn't seem to matter to me after I knew that she was no longer alive. Let the money sit in a box held by the Indian Agent I thought. I certainly did not need any money in the hole in the ground I called home at any particular moment. I just supposed I could always have it when I returned home if I ever did get home again.

Anyway, with some sense of finality I remember thinking, what the hell difference will it mean to anyone in the long run if one Canadian soldier has gone from being part of a family to being an orphan on the battlefield. My attitude, from the moment I learned that Ma had died, had undergone a large shift.

I was here because I wanted to be here. I was no longer in uniform because there was someone back home expecting me to do my duty and all that sort of crap. Anyway, the hard cold fact was that every soldier on the front had to confront at least one or more dead bodies every day they were in the line. The line was really just a trench dug through a large existing cemetery. Bodies had been buried, the war had moved forward or back and soon the burial place was part of the line again. Thousands of bodies had never been recovered or uncovered from the shell holes, collapsed underground tunnels, and old trenches.

Everywhere you looked or dug you were always expecting to find a body or two that had never been recovered to a cemetery. Where you lived today was going to be the place you were buried tomorrow; it was that simple. The war specialized in making families into fatherless families. If I were killed someone back in Canada would have to take my file and put whatever money was left in it back into the pockets of the government. That would make some bureaucrat happy I supposed.

So in the end I just left everything the way it was as far as my records were concerned. The monthly payment I was required to make to Cold Dawn would still arrive, by mail, at Saddle Lake. There was no doubt whatsoever my mail would be waiting for me when I returned. No one except me would ever receive a letter to say I was wounded or killed. And even more important, who was left in Saddle Lake to care one way or the other?

***

It had been snowing for more than an hour. The snow brought with it some sense of freshness. It covered the swill of death, human shit, and the muck and mortar of the trenches that were filled with fear and beating hearts. Arthur and I stayed close together threading our way against the constant flow of men moving along the duck work.

Canadian soldiers were like a river flowing towards the final pre-attack positions that they would live or die in. We, Arthur and I, were starting our long patrol, which would take us to the sniping position we had been assigned. The ice jam of preparation leading up to our planned attack on Vimy Ridge had broken. Soldiers, citizen soldiers really, only but a few of the total had even been in the army when this war had started, were finally on the move forward. Very few of the permanent soldiers that had accompanied the original deployment of the First Division were alive today. Almost every single one of the original soldiers that sailed with the First Division had been killed, wounded, or returned to Canada in the three years we had been fighting. We who were left were numbered amongst those who had been recruited and trained since 1914. The army on the move with me now was a very different army then the one that had been killed, wounded and gassed at the Somme. That original army had taken a terrible pounding. Their bodies filled graveyards and lay unknown in collapsed tunnels and trenches. At home, telegrams and letters notifying families of their loss had saddened thousands of hearts. But today, a new army, a new army with old eyes and mud filled boots started to gather as the First Canadian Corps. Four full divisions of Canadians would stand together in a waiting dawn to win or die trying to do what the French and British Armies had failed to do, to take and hold Vimy Ridge.

Arthur and I stood aside briefly as a small resupply column of twenty or so soldiers staggered and slipped their way around, sometimes between but eventually past us. Each man was heavily burdened with pack boards or sandbags tied around their necks. They carried water in gallon tins, boxes of machine gun or rifle ammunition. Each of them, to a man, bore an expression of entrenched weariness. I knew from experience, having done this job myself, the sandbags would be filled with rations that had been divided into infantry section allotments and topped up to full weight with medical or other necessary war like items.

At this point of our journey, the shallow pits and scrapings known as 'reserve trenches' were mud filled with watery bottoms. In platoon areas entire sections of men had tunnelled or carved into the sides of their allocated defensive waiting areas. The water and filth-filled earthen sides of the trench lines threatened to collapse at any moment and all it took was one nearby arrival of an artillery shell to cause landslides and burials of anyone within the area of ground shock. The chalky clay soil extracted from the trench lines had been thrown up in low banks on either side of the trenches, men's feet and sometimes even entire legs were sticking out in comical angles from the lower levels of the dugouts.

This was not hell, it was the road up and back from hell, and everyone knew it. Hell was a lot worse than this road could ever be. Hell was what awaited them once they stood up, forced their way over the wall of the trench, and started their heart pounding assault on the German line.

The smell of these forward areas was horrendous. Human funk, human excrement, rotting remains of animals, humans, and every discarded piece of useful equipment decayed and fermented into a cloud of indescribable odour.

The days and weeks and months that men had spent enfolded in this cavernous sewer called the front line had helped to deaden the normal sensitivity that mankind held for putrid air.

Every man-jack soldier knew it would only be a short time before they were answering to the screaming anxiety of the platoon commander's whistle. From the second that the order to attack was given their life became a ritual governed by a convention that could not be questioned. Once the whistle blew every single man hung on getting 'up and over the wall' and on his measured and purposeful mission to kill or die doing it. There would be no turning back; there could be no permissible hesitation. There was no 'letting down the side'. The convention of attack called for unquestioned bravery and conformation to issued orders. Every man was expected to execute his duty until death or compelling wounds precluded further forward movement. Their officers could shoot men that hesitated; men that stumbled into and then found refuge in a shell hole would be considered to be cowards. The searing fear of death they faced while clawing their way forward was no worse than the crippling dread of being called a coward by the men they fought with and for.

The dirt, ground, and space that were this part of the line had been farmers' fields for hundreds of years. This land had known the labour of farmers and their sons and the sons of those that followed ever since mankind had learned to turn the land over for the planting of grain and gardens. It had always been fertilized with pig, cow and animal shit and now, for the last few months, thousands of pounds of human waste had been added to it daily as over 120,000 men awaited the whistle that would call for them to advance towards the hill; the dominating high ground or 'whales back' known as Vimy Ridge.

No part of earth here, no spade full nor dugout filled with wet and dirty soldiers smelled at all like any earth or field you would have ever walked over.

Here the ground gave back what it had received. Here the very ground itself was so churned and mixed, tossed and torn, that every foot of digging only exposed more of the horror that man was wreaking upon man. Here, graves had been dug and ceremonies of remembrance had been held. Here the tides of battle had flowed over and back much like the ocean does with the resultant constant changing of the beach. Here the beach was not sand but clay, chalk, and body parts, lost or discarded equipment and always, always the centuries of shit and waste that man had left behind. This was not just hell. No, no, far from it. This ground that surrounded the hill called Vimy Ridge was so much more than hell. It had been consecrated by the farmers and occupied since the very beginning of the war by tens of thousands of French then British then German and now Canadian soldiers. No one, not even those that lived in this hell, could ever form words that did justice to the nightmare that was the ground surrounding and extending to and from Vimy Ridge.

We lived with gunshot, machine gun staccato, and shrapnel as companions. We did not huddle; we tried, mostly succeeding, to sink into the ground. From the earth we sought the comfort that a dog might find while being beaten in a field. The dog's pain was the same but in some small and almost closed part of his mind the dog thought that as soon as the beating was over he might be fed. Soldiers would, in the same macabre way, always know that if they lived through the attack they could expect to eat at the end of the consolidation.

Once we were in a sniping position, Arthur and I did not talk, we did not think of deeds or honour. We did not whisper about nor did we covet medals won through great deeds or acts of heroism. We did none of those things as far as I can remember but what we did very well was to sink into and become part of the shell hole or torn piece of earth that we occupied at that moment. We would shield ourselves with our top cover and all the time that we searched for targets and range indicators we would pray. We would pray in silence or in whispered words that always seemed to repeat themselves as we waited and watched. Arthur would pray to his Jesus; I would pray to my Manitou. Both hoping, I suppose, that one or both would save us from the death that hung above us, crawled beside us and burrowed beneath us. We had become experts in bringing death to someone else and yet we remained gripped by and nearly overwhelmed by the possibility, nay the probability that it would happen to us.

No one asked Arthur and me, "Who are you"? No one said, "Where are you going"? We were but two of over sixty thousand Canadian soldiers moving into positions along the Vimy Ridge assault line; all moving forward each to their own unit orders and instructions. We were an army then, dirty, muddy, cold and hungry, but an army with a purpose and a will. Something magical had happened to the soldiers of the Corps. We had begun to realize that we were special. That Canadians and being Canadian had some special meaning. That feeling invaded, gripped, and held all of us closer together.
All four of the Canadian divisions, for the first time our history, would move and act as one. Arthur and I were just a small part of that oneness and yet that night Arthur and I were the only two soldiers seemingly moving away from the front line.

Nobody even gave us a second glance. There was an overwhelming sense of understanding between all of us; a trust I suppose you could call it. A trust that each of us would do our duty according to our orders and on the morning of the 9th of April we would stand and do our part.

* * *

Vimy Ridge   Dying to Get There

Sometime around three o'clock in the morning of the 8th of April, Arthur and I had arrived at a Fourth Division rear area control point. For every step we had taken a muddy demon had sucked at our boots. Hundreds of guns and howitzers had sung the gunner's choir over our torturous path. Our ears stung with pain and the shock of concussion as round after round drove their flight into the German positions. A squally snow and rain whipped under our soaked woollen coats and uniforms. Every part of the world we walked and lived in was filled to overflowing with the sounds and smells of death. Rain, snow, mud, fear, constant movement of men and arms; everywhere you looked or went the very worst that men could do, the very best that man can be, flooded every sense of who we were. The smell of the demise and the rotting of hope, all this was mixed with duty and orders and the will to live in spite of death. I remember very clearly, just after we had confirmed that we had actually arrived within the area that we intended to deploy from, Arthur pulled gently on my shoulder strap and said,

"Well, that was a piece of cake, are you ready to do a little work now"? He did not bother to make eye contact but I could see a small slice of humour sliding across his face

I tried to find someone, anyone who might have cared about our being inside his unit lines. We were just two soldiers; they were many soldiers. There were unit guides with maps and written orders for officers in command. There were military police checkpoints that everyone just ignored.

There was a chaplain and a small burial party that seemed unconvinced that rearward would be any different from forward. Everyone, even the officers were white faced and silent.

Everyone seemed to understand that a large-scale killing had just been postponed for twenty-four hours. Someone said the French had requested the attack be put back until after the soldiers had time to celebrate Easter. Now, it seemed, those half ready and those half moved were only half prepared to accept the reality they might live to see another dawn.

Arthur and I just stepped off the road, turned north, and started to walk again. We followed a narrow trench that charted the boundary between the Canadian corps on the right and the British division on the left. In my mind I knew that I had walked this trench before. I had walked it with my eye and with my thumb as I had followed the countless air photographs that I had put together and helped to film with 16 Squadron RFC. In my mind at night, when I closed my eyes to think about how we go from the map to the real trench, these were the trenches that I had seen and walked in my mind. These duckboards were covered with inches of mud and man sweat. We did not know where we were going but I knew how to get there.

Every hundred yards or so we would come to a branch trench leading off into the Canadian Fourth Division area on the right or into the British First Division area on the left. Once in a while, every fifty yards or so, we would pass young men with old eyes, their rifles loosely held in their hands. Their bodies wrapped in blankets and old wool in an attempt to keep body and soul in the same frame.

They knew us for what we were. We did not wear helmets. Our outerwear was individually made of fashioned strips and coverings of camouflage. Our heads were bare now but behind our heads we wore large irregular hoods of sackcloth with tattered tails of grey, brown and blue cotton. Strung like capes around our shoulders, ready to put on when the time came, we wore the handmade smocks of snipers.

Arthur carried a large pack on his back. He had fashioned it himself so that it could look like a rock or a tossed up mound of dirt. In it he carried three days' food for himself and me, two large ground sheets, a small first aid kit and one hundred rounds of .303 ammunition. Every round had been cleaned, weighed, and 'matched'. Every round had been oiled and wiped; each had been chambered in my rifle and marked with a small pencil mark as having met with my approval. The Ross rifle did not tolerate mud, water, dirt, or ill-fitting ammunition. The infantry soldiers hated it because it just did not work consistently unless it was clean and oiled and free of all the different kinds of shit and mud that soldiers immersed it in. Snipers and marksmen loved it because if you oiled it, cleaned it and carried it in a special carrying bag, the Ross was an excellent marksman's rifle. Arthur also carried one ten-power set of binoculars around his neck with another one in his pack.

Finally, Arthur wore a holstered Wembley 445 calibre pistol on his right hip. He would use the Wembley if needed until only two rounds remained. One round would be for me, the last one round for him, in that order; nobody liked snipers. It was better to die at your own hand than to be captured.

I carried a similar large pack with two gallons of water, about sixteen pounds, in leather bags, some food, fifty rounds of matched .303 ammunition and ten trench grenades. The most precious item, disassembled and wrapped in a carrying bag, was my rifle. It was one of only five hundred Ross Mark II rifles specially built for long distance shooting. It was mated with a Warner and Swasey model 1913 prismatic telescope sight having 5.2X magnification. The sight was mounted offset to allow the "iron sights" to be used if necessary. In my hands the rifle was accurate out to 600 yards and I had killed beyond that. I had designed the rifle carrying bag so it could be unfolded and used as extra top cover once we had settled into our nest. In a roll on my back I had a small gas tarp, which we could use if required and it was a good rifle cover in the rain. Also in a roll hung over a shoulder I had a ten by twelve foot handmade camouflage blanket. It was made using thickly corded cotton netting. Strung through it and into it were hundreds of earth coloured pieces of cloth, parts of plants and pieces of common battlefield junk. It was our main daytime top cover sheet; we used it to become part of the ground, to make us disappear to the naked eye. Once into our position we would pull the top cover over us and settle in to kill or to die. We had already spent hundreds of hours under it; it had served us well.

It was as if all of the darkness of the night had gathered in just one place. Neither the glow of the lamps nor the bursting of star shells could penetrate the gathered gloom. The night was a nightmare itself. We leaned into the surrounding blackness like cattle lean into a storm. Rain fell in curtains driven relentlessly by a fickle wind that could not or did not know its own destination.

The mud and slime and shattered earth leaked and ran and swam into the bottom of putrid trenches. The sounds of distant guns were muted and hollow. The fall of shot was quickly covered and hidden with the voluminous towers of water and mud thrown up in stinking, lethal columns of steel edged spray. Even the bravest of those amongst us shuddered at the thought of being wounded or killed in a place such as the one that this war had provided for us.

The air and darkness conspired until they were thick and heavy; they were so impenetrable and hostile that even the glow from nearby cigarettes could not be seen beyond the length of a rusting rifle barrel.

I had a hand made map and pieces from an air photograph. I knew where I wanted to be; the problem was getting from here to there. We had to follow, for as long as circumstances and reality permitted, the existing trenches and communication lines. The route we had selected was on the very shoulder between the Canadian corps area and the British division that was dug in on its left. The usual three lines of defence were very well developed all along our route. The existing trenches in the third defensive line were well constructed, deep and wide with many dugouts and support areas. They were filled with activities and men. As we moved forward into the last trench line, the one closest to the German lines, the walls showed the signs of final preparations. Fire steps and additional wire had been recently added. Ladders and stepping off places were in place, lanes through our own wire were already marked, and the wire remaining in the gaps was ready to be hauled down. Sandbags clearly marked first aid posts and ammunition stores. The front awaited the arrival of men ordered into the greatest attack Canadians soldiers had ever made as a nation.

The step-off should have been in just hours but now another twenty-four hours had been added to the waiting. Arthur and I could not wait; we had to be in our position when the first whistles were blown.

The night was a complete and utter earthquake. Guns and howitzers of every calibre spat out their sounds of hate. The smaller field guns were layered with the large; the heavy and longer range ones were the furthest back; the smaller, fitful, and faster firing batteries were forward. I could have sworn that some of the guns were on the duckboards with us so that everywhere, over and around us, the air was torn asunder with the passing of the projectiles. The shock of their muzzles had been over our left shoulders for all the time that we had been traversing the rear area of the Fourth Division. Now that we had turned right and east north east to cling to the small seam of ground that was the inter-divisional boundary the pounding pressure of over nine hundred guns pushed against our backs forcing every next step closer to our chosen position. I could see our final objective in my mind; we were slowly getting closer to the forward outposts of the 10th Battalion. There we would step out into the no man's land that used to be the Bois De Givenchy.

This wooded area had long since been pounded into the mud and mixed with the flesh and bones and battlefield debris of the British, French, and German soldiers who had fought over it. No single part of anything we had seen so far was untouched by the relentless rain of bombardment. Shrapnel seemed to have sifted every inch of soil until nothing of the former surface remained.

Somewhere, just a few hundred yards forward of the 10th Battalion was the German line and a sharp little hill now called 'The Pimple'. Our sniper's nest was meant to look up and into that small overlooking feature. Our mission was to kill or wound as many careless defenders that presented themselves as targets.

All Arthur and I had to do now was to locate and inform the forward, left hand platoon of the 10th Battalion where we intended to be. Those soldiers, all of them, needed to know we were going to be out there in front of them. They needed to know that when they stepped over the wall in the early pre-dawn of tomorrow we would be there to protect them. From our point of view, a Canadian soldier, out in that first one hundred yards of no man's land, would not think twice about shooting anything and everything that moved in front of him. Still, a sniper's life hung on a thread of trust that the Canadians behind them knew there were Canadians in front of them. Once we were convinced that number four platoon of D Company the 10th Battalion knew that their snipers were active just in front of their step-off point we would slip over their parapet and into the darkness. Hopefully we would live long enough to kill.

Once confirming we were inside the forward battalion area we were escorted through to a deep and sharply stepped underground entrance. A muddy, youthful face, filled with tension and exhaustion poked out of a candle lit corner. His uniform was a mess of muddy wool but his Lieutenants pips were still visible. I spoke quickly not wanting to waste either his time nor mine.

"We are a sniper section Sir; we have orders from Divisional Headquarters to establish a position just left and slightly forward of your line by first light. I can mark your map if you like to show you where we think we will be for the next day or so".

I just let it all hang there. No need for names or Units, he only needed to know that he had us in his area so hopefully none of his rifleman would shoot us before the Germans had the first chance.

"We are not moving out of here until 0527 hrs on the 9th"; he said turning to pull a small map out of a pack that hung from a rifle barrel leaning against the wall of the dugout. "That's a long time for you to be out there between the Germans and my own men".

I just nodded, no use saying we had been through all this before. He knew that we knew our job came with no guarantees; with a shrug he added "I cannot offer you more than good luck", he stopped again and wiped a piece of dirt out of his mouth before pointing with a grimy finger at his map; "Try to stay behind this line, my machine gun section on this side is covering forward and up to The Pimple. If you get caught in their zone it will make it hard to get out". All I could say was "Yes Sir".

I quickly marked my small map with what information I could use from his large scale defensive map. We just nodded at one another as I left. He didn't have any confidence in his eyes that Arthur and I had any more than a snowball's chance in hell of getting safely over the wall and into the darkness that still existed to the left of his platoon's position.

I wasn't at all concerned about the German's catching us in the act; the real danger was some gun happy Canadian rifleman would see the movement as we slipped over the firing step and loose a few rounds out of fear, procedure and routine.

Arthur and I went over and huddled together leaning into the forward wall of the trench beneath the front firing step. Once we crawled over the wall we would be on our own with a lot of men, men on both sides of this trench, trained and ready to shoot us.

Sniper teams had a lot of experience with doing this very same manoeuvre. The answer to being successful was to get the men on your own side of the trench on your team before you ventured out. No one talked this far forward, no one purposely moved and looked over the trench walls and no one, who lived to talk about it, ever showed their head or any other part of their bodies over the firing step.

Arthur and I sat down on the edge of the duckboards. We reached into our packs and each of us took out an apple. Apples being eaten have a very peculiar sound, a sound that evokes warm memories and interest in any soldier that is within hearing distance. Make a deep and hard bite. Make a smacking as loud as you can without extreme exaggeration and wait about 30 seconds and one or two heads from the nearby soldiers will poke out from where they are hidden from view behind their ground sheets covering their individual indents in the walls. Two bites later we had six soldiers all crawling over with their tongues hanging out looking to see what kind of soldiers had apples that far forward. We shared the four remaining apples with the soldiers that came forward. We told them in hushed tones who we were and why we were there. I pointed a few times at the map and in a couple of different ways I said, "Tell your section where we will be and good luck on the way over". We now had the riflemen from the immediate area on our side and aware that two fellow soldiers were about to go out and over the wall doing something they would not wish on their worst enemy. Such frankly, was the life of a sniper.

***

At four in the morning, with one motion, Arthur and I stood as one. His hard, firm hand gave a short and reassuring squeeze to my upper right arm. I knew that he was smiling. These were the perfect conditions for snipers to leave the questionable security of their own lines to strive to turn the existence of nearby German soldiers into something beyond the very confines of human thought. For just a second I stood above myself looking down at the two us as we stepped through the door of Dante's hell.

We were a team, a team of killers bonded in purpose and the impossible magic that sometimes happens between two souls bent on accomplishing some common mission or effort. Neither Arthur nor I were talkers. When we were 'over the wall' we hardly ever exchanged a word. Just a touch, a slight effort, an almost unperceivable head movement was enough to indicate a target. We were good at what we did. He found the targets; I shot them. Everything we carried had a purpose. Our purpose was to kill and not be killed. We were good at what we did. We were snipers.

I sincerely wish that I could clearly remember every minute of the next two days but I cannot. I truthfully wish I could say that the time we were forward of 10th Battalion passed in the blinking of an eye but I cannot.

From the moment Arthur and I stood up on the firing step, we turned and gave the smallest of waves to the foursome that waited with us, all of the trappings of bravery fell away. My heart pounded, we crawled, and huddled and moved on, time after time; horrible things were under our hands or knees. We attempted to crawl a straight line but we could not; deep craters of water turned us left or right. Remnants of wire and posts required cutting or pushing aside. Both of us were surprised at how much wire remained; we had thought the artillery rounds would have cleared the area of everything standing.

Twice German voices seemed to be on our shoulders only to prove later they were voices above us carrying down into the sewer we crawled through. Time collapsed and stalled as we hunted for our final position, our own artillery seemed to follow us; dirt and screaming steel came within inches of our bodies. Arthur twice pushed me from behind when I just could not force myself out of the relative safety of deep sodden shell holes. I can still close my eyes and play the newsreel that followed us as we crawled, cut, hacked, and prayed our way into the edge of daylight that finally decided where we would make our final nest.

Daylight brought us images of a fearful landscape. We lay together, under our covers. Our hooded heads held down into the stinking mud of our furrow that we had selected to hide us. There was a quality of memory burned into the moment I first saw The Pimple rising above us that would stay in my mind until the moment of my death. And to this day I cannot remember time passing, I can only remember the images that assailed my eyes.

Just a foot or so from where we chose to nest was a hugely bloated and disfigured body of a young German soldier. His remains must have been there for two weeks or more. Shell shrapnel had pinned him to the ground. His arms were raised up above him as if he were reaching for the sky. A large fat and slimy rat turned and returned and turned again, time after time through his open mouth as it fed from what ever it found behind the now exposed teeth.

We passed the entire day of the 8th of April pressed together, not moving except to turn and pee into the ground beside us. Trying not to create a flutter or a movement in our top cover we took turns having a drink of water or nourishment that we had at hand.
Arthur noted details of possible targets we could identify. I planned to raise a small Union Jack on a short stick as soon as the battalion, now coiling in readiness behind us, was up and over the wall. Their movement and covering fire would be the first and immediate concern of the German machine gunners and snipers still alive on the top of the hill. We, Arthur and I, could only kill those that we could see, we worked hard to see as many as we could. The day passed.

During the night of the 9th, the Canadian and British Batteries increased their rate of fire. Rounds seemed to pour into the hilltop above us; the ground shook and lifted as medium and heavy rounds sought to remove 'The Pimple' from the map. First light brought our Ross rifle out of its canvas bag and into the hardness of arm and shoulder. Our first target was stirring near a trench line that had been fairly struck by a field gun during the night. Some poor bastard stood for just a second to push his machine gun back into place so he could shoot down into the direction our advancing soldiers would be forced to follow. The Ross kicked hard as I watch a large red cloud appear where his head had been just an instant before. I whispered to Arthur,

"Even if that is our only shot Arthur we have paid for our rations today".

Arthur's short and immediate grunt of appreciation caused our top cover to flutter just the smallest amount. We both squirmed slightly; adjusting our position to be ready for the second target we had chosen. I adjusted the barrel direction slowly to the left, my eye seeking the sniper position we suspected existed just beneath the machine gun post we had just engaged. I clearly saw the flash and hidden smoke from the German sniper's first round. A sickening breaking sound to my right reminded me of dropping a watermelon from a short height.

I looked down and along my rifle barrel and bolt; a large piece of Arthur's left face, most of one eye, and piece of his nose was hanging from the top part of my telescopic sight.

Almost without sighting I returned fire at the point where I had seen the flash. I was rewarded with a sudden small eruption of movement as the German sniper involuntarily jerked in his last second of life. Seconds passed. I slowly and carefully laid down my rifle. I pushed my hand down the rifle barrel in an attempt to put Arthur back together. He had not moved. He would never move again and all I could think of was that he would never know if she had waited for him in La Havre.

Arthur and I spent the next few minutes trying to remember where to find the other targets. I say Arthur because I found and used the symbols and notes he had made the day before. I was not careless but I had lost my sense of professionalism. I only wanted to engage and to kill as many German soldiers as I could see and find along the length of the slightly raising high ground spread out a couple of hundred yards to my front. I do not recollect changing magazines so I must have shot under ten times but I do know that at least two machine guns would have needed to have found replacement gunners before they could reengage.

Then suddenly the friendly close fire of the artillery lifted. It started higher on the hill and further out in front of our own lines. Whistles were blowing, voices injected fresh sounds into the shattered air around the massive length of our lines. The attack, the long awaited attack had started. Without even thinking I reached out and planted the little flag next to Arthurs right side. I placed it almost in his open hand as if he were reaching for it.

Then I turned again and scanned the Pimple for any sign of movement or for the open mouths of machine guns that were being made ready to sweep away the lines of forming Canadians that were now spewing out of pre-dug tunnels, trenches and holding areas all along the area in front of the ripe and waiting Germans determined to hold their positions at all costs.

Again time did not stay with me. I have no idea how long I lay there loading, shooting, and waiting for the Canadian lines to wash over me. A couple of times soldiers came near me, then they seemed to melt away and the ferocity of battle swirled in some other direction. I could hear the pitch of artillery fire moving forward, rifle fire getting further and further away on the right side of our line. German targets kept appearing and disappearing during the morning as new interest was shown from those still holding the heights above me. Five or six times I know that my rifle found willing flesh as they exposed themselves.

I had long since taken down my little flag marker; I knew that a Canadian soldier would not step on me any time soon. No one seemed to be interested in locating me; there were just too many other targets behind me in the distance where our original starting point had been. I remember thinking that the fire coming from the very top of The Pimple, the parts that I could not see, was withering and had probably stopped the Fourth Division from moving forward out of their forward lines.

Everything seemed to stop. The battle swirled and growled but not here. Far off towards the heights at Vimy the sounds of battle built and ebbed. Overhead British aircraft flew; I could imagine that someone from 16 Squadron had me in their camera's eye as they passed over.

Night came and went, I spent most of the tenth of April talking to Arthur as if I expected him to answer. I knew that at some time, at some time soon, the Fourth Division would rise from their trenches and claw and dig their way to the top of The Pimple. I just did not have anyway of knowing when that might be.

The eleventh of April was long and cold. The snow had lifted but the constant pounding of our own artillery had returned. The hill in front of me heaved and spewed volcanoes of earth and hillside. I helped myself to Arthur's food and water, time crawled with every cloud that covered and uncovered the pale and feeble face of the sun. From somewhere behind me a constant finger of machine gun fire poked and scrawled its name with lead along the features of The Pimple. At some point during the following night I moved Arthurs remains closer to the front of the lip of the shell hole we had lain in. He was no longer worried about being shot at from the heights of the hill but I was.

The dawn on the Twelfth of April, the whole scene started to repeat itself. The artillery fire was so intense I could not begin to distinguish one rounds howl and agony of death from the next. I just could not imagine how anyone could stay alive or if alive how they could remain sane up there on the German held crest. Then, at last, the unmistakeable sounds that battalions make as they break cover and start their clawing across the ground.

I concentrated every fibre of my attention at what was at my front. I could not change nor help what was going on behind me as my fellow Canadians started to advance in my direction on their way forward to take The Pimple. Some minutes passed, the sounds of whistles and orders being shouted out all along the closest lines spread out behind me.

Finally, I thought, finally the Fourth Division was getting close to me and to their assault on The Pimple. I turned on my hip so that I could get a better view of advancing soldiers. The last thing I wanted was for someone to see me and assume I was a German soldier. Minutes crept by; the volume of fire from The Pimple decreased for a while as renewed artillery fire started to creep up the face of the hill and pound the rear areas beyond my vision. Suddenly five or six Canadian soldiers appeared in a shortened line just yards to my right. Their complete attention seemed to be focussed on finding ways through the German barbed wire that still clung maddeningly to their posts all along the bottom of the hill. It seemed as if that part of the hill had been almost completely missed being engaged by friendly fire. Suddenly, a machine gun, out of sight to me because of its height, opened up and four of the five soldiers fell, soundlessly, into the craters and churned soil. Only one young soldier remained standing. He was about ten yards from me, line abreast; his face had lost all expression.

Because fear had turned him into something he was not, his mind, all on its own and for its own reasons, told him he was someone he could not be. In that instant he became a hero. In his mind he became a hero that must take a life because it was a life that must end. Must end because he could not face another minute of walking through a terror that he could see and hear, taste and feel but could not control. He knew that if he took a life then the moment he pulled the trigger he would be just what he had been before. He would become a lonely farm boy again; just an ordinary, young, Canadian farm boy, from somewhere near Wetaskiwin Alberta.

He, without even knowing it, had fallen to his knees. His eyes had lost their screaming edge of fear that had gripped him ever since he had stridden over the firing step and out into the endless pain that was no man's land. With Sunday precision he made the sign of the cross, the Father, the Son and Holy Ghost. Without a moments hesitation he reached down and took his Lee Enfield by the front of its fore grip and placed the maw of the barrel into his open mouth. His right hand was working down the fore stock in search of the trigger guard that protected the trigger from accidental discharge and damage.

No longer a sniper I was now a helpless witness to what certainly was going to end in a way that even I could not condone. Involuntarily my legs were in motion, I threw aside the weight of my top cover and lunged forward out of the safety and security of my sniper's nest. He was only a few short yards from me, my voice screamed at him, begging him to listen. Charging him, I plucked my hood from my head and hurled it at him as an airborne messenger meant to stop his hand from its sure and final act. Slowly, as if in a dream he saw my frantic scramble to reach him before his hand found the trigger. His eyes were narrowing, he realized I was there and I was about to run him over, knock him down, take away his rifle, and stop him from being the hero he wanted to be.

Three more steps I thought, my knees were churning, mud flying off my sniper's cape as I ran, screaming for him to stop. Two steps remained; his hands had reluctantly jerked the barrel out of his mouth bringing the barrel down and out, away from his head and in the general path of my approach. His right hand had found the trigger; his face was twisted and deeply furrowed with the anguish of his mind and the moment.

One more step; I launched my body straight at him in an attempt to strike him as an arrow would; I wanted to bowl him over, knock him down, save him from himself. Just inches from our imminent collision his rifle discharged, the bullet struck home, penetrated and exited before I even knew that I had found a way to save him.

* * *

A Sanctuary of Sorts

I heard the sound the rifle made but I was separate from the event itself. My life and light seemed to float in and out much like a distant bonfire would seem to if you approached it at night, walking towards it through a thick and changing forest of trees and branches. My existence, my very life itself was disconnected from where I seemed to be. I imagined I was far above the ground, detached and looking down to find myself but I could not see anything that I recognized amongst the changing scene below. For a while I was carried aloft, as if on silent, strong wings, which made no sound except for the slightest whispering a playful wind might make in a tall pine tree. I listened hard, straining to hear the words the wind might make; over and over again I heard one single word; it was the word stay, stay, stay.

Then, I awoke again as in a dream. I had returned to ground level and I believed I was in a birch bark canoe. It was a canoe much like the one that I helped Johnny Snake Eye build for all of the summer that I was fourteen. I was in that canoe for a long while. Every time the canoe moved a wave of pain, deep and intense, washed over me, forcing me to close my mind to everything until the next wave would collide with me again.

At some level I knew I would be unable to paddle; I was unable to do anything at all. I could not even will myself to change direction as I drifted, all alone, on a lake wracked by a storm that churned and crafted wave after following wave.
The canoe and I drifted in and out of small shafts of light and far away, maybe as far away as the shoreline might be, there were sounds of voices.

The first voice said, "I shot him". A different voice said "stretcher" and another said "still alive". All the while the canoe moved and rocked and a deep and indescribable pain moved and rocked in me and with me.

Then the voices spoke in single words as a daylight turned to dark and light again. Words like, "gentle", or "lift". Some man said "slowly", another said "stitch". In the dark again a train track ran in my canoe and the rails brought new pain and voices said, "Canadian" and "ship". Light changed from grey into white and dark again. A woman said, "lift", another said, "clean". That is all I can remember except for the pain. The pain was well beyond what I had ever imagined. I dreamed I was being carried away somewhere on a flood of sharp, deep, sweeping waves of pain. It was so real I thought it was actually happening to me.

Then after some time I can remember knowing my canoe was motionless and if I remained still the pain would go away. I remember Ma talking to me, telling me to be proud I had learned to push the waves away. I could feel myself moving again, moving to somewhere where there would be no pain left to dread. I drove the words away too and I only listened for the soft voice that said, "gentle". A spoon seemed to come and go. The spoon was warm and a single word drifted around in my dream. "Drink", the word was said again and again.

I fought against the urge to open my eyes. I thought I heard Tears whispering to me; somewhere near her voice was asking me to open my eyes because if I did they would see she was happy. But I was afraid, both to listen and to believe. I thought if opened my eyes I would see Askuwheteau in his box and he would be crying.

I struggled to move but it was as if I had been enclosed so tightly in a blanket it was impossible to free myself. I dreamed of being in a winter night camp. I had built my fire pit too close to my sleeping place and now the blanket was too hot and I was burning up. I was dreaming again; I had lost my way and now I was in a very hot place. The sun shone constantly and I could not escape the heat. I thought I had caught myself in one of my snares and I struggled to move, to move my arms but I could not. I could not find the slipknot on the snare, which held me. I kept fading into darkness; darkness, but not one filled with peace or sleep. I was too fiery to sleep and someone was putting cold water on my forehead. A voice said, "infection", another said, "dying".

In my dream I laughed at the voices. They were so serious those voices. It became light again before I heard the voices return. A man with a soft voice spoke Latin. Latin words from a verse I recognized; Latin words made me wonder if the Priest was dying?
"Per istam sanctum unctionem et suam piissimam misericordiam".

The next thing I remember were the waves returning. Wave after wave of pain returned but it was worse now because I could not move. I could smell the strong and constant odour of alcohol; I tried to fight my way out of the snare that held me.

I felt trapped; there seemed no way to escape. It was as if some great force held me with a hard and painful hand pressing down over my eyes so that I could not open my eyes to see. My eyes seemed to be sewn shut like the deerskin we had wrapped Johnny Snake Eye in before I lifted him onto the platform beneath the forest and the sky. I was lying on my back but I could neither stand to run nor could I turn away from the constant pain. And yet, at some level, I knew I could not be like Johnny Snake Eye; I had too much to understand, too much to tell to Manitou.

Then I opened my eyes and I saw her. A young woman stood close to me, she was dressed all in white like a bride would be. Her dress was long and her hair was covered with a white hat that had a blue stripe. She was looking intently at a small stick that seemed to be made of glass; the stick had small red lines and numbers written on it. Her mouth moved but no words came out. I said,
"Are you the Virgin"?

It was as if a shot had gone off somewhere near to her. She dropped the glass stick and turning quickly, she ran away so swiftly I did not register that she had disappeared from my view. My eyes were trying to focus on the room. I tried to identify something that would reassure me I was safe when suddenly a strong face with a small white beard appeared over me. His face was close, his eyes danced around my eyes, he seemed to look deep within me, searching for something.

"So", he said with a soft British accent, "You have come back to us". He paused for a moment as if gauging my reaction to his spoken words. "We thought you might not be able to find your way back".

I must have been staring at him, I know that my mind was a complete fog; the last thing I could clearly remember was cleaning Arthur off the side of my Ross rifle.

"You have come to us from a place they are calling the greatest Canadian victory of the war. Do you remember anything about how you got here and, more importantly I suppose...", he paused again as if reluctant to go on. Then in a much softer tone he said, "do you have any idea why you are in this hospital in London"?

It only took a few seconds for me to begin wishing that I had stayed wrapped securely inside my long and painful dream. There seemed to be a ragged edge of comfort in the small parts that I could still remember about where that dream had taken me. It had been a dark dream but someone had kept saying "gentle", "nearly over", and "handsome". Until I had opened my eyes it had really and truly only been a dream and now, sadly the truth came crushing down on me. My dream, at least, had been a sanctuary of sorts. Now that I was awake again I saw the pity in their eyes and I knew their pity would come to haunt me.

* * *

Nursing Sister Elizabeth Grace Bain was a Londoner. She had been born and raised within a mile of the Bow Bells and from her earliest memories she had always wanted to be a nurse. When the war started she packed her meagre wardrobe and inconsequential belongings into a rented wagon and asked the driver to deliver them to her mother's house near St. Martin's in the Field. She watched the wagon drive away, her heart not knowing exactly what her mother would think and she then turned and made her way to the nearest Army Recruiting Station to enlist. For the next two years she had worked twelve to fourteen hours a day at the General Field Hospital at Salisbury Camp. Every single working day that she worked there she saw sick men, boys mostly, and none of them were ever anything to her except soldiers needing her attention in order to get well again. Never once had she ever let her heart beat with any emotion stronger than sympathy. Not even once had her body betrayed her strong female awareness of the unremitting looks and longings openly displayed by the constantly changing cast of men under her care. By days end she was habitually worn out, physically exhausted, her very soul begged for rest and rehabilitation prior to the morning's early call to duty. For two full years Elizabeth Grace was the classic devoted, single minded, professional Sister of Mercy that the war wounded relied on. Days faded into weeks, routine became the master she marched to. Short, regulated meetings held by changing medical shifts and staffs were the only punctuated time breaks for the hospital staff. Hurried trips to the dispensary, the constant filling out and keeping of medical records, the hurried and monotonous partaking of meals and the robotic dressing and undressing from soiled clothes to freshly provided hospital gowns and clothing were her only other breaks from the constant pain, death and healing of the ward. Only the regular monthly arrival of her periods reminded her that her soul and spirit lived within a temple completely capable of loving, being loved and making love.

After two years of being away from her mom and family in London while she slaved away in Salisbury she applied for and won a nursing position at a well known hospital for seriously wounded soldiers being transferred to advanced facilities in London. She now found herself as a Ward Sister at Queen Alexandra Military Hospital only a mile or so from where her mom lived.

Sister Bain had been on duty since six that morning. At each bed she nodded, said the professionally formatted words required to assure, solicit cooperation and achieve her mission of mercy so that she could move on to the next poor bastard needing his dressing changed or bedding rearranged. Her heart was filled with pity for every man she served and there had been thousands of them over the past two years alone. Men without eyes, men without one or more limbs, men without touch with reality, and most often, men without hope. Her ward received the wounded just after they had passed through the surgery or emergency ward.

"Those poor buggers", she had been told, "are here to heal or die". She took her role seriously, professionally. Her heart wished recovery for every body she worked on. Her lips said only those words, which pragmatically enabled her to perform, time after time, the nursing care that it was her duty to fulfill.

It was not always like that; there had been a time when she gave a piece of herself, a pound of flesh, to every single wounded soldier that she had come in contact with. But slowly, almost imperceptibly, she had hardened into the professional shell that she was now. She was as battle shocked as any soldier who came out screaming from underneath the countless rain of falling steel of a week long German bombardment at the Somme.

Her mind was emotionally closed, as closed as those hearts that beat within the chests of the Priests and Chaplains that repeated, day after day, the last rites for soldiers who had not recovered from their wounds. These men and the medical staffs in all of the military hospitals stretching from battalion dressing stations, to casualty clearing stations within divisional lines and all the way back to England and then as far as Canada, or Australia, or India; they had all learned to hide themselves behind shields built by minds over used and over insulted by what their duties demanded of them.

Elizabeth Grace had learned to hold her mind away from the constant fire of grief that lapped away at her very being as day after day, week after week, she spoke the words required to perform the commitment that she had wed and promised the day she had joined the Queen Alexandra's Imperial Military Nursing Service.

But when I refused to die, Nursing Sister Elizabeth Grace Bain started to change. When she came to my bedside she found herself praying she would find me continuing to float along in the long dream I thought I was having but was not. And for each of those days the Priest had said to her, "Today, not longer than today", she would work all the harder with a spoon to force liquid into my mouth. And when the doctors said, "Standard treatment Sister, he will soon expire from this infection", she would change my dressings, wash and clean my wounds with alcohol and spend precious time putting cooling towels dipped in clean, cold, water on my forehead to help bring my temperature down. Later, during my recovery period, she told me when she had heard someone whom she thought was dying speak to her and ask her if she was The Virgin, she knew God Himself had answered her prayers for me.

* * *

Picking up the Pieces

I started to make and keep notes on the 21st of May 1917. I still have those scribbled pages in longhand. Nurse Bain acquired the note pad and pencil I used from a stationery store very near to where she was quartered at 20 John Islip Street. She lived just around the corner really from the hospital.

In my first few attempts to make a record of my journey from France to England I always started with the fact that I was now a man with only one arm. The second time I started to write I had even described how incredibly shocked I was to discover that almost all of my entire left shoulder had been removed as well and for a long time I just could not even begin to understand how life could or would go on for me without having both arms and both hands.

For a few days I could not even begin to look at myself. But then, after days of being told to get up out of bed and dress myself; after miles of walking, first around the hospital bed, later around the ward and even later outside and along the sidewalks near to and around the hospital, I started to see just how damn lucky I was to be alive. I had, nurse Bain told me, survived a .303 round through the shoulder, a crude but expedient amputation of the left arm, followed a few days later by removal of a large portion of my shoulder muscle and infected tissue. Had those medical interventions not been performed, I would surely have died, not of the wound but of the substantial infection that followed.

But I am ahead of myself. On the 19th of May a minor miracle occurred in the hallway just outside the door leading into the common hospital room, which I shared, with twenty-four other patient beds. The wards, most named after Victoria Cross winners, were filled, as was mine, with soldiers that had recently returned from France. Each of us were considered to have suffered serious wounds, the majority of us were amputees and all of us suffered from lingering and severe infection associated with the length of time or the physical location our bodies had lain in or had travelled through during our recovery from the battlefield. The military required individual soldiers' medical records to contain details concerning all of the known medical treatments and procedures administered at each medical facility. That said, only our names, regimental numbers and the title of our units, were written on a small removable card posted on our bed-end.

Every soldier had records; records followed you to wherever you were posted. The Army knew where every living and dead soldier was in terms of which unit or cemetery he was in. I was currently in the Queen Alexandra Military Hospital, Millbank, London, SW 1. The hospital was very central, only two city blocks from the River Thames, next door to the Tate National Gallery, in front of Millbank Gardens, close to Grosvenor Road Wharf with the Royal Doulton Pottery factory just across the river. How in the name of hell Captain Johnson from the 49th Battalion found me in that hospital remains a complete mystery.

Captain Johnson had followed more or less the same medical path as I. Though the ground over which we had travelled was similar he had been conscious for every step, every tramcar, the ambulances and the Casualty Clearing Stations.

He had been wounded by a German sniper while standing overlooking work he had ordered to be carried out on the forward A Company section of our Vimy position communications trench. He had received his first attention at the Battalion Aid Post located back in the reserve area. From there, just like I was, he was escorted, I was carried on a stretcher, and he walked to a brigade dressing station that had already been established prior to our attack on Vimy Ridge. Next he was sent through to the divisional area where he was assessed at the Casualty Clearing Station. Here decisions were made regarding what kind of future medical attention would be required to save the patient's life or return him to the battlefield. Seriously wounded men, like Johnson and me were then handed over to various methods of medical transport. Both of us travelled under medical escort by tramway and rail line to Le Havre where we were put on a Hospital ship. We landed in England, I went, because there was room available in the operating theatre, to the Queen Alexandra Military Hospital; Johnson went to the Michie Hospital in London, a hospital set up at 184 Queens Gate. Captain Johnson was told, during his recovery, that some Canadian casualties from the battle at Vimy had been sent to the QA Hospital and by sheer luck and chance he walked into my room and asked if anyone was from the 49th Battalion.

"So", he said looking over the back of my bed, "What the hell happened to you"? He tossed his Army Forage Hat onto the foot of my bed and slowly walked around to right side of bed and stood looking down at me. His eyes narrowed as he scanned the deformed thing that I had become.

"Looks like you lost a wing Giorgio, could have been worse, you could have been in the same cemetery as the Company Commander, poor bastard". With an audible sigh he added, "He never knew what happened".

Johnson slowly reached over and pulled the sheet down covering the remainder of my left shoulder. The bandage hid the damage but it clearly indicated to a trained eye the extent to which the medical staff had removed bone and muscle in their fight to safe my life. His eyes met mine again; he reached over and hauled up a chair so that he could sit next to my bed. Force of habit made him hold his damaged and bandaged hand out in front of him and this served as a notice to me that we both had returned to England significantly different than when we served the 49th.

"Ok, now you listen to me Giorgio or Askuwheteau or whatever your real name is". He shifted his ass on the chair a little so that he could get his face closer to mine and lowered his voice so that only he and I are were part of what would follow. "You are one of the strongest and most independent men that I have served with. Whenever I needed someone to step up to the plate and get something done or whenever I needed a fresh point of view of how to solve a problem, I knew that I could count on you".

He very gently rearranged the sheet that he had moved when he first looked at the extent of my wound. With a small shrug, a sheepish sort of smile taking control of the left corner of his mouth he added, "That has not changed just because you lost your left arm. You are wounded yes, you are recovering yes, but you are the same smart, independent man that you were on the morning of the 8th of April when you and Arthur crossed the firing step to do a sniping mission that you designed and executed on your own initiative".

With that he sat back into the chair and continued to just stare at me as if the next move was entirely up to me. And those few words from a man I truly admired and respected started to put my feet back on the road to recovery.

Every day for nearly two weeks Robert James Johnson would wander into my room and remind me that I was alive. His right hand was a mangled mess of scar tissue and bullet wound. He was absolutely driven to regain complete movement and use of his hand. He did not and some weeks later he ended up being transferred out of active duty with the Battalion, staying in London on staff of The Office of the Minister, Overseas Military Forces of Canada.

I introduced him to Nurse Bain. Together they schemed and plotted to get me moving and motivated. A little bit at a time I told him the entire story of my time spent with 16 Squadron. I even shared with him how I had begun to believe the words my grandmother had said about me being the reincarnation of the great Cree legend Askuwheteau. On one of our very first walks together around the streets framing our 200 bed hospital I related how Arthur and I had walked nearly all day to get into a position to begin our sniping patrol below the Pimple. I did not spare any detail on how devastated and alone I felt after Arthur had been killed. I recalled how for the next nearly seventy-two hours, I had continued to fulfil my sniper's role, shooting and killing targets time and time again as they presented themselves on the high ground overlooking the route of the Canadian advance.

"On the next day, the tenth, the Fourth Division still had not even come close to getting out of their trenches and attacking the Germans who had reinforced and continued to hold The Pimple.

Every time Canadians moved behind me the German artillery observers, machine gunners and snipers would blanket the entire approach lanes through the wire. I was pretty much the only Canadian forward still alive as far as I could tell".

We both stopped and leaned against the sheltered side of the hospital wall looking into the streets, now filled with wagons and ambulances busy carrying supplies, fresh linens, and additional patients to and from the hospital wards.

"I knew in my heart that something had gone wrong with the plan to take the entire ridge on the 9th of April. I was nearly out of ammunition, water, and food. It had been snowing with fairly high winds and rain for those two nights. Early on the morning of the twelfth the guns started all over again. A huge artillery fire plan was concentrated on The Pimple, all kinds of rounds landed within just a few yards of my position but luckily most of the shrapnel carried forward into the slope and hill side. I had a busy night and early morning staying alive and engaging targets until the artillery bombardment started to move up the hill, into and over the top. Suddenly there were two or three Canadian battalions, all in lines, coming straight at me. Men were falling; they were shooting and finding lanes through the wire. There was a lot of wire still standing, it was an awful sight let me tell you".

Captain Johnson just stared at me, shaking his head. I supposed, after all he had been through himself at the Somme, he had a very clear understanding what it was like being out there with Arthur lying dead beside me for over three days and then watching the final attack going in right over where I had been hiding in my sniper's nest.

"I did not expose myself to either the German snipers or to the approaching Canadian Companies. I knew there was no way in hell the Canadians would know I was one of theirs. I was clearly all alone out front and lying in their path. I knew it was best to just hope they would walk by me without noticing me on their way up to attack The Pimple. All I could do was wait until they were beyond me before I could stand up and make my way back to the reserve trenches. It was the only way that I would be able to get out of the hole I was in and get Arthur to a Chaplain and a burial party".

Captain Johnson had stopped walking and turned back towards the way we had come. His broad forehead wore a deep mask of concern. "Four days; you were gone from the Battalion and out there alone for almost four full days. Jesus Christ, how did you manage to stay alive for that period of time with all the artillery and shooting going on from both sides"?

"Well", I said, "There were three things going right for me. First there was a dead German soldier hanging from wire right in front of my position. I believe that kept the Germans from firing down and into the place where his body was. Secondly, there were fairly deep artillery shell craters Arthur I had occupied and developed into our snipers' nest. During the next three days I used Arthur's body and a lot of mud and dirt to provide cover and protection to hide any movement I might make as I changed from one target to another. And thirdly, the weather was perfect. It was snowing and blowing for almost the entire time, the snow was at my back, blowing up and into the faces of the Germans defending The Pimple. They were damned afraid of what would come next and I was certain the Canadians were going to come and walk right through where I was hiding. I had the advantage for all of that time".

The next afternoon Johnson took Nurse Bain out for a short walk around the hospital grounds. I knew they were talking about me but frankly I was far too preoccupied trying to learn how to dress and wash and shave one-handed to worry much about their chitter and chatter. They looked good together, both had expressive faces, and both shared a real and growing concern that I might re-infect my wounds. The hospital was filled with men, men in every ward, who had deep and seemingly incurable infections.

At about three in the afternoon, Johnson and Bain and a couple of other Army officers that I had not seen before came into the ward. Some discussions were held between them and the hospital staff and shortly afterwards I was put into a chair with wheels and pushed down the hallway and into a small sort of waiting room. The waiting room was crowded with chairs occupied mostly by young Canadian Officers in well tailored uniforms without any insignia except rank. That meant they were staff officers who had spent their entire wartime careers here in London, living the good life, employed on one of the many staffs that occupied hundreds and hundreds of officers for whom there were no field positions with the Canadian Corps. Do you remember how I told you that the Army consisted of two parts? Well these guys were definitely from Part One. Two of these officers, Colonels I believe, one British, and one Canadian, were sitting on chairs behind a small writing desk. It looked rather like an inquisition or a disciplinary hearing.

I was introduced to those gathered and without ceremony I was asked to relate the history of my tour with 16 Squadron and the extent to which I had developed and planned the sniper coverage for the 10th Battalion front looking up at The Pimple feature.

The Canadian Colonel asked a lot of questions about how I managed to stay alive out in no mans land and how I came to be wounded. I kept the story short and simple, trying to keep the horror and pain of Arthur's death from spilling out of my memory into the room.

"Staying alive in no man's land is not difficult, doing a sniper's job in no man's land is the difficult thing to do. I knew from the very beginning that the Germans firing down from the heights of The Pimple would have the advantage over any position Arthur and I chose below them. What we had to do was to study the air photographs and pick the very best position that gave us the best possible cover and also would provide firing lanes up into the hill side without exposing our position to their counter fire".

I noticed that most of the hands that been taking notes had stopped writing. I continued anyway.

"Unfortunately for Arthur it seems that one new German sniper position had been moved down from the hill top and it looked right into the shell hole and position we had chosen. That sniper detected the movement of our top cover and he fired at the movement. His first round hit and killed Arthur".

I remember pausing there for a second or two before convincing myself that there was nothing to gain from adding any of details about having to remove part of Arthur's head from my rifle. "I had seen the position from which he had fired, I fired next and killed him".

I could feel the weight of eyes pressing on me as I spoke, I remember thinking that not one of the officers in that room with the exception of Johnson had any real idea of what existence had been like for Arthur and me as Arthur died and I struggled to live.

"It was shot for shot. One life for one life", I told them. "That is often the way an engagement goes when snipers exchange fire, someone shoots first and if he does not kill the rifleman there is a pretty good possibility that the next round fired will kill or wound the first sniper".

I let my eyes wander over the faces in that room. There were ten or so men that quickly dropped their eyes in order to avoid contact with someone who had been there while they had not.

"Over the next nearly three nights and days I fired over eighty aimed shots into the summit of The Pimple, I believe that the majority of my shots would have killed or wounded the intended target".

A whispered voice from the back of the room said, "Eighty! Fuck me, eighty dead Germans all killed by one rifleman in three days"!

A Colonel asked me to tell him about how I had been wounded and if I could recall anything about how I had been evacuated out from below The Pimple.

"In a nut shell, Sir, I can answer the last part with one word, nothing. I remember nothing about how I got here and I have no idea who might have been involved. I remember some stretches when I was aware it was daytime or night time. I remember hearing train wheels running on a track. I think someone said the word 'ship' and I remember a lot of pain and trying to get away from the smell of alcohol. That is about all that I can remember. I know that a lot of people were very involved in getting me back here and I am thankful to be alive but I think it is fair to say that time sort of evaporated just after I was wounded".

One of the medical officers in the room added that he had a more or less complete set of my medical records. He added they contained the notes that had been written by every medical aid station and medical facility I had passed through on my way to this hospital in London. There was a general nodding of heads as he read from a long list of notes scribbled and written into my records. I was very surprised to learn I had been operated on three times along the way, the first to remove my left arm at the shoulder. The second time on board the hospital ship to remove some infected bone fragments from the area of my shoulder and a much longer and more detailed operation to remove additional bone and flesh that had become infected which had been done here at the hospital in London shortly after my arrival.

I then gave a short description of the assault on The Pimple on the morning of the 12th of April. I related how the attacking Canadians appeared through the very early dawn rain and snow and how I watched as they advanced forward behind massive artillery bombardment being conducted on to The Pimple in front of them.

I described, as best I could, how the remaining and still standing German wire had forced the majority of advancing soldiers to move to my left through lanes they used or improved as they moved forward. The attack took about thirty minutes I thought and only two other Canadian soldiers managed to get through the wire lane in my immediate area. One was shot and killed very close to where I lay with Arthur as my marker and protector.

I told them the other soldier had stopped, gone to his knees and then had preceded to hold his service rifle in his hands pointing the rifle at his own head as if he intended to end his own life. I admitted at that point I had lost my sense of purpose and professionalism and broke cover and ran to try to intercede as quickly I could.

I related shouting and throwing my hood in his direction to distract him from his intent. I told them I believed the soldier had only realized I was running at him for the last few seconds. He may have seen me running at him but he was actually attempting to pull the trigger that would have ended his life. "As I got within a few feet of him he pulled the rifle barrel down as if trying to protect himself from my charge. The rifle discharged, striking me".

The medical officer in the back of the room again referred to my medical records, which recorded that the .303 round had entered in the upper part of my left chest, the bullet tracked through my shoulder, separating my arm from the shoulder joint. The shock of impact had rendered me unconscious and apparently I never did really regain consciousness again due to loss of blood and later infection until I had arrived, at the point of death, at the QA Hospital.

* * *

Nurse Bain escorted me back to my room and frankly I never gave much thought as to why anyone would come from a headquarters on the other side of London to speak to a soldier about how he received his wounds at Vimy Ridge. I was only one of thousands of Canadians wounded; I was beginning to believe Captain Johnson when he had said how lucky I was to be alive.

Later on that evening after the dinner meal, Nurse Bain came again to sit for a few minutes at the side of my bed. It had been a long day, her face was drawn; her uniform no longer held the sharp, just starched, pressed look it had at the beginning of every new day.

"Snipe", she said, "All that stuff that happened today was about some possible disciplinary action that might be taken by your Army against the soldier that shot you".

She looked down at her hands; they were restless in her lap as if they were expressing something her mouth would not issue. Her eyes found mine again. "You may not have been told everything about how and why you ended up here in London in a British military hospital and I guess that isn't really very important for you to know all about that".

She paused again; I suppose she was trying to judge my reaction to her words. "All that you really need to know Snipe is that your own Canadian medical system was very overloaded with causalities immediately following your Corps attack on Vimy Ridge and whenever individual Commonwealth systems start to fill up their patients are sent to hospitals and facilities within the British system. You ended up with us and now there is discussion about where to send you until you can be released and sent back home to Canada".

She paused there. Her eyes centered on mine. Her mouth worked for a few seconds before she added, "I think you will remain here in England for about three or four months. I cannot say where you will go from here but for now Capt. Johnson and I are working on a plan that might keep you here in London or at least somewhere close to us in the London area".

She paused there, fatigue approaching exhaustion was not uncommon amongst nursing sisters forced to work twelve or more hours a day on their wards during periods of time when large numbers of casualties were arriving from the slaughter fields of Europe. Her face had lost some of its youth. She looked down at her uniform and for a few seconds her hands fluttered trying to remove the day's wrinkles from her apron and dress. "I have been working extremely long hours for an incredibly long time Snipe, I am tired and I know that my personal judgement may not be the very best at this moment".

I raised my hand to signal my disagreement but she just waved my objection aside and continued.
"The Head of Nursing has ordered that I take a fortnight's leave, that is two weeks to you in Canadian. I have a small two bedroom flat near here that a friend lets me use. She is in France at the moment working with another of the forward military hospitals so it is available and I intend to go there, rest and try to find some of the enthusiasm I possessed when I joined Queen Alexandra's Nursing Corps over two years ago now".

She stood up and walked around my bed for a time, pulling, straightening, and pushing at my bedding, more from habit than requirement. She stopped her migration and stood over me as I lay awaiting her words.

"I am going to take you with me as a house guest when I leave here tomorrow. Your friend Captain Johnson and I think it is in your best interest to get away from this hospital before you re-engage some infection in your existing wound. By staying with me, I believe that you will get better care and better food than you are getting here. I have checked with the Head of Nursing and she has agreed to let me sign you out tomorrow morning into my and Captain Johnson's care".

She sighed a deep sigh as if admitting to herself that she had finally gathered enough nerve to ask a man to do anything with her or to her for the first time in her entire life. "So that is what is going to happen to you tomorrow".

She stopped there, in mid thought, as if gathering strength and words with which to go on. She reached down and took my hand in hers, her eyes firmly fixed on mine as if to ensure that I was listening and agreeing.

"Tomorrow morning you will go through a series of early morning doctor's rounds. They will want to check how your amputation and wounds are healing and if you are clear from infection. You know that there is always a very big possibility of reinfection with your type of wounds and that would not be a good thing for you right now".

She was open and emotionally vulnerable. Just the slightest of tears had gathered at the corner of her left eye. She wiped at it as if annoyed at herself for exposing the soul that lay beneath her uniform. "One of the biggest sources of infection is just being here in this hospital with all of the other soldiers that are fighting infections of their own. Getting you away from here for a couple of weeks should ensure that you will continue to heal and your shoulder wounds will continue to close and repair themselves without having another removal of surrounding flesh".

She pulled some of my bedcovers up around my chest and walked a small circle. Some of the other soldiers sharing my ward room were now interested in why a nurse was spending extra time with one of their ward mates. Any female in the room always attracted attention even amongst those men seriously wounded. It was strange I had thought, even the possibility of dying from one's wounds did not impede the stiffening of a soldiers penis when a pretty young nurse came to administer health and understanding.

She came back to my bedside and stood over me, her voice lowered and direct, "If the medical staff will agree to discharge you into my care tomorrow, Capt. Johnson and I are going to get you into an ambulance and deliver you just down the street to my apartment. I will be absent from my unit on leave, Capt. Johnson has agreed to visit you and assist me in doing what ever needs to be done as far as providing you with proper care while you are staying with me under my medical supervision. I hope you will agree with all of this Snipe or else I am going to look pretty silly getting the Hospital to undo what we have put in place".

"Well I'll be damned", was all that I could think to say.

* * *

Falling In Love In London Again

Getting a temporary reprieve from Millbank Hospital was the easiest thing about getting well. Nurse Bain had spoken with the medical staff and the Head of Nursing. They, in turn, had agreed to let her move me into a second floor apartment that was only about a quarter of a mile from the hospital door. They even provided her with bed linens and bandages. Captain Johnson helped make the physical move. It seems that nearly all of the hospital staff and certainly most of the doctors were well aware that a patient's chances of survival from battle wounds and injuries greatly increased if they did not get infection. Most of them also understood that a wounded soldier lying in a hospital bed had about a seventy percent chance of reinfection.

By noon on Monday, the eighteenth of June 1917, holding tightly to the arm of Capt. Johnson, I was looking out of my bedroom window. The 'flat', as Elizabeth called it, was on Horseferry Road overlooking St. John's Gardens. It was a pleasant apartment consisting of two bedrooms and a bath in the rear of the apartment. It fronted on to Horseferry Road; there were tall, high windows on to the street. The kitchen was like a small galley on a ship but modern with an icebox and a small kitchen stove that used gas instead of wood to cook food.

I remember telling Elizabeth that my appetite for food had not been in the least dependent on whether it had been cooked or not. Most often Canadian soldiers, Brits too for that matter, had learned to live on bully beef right out of tin cans, Tickler's apple or plum pudding, and anything else that might have arrived in a soldier's parcel sent by mail from Canada.

I quickly learned it was a really good thing that I did not have a finicky stomach because although Elizabeth had spent a lot of her young life learning to be an outstanding and caring nurse, she had not mastered much cooking expertise in the kitchen beyond making tea.

It was wartime; London's streets were filled with uniforms. Citizens of all ranks and social climates came and went along her streets, most without notice and nearly all without rancour. There were hundreds of thousands of soldiers; there were thousands of men not of military age that had sought and found work amongst London's shops and factories. The war had changed the very face of the local boroughs. Whereas before hostilities, Londoners had lived and played, those now consumed by the plots and lots of war shuffled and scuffled. A nurse in military uniform returning from a hard day's duty at the local hospital went without notice as she entered or exited her residence. Men, in their droves, came and went into and out of apartments all over London. No one even raised an eyebrow when two wounded Canadian soldiers trundled out of a military ambulance, down the street and up the stairwell into flat number four.

The next ten days seemed to melt away into hours. Hours spent sitting in a chair looking out the front parlour window or sleeping in the quiet and solitude of my bedroom. The window offered reality; the bedroom presented me with time in which I could escape into fantasy. For some time each morning and usually for an hour or so in the afternoons, I used the window to remind myself that life went on.

Beyond the glass life went on. People and horses, women and children, wagons and automobiles, all became a snake of life and traffic that wound their way up and down Horseferry Road.

I would sit there, huddled in my pain, conscious of my physical condition; trying to make reason of who and what I might be when it came time to leave the safety and sanctity of the apartment.

Time spent in my bedroom was an entirely different matter. The bedroom was the place where I had to face both myself, as I existed, and the person that I wished to be. I knew how dreadful were my wounds. Slowly, as Elizabeth taught me how to clean and wind bandages and repack the gaping hole that had been my left shoulder, I learned how hideous my beautiful body had become. My entire left arm and later the shoulder muscles and bones had been removed. The arm was amputated at a forward Casualty Clearing Station due to medical expediency and battlefield trauma. The doctor that performed that operation had been working over thirty hours without sleep or without even a break from the butcher shop that Vimy Ridge had presented to him. Later, on the hospital ship on its way to Portsmouth, the medical team had deemed it necessary to attempt to save me from the advance of infection that had spread into what remained of my shoulder bones and tissue. What remained was a sunken hole where my shoulder had been. The constant pain associated with the surgeries and the yet to be completely healed skin stretching over the wound left me in a continuing fight to control the urge to jump out of the window and end it all at the completion of the fall.

In an attempt to compensate and alleviate the pain that came and went I found myself relying on a game, long played as a child, of being someone else in some place of greater pleasure or more adventurous possibilities. You may call it day dreaming, I called it existence. For as long as I could hold fantasy as being real, I could be whole again.

In early mornings I imagined my arms held Tears in love and passion. For hours in the afternoons I would hunt the forests with my rifle and traps. Each easy prey became a beautiful pelt under the hands of Cold Dawn as she stretched and hung the marten and mink under the eaves of our lodge at Saddle Lake. For five nights I played a continuing game with Arthur as we silently crossed over the stinking trench lines to make the perfect shot on some poor unsuspecting German machine gunner.

Captain Johnson came and went. He always arrived with a large bundle or a kit bag filled with linens and food. He was a strong man with deep blue eyes that quickly filled with concern or laughter. He was tall, five foot ten at least and his drive and sense of duty kept him slim and physically fit. He had joined the 49th as a Private soldier on the very first day that it had started to recruit. He had quickly been singled out as a man with leadership abilities and soon after the battalion was assigned to the Third Division in December 1915 he had been sent off to Officer training. He had won the complete respect of everyone he led during the Battalion's first few months of initiation by fire at the Somme. I had learned soon after meeting him for the first time that just a mention of Courcelette was enough to cause deep furrows of grief and pain to carve his face into a mask that would not discuss the unspeakable carnage and loss of life the 49th had suffered at the Sugar Factory and Candy Trench.

On one day, in just minutes, Johnson had gone from Platoon Commander to Company Commander as men and officers fell in the seesaw battles for objectives with names like Regina, Sudbury, and Kenora. By the end of October 1916 the Battalion had lost almost fifty percent of its initial intake of soldiers. By then Johnson was a senior Captain with almost one year of combat experience. I had learned to trust his every word when I served with him and for him.

Now, here in London, he was the continuing reminder of what we had been and seen during our months in the trenches together. There was simply not a single solitary thing that I would not have given him or done for him if he would have but asked. He asked for nothing; between himself and Nurse Bain they were at my every turn, they cleaned, encouraged, cooked, and cajoled. He never once complained about his own badly damaged hand and he went about his day much as any completely uninjured man would have done. He inspired me to wellness and recovery.

He had come into my bedroom one early morning before I had finished dressing; I was readying myself for my hour at the windowpanes. He seemed totally relaxed, I had heard the two of them laughing and joking about what a bad cook Elizabeth was and their laughter seemed to rub off on the yellowed wall paper that encased the room which I now called 'Ward One'. He threw some clean hospital gowns at me playfully; his long legs curled up under a bedside chair as he continued to talk about news from the front and how he had taken a walk the night before around a great park filled with a lake called the Serpentine. I suppose I should not have been shocked that Johnson would have made that walk. London was still out there in all of Her beauty. It was June after all. Even in wartime, soldiers and even wounded soldiers found beauty and some sense of home as they discovered what Londoners had always known about the beauty that lay just behind some great teeming street.

Suddenly, as if a dam had broken, I began to recall and recount the wonderful days I had spent here in London in what seemed to be just a few days past. I told him how I had been selected to attend a snipers' course; everyone selected was given a free transportation warrant to almost anywhere in England and told not to come back for five days.

I spoke about how I had chosen London as my destination. I am not even sure at what part of my story telling Elizabeth had come into the room and sat, listening, by the end of my bed.

I cannot imagine now, looking back, why I thought I needed to tell the entire story, but I did. I suppose it had something to do with all the fantasies that I had conjured up while lying in that bedroom by myself, feeling sorry for myself and hiding my real soul behind the mind games I had played. I told them all about how John Edward Martin and I had agreed to share a hotel room. I banged on about how grand my very first impressions of London were; I talked to my surprise at the immensity of Westminster and the Parliament. I did not spare them any of the childish emotions I had felt when I met and got to know Sarah Ruth Middleton, the driver for a General at the British Army headquarters at Whitehall. We all laughed together at the senselessness of John Edward as he fell pants over boots for the greedy Eleanor and how she and her friends had bilked him out of every penny he carried and left him with a medical gift that kept on giving. I remember sobering only slightly when I remembered that John had been posted missing in action very early in our first engagements in France in September of 1916.

Elizabeth, always the practical one, enquired if I had kept in touch with Sarah, had we exchanged letters, or had we ever met again following our dream like nights together in a hotel room overlooking London Bridge. No, I told them truthfully, I had not written nor had I received any letters from Sarah. I remember saying that my sudden thrust into being a sniper and the fact that my only living relative had died in Canada had taken away my thirst for continued contact.

Besides that, the sheer and grinding hell of day to day killing and avoiding being killed did not seem to me to be the kind of hope and fellowship I had wanted to share with a sweet and tender heart that beat for an instant in trust that I would continue our relationship.

I did relate to them though the wonderful emotion that Sarah and I shared as we had parted. I told them how Sarah had given me her parents home telephone number saying if I called and asked for her mother and told her that the hat Sarah had ordered was ready for pick up she would know I was coming to London. I suppose I must have mentioned I kept the telephone number in my Italian Bible.

That Bible had somehow survived all of my evacuation and hospitalization along with my blood stained, all important Pay Book. Everything else I had gone to battle with, all of the covers and hoods, all of the kit and caboodle that Arthur and I had carried into our sniper's nest in front of the 10th Battalion now lay trapped and forgotten in the mud that was that battlefield. And yet, here in London, here in my bedroom, alongside of my hospital pillow and my hospital gowns were my Bible and my Pay Book. You try to imagine how many hands and eyes and hospital staffs along the pain filled road I had followed were involved in keeping my shattered body and those two documents together.

Robert James Johnson reached over my right shoulder to pick up the Bible that sat, unopened, on the bedside table next to my bed. He quickly thumbed it, opening and turning a few pages here and there, a puzzled look on his face.

"Giorgio"? He said looking up from the book that now lay open in his lap, "Do you read Latin"?

"It is not Latin", I said, a note of lightness had crept into my voice that surprised even me. "It is an Italian version of the Bible, I got it from a book shop that sold Italian books and religious articles in Edmonton Alberta". I reached out and took the Bible back from his hand and quickly turned to a page near the back where I had written Sarah's name and her mother's telephone number.

"Here it is; here is where I put the telephone number that she gave me in case I ever made it back here to London".

The room went silent with unspoken realization that an elephant had just walked into that little bedroom with just one window that looked out onto the back alley behind the apartment block we were staying in.

"No use calling anyone at that number now", I said with an edge of finality in my voice. "I am a completely different man now from what I was then". That at least was a truth that no one would dispute.

Both Robert and Elizabeth squirmed a bit in their chairs. Their eyes met and then they both quickly looked down at the floor as if in search of something which had suddenly caused the air to go out of the room.

"I would imagine that Sarah has long since moved on", I said more as if trying to fill an empty space in the conversation. "She would have had lots of opportunities to meet other soldiers since I left town and besides a pretty girl like that would have forgotten all about me the day after I got on the train to return to Aldershot".

As I remember, we tried to avoid speaking to one another for the next two or three hours, each of us busy with trying to reimagine what life would have been like had we only had enough common sense to stay at home instead of rushing off to save the world and every Brit in it.

* * *

I had awakened very early the next morning. An unrelenting sort of mood had held me all night long. The entire night had filled an eternity. My mind had worked trying to remember every casual conversation that Elizabeth and I had exchanged; when was it that we had gone from being a nurse in a recovery ward and a severely wounded patient. What, I wondered had driven a wonderful, pleasant and very attractive woman like Elizabeth to inexplicably attach herself to my cause. After all the soldiers and all the pain that she had encountered, why had she suddenly seized on me to spoon feed, coax and cajole to stay alive.

The person that I had become was only hours from certain death. My body was in shock. I had not been mindfully aware enough to eat or drink and therefore to sustain life. My shoulder had been shattered; slowly over some days, successive medical teams had tried to keep ahead of a gathering infection. By the time I had arrived on her ward, in her care, I was far too weak to care, far too far gone to understand the passion that she gathered and expended to keep my body and soul together. Over and over again my mind returned to the same conclusion; I could not for the life of me even begin to understand why Nursing Sister Elizabeth Grace Bain had made me her soul to save.

I had gone to bed early, leaving Elizabeth and Robert alone in the sitting room that overlooked the street in front of the tenement. I understood they both were very concerned about the next stage of my recovery. Elizabeth had slipped out a couple of days earlier and I knew, when she returned to the apartment, that the meeting or purpose of her business had left her troubled. She tried to smile sweetly at me when she popped her head into my bedroom to say she had returned but her eyes and tone of voice gave her away.

Robert mentioned casually the next day that he had met with someone who was part of the Canadian headquarters responsible for staff decisions affecting medical cases. He was his normal blunt and direct self.

"Seems the Canadian medical staff wants to put you on a ship and return you to Halifax as soon as you are capable of travelling Giorgio".

Robert had taken to rubbing his wounded right hand with his left whenever he was preoccupied with life in general or something needed to be worked out before he could proceed. I knew that he was due to return to active duty soon even though his next position would be in a non-combat role within the Canadian staff in here in London.

"Both Elizabeth and I would like to extend your stay in England until you have completely recovered and that would mean you should be sent to a convalescent hospital somewhere near here until you are physically better able to travel".

He closed the bedroom door quickly, and spoke in a hushed tone, one that would make sure his words did not leak out down the hallway and into the waiting ears of Elizabeth.

"The stupid bloody system has no idea what it is like to be wounded. They think that guys like you and me are just numbers that need to be pushed around until the boxes and the columns add up and then they can write some neat little note that says they have done their jobs".

He sat down on the chair close to the head of my bed. Once seated he quickly stood up again and returned to the door. He opened it slowly, peeking left and right. He seemed satisfied that Elizabeth was not within earshot before continuing. "Elizabeth has gone out on a limb for you Giorgio. Her Matron thinks she is in love with you and that she is doing all this for her own personal reasons".

He walked a tight circle, clearly agitated, all the while rubbing, and messaging his hand. He stopped suddenly, turning to me lying on my back, covered with the bed sheet, quietly waiting for the penny to drop. "I am in big trouble here Giorgio". He sat down again, putting his head closer to mine, his head drooping slightly as if the weight of his concerns was too heavy to bear for the moment. After a short pause, his eyes came up to lock with mine. His mouth worked for a second, the very words that he wanted to say seemed just too weighty to push past his lips.

"I think that I am in love with her Giorgio, can you imagine that? Can you imagine how stupid it is to fall in love with someone who is so madly in love with her job that she can not imagine herself in love with anything else"?

Oh my Dear God I thought, he could be talking about me. Does he know that at another level, at a level of gratitude and professional admiration, I love her too?

Just then a muted little feminine voice called out from the general direction of the kitchen; "Robert come quickly I think I burned the mutton joint". That was followed by high pitched words that I could not understand because of Robert's quick efforts to push back the chair he sat in.

The squeaking of his boots on the wooden floor as he pivoted to exit and the sounds associated with the opening and closing of the door completely shielded my ears from what very well could have been a very unladylike string of words centred on how incompetent she was when it came to cooking something in the little gas oven.

I remember reluctantly pushing myself out of bed with my right hand and arm. Some traces of smoke from the kitchen had already invaded the hallway and were wafting their way into my bedroom through the top two feet of the open doorway. I pulled a hospital housecoat around my shoulder, no pun intended, and was preparing to make my way to the bathroom and, from there, towards the now open sitting room window that faced onto the street below. Just then, a steady and loud knocking ensued on our apartment door leading onto the second floor hallway. The building entrance was down a greenish, grey, wallpapered hallway, to the stairwell and from there down to the main floor.

With both Robert and Elizabeth standing by to rescue whatever remained of tonight's dinner I was self nominated to attend to the visitor demanding attention at the large oak panelled door that fronted onto our hallway and separated the lives that lived within from the world of strangers that lived elsewhere.

Without knowing the consequences; without any idea of the life changing effect that my action would have, I reached down with my one remaining hand and slowly turned the door lever. The lever worked with well oiled precision, the door nearly sprung open on its own, so well balanced was the weight on its hinges.

And there, smiling sweetly, dressed in a summer weight long nursing dress, capped in a white lace bonnet with matching blue ribboned booties to help protect his skin from the afternoon sun, held and protected in the arms of his beautiful mother, was my six month old son.

* * *

Sarah Ruth Middleton's mother had received a telephone call from a Canadian Officer; at first she had refused to speak with the caller and told her butler who immediately spoke to the Lady's personal maid who in turn refused to tell the caller the whereabouts of Sarah.

Sarah, it seems, had overheard some of the conversation occurring on the phone, and intervened. The result was that after just a few minutes of waiting, Robert James Johnson was informing Sarah that a Canadian soldier she had met some time ago in London, was wounded, suffering, and recovering in an apartment not far from the Thames River, on Horseferry Road.

Sarah, after confirming the soldier's name was Giorgio Askuwheteau Costello from Edmonton, Alberta, immediately told Robert that she had spent some considerable effort over the past year trying to inform that self same Canadian soldier that he was the father of her child, Master Barton Andrew Middleton the Third.

An exchange of an invitation to dinner and timings had followed, which Sarah's entire family, including her mother and the maids, completely refused to accept when informed. The result was a huge argument and considerable acrimony which ended in much slamming of doors, finger pointing about getting pregnant in the first case, who was this Canadian soldier anyway and more raised voices and finger pointing.

Since, as Sarah later confessed, the invitation was set for only two days hence she had little time to really think about the consequences, nor had she really had any time to plan what she would say or do at this reunion with a man that even she agreed had been known on a pretty casual, albeit intimate, level.

As for Elizabeth and Robert, they had chosen, rightly or wrongly, to leave me completely in the dark, in my pyjamas and housecoat, standing at the door that they had intended to open in welcome to a stranger that I had once loved.

I had opened the door, looking for the entire world like a skeletal image of the soldier Sarah had known fifteen months before. There was a large and nasty volume of smoke and the nauseating odour of burnt mutton holding court throughout the length and breadth of the hallway. Robert's voice, somewhat raised in volume due to the fact that he had somehow managed to burn his hand on the pan holding the now blackened mutton, was echoing in the background.

Elizabeth exited the kitchen at that exact moment on her way to find some sort of bandage for Robert's arm. On becoming aware that her guest had arrived and was now standing just without the premises, Elizabeth stopped dead in her tracks, gave the smallest of shrieks, and said, "Oh Bugger". The words tumbled out on the floor and rattled around, failing to add elegance to the moment of our meeting.

Sarah, in her excitement, confusion, and sheer expectant emotion of the past thirty eight hours or so had succeeded in passing on some of her nervous tension to her child.

Master Barton Andrew Middleton the Third chose that precise and inappropriate moment to soil himself from top to bottom. He was still being held in the loving arms of the woman whose beautiful face reminded me just how much I had loved and needed her the last time I had seen her.

The remainder of the evening was pretty much a complete disaster as well. Elizabeth recovered first and took charge of the shitty situation that existed at the doorsill. The two ladies and young Barton disappeared into Elizabeth's bedroom. They did not emerge until well over an hour had transpired.

Robert and I had plenty of time to open kitchen windows in an attempt to release the remaining oily smoke from the ruin of the unserved dinner. Robert explained how he had helped himself to the telephone number I had in my Bible and gave me a short and factual rendition of the conversation he had held with Sarah including the impulsive act of inviting her over to Elizabeth's apartment for dinner. He did mention Elizabeth had not been impressed with that idea since she had previously confessed to possessing little or no ability to actually cook, serve and host such an event.

Taking advantage of the fact that the two ladies had obviously found some kindredship in the sanctity of the bedroom, in typical soldier fashion, Robert managed to produce something that closely resembled cold mutton sandwiches on day old bread. That, served with a very nice bottle of French red wine was dinner for four when the ladies finally exited the bedroom.

Elizabeth had found and offered a completely different dress to replace the one that Sarah had been wearing during the amazing demonstration of bowel emptying that Barton had displayed. Apparently the two had found ample use for hospital bandages that were plentiful because of Elizabeth's access to the same in order to provide for my daily medical necessities.

The four of us sat stiffly on hard back chairs in the parlour speaking in generalities about where we had been and what had occurred to each of us.

Robert gave a very elegant and convincing introduction to the time that he and I had served together in Belgium and France as part of the 49th Battalion. Elizabeth explained to myself and Robert that she and Sarah had time to discuss and understand the extent of my injuries and the length of time that it might take for my recovery. Sarah explained in a very few words that she had been forced to resign her position as a driver in the British Women's Army Auxiliary Corps as soon as she had confessed to her condition.

She made little if any excuse when explaining that living at home with mother was less than perfect and that she had tried and failed to locate me, the father of the child, because all she had was an address in Aldershot that had continued to return all mail sent to that address.

It was as if we were four complete strangers trying to ignore the fact that two of the people were parents to the child that I never even got to hold. Only twice that I could remember did I ever hold and capture Sarah's eyes as I tried to say something like, 'I had no idea'. I never got or at least I never took the opportunity to tell Sarah how much I had loved her all those many months before. Barton became fussy; Sarah said he was hungry and that she should return to her mother's so that she could nurse him. We promised to meet again, here in the parlour at two the following afternoon.

I never got to hold Barton in my strong right arm and I never got to look him in the eye and talk to him about the day the fox watched over the lake with me while we waited for the deer to come and drink. All that had to wait until tomorrow. Tomorrow never came.

* * *

Waiting For Tomorrow

Elizabeth, Robert and I huddled amongst the ruins of a few mean looking sandwiches that remained uneaten on the parlour table. They were sorry for the way it had turned out. I was sorry that I had not seen it coming. None of us shared a shred of confidence or pride in what had been planned as a great reunion between young lovers and their bouncing baby boy. Our heads and hearts seemed to hang in disbelief of the bee sting of events that had transpired earlier. From the moment that I had opened the door to a lovely and anxious Sarah, an oven on fire, a planned dinner ruined, a beautiful baby leaking his morning's milk in various colours of yellow over his mother's very fresh looking peach dress and himself, there seemed to be no corner of Sarah's visit that had not been filled by awkwardness or embarrassed silence.

"Wasn't she beautiful", was about all that I could add as I excused myself and went despondently alone and dejectedly sullen into my bedroom. That night I dreamed of competing wolf packs singing challenges across the valley floors separated by hills with trails that only they could navigate. Just after sunrise a loud and consistent knocking on the apartment door awakened me.

Elizabeth responded; I did not actually enter into the hallway area of confrontation but the tone and volume of the encounter was easily understood by anyone with half an ear. The visitors were the Head of Nursing from the Queen Alexandra Hospital and some senior representative from the medical staff. From what I heard it was what you might call a one-way conversation.

In very short order the visitors made it perfectly clear that someone, no names, no pack drill, had made a very serious complaint with regard to the arrangements previously agreed to by the hospital staff which had given permission for Nursing Sister Elizabeth Bain to offer and perform specialized medical recovery care within her own residence to a member of the Canadian Army.

One voice, I believed it to be the Head of Nursing herself, was banging on about how in the late part of yesterday afternoon the Head of Nursing had been called to account. It seemed, regardless of argument provided, the seriousness and the level from which the complaint had been offered could not be ignored. The 'so called complaint' had been passed to the Surgeon General of the Canadian Army in the late part of yesterday afternoon. By this morning, he, that is the Surgeon General, had decided that I, the patient, was to be returned without further hesitation or delay to the QA hospital within minutes of having been told or else. God only knows what 'Or Else' would have meant but there was an ambulance sitting waiting outside of our apartment on Horseferry Road at that very moment.

I didn't even have to worry about packing the very few items that I still possessed. With my pay book and my Bible in hand, I gave Elizabeth a hug and sullenly made my way back via ambulance to a familiar Victoria Cross winner ward and bed and hospital food.

Two days later Elizabeth was posted effective immediately to Number 7 General Hospital, in Saint Omer, France. She did get a very short opportunity to visit with me at the QA hospital; we promised to keep in touch no matter what transpired and in fact we did just that.

Elizabeth, with a large kit bag and a sailing trunk packed with personal items and clothing was on a hospital ship sailing to France within four days of being marched into the Chief Surgeon's office. There was some mention of apology offered by the Head of Nursing but due to circumstances beyond all of their control they thought it best that she quietly accept this new overseas duty without delay or comment. In her first letter to me, which I received one week later, Elizabeth related that she was on duty in casualty care in France and Robert had been required to report to Portsmouth for repatriation to Canada and subsequent reassignment, due to injuries, from his beloved battalion.

In another letter, that I received about ten days later, Capt. Robert Johnson informed me that Sarah's father had articled and worked for a firm of solicitors in Porthmadog, Wales. While there he had befriended a rather well known Englishman with the name David Lloyd George; that would be 1st Earl Lloyd-George of Dwyfor, OM PC, and Prime Minister of the wartime coalition government of the United Kingdom. Mr. Middleton, a man of considerable wealth and position within the English industrial community had decided that he would not be pleased to have his daughter associated with a wounded, untitled, other rank from one of the many Commonwealth Armies that were currently present within the territorial boundaries of the United Kingdom. His personal telephone call to the Prime Minister had raised a number of questions and suggested several workable solutions to what he saw as the problem.

The end result was an official from the office of the Prime Minister had 'unofficially observed' during a telephone call to the Canadian Army Headquarters in London that an individual or two, one British citizen and one Canadian Officer might have overstepped their loyalty and concern for the medical care of one of their comrades. Further, the Office of the Prime Minister of England suggested that the patient, namely myself, should be afforded the very best of English medical attention at a convalescent hospital near London until a suitable time and opportunity occurred which would allow my transfer to a Canadian facility.

Now then, who could argue with the logic of Mr. Middleton and the 1st Earl Lloyd-George of Dwyfor, OM PC, and Prime Minister of the wartime coalition government of the United Kingdom? The answer, apparently, was no one. The QA Hospital made immediate plans for my transfer out from under their care. The Canadian Staff made some comments about ensuring that there would be no break or detrition of my recovery process.

The Canadian Surgeon General sent a young doctor around almost immediately to assess my recovery, prognosis, and mental state. The visiting doctor thought that I was ready for immediate transfer to a hospital that could offer a higher state of orthopaedic reconstruction and care and left with the comment, "Well Corporal Costello, I have never met a man like you before. In just two months of being a patient here in England you have managed to get everyone from the Surgeon General up to the Prime Minister of England interested in your welfare".

He neither smiled nor offered his hand as he turned on his young, well polished heel, and fled the ward room, presumably to brief the Surgeon General on my readiness for return to Canada.

On the First of August 1917, I was transferred, without ceremony or so much as a goodbye, from the QA Hospital to the Royal National Orthopaedic Hospital, located in Stanmore, a part of London, in the Borough of Harrow. It was about an hour's ride by motor ambulance through busy streets filled with everything from handcarts to fishmongers.

The Royal Hospital was pleasant enough; it was to be my home for the next nearly three months. The staffs there were learning to be experts at dealing with amputations that had taken more than just a limb. Men like me who have lost a shoulder as well needed special support and training on how to live, how to look after themselves and more importantly, how to face a world filled with men with two arms and two hands who expected everyone else to work and look just like they did.

Later that same week, Captain Robert Johnson, was Gazetted in the London Times for valour and conspicuous bravery on the battlefield. His citation mentioned that although seriously wounded, he had immediately assumed command of the Battalion on the death of his Commanding Officer and had provided essential leadership to his battalion, the 49th Canadian. For his actions he was awarded the Military Cross. The Times also offered a short addendum mentioning that the newly promoted Major Robert Johnson was returning to Canada for staff employment in Ottawa due to wounds received during the lead up to the Battle of Vimy Ridge.

On the same page of the Times, amongst ten other names, was a similar citation in the name of Corporal Giorgio Costello, a sniper with the 49th Battalion who was awarded the Military Medal for conspicuous bravery and individual initiative in the face of enemy. The Citation read:

Costello, G., 43391, Corporal, "B" Company, 49th Canadian Battalion, Vimy Ridge, 1917. – From 8 until 13 April, near Vimy Ridge, Corporal Costello was in charge of a sniper party tasked with harassing and observing enemy actions originating from the area of a feature, "The Pimple". He boldly and aggressively brought his marksmanship into action during an exceptional period of four days and was credited with making over sixty kills, thus enabling the advance of other units and men of the Canadian Corps as they successfully captured the feature. His resolute courage and admirable disposition instilled confidence into officers and men of the attacking force. (M.M. (immediate) 23/7/17).

Here, in a hospital, far away from everything and everyone I knew, I was challenged to become a two armed man with only one arm. Here, in a part of London that I did not know, there were caring and professionally motivated staffs that were beginning to understand what they could add and what they could do to make my recovery and return to Civilian Street a success. But until all that happened I had a lot of work to do. I had to work with a body I no longer even wanted to touch or look at. I had to work with a mind that kept reminding me that I had no other skills other than the ones that Johnny Snake Eye had passed on to me through the urgings of Cold Dawn.

As a bitter solace, the Army had used my skills and improved my skills until I had been given a medal. An award that clearly said I could shoot and kill other human beings at a better rate and with more aplomb than the Germans could muster against me. Frankly I had one hell of a time starting to realize I was going to be an entirely different man when I finally returned to Canada and my village of Saddle Lake.

What could a hunter with one arm do to help his people feed and build and grow? How could I hold a knife to skin an animal that someone else had brought home for me? How and why would anyone ever want to look at me again in the way that they had looked at me before I left for the Army?

And as for my friendship with Elizabeth and Robert, where had that taken me? And for that matter, how about the entire first part of my recovery process, what about all that? What had started as an unbelievable dream had ended in a nightmare. I had almost pinched myself when Elizabeth had first introduced the thought that she might be able to convince the hospital authorities to allow her to provide specialized home care for me while she was on two weeks rest and 'military leave' from her place of duty. Then when I found out that she and Robert had been scheming all along to work together so that I might have an increased chance of recovery without having to worry about the possibility of re-contracting an infection while in one of wards, why I was really blown away. My entire stay at the borrowed apartment on Horseferry Road was a dream from which I dreaded to awake. And true to form, if things can go wrong they will go wrong.

In a casual conversation about having already visited London I had mentioned to both Robert and Elizabeth the fact that just over a year before I had met and fallen hard for a wonderful young British service woman. Looking back on that conversation I suppose it was fate or maybe Manitou was intervening in my life again to make sure that I had seen what needed to be seen in order for me to relate how the world was changing. But instead of being just another wonderful part of a dream that cuddled and coddled the slow process of my recovery it too blossomed and bloomed into yet an even bigger outlandish episode.

Sarah had arrived in the very midst of a domestic melt down in the kitchen. My nearly newborn son chose that moment to have an explosive discharge, which almost completely covered poor, beautiful, and embarrassed Sarah, with the resultant residue. On the plus side I must say, Elizabeth and Sarah had a great introduction and enjoyed an opportunity to discuss in detail my physical, mental and recovery state. All to no avail however. It seems that on return to her parents' home in Knightsbridge, she told them the entirety of her fears and concerns about me and my friends and they, all of them together, must have reached the conclusion that it was essential this affair be ended and ended immediately.

And then, on the 17th of August, another bizarre and straight out of the blue arrow was shot from the highest cloud, landing with a resounding impact into my hands in the form of a very formal looking letter. It was so formal that the Chief of Surgery himself with two of his attending Orthopaedic specialists hand carried the letter all the way from their offices to my bedside where I sat playing cards with three other fellow soldiers.

"Got a letter this morning Costello, I also received a telephone call yesterday afternoon informing me that it was on its way".

Colonel Randal Hemingworth, OBE, MD, paused. In his hand was a very impressive looking letter; fancy handwriting filled most of the front. The back was centered with a large and formal looking red wax seal. The Colonel was clearly more impressed than I was because I had no idea whatsoever what all the fuss was over a letter. "It seems that someone from Buckingham Palace has heard of you Costello and they intend to invite you for tea or something".

His face looked very serious and there was not even the slightest hint of a smirk. My God, I thought, reaching out and taking possession of the offered envelope, I do believe that he is serious.

"Wait", he said, "I was informed by the Commander of the Royal Flying Corps to make sure that you receive and read this letter before you open the other".

With that he reached into his left inside uniform jacket pocket and extracted what appeared to be an already opened envelope that had been addressed to the Surgeon General and the hospital itself.

Expectant faces awaited my clumsy attempt to put down my cards, hold the opened envelop against my right hip and extract the letter. It opened with a short snap and flutter; it read in part,

"I am therefore delighted to inform you that today His Majesty the King has approved my recommendation to award you the Distinguished Conduct Metal for conspicuous service whilst employed as an acting Air Observer with 16 Squadron, RFC. The Citation will read:

"For continuous gallantry and devotion to duty during photographic missions into enemy territory including one flight directly over the battlefield of Vimy Ridge. Cpl Costello, during his time as observer, had a fine record of carrying out his mission successfully. On the morning of 21 March 1917, he and his pilot took off on an operational sortie. 10 minutes after leaving their base, a German scout attempted to attack from below and out of the sight of the pilot. Costello's immediate warning and directions given to the pilot undoubtedly saved both the aircraft and the life of the crew.

On landing, he requested that he might immediately be allowed to conduct a photographic mission in another aircraft. On this being arranged, he took off and carried out a highly successful photographic mission, which in no small way improved air photographic coverage for the successful Canadian Attack on Vimy Ridge."

My mind was reeling. That was not how the whole thing had happened at all. I had been so lost in the movement and beauty of the flight that my finger pointing had been an indication of a shadow I had seen beneath us and my joy that I was now over my mates in the 49th Battalion. My mind, at the time, was filled with childish humour about what a sorry bunch of wet assed soldiers they all were while I sailed merrily above them on wings of wood and cloth.

By the time I had reread the entire letter I realized that once put in motion this medal thing was going to occur no matter how I twisted or turned. Damn, I thought, that will look nice next to my MM.

One of the attending Residence doctors had brought a proper letter opener and offered to open the letter from the Palace. Much discussion was being offered around the notion that, 'I would want to keep this envelop as a souvenir long after it was opened', and, 'It would be a shame to ruin a fine wax seal from Buckingham Palace and all that'.

To be perfectly honest, I certainly was not and I suspected that no one else in that room was used to receiving a letter from Buckingham Palace. It was a very classy and posh envelope I certainly must say. Both the envelope and the letter within were of an ivory white with a smooth velour texture and certainly of a much higher quality than I am generally used to receiving.

On the cover front were the words the '*Office of the Lord Chamberlain*' and a small return address in the upper right hand corner said '*Buckingham Palace, London*'. Inside the envelope there were even more special stationery and an expensive invitation card from the Lord Chamberlain himself stating that he had been commanded by His Majesty to invite me to attend a medal ceremony to be held in my honour, on Thursday, 25 October, 1917, at the Palace.

Well, I thought, as I read the invitation out loud to the admiring crowd that had gathered, I guess I know where I will be staying until after all this Royal stuff is over.

It took until the next morning to sort out and begin to understand the importance of having been awarded both the Military Medal and the Distinguished Conduct Metal. Not many men would have been given the opportunity to be in such a position, first flying with the Flying Corps and then, almost immediately afterwards, in action with the Army at Vimy Ridge. But, even more important, it seemed, was that my date with the King was now scheduled and obviously would not change, so therefore I could at least expect to remain in England, in one place or another, until that auspicious day.

Following morning ablutions, dressing practice, breakfast and medical rounds inspections I sat and composed a cheery little letter to Major Hugh Mills, the Squadron Commander of 16 Squadron RFC. I expressed a genuine gratitude to him, his adjutant and his officers for their for unexpected commendation which had resulted in my being awarded the DFM. I gave a brief description of my current situation and location, requesting that I be remembered to Sgt Major William Wilcox and of course to Liam Ward.

I am continually driven to remember the day I wrote that letter. I was feeling a sense of smugness I suppose. I had been there and returned. I had suffered with the men of the Canadian Corps. As with them there was something special in the knowing that the violence and sickening fear that gripped everyone was over for us now, over for good. Looking down at myself, I was sickened in spirit at what I had become, but on a completely different level there was a satisfaction that I had survived battlefields filled with hideously bloated bodies and smashed forms that had suffered even worse. I had seen them there, I had seen them dead and twisted and pawing at the dawn. But I had seen them and they, the ones that would remain forever as a part of the battlefields on which they died, they were the ones that would only be remembered. While I still drew breath I was resolved to celebrate how much I had and not lose myself in mourning the abilities I had lost.

Late summer bees filled the gardens of the Royal National Orthopaedic Hospital in Stanmore. Canadian and few other Commonwealth soldiers with very serious amputations came and went. The routine of wakening, washing, and wishing for improvement became a numbing grind that settled over me like a swan's wing covers a cygnet.

I made friends in late August that were transferred home in September. Faces I liked in September were gone by mid October. Looking back on my nine week stay I remember very little of the hours and days. I remember more of the milestones like mastering tying boots with one hand, cutting food without having a fork to hold down a difficult piece of over cooked beef, and learning to face myself naked in a mirror. You must believe me when I say that your mind might remember your youth running through green glens filled with dandelions, but your eyes tell the truth when you are as disfigured as I am.

The 25th of October marched steadily forward on the calendar that held complete and total sway over everything that happened to my life while at the Royal National Orthopaedic Hospital. I believe there was reason for some people and staff at the hospital to be almost as excited as I was. For them it was enough just to know someone called to Buckingham Palace to stand before the King of England. Looking back on the event I suppose I really should have been slightly more in awe, slightly more attentive to the ceremony; because, in truth, it really was a show unlike anything I had ever imagined or will ever see again.

On the morning of the investiture the hospital staff presented me with a brand new, incredibly well pressed and tailored Canadian Army uniform, rank, badges and ribbons properly inspected and in order. The Commanding Officer of the Hospital had volunteered to be my escort; a lovely British Army Rolls Royce and driver drove us, on a very controlled route and schedule to the Palace gates where each car in turn was checked by protocol staff. The Brigadier was whisked away by the household staff towards the Ballroom and his allocated seat. He had confessed to me that he had been through all of this before and that he never tired of the pomp and ceremony as well as the opportunity to see and be seen in such noteworthy company.

My guide, a young Cavalry Officer, part of the ceremonial staff I would suppose, bundled me, at a soldier like pace, through hallways with ceilings towering above us, around corners guarded by uniformed soldiers in all of their best shiny breastplates and swords. Along the route my cheery Captain explained the program. We were, he informed me, on our way to the Picture Gallery where I would be briefed on the protocol and schedule of the ceremony that I would soon be part of. Most of our quick march up to and into the Picture Gallery and the very detailed briefing given on how to respond and answer questions from the King goes unremembered.

However, I certainly do remember the complete shock and wonder, which struck me the moment we entered the 155-foot-long Picture Gallery. The walls were hung with silk damask and covered with what seemed to be hundreds of remarkable paintings by people that hundreds of books have been written about.

There were over a hundred of us being presented medals, many were of Orders much higher than mine, but I was the only soldier being awarded both the Military Medal and the Distinguished Conduct Medal at the same time. I was introduced to the other recipients for that honour; everyone was very kind in their nodding and smiles.

Then, in the order that we would be presented to the King, we were lined up like good little boys and herded down magnificent hallways and into what I am told is one of the most beautiful rooms in the world. To my mind, a mind that had seen nothing grander then a few hotels in London and Arras, the Grand Hall left me absolutely dumbstruck. Marble and bronze statues and a huge fireplace, astounding floral embellishments and troops of soldiers in full dress uniforms standing like the statues they guarded. And then, finally, as a group we entered together into the Ballroom. A small orchestra was hidden somewhere high above the marble floor. The room was filled with men and women all wearing formal day dress, morning coat or service uniform. All were looking very smug to be seated into their gilt chairs on raised banquettes on either side of the room. The room was filled with soft and respectful voices, some noting, or softly greeting recipients whom they recognized or escorted.

Then, as I remember, the room became very quiet, the King and a small party of aides and staff entered the room.

His Majesty, in a strong voice, asked all the guests to be seated and then, one after the other, we were called forward, the individual award was announced and the King presented each with their medal or honours.

A short and very courteous exchange between the King and the individual recipient took place and each in order then moved on to join their own party of guests or escort. When my name was called, the King broke protocol only slightly; he turned, just after he had extended his hand to meet me, and said to the assembled room:

"Corporal Giorgio Costello, a Canadian Métis from the 49th Battalion of the First Canadian Corps, deserves my special recognition for having won both the Military Medal and the Distinguished Conduct Medal for conspicuous bravery prior to and during the glorious Canadian Victory at Vimy Ridge". To which the crowd responded with a very polite and subdued applause. To me he said:

"Corporal, let me extend my most sincerely gratitude for your service to Great Britain and the Commonwealth. Your outstanding bravery has been brought to the attention of both the Queen and myself and both of us extend our congratulations as you receive these awards today. Let me also express my personal sorrow for the extent of your wounds and injury and may I wish you a speedy recovery and a safe return to Canada".

To which I replied: "Thank you Your Majesty, I will look forward to greeting you personally on your next visit to Canada".

"By Jove", he said, "What a fine thing to say"! He turned away to greet the next person in line and I, with two felt covered metal boxes in my hand turned to walk towards the Brigadier who was smiling away in the fourth row of the assembled crowd of well wishers. If everyone in this world gets one minute on the stage of glory, I supposed that time was mine.

* * *

Return to Sender Address Unknown

The Army had provided me with a well tailored uniform in which to stand before the King. The hospital staff had taken a collection from amongst the staff and purchased a fetching pair of boots, made in England, to wear with it. My medals themselves are nice enough, not that anyone except a few soldiers or airmen would be able to recognize them. I did get sincere and polite letters from the Commanding Officer of the 49th Battalion, the Brigade Commander of the Seventh Brigade, the Division Commander of Third Division and even one signed by the Corps Commander himself. All were congratulatory in nature and expressed their thanks for my service and contained words like 'proud' and 'exemplary', not one of them said, "herewith please find enclosed a cheque payable to you to cover the loss of your arm and shoulder". And as for the medals, well they mean a lot to me but if I were to sell them they would only bring the price of a few beers for the two of them.

As so often happens, it was neither meeting the King nor the award of the medals that helped to change my little world at that time of my recovery. Fate did intervene again but not because of anything I had done but rather because I happened to have been noticed for having been present in the halls of Buckingham Palace.

You may recall that I related how His Majesty had taken the opportunity to turn to the crowd of special guests and families that day to mention my awards by way of special recognition. That magnanimous gesture prompted someone from the newspaper to write a short but rather nice little article in the London Times, which stated in part:

"His Majesty was moved to mention during the ceremony the outstanding bravery of Corporal Costello, a Canadian Métis individual soldier having been awarded both the D.C.M., for conspicuous gallantry while employed as an Air Observer with the 16th Squadron RAF, and the M.M., awarded for gallantry in the presence of the enemy at the Battle of Vimy Ridge."

Now just to add a little excitement to my otherwise boring life of lying around a British hospital trying to recuperate from my wounds, someone else's eyes seized the same lines. My really good friend, the man who had worked so hard to have me rushed out of London in the first place, none other than Sarah Ruth Middleton's father, Mr. Barton Andrew Middleton the Second, read the newspaper and the very same article.

Barton Andrew Middleton was a man of action. He had heard quite enough, I would suppose, about a Métis soldier from Canada. That damned half breed was the very man his daughter claimed she loved enough to get pregnant with and that love had produced a bastard grandson who now bore not only his family name but his first and second names as well. He thought, I guess, with irritating sincerity, it was time he made another telephone call to his good friend and classmate, the Prime Minister of England, to inquire if England's medical system was doing its utmost to return wounded Canadian Servicemen back to the loving arms of their families and friends. It would seem Middleton's inquiry to the Prime Minister energized someone on his staff to follow up on that question. Since my name had once again been mentioned as an example of one of the poor suffering Canadian soldiers that would benefit from immediate transfer to the country of my birth, the Commanding Officer of the Royal Hospital was asked to expedite my transfer home as soon as practical.

But, and there is always a but, the story does not end there, even though it took some considerable time for me to hear of all of this. Later, much later, as you will see, I did find out how the over-stuffed and full of himself Mr. Middleton came home from his day of briefing the Prime Minister on how politically sensitive the entire issue of wounded Commonwealth soldiers had become in some of the Capitals like Canberra and Ottawa.

"Well", he had told Lloyd George, "the families of wounded Commonwealth soldiers are absolutely up in arms over the fact that their sons and husbands could very well be recovering at home in Canada or Australia rather than being given the opportunity to bother high ranking English Ladies and their daughters over here".

Middleton had made the mistake of gloating to his wife about how he had recently read in the Times that the very man their beautiful daughter had an affair with had been decorated by the King at Buckingham Palace. Further, he bragged, he had taken his good friend to task forthwith, and had been assured as soon as physically and medically possible the Canadian bounder would be placed on an outgoing steamer for Halifax.

"Good riddance to the bastard that stole the heart and maidenhead of our beautiful and innocent daughter. And do not forget, my darling wife, since we are doing the work of the Lord, He will help us to do it".

All this information and rightful retribution was far too much for mother to bear in silence so at the next possible opportunity she ran to the nursery to 'once again point her finger at the shame that Sarah had brought upon their good family name'.

Thinking that Sarah would be finally 'well done and over with the likes of me', Mrs. Middleton went on to hiss the entire story of the always patriotic father searching the press for news of English heroes. Well just imagine the shock and surprise he had been exposed to when he discovered that Costello was still in England convalescing at some English Hospital and even worse, had been decorated for some act or another by none less than the King himself.

"Your Father though", she said, "always a man of grace and common sense, has once again prevailed on the Prime Minister to ensure that the father of our bastard grandson will be dispatched immediately to Halifax and home to whatever slum he must have lived in".

Poor Sarah, once again raked over the emotional edge for her follies and indiscretions. Nevertheless, her father's rant and her mother's tongue had one beneficial outcome. Sarah now knew I was still alive, improving, still in England, soon on my way home. What was more, my number, rank, name, and battalion were clearly available through the London Times or by checking for Canadian recipients of medals presented by the King of England. At least, she thought, if needed, she would now know how to get a message through to Canada and the father of her son.

* * *

The sky over Liverpool was filled with November fog; shifting clouds reached down and touched the stone clad streets. The Mersey River ran brown and disinterested full of hospital ships and their cargos. Only the seagulls seemed to complain that I was finally on my way home.

I felt little if any remorse or anticipation as I wriggled and writhed up the gangplank of His Majesty's Ambulance Transport Araguaya about to embark for Halifax, Nova Scotia. The ship was a converted mail carrier turned into a floating convalescent hospital. She was painted in a dazzle camouflage pattern; her paint and railings patched and repatched by the frequent visit of paint brushes.

The Royal Hospital had reportedly fought a hard but losing battle to have me remain in their recovery program until after Christmas. The ward staff had even been so bold as to tell me that they were not sure that I was ready mentally to return to the harsh and cold reality of being a one armed man in a two armed world. Even the Commanding Surgeon came down to my shared ward room the day before my train trip out to Liverpool. He spoke of the pleasure that it had been to have met me and accompany me to Buckingham Palace. He did mention, rather as a side comment, that someone much higher placed than he seemed to think that my personal welfare would improve immensely once I returned to the care of my countrymen.

I thanked everyone, generally, for his or her professional care and personal friendships and continued to pack my few meagre belongings into my new kit bag. I never did recover the original one, which must have remained mysteriously missing forever in the system somewhere between Vimy Ridge and England. Perhaps the Prime Minister or Mr. Middleton, the two men most interested in seeing me returned to Canada would forward it to me should it ever show up.

There were eight Canadians, including myself on our way from the Royal. We were called an invalid parade but believe me when I say it was not a parade at all. Along the way, from many of the different hospitals and recovery homes, another five hundred and ten patients joined the little stream, all bound for Halifax. At about eight in the morning all, including myself, were taken from the hospital train in one large group and we were pushed, helped, limped, and struggled to get up the gangway and into our 'amputee ward'. Some of the soldiers that were missing legs proudly marched, to the best of their individual abilities, using canes to aid their shattered bodies. Recently fitted prosthetics appeared ill fitting but at least they allowed proud soldiers to make their way up from the dock side into the coal smoke scented ward rooms that awaited their arrival.

A spectacle of mechanized and horse drawn ambulances had by now drawn up, tens deep, each awaiting their turn to disgorge their cargo of blinded, blistered, maimed, gassed, shell shocked, tubercular, and mentally ill Canadian soldiers. My dear God, I thought, as I struggled on my own to gain the main deck greeting party, aren't we just a pretty kettle of fish. One by one, nearly 500 hundred of us, all of whom had been physically fit, handsome and optimistic young men, struggled down the stairways, gangways and ladders.

All of us had made at least one other cross Atlantic trip. All of us had come to England from Canada so everyone had the common experience of having been soldiers on board their troop ships.

On the Araguaya we were reintroduced to the language of sailors and men who made their living sailing on ships. Floors became decks. What land lubbers would call hallways became companion ways. The new vocabulary assailed the ear and the mind. Signs referred to holds and hatches; we walked through bulkheads into compartments and cabins. Saloons were not for drinking in and there were fore and aft gangways; there was a forecastle and mess decks. Some men were assigned to quarters, others to wards. There were skylights and no lights at all. There was so much to learn and so much to remember and some of us had so many wounds and problems that our minds would not allow us to give even a little shit about learning what to call a door or a wall.

Many if not most of us, before we were ground into invalid soldiers, had suffered and sustained months of facing death without blinking. Artillery fire had been a constant fact of life; snipers, food poisoning, frost bite, infections from lice and vermin bites had slowly but surely taken some minds and turned them into a crooked pot of sharp edged ledges on which sat and sang their very worst fears. From having been the sun warmed harvest of Canada's very best and fittest, here we swam on the Liverpool quay, a twisted lot of men who had put our lives on the line and had lost. Lost and for some, lost to the point of never ever again being sane enough even to sign their own names.

Were we ready to return to Canada? Even more important, was Canada ready to receive her wounded sons back into her arms? Ten days at sea would test a saint. Two more weeks in a Canadian convalescent hospital in Halifax or some other city and then the long train ride home awaited each and every one of us. And we hadn't even set sail yet.

It took over a day to load and prepare the Araguaya for sailing. Finally, those of us who were able walked up to stand at the rails and watch the ship's hands release their grip on land. We churned our way slowly, cautiously out and into the Mersey River. I had gone down to sort out my bed space and meet with my fellow passengers before we met up with our British destroyer that would escort us out to sea where we would join up with three other ships also on their way to Halifax. I will make no attempt to hide that every soldiers' eye was filled with the unseen horror of what would happen to them if we were unfortunate enough to be ambushed by a U-boat anywhere along our long and salty 10-day sail.

Almost as soon as we started our journey on the 2nd of November, the crew began the slow but necessary 'life boat and emergency exercises'. It took hours to acquaint most of the passengers, disabled men alike, how and where to gather, who would be in charge, how the crew would get them into lifeboats and where their individual lifeboat stations were located. At the end, without ceremony, the psychiatric cases were escorted back to their locked and secluded ward on the lower deck. Poor bastards I thought, as the remainder of us made our way to our beds, their return trip would be a lot different than the one that carried them triumphantly to England and the killing fields of France.

Wind and waves pulled and pushed at the sides of our little ship as we rounded the coast of Northern Ireland and turned our bow towards the open sea. The next ten days certainly could not be classified as a holiday.

Men were constantly sea sick. Those that wrapped themselves in heavy blankets and slickers and braved a walk or a short stop in the lounge chairs on the promenade deck soon found themselves soaked to the very core.

The small troop of Nursing Sisters was run ragged trying to keep up with bandage changes, new bumps and bangs due to collisions with hard metal walls and normal routines.

It was late at night on the 10th of November before someone reported having seen the Sable Island light. The weather improved as we approached Halifax. The ship was able to radio our casualty list. That at least would give the shore based authorities time to arrange seats on trains or beds in hospitals for the sorry looking lot that we had all become.

I was on deck with many of my new acquaintances as we reached the approach to Halifax. The huge submarine nets that stretched out from McNabs Island to Point Pleasant Park had been opened to allow us to sneak through and into the harbour. A pilot came aboard some time later as we became just one of the many other ships coming or going through the narrows.

At near noon on the 12th, tugboats alongside Pier 2 nudged us in and we were once again secured to Canada.

Almost immediately the parades of disembarking soldiers started to leave the ship. Those with infectious diseases were whisked off to the Halifax Infectious Diseases Hospital. The boys going on to New Brunswick, Nova Scotia and Prince Edward Island were next. Then a large group of walking wounded made their way to a waiting passenger train that was sitting in her steam waiting to start a cross Canada dash letting soldiers return to the cities of their recruitment.

Finally, some others and I were herded off into ambulances and buses on our way to the Halifax Camp Hill Hospital. Each of us would have a different schedule.

I would spend another nearly two weeks with a superb group of doctors and staff. They really seemed concerned about the fact that so much of my left shoulder and upper body bone and muscle had been removed during the four or five operations I had gone through in order to save my life from the infection which nearly claimed me for its own.

Christmas was coming. The staffs were trying to get everyone they could out of Halifax and at least closer to individual homes and families. I didn't even bother to tell them that none of that really mattered to me. The truth was, no matter how long it took them to finally release me for the train trip back to Edmonton, no one would be there to meet a half breed with only one arm.

* * *

The Legend Ends The Legend Begins

And so, as I first wrote at the very beginning, "I was starting near the end", and we are nearly there now. At the very beginning I described how I had departed England as I had arrived, on a ship without sails. In those days being a soldier and living with soldiers had been the determining factor in my life. During both my coming home to Halifax and my going out to Portsmouth, the ships that carried me had also transported hundreds of other Canadian soldiers. On both legs of my sea adventures the ships had been old and near the very end of their sea going lives. On both of the crossings the Atlantic had been ploughed and raked by heavy winds which whipped the surface into long, continuous furrows that pounded on the steel walls of our below decks quarters. But that was pretty much where the similarities ended.

On the voyage over, from Quebec City to Portsmouth, the soldiers had been young and whole and filled with the wonder youth imparts to those who cannot know the future. The returning ship was filled with red crosses and broken soldiers with broken bodies and shattered spirits. Many of us had been washed in and stained by the despair and anguish brought about by the intimate knowledge one acquires when introduced to hell incarnate.

So powerful had been the pain experienced in the past that many of us struggled to face what the future held for us. Only a few had hope; on the far right of the scale only a very small number of us could expect family support and the resources through which one could imagine returning to some sense of normalcy. Now turn and see, the other end of the scale where some were so shattered even medicine and a loving family could not offer a licence to hold much hope. And finally, as it always is in real life, in the middle of the scale there were a number of soldiers, myself included, who had nothing else to cling to except our own strength of imagination and courage. We, all of us, every single soldier that served, had understood on signing that we were prepared to give everything we had, up to and including our very lives, in the service of King and Country. Here then we stood, the wounded and the mentally anguished; here we stood about to become plain and simple citizens again. We had done our duties; we had stood our ground and taken our chances. Now, as it always is for the proud and unbowed, it was up to us as individuals to find, secure, and redefine our places in the society that we wanted to reengage.

It was almost two years since I had travelled from Edmonton to Valcartier and then to Quebec City by train. Those trains had been filled with youth, energy, optimism; the trains themselves had spread hot coals and steamy expectations of adventure. Just like 'The Tale of Two Cities', these were the very best of times. But my return to Edmonton had been the other side of the coin. I returned to Edmonton in a train filled with wounded and damaged men in bandages and dressings. We were the ones who had suffered more than we had even imagined could befall anyone. In comparison to the beginning, the ending was the very worst of times.

There had been a sizeable crowd of people at the Edmonton Canadian National Railroad station as our train pulled in. The Army had sent telegrams to advise family members of the imminent arrival of their son or husband or loved one. The people meeting that train knew it was a hospital train; some would have even known the extent of injuries the soldier they were waiting for had experienced. Some of these soldiers, not unlike myself, had been in the medical chain for some time already. Many others and I had been wounded in April; seven months had passed since we had transitioned from warrior to wounded. Letters had been exchanged; the truth would be discovered at the meeting. But those that waited knew the edges of reality. Most of those waiting for the train were respectfully and quietly anticipating their loved one to be carried or assisted from the hospital cars.

The train had stopped; the engine sat lifting her skirts of steam to show the power and beauty of her design. A voice said we could disembark. I stepped into the commotion of words from the crowd; silent eddies of steam from the engine and the gathering darkness of an late, snow filled Alberta autumn were lined up to add to the drama of arrival home.

I was alone amongst hundreds of other soldiers and unassisted as I had been on my departure. I was returning to the place I had departed from almost two years before but everything I knew then, everything I had been then, had changed. I was returning however I was not the same man that had departed. The war had changed not only who I was but also what I was.

I could feel waiting eyes following me as I obeyed signs pointing to 'Walking Wounded Report Here'. A man, deeply sheathed in an expensive looking wool coat, had pushed his way forward and stood in my way. There was something in his manner and dress that set him apart from the others in the waiting room. He wore a dark, stylish homburg hat, which had acquired of late a lot of admiration amongst the well heeled of Europe. His skin was pale and shallow like someone who spent little time outdoors. In his hands he carried a large camera and a notebook, a nameplate pinned on his collar said, 'Edmonton Bulletin'.

"You look like an Indian". He said as he suddenly realized I might not be one of the white soldiers he had been waiting for. "Are you an Indian? "Where are you from? What unit are you from"? He was aggressively standing in my way, blocking my advance; I could feel my own bile rising to the occasion.

I turned slightly, pushing out a little with my right hand in an attempt to go around him.

"Wait"! He exclaimed, almost as an order. Again he turned as I had turned; there was no way through or around him without being equally as rude or assertive.

The crowd began to slowly push forward; some of the stretchers were being unloaded. These were ordinary people, mothers and fathers, sisters and brothers and maybe even friends awaiting the arrival of a loved one. Their clothes and manner reflected what Edmonton was, a working city with a widely mixed cultural base of recently arrived immigrants from Europe and Great Britain. The curious struggled for a look; waiting families pushed to find the heart they had been waiting for.

I stopped my attempt to continue and turned to face him. My initial impulse had been to be polite and accommodating. He could have the very best of intentions. We soldiers were a news item, not one that happened every day I guessed. I sought his eyes, trying to establish a contact, a rapport. He was scanning the crowd, his attention drawn towards bigger game than the one he had trapped behind his bulky frame and aggressive stance. He had cold, ice blue eyes that instantly expressed the surging energy of a man with a short time frame to capture what he wanted and then to move on to some other part that he had to play.

"Do you really care who I am or are you just here for a story"? I had quickly realized he did not care who we were or why we were on that train; to him we wounded soldiers only represented an opportunity for a headline, a few lines in tomorrow's paper, nothing more. I tried to keep my tone unemotional and frank.

"I am from here; I was born in Edmonton". His eyes never even wavered from the task he had assigned them which was to locate someone with a story that he could use. Undaunted I continued, 'I enlisted in Edmonton and if I have any real family left they are here in Edmonton. What do you want to know? How was the war? Where was I wounded? How long did it take the ship to cross the Atlantic? What do you want to know"?

Other walking wounded pushed past, some with nurses, some with families who had found them from amongst the many. His eyes followed them as he searched faces for a story he could use.

"No", he said, without even looking at me, "I was looking for someone else, an Englishman or at least a white man". He made no effort whatsoever to hide or disguise the cultural contempt in his voice. Now it was his turn to attempt to push away from me, to find a new vantage point not soiled by my presence.

I had tried hard to anticipate my coming home. My home had changed but then again, so had I. The army had provided me with an arena in which I had learned a lot about myself and even more about the world I lived in. I had come home with a sort of confidence that I had paid my dues; the world would accept me for who I was and just look and see what I was. Even though I knew no one would be there to meet me still I held a strong hope everyone there to meet us would show a general acceptance for what we all, as a group, represented. All of us were Canadians. All of us were returning wounded from one of greatest battlefields of the war. Surely, I had thought, just our being together in one place, all wearing the same uniform and bandages would mark us as equals amongst equals.

I could no longer swallow the resentment I felt. I pushed my chin into the journalist's face with a firmness and resolve he could not ignore.

"My grandfather was an English man who called himself a gentleman. Some gentleman! He got my grandmother pregnant and abandoned her and his new born child in Lac La Biche. My father was a white man from this very city. He wasn't a gentleman either, he abandoned my mother when she was pregnant and carrying me. He left my mother without money or hope.

I am told he bragged about selling my mother to his white man friends before he drank himself to death. I am a half-breed soldier returning home wounded from the battle of Vimy Ridge. I may be the first man from my family that did not abandon anybody, not even Canada, when they needed my help. Why don't you write a story about that"?

The journalist was a big man with the soft hands of a lady and the hard eyes of a cynic. There was arrogance in his manner that reached out like an unprovoked slap in the face. Roughly, he put his hand on my hand pulling it away from his coat front. He leaned forward so that his hiss and hatred could be close enough to scar my memory.

"Listen", he derided, "no one wants to read a story about a fucking wounded Indian no matter where you are from or what you have done".

I stepped back in utter revulsion; he pulled his camera closer to his body and turned into the crowd. I stood in shock staring at his disappearing back. It took a moment to realize just how alone and isolated I was. I was not a returning soldier as all the rest of the soldiers here were; I stood surrounded by fellow wounded soldiers and the faces of their families but I had returned as a wounded Indian. These fellow passengers were strangers now that we were on the railroad station platform. My service had changed nothing. They were white Canadian soldiers I was just a half-breed.

Like the sailboat I had watched which had lost its way on the River Thames, I had lost the wind that had driven my hopes. I had lost the energy of purpose that had lain sheltered in my soul.

My eyes filled with tears; my heart swam in the panic of despair. I could no longer see to read the signs I had been following. It was then, as if the Mighty One had touched me, I saw the truth.

The truth was grandmother had been right all along. My grandmother knew and she had told me I was the 'Askuwheteau'. Grandmother's words reminded me Manitou had appeared to her and told her I would go out into the world again. I would go out and see with my eyes; I would see the world as it was and only then, through my eyes, could the Creator know the way the world had changed.

I had gone out alone just as the Askuwheteau had gone out. I had walked from Lac La Biche to Edmonton. I had seen, first hand, the way the white man lived. I had seen the troubles my people lived with in Whiteman's villages. I had joined the Canadian Expeditionary Force as a soldier and I tried to become like all of the thousands that had done so. But being a soldier does not change who you were, it only impacts what you have done. But through the Army, with the Army, by being part of the Army, I had ridden on the great steel rail and saw a thousand villages and rivers that did not have Cree names. My journey made me understand that Lac La Biche was not the center of the universe. It made me understand that the Nation of Cree people were only one of many great nations which Manitou had created.

It was then, at that moment, I started to understand the entirety of what I lived through over the two years I had been away. I lived with and watched the white soldiers in their army camps. I became one of them. I ate what they ate and I dressed as they dressed. I trained with and became a soldier with them. Together we laughed and sang and shouldered our way onto the dockyards. The sounds of our heels marching together up long streets and into the waiting harbour made large crowds cheer our youth; so sure we were of victory. Together as brothers in uniform we floated on ships without sails. Ships that carried us to England where we learned to live with death. From army camps filled to overflowing we Canadian youth sailed again and rode trains together into lands so strange and far away only the Great Manitou knew of them and the languages spoken in them. I watched hundreds of my new friends die in the hell they called Vimy Ridge. And like Askuwheteau before me I had flown above the land of Europe. I saw the battlefields as Askuwheteau had seen them; battlefields that were twisted, broken, smashed and tossed by nations of white men now buried in those self same fields.

I had seen with my own eyes the death and destruction war brought to those people and their villages. Indescribable muddle and confusion, individual bravery and self sacrifice, all these things had marched past my eyes and while watching them I had learned to think, thank God their lot is not mine as I slunk past on my way to some hell that I would try to control. I had witnessed countless beasts of burden so overworked by constant hauling and pulling that when their drivers stopped beating them they simply sank into the mud and grime that surrounded them and slept without even a hint of the fear of death.

I had been wounded, lost a wing and could never fly again. But even after all of that I had a purpose unfulfilled. Because I needed time to heal, Manitou had sent me to know the land and village where my Grandfather had built his nest. It was there I learned how much pain, hate and prejudice filled the hearts of his English family who had lived before me.

Now I was nearly home again; home in Alberta. Again, the Great Mystery reached out and provided a lasting and knowing lesson. This journalist, this self centered Canadian had no interest whatsoever in who we were as a Cree Nation. The journalist only represented a great mistake I had made, a mistake that only I was responsible for. I had thought my decision to travel into the crucible of war, to reach into and hold a weapon in the name of the British civilization, would make a difference to who and what I was.

It was clear to me now. I heard the very word of Manitou, the word 'NO' resounded loudly on that rail station platform. Then softly, like my Grandmother Cold Dawn would speak to me when I was still a restless child; I heard, in my heart, the truth as it was spoken.

"You have not learned what I, the Great One would have you know".

No one, no one except the Spirit would ever hear the story of my travels. I stood there on the station platform; my heart filled with the knowledge that Manitou already knew everything I carried in my heart and in my words.

The Great One knew the pain that comes from knowledge. The same pain that comes from knowing what war had shown me, took away those words from my lips. Where there had been hope there now existed a bitter truth. It was the truth of who I was now compared to what I had been when I left Lac La Biche. This final piece of truth came crashing down on me like a fire stone falling to earth from a night darkened sky.

Tears blinded me until I could not see. Words were ripped from my tongue. I had become the Askuwheteau as he had been in the 'Box Full of Tears'.

I stood on the railway platform until a soldier from my train reached out with the only good hand he had. Taking my arm, he led me down the platform. At the far end of the station building there was a small group of Army Staff, some medical nurses, onlookers; all gathered around a short line of tables filled with boxes marked with various signs. We soldiers stood together, in silence, until the hospital and military staff asked us to line up and present our medical papers and identifications.

Every soldier carried a file; in those files were words recording where they had been and what they had done. Every soldier had a different file; some files were handed to doctors or nurses standing waiting. My records, the records of my travels, were quickly examined and put into a box. The box was labelled, "No further treatment required". My file was the only one I saw to go into that box. Someone at the next desk spoke.

"You are a veteran now; Canada will give you money every month. Here are instructions on how to apply for your pension".

And so it was, desk after desk, until we reached the end of the line. When the people at each desk were finished saying everything that needed saying they would turn to the next soldier in line and repeated those same things he needed to know. As I stood in the line, shuffling forward, one desk after the other, I already knew all the information and questions that the person at the next stop would ask. The same shuffle forward, the same listen to the words being spoken, soldier after soldier. A few of the wounded were led away or carried away to waiting medical ambulances. Some others, a few others, the walking wounded like myself, were told to go away to their homes or local hotels; we were told we should be filled with hope during our weeks of recovery or release. Some were given schedules of when and where to report for further medical treatment and training.

Someone said to me, "Your amputation has healed well; there is nothing more we can do for you. You are free to go home". The papers they handed to me said I was cured and would not need to go into the hospital again. I was told I should report back after two weeks and the Army would arrange for me to sign my release papers. They gave me the address of an office in Edmonton where I should report. They said I could wear civilian clothes. They gave me some money and said do not forget to pick up my kit bag. Their job was done for the day or the night, it depends I suppose on what you think their job was. Mine, my job, my new job was to become a civilian again, a Canadian again, a half-breed again. All that becoming like I was, like a circle, was just beginning.

Someone came, a younger lady with auburn hair, and took my hand and led me down a long corridor into a room filled with the smells of coffee and real beef. A man said I could have as much food as I wanted. An older lady with little hand written tag pinned to her sweater smiled at me and said I should try to relax and enjoy my family. Some women walked amongst us and brought us more of the drinks and food that were piled high on the tables. A few waiting families were gathered around their soldiers; many were smiling now; the fear of what they would find in their soldier had now been faced. I could see the pain they felt for the man they loved but I could also see the anxiety washing away in the soap of hope and the future. Here and there the smallest sounds of laughter escaped from the room.

Of all the others I was different; I alone was different from all the rest. Only I was the Askuwheteau; that and the fact that I was lost and in pain made me different from the rest. I was a half-breed Indian without any family and nowhere to go. The others were white men with homes and families with soft hearts waiting to hold them until they were well again. No one came and talked to me, no one smiled and said, "Welcome home soldier".

I had never felt so utterly alone; even in the deepest forests of Alberta where I spent my youth I had wolves to watch over me. Now I had no one, not even myself, who had any love or kind thoughts for me at all. I stood up from the table where I had sat not knowing where to go or what to do. My mind was a fog of pain; somewhere deep inside my head there was a presence, a hand, a pressure, reaching out and taking all of the light and breath away. I remember stumbling out of that meeting room. I found and shouldered my kit bag, which had been piled in a heap of hundreds of kit bags just like it.

Without knowing I had a plan at all I realized I had made my way across the station platform and out through the wide-open doorways. The area of the station was just as I had remembered it. A wide road and large parking lot stood out as I exited. I could see the grain elevators standing alongside of the tracks on the west and behind the station a large chimney continued to spew cinders and smoke into the surrounding neighbourhood. The uneven sidewalk represented the streets of Edmonton and life as it was on that day. I could not focus. I only knew I needed a place to camp, a quiet corner where I could awake the next morning and find time to push the edges of where to begin the days ahead of me.

I took my first few steps out into the night, the cruelty of the evening jabbed me with its cold fingers. The weight of the kit bag over my only shoulder and the bulk of a suitcase scraping against my right leg seemed like chains meant to impede my progress. Nothing seemed to make any sense. I had been away and everything in my life had changed but nothing here had changed. I had left from here as a healthy half-breed man and I had returned as a white man in an empty shell. I had stepped onto a train that had taken me to Valcartier, a man with clear eyes, and two strong arms; I had returned home broken with a mind filled with horrors of what I had seen and done.

When I had departed Edmonton it seemed as if there was not anything I could not do. Now, it seemed as if there was very little that I could do. I had departed as a complete man and returned as a man with one arm and one hand. What would Alberta do with a half-white man without any skills or white friends? What would a half-breed Indian do with a mind filled with tears and only one arm with which to hold a rifle or a knife?

I had stepped off the train that brought me back as a man with no sense of purpose, with no understanding of who I would be in the future.

A gloomy and downward wind pressed hard upon my every fibre. In my present state it seemed clear that Askuwheteau could now return to the empty box that once had been so over filled with youth and unimagined pleasures. The box that lay before me was empty, dark, and careless. I had the feeling my body would slowly become a torrent of tears. I knew that there would be tears enough to fill a box.

I became possessed by the need to get out of that station. I had to leave this place behind me and find some abode where I could cleanse myself, become myself, put some frame around what my life would mean in the future. First, above many things, before I flowed away in self pity and sorrow, I had to write my story and put it into a box. It was the box I intended to leave behind when I left this life to join my grandmother, Cold Dawn.

Alone in the uniform of a Canadian soldier, unaided and unique amongst every other Canadian citizen walking the streets of Edmonton that night, I turned away from the railway station and walked into the night. Barely aware of why or where I stumbled under the awkward weight of my luggage without sense of direction through a large stretch of concrete parking lot. On my left a grain elevator stood over the streets below casting it's tall attendance through the streetlights. Cars and trucks fiddled and farted, this way and that; nothing beckoned or pointed a way to turn. A nearby hotel with a small dirty sign above some broken steps leading to double doors that needed painting offered a refuge.

My mind cried out for silence; my body cried out for rest. I lurched, like a crab with only one claw, carrying my heavy kit bag into the hotel lobby. I had over a hundred dollars in my jacket pocket. No one would decline a room to a soldier with money.

The man behind the desk only asked that I sign my name to the Hotel register. He pointed the way to a stairway leading to my room. He did not offer any information about breakfast, dining room, or other services that they provided. He did take my ten-dollar bill and he told me that would secure five nights lodgings; clean linen every second day, and no room guests. I remember nodding my head and turning to seek the sleep I so desperately needed; I did not tell him that I was an Indian or that I still had my beautiful German pistol in my kit bag.

* * *

I went up two flights of stairs and opened the door to a rented room that still had the smell of the last one hundred people that had slept there. A twin sized bed occupied one corner. A small bedside table supported a Pequegnat clock that had long since lost its ability to either tick or talk. A large clothes closet with an open door yawned at me; there were only two hangers and they were bent and malformed. A small area rug had been thrown on the floor in front of the bed and the cleaner must have thought that it would straighten itself to be in line with the remainder of the furnishings. Only the two pillows on the bed seemed new, that was because neither had a pillowslip.

For a while I sat in the only chair my room contained; it was an old Hudson's Bay special, scratched, sway legged and threatening to collapse under even my modest weight. The near winter night had fallen in on the street lamps. Snow dusted an empty street; the parking lot stared back from behind the Hotel front sidewalk. Two men dressed in long coats, their breaths trailing like scarves behind them leaned into the windy street and disappeared into the edges of dark shadow that lay beyond my view. I threw my kit bag and my suitcase into the corner and peeled off my travel worn uniform. The uniform formed a small, wool smelling pile of yesterday at the end of my bed. I would never need to put that uniform on again. I was an Indian again, I would have to buy new clothes that better suited what I intended to do in the weeks that followed.

Naked and shivering in the coldness of that hotel room I sat behind the window and reviewed my options. I had no problem being who I was now. The Army saw me as someone who had served and now that service had ended. Nearly seven hundred thousand men and women had served or were still serving Canada in uniform. That is more people then I could count if I sat in my hotel room and did nothing but count for a whole week.

My soldier days were over now that I was here again. Tomorrow I would be a veteran, a veteran that would get a pension, and if needed, medical attention. Veterans Affairs saw no requirement for them to be involved in my life and frankly nether did I. My encounter with the newspaper journalist had seared my mind with indelible ink. He saw me as nearly everyone in Canada would see me. I was just a returning wounded veteran without a past or a future. I was Askuwheteau, a legend without a story. I was a half breed Indian from Saddle Lake. I had neither treaty rights nor Whiteman's rights. I had a Veterans Affairs pension, some memories, and a handful of medals. What I did from here on in was up to me. The truth became clear to me as I stared at the walls of the dingy hotel room I had hired as a hole to crawl into and hide. My problem did not rest with what I had done or how I had served. I had served my country well, I had served my country in good faith, and the other soldiers around me had been happy that I was there at their shoulder.

No, my problem was not with the Army. My problem was not with Veterans Affairs. My problem was that I was neither a treaty Indian nor a white man. Now that I was out of uniform I was a nobody in a country where being white was the only thing that people didn't notice.

If I would have had a bottle of whiskey I would have drunk it and pissed in the corner of the room in just about the same place where someone else had seemed to have done recently. Since I did not drink and did not have such a luxury I carefully pulled the blankets up over my left side, the side with a gaping hole where my shoulder had been, and without any hesitation I slept as if I had died. And in some small way, the person that I was before, the soldier who had come and gone on trains from Edmonton to the East Coast of Canada and returned really did die in that lumpy bed.

I slept in until well past eight the next morning. When I awoke I was a different man than the one that pulled those blankets over a wounded shoulder. When I awoke I could not even remember anything about how my life had been while I was in the army. Those days, all of those days, just seemed to be lost, I did not know where I had put them, and I was not sure that I would ever want to find them again.

* * *

Unravelling the Wind

I spent the first three days of my new life learning a lot of up-to-the-minute things. I walked the streets of Edmonton looking into windows that lined the main streets marvelling at how many different kinds of articles there were hidden behind the windowpanes. Hundreds of people were hidden in plain view as they opened doors that were closed and closed doors that were open. There were entire storefronts with windows filled with women's clothes and some with just women's hats and gloves. Edmonton was not London and Jasper Avenue was not Regent Street but nevertheless, the city had certainly responded to having fewer people and more money than there were before the war.

I made three visits to the Hudson's Bay Company store; my first buying spree must have been done with my eyes closed. I was a man with a purpose and a pocket filled with dollars. I had paid pretty close attention to what the white men were wearing on the train we had arrived on. I had sat looking out of the hotel window for most of the first morning just observing how people looked and what they wore. On exiting HBC I was just another man bending into the winter wind.

The street was filled to overflowing with a wind that climbed walls and played games as the tumbling snowflakes assembled and rolled along Jasper Avenue. Two hours of trying on and buying boots, underwear, socks, pants, sweaters, shirts and two different weights of coats and scarves had slowly transformed the outward me into someone that could be as lost in a crowd as everyone else was in the downtown winter shortened daylight.

Drivers of horse drawn wagons paid me no attention at all; the drivers of the conveyor belt of streetcars and automobiles paid not the slightest attention to me as I relentlessly strode from corner to corner looking for wool or cotton that would hide me from myself.

At noon I joined a small band of sullen and cold men in a small but cozy diner. I marvelled at how good the beef was, soaked in real gravy with a heap of potatoes on the side. I struggled to cut the steak with one hand but no one offered to help or for that matter even looked up from their plates. I had a lot to learn about being who I wanted to be.

A very short streetcar ride took me to a door that I had knocked on before. Nothing had changed on the street that I had sought all those many months before. The very same brass bell and the very same bronze door handle pushed out into the space between me and the rooms beyond. Father Luciano Capono, his soft, feminine face and hands, both showing their surprise at my appearance, answered the door.

"Father Capono", I said, offering my right hand, "How nice to see you again, almost two years isn't it"?

His mouth had fallen open in surprise to see me standing there; his first impulse had been to offer his hand but surprise and suspicion recoiled through his body as he withdrew his hand.

"Do I know you"? Was the best he could muster at the moment.

"Askuwheteau, Father", I said, pushing my way around his narrow frame, my right arm pulling him around with me as I boldly stepped over the hearth and strode, my arm around his shoulder, towards the comfort of the drawing room I remembered just through the foyer and past the gloom of the hallway that awaited our footsteps. "I need your help again Father and I will not take no for an answer".

My plan was to give him no room to wiggle, no room to step into the 'priestly world' of being there without being there at all. My memories of being a child in the Saddle Lake Residential School had filled in every possible wrinkle that he could use to escape my need and intention. He was trapped like a marten that I remembered dining on with Tears not all that long ago. A Tear was gone, the marten was no more, and poor Father Capono was taking deep breaths like a man with a heart condition.

Without hesitation and without giving up an ounce of the advantage of surprise that I held at that moment I pushed him firmly but with purpose towards a large, soft, and overstuffed chair I had remembered filling a corner in a large but private room just off the main hallway. We two had sat there one morning after descending the stairwell leading from the private quarters allocated to the three or more priests who comprised the Bishop's staff in the Catholic Archdiocese of Edmonton.

"Sit down Father, I have a long story to tell you about the travels that the Bible you gave me has taken". Slowly, almost as if a shadow had passed over the soft and self indulged life he lived, a recollection of my visit and his impulsive gift of an Italian language Bible must have swum into his mind. "Ah yes", he said, a new light pressing out from his inquisitive eyes, "Ah yes, now I remember, the boy that slept with a knife in his hand".

I stood, slowly and deliberately in front of him, centring both his chair and his eyes. I wanted to watch his face and his expression as I undressed in front of him. Without any haste, without any inhibitions, I performed the act that I suspected he had asked many young boys and men to do during his years of priesthood.

I started with my shoes and I ended with my underwear until I was completely and unashamedly naked in front of him. Not once did he take his eyes off me, not once did he exhibit, not even the tiniest hint of lust or passion. He managed to keep his face immobile, expressionless, only his fingers gave him away. His hands gripped the sides of the soft upholstered chair so tightly that his fingers, up to the end of his fingernails, had disappeared into the material. Not once did I ever touch nor did I remove the beautiful, brand new skinning knife I wore, in a scabbard, on a small belt around my now naked waist.

The afternoon sun had broken out behind the parlour window and it must have streamed in behind me to form a bit of a backdrop between my now mutilated but still physically fit frame. Not a word had been exchanged between us until I started to talk.

"Two years ago I came to you as a young half breed boy wanting to join the army. I know you remember my coming here and I also remember the way you looked at me as you pretended to be interested in helping me enlist in the Canadian Expeditionary Force".

His eyes never left mine, his attention was no longer a sexual thing; real and palpable fear had fallen over his face like a like a tourniquet on a femoral artery. "I was not your normal Indian boy then was I Father"? I paused to let my words sink in, he was starting to squirm a little in his seat wondering where all this was going to lead.

"I needed your help, the kind of help my Grandmother Cold Dawn had asked her priest at Saddle Lake to arrange. Do you remember getting that letter Father"?

I leaned slightly forward, staring hard at his eyes. I wanted to make him squirm in the same way he must have made tens and tens of young Indian boys squirm on those occasions when he forgot his priestly vows and crossed the line from being a priest to being a predator.

"I am not your normal Indian man today either am I Father? All of your young boys would have had two arms and two hands and you would have thought them very pretty I suspect". Some of my disgust had started to leak out of my voice like shit finds a way to escape from even the very best fastened diaper.

His eyes had widened. His face had grown pallid in the shaded room behind the white lace curtains, though opened, partially covered most of the west facing window. For at least a minute I defiantly stood there, only a few yards in front of him, daring him to deny or offer some plausible excuse.

"Well as you can see Father I am no longer a pretty boy. A Canadian soldier accidently shot me in the upper part of my left arm just as the battle for Vimy Ridge was closing. Our medical system fought for nearly two months to keep me alive and somehow Manitou and maybe the spirit you call God found reason to keep me alive. The doctors had to take more and more of my flesh away as fever and infection raced through my body and now I stand here. This is the way I will be for the rest of my life. Do you see me Father Capono? Do you really see me"?

A great heavy weight of silence crushed the room. Not even the sounds of the wind blowing snow around the street outside could penetrate the blanket of shame and fear shining through Capono's eyes as he stared at what I had become.

His mouth worked but no sound emerged. I allowed just an edge of cynicism to creep into my voice. " Even so Father, even so, I am still a whole man. I want you to know that in my mind, where I live, I am still a whole man. I will always be a whole man because no one, not you, or anyone else ever violated my soul. I have lost an arm and a shoulder but I have not lost my pride. No one every forced themselves on my body and took away from me the ability to think of myself as a whole man".

The very first of many small sobs bubbled up out from somewhere deep inside his chest. The sound he made was like that of a spent bullet singing somewhere near your ear as it slides away without purpose or intent. I could not yet tell if it was fear or repentance that coiled and squeezed his very psyche.

"But those innocent Indian boys, your boys Father, the boys you forced yourself on just like you would have forced yourself on me two years ago if I had been weak. What about them Father? How do you think they feel now? Today? How whole do they feel about themselves? What do you think Father"?

Another sort of low and slow, almost primeval, whine escaped his throat, his eyes were now wide, nearly glazed by the turmoil of remorse and self incrimination that absorbed him. Slowly, like a balloon with a fatal leak, his body crumpled within itself. His head and arms gradually fell into his chest and lap until, in a short few seconds, he was just a human lump in the black day dress of a Catholic priest, supported by the shadows that crept across the corner of the chair he sat in.

I moved closer to him, my voice in almost a whisper, "Do you think your God will ever forgive you Father for the innocence that you and men like you have taken from the children of my people? Who will give their innocence back to them? What part of your culture will they cling to do you suppose in order to find a way to forgive you for what you have done to them"?

He spoke in Latin, "Deus indulgeo mihi". Over and over again he was asking God to forgive him. His initial fear had now coalesced into a gathered storm of shame. Slowly and deliberately I started to dress, one item at a time, hoping that if he had a mind to watch he would see how difficult it could be for a man with one arm to manage buttons and shoestrings. Finally, after at least five minutes without a word being exchanged the room was seized and held in the hand of utter silence. I turned and sat in the large over-stuffed chair, just opposite from the one he sweated and cringed in.

"Now then Father", I said with great purpose, "There is something you can help me with again. Are you ready to listen"? The silent but rapid nodding of his balding head told me all I needed to know.

* * *

Father Capono and I met with the Bishop at ten o'clock on the 7th of December. Capono had briefed him on the purpose of my request to meet and when I had arrived, nearly frozen from my long walk over to the Residence, hot coffee and a cordial greeting awaited.

The Archbishop, Emile-Joseph Legal, spoke only passing English so we conducted most of our meeting in French. He was originally from France but he had lived and worked for nearly twenty years with the Blackfoot tribes of southern Alberta. The Blackfoot language is an Algonquian dialect so we managed to get along very well in both of our second languages.

I spoke at length about something that Father Capono and the Bishop probably knew very little about. I spoke about natural love between men and women and the children that their love brings into the world. I spoke about the magic that was my grandmother. I related how she had managed not just to raise me but also to instil in me the singular purpose of being a Cree. I told them, without hiding even one tiny bit of the incredible love and lust that I had shared with Tears and how devastating her death and my loss of her love had been to me.

I spared no emotion and none of the main details about how soul destroying it was to the children of Saddle Lake and all the surrounding Reserves when the Government of Canada ordered that their families must give up every single Indian child to be sent into the residential schools.

For a few minutes I spoke in all four of the aboriginal languages that I knew and understood. Then, to the best of my ability I spoke the same message in English, in French. I was direct and forcible as I pointed out that the learning of languages and the skill of using them was only possible if an Indian child was allowed to swim and play inside the hearts of the families that loved them and cherished them and honoured their cultural backgrounds and heritage.

I spoke until the hour had long passed that the Archbishop had allotted to me for the meeting. Not once did I ever receive even the slightest nodding of the head of understanding of where my message had hoped to land.

"Your Excellency, I can see by your very apparent disinterest that I have completely failed to convince you that the current Residential School policy of Ottawa is a sin against my people and that it will lead to the total destruction of native culture and languages. Can I do nothing else to convince you of the evils of these practices"?

"My Son, I do not intend to be rude", the Bishop said, rising stiffly from his chair, "I have heard all this argued before and although I feel great sorrow for the mothers and fathers of all Indian children so affected by this program I hold firm to the belief that by becoming civilized and educated the Indian children of Alberta and Canada will become better citizens of Canada in the near future".

"Your Excellency", I said rising from the chair that centred the desk in his official office and stood before him. The office walls were neatly squared with both paintings and photographs of churches, important people and of course the tens of saints and heavenly figures to whom the Bishop prayed to on a daily basis.

"I am not in the least surprised at your response. As a child and as a man I have heard it said, from Bishops down to the ordinary man on the streets of Lac La Biche, that the salvation of First Nations will be complete only when our culture is completely submerged within the wishes of the Government".

I paused there, allowing my words to find root in his attention.

"You of all the people have a great responsibility for the future welfare of our Nations and you must have an excellent understanding of the powers and beauty of our First Nations history. You know and have lived amongst our people; you speak enough of our language that you can sit in understanding at our circles when we speak amongst ourselves."

He raised his hand as if to silence me. I raised my hand as well to show I was not inclined to be treated like a bad little boy speaking out in a classroom in which the teacher had already made the decision to move into the next subject. "Just one more minute Your Excellency, hear me out and then I will leave".
I walked around my chair and stood beside the chair occupied by Father Capono. His face suddenly lost all colour, his eyes were wide with an unspoken fear.

"This man", I said, "Can be of great help to both you and me if you permit him to travel with me to Saddle Lake. There he can see for himself, as you have seen, how the schools impart education and treat our children. He perhaps can bring you new information on how well or how poorly the church and the school are doing with their mission to assimilate the Cree into the white man's vision for my people.

I only ask that you allow Father Capono to see with his own eyes the successes and the failures that may exist in my Reserve. He will form his own opinion and he can be your eyes and ears if you so wish. Please, Your Excellency, I beg you, give me an opportunity to speak to you again through the eyes and mouth of one of your respected priests. The Father has much to learn but I know that he will give his complete attention to doing the right thing if he is given this opportunity".

At my right shoulder, Father Capono swallowed hard; his Adam's apple bobbing up and down he tried hard to keep breathing enough air to maintain his upright position in his chair.

The Bishop's eyes narrowed as they focused on the still seated Priest. "What do you think Father"? The Bishop's tone was questioning, he was clearly trying to find a solution to my request that would leave him time to restate the hard and unchangeable position that he and men like him had held ever since the Government had written the Indian's future away with their laws of residential schooling.

Father Capono stood, one hand firmly on the chair back and one hand pressed firmly into my good right arm. He spoke slowly and deliberately as he had just been given an unexpected reprieve. "We all have greater missions in our lives Your Excellency. I believe that Askuwheteau has presented me with a mission that could help me and perhaps you to better see God's plan for our people of Saddle Lake and our wonderful church at Lac La Biche. Perhaps a few weeks away from Edmonton would be an ideal way for the Lord Jesus to speak to me. I am ready to do your bidding should you agree to let me travel with Askuwheteau".

A long minute passed with the three of us standing, motionless, our eyes touching, without any sign of how the Bishop would rule. Slowly, but with agreement, he nodded his head.

"You may go and see as my eyes would see. I expect that you will find that all is, as we already know it to be. I expect that you will also have much to learn from Askuwheteau and his people and that is why I will agree to this mission. The Lord has seen fit to speak to me about the concerns of our native brothers and sisters. You may have one month Father; we will work together to better understand the form that your report will take when it is written and how we might work to use it in the improvement of our administrations of the Church and the Residential Schools".

Then turning to me he said, "You have given much to your country Askuwheteau. You have served well and you are a returning hero with the recognition of the King of England and of the Government of Canada of your value to the Nation".

He stood, hands together, eyes slightly closed as he spoke as if he was trying hard to get a better vision of who I was and how he might make better use of me in his service.

"I must inform the Diocese of Lac La Biche of the form and purpose of my mission and the task that I will assign to Father Capono. I will send letters this week to Saddle Lake to make arrangements in preparation for your and the Father's journey. Please return on Monday next and I will inform you of the arrangements that we have agreed to on where and how long you will travel with and act as a guide to Father Capono".

With a handshake I was dismissed from the office, I could feel Capono's eyes following my footsteps. I knew that I had won a small but important battle in that room. It would take them a little longer to agree between them just what the hell they were going to do in order to keep me from overrunning their position as keeper of the Residential School gate in Saddle Lake. Winning a battle is not winning a war but it is a start. I didn't know how to proceed at that point in time but I was resolved to think hard and work with purpose on the next phase.

As I closed the large and impressive front door of the Bishop's residence and started down the long wide sidewalk leading to the street I was aware of the sounds and smells that are part of a large city like Edmonton. Horse hoofs on frozen roads. The gasoline smells that car engines leave in their wake. There were no bombs or artillery shells here or in the distance. There were no ragged fields twisted and torn by battles and the efforts that men make to hide themselves while they wait for death to find them.

The streets of Edmonton may not have been a battlefield but I was still at war. My culture and my Nation needed someone to stand up and make a line in the sand. Maybe Manitou was not through with me yet. I returned to my hotel room with a feeling of having discovered a little more about who I really was.

In the fading afternoon light, I undressed again. I carefully removed the street clothes that I had purchased to make me appear more like anyone of the many European immigrants that now called themselves Albertans. I stood, quietly and proudly naked until I managed to feel unashamed of who I was. That, I swore to myself, was the last time I would ever try to be a white man. Whatever it was that I could do in the future would be done by me not by someone that I pretended to be.

The people that I faced must see me for what and who I was. I was Askuwheteau. I was a native Canadian with a long and proud history of blood flowing through my veins. I, as a person, was finally ready to accept my birthright. I had an English grandfather and an English father. I could no more change that than I would want to change the fact that my grandmother had been a full blood Cree. If someone could not see me as an equal, then I must work harder and be bolder with both my actions and my words to make them see me as a spokesman and advocate for the indigenous peoples of this nation we called Kanata.

The next time I went shopping I bought clothing for the person that I was and for the places and purposes that I would use them. In the far north corner of the third floor of the Hudson's Bay Company store was a large area devoted solely to the sale and display of furs of various types. Beautiful fur coats, wonderful beaver hats for both men and women stood waiting for eager eyes and wallets. Buffalo skins had become extremely scarce over the last thirty years and yet the Royal Canadian Mounted Police continued proudly to clothe themselves with beautiful buffalo skin winter coats and jackets. Thousands of skins were sold every year to fill the market for warm, buffalo skin winter blankets.

Buffalo coats were the favourite of everyday folk during the harsh Alberta and western Canada winters as covers for passengers in very popular winter sleighs. These fashionable blankets thrilled young and old alike as they made their way from farms and town homes to shop, school, and social events.

I had struggled to carry one from the store to my room but I smiled with sin alight as I covered myself in my hotel bed that night. I think that night was the first time in a long time that I had slept without being mindful of being a man without an arm. The Bishop had given one week until he would disclose his purpose for Father Capono and I to proceed to Lac La Biche and Saddle Lake. One week was not a long time for me to get my mind around the enormous and emotional workload I had committed myself to undertake.

* * *

It was the 18th of December 1917 when Father Capono and I stepped up from the train station platform through the cold iron doorway of the train that would take us to Lac La Biche. Capono carried two large bags. One was for his clothing and habit; the other was full of books, literature, and Christmas gifts that the Bishop had arranged to be assembled as favours for the various priests and staffs at the Lac La Biche Mission. Notre Dame des Victoires, better known as The Mission, had agreed to provide the two of us room and board for a few days while we visited with and spoke to First Nations and Métis children that still attended the Mission school. Following that, we planned to move into the Alberta Inn, in the town of Lac La Biche, for the remainder of our undertaking. The Catholic churches in both locations would of course welcome Capono to celebrate mass at his wish. Our plan was to spend until New Year's Day in Lac La Biche and then move on by automobile for an additional two weeks with the Residential School and my old village at Saddle Lake.

I carried only my old, well travelled army kit bag. I had packed the very few things that were important to me now. Most of my belongings were winter clothing and a new pair of snowshoes; the exceptions were my army records, my battle worn Bible and a small canvas case which held a supply of writing paper, an address book and some pens and ink. Hidden, along with the nearly eight hundred dollars the Army had paid me as I was discharged from the Service, was a small leather case which contained my well oiled German pistol.

I had time, while in Edmonton to take stock of my financial situation. I was not a rich man by anyone's definition but I did have most of the money that I had earned while serving in Canada and in Europe. Army pay was one dollar and twenty five cents for every day of overseas service, one dollar a day for service in Canada, a thirty five dollar allowance to purchase civilian clothes on release and a small grant of nearly three hundred dollars given to all soldiers as they re-entered civilian life. Yet to come was a small monthly pension that I was sure to get for being permanently disabled. Now granted, I had spent some of my monthly pay on such nonsense as hotels and food while I was on service leave in England and France. I did buy a trinket or two but God knows where they were now that I had been evacuated from my unit. Of course, the Indian Agent in Saddle Lake would also have nearly three hundred dollars in various monthly allotments that I had sent to Cold Dawn. My total fortune would not buy a fine house in uptown Edmonton but it would see me through a university degree if I could talk the Department of Education into taking a Métis as a possible student. All in all, it was not very much money for an arm. Money was not all I had on my mind as I had packed my clothes for this important first attack. The real question I had was how could I make a difference for my culture.

* * *

Lost Amongst The Tents Of My People

I do not want to speak of Lac La Biche as if it was London, England or Paris, France, or any other European city because it certainly was not. Although the farming community must have grown a little larger with every newly arrived white family that came to the area in search of farmland, Lac La Biche, was a small cluster of wooden, board and plank buildings. The Alberta Inn, the Lac La Biche Hotel and a very few other buildings were two stories. The rest, just shacks really, squatted on a rutted, muddy, horseshit covered street that came up from the lake and led to the only building of industrial consequence, the railroad station. Commercial buildings or at least the parts of the buildings open for business, carried signs on their fronts that announced things like food store, hardware, post office upstairs, a bakery, and the Royal Café.

Although I was on my own ground here in Lac La Biche my eye judged what I saw based on my European experience. There was no doubt in my mind that many of thousands of returning soldiers would be quick to compare what they had seen in the years spent in England and France. Lac La Biche had no roads with paving stones to amplify the sounds of iron shoes on horse's hooves.

A narrow strip of land between the river and main street and another over near the railroad track hosted groups of old wooden houses. The majority, shacks really, had changed hands many times and nobody really remembered or cared who had built them or when.

Most of these houses, those with a family living in them, had a fairly large garden plot as part of the property.

Gardens formed a major part of the food source for white families. They grew vegetables and potatoes and tried to keep them from freezing during the long, dark, cold, and miserable days of winter. Wild game and fish were the main meat sources. The lake provided fish for just about anyone that could venture near with a hook and a pole. Holes were cut in the ice during the winter to provide access for the hooks, the fish didn't seem to care whether the hands that caught and cleaned them were brown like mine or the more pale, calloused, hands of eager white men. For the most part the town was a quiet place. Only the arrival of trains, church bells, and drunken singing from the bars ever caused anyone to take much notice of the daily routine of the townspeople. Those just arriving, after having spent weeks on the wagon tracks coming to town might almost have missed the whole village had it not been for their requirement to buy flour and beans before passing through to take up homesteads somewhere on former Indian land. And just like any other frontier village struggling to become a town there was a small, upscale residential area where the storeowners, the railroad stationmaster, the hotel manager, and a few other acceptable white folks lived.

What was missing was the Indian population. There was not a village street that had a Cree name where First Nations people lived and contributed to the culture and the day to day life of Lac La Biche. Whiteman had moved in and had moved on with his life. The First Nations people had fallen aside; they had surrendered their land and lost their culture. Only the stories and legends told by the storytellers such as Cold Dawn would ever remember what a grand and wonderful life Manitou had given us to bring our babies into.

All of this land had once been the playground, the fishing banks, and the living room for the confederation of Cree and Assiniboine bands. All of them together had signed Treaty 6. Chief Onchaminahos had signed for the Saddle Lake band of Cree. Chief Pakan had signed for the Whitefish Lake band of Cree who represented the ancestors of the Saddle Lake Cree Nation at negotiations and the signing at Fort Pitt. Chief Pakan, along with Big Bear had fought hard and had argued long to have one large reserve of 1,000 square miles on which all the Plains and Wood Cree in the West of Canada could live, hunt and farm together as a nation of people.

For many years the Canadian government had not seen it possible to grant that much of the Indian lands back to the control of the First Nations people that had owned it in the first place. So in 1902, years after the 6th Treaty had been signed, the four traditional and historical Cree bands agreed to be amalgamated and they were given the name of Saddle Lake Cree Nation. It was to that amalgamated site that the Mission Residential School had moved. That was going to be my first place to visit.

There had been an enormous bush fire north and east of Lac La Biche in 1905. The fire had burned hundreds of thousands of acres of forests, riverbanks, and rocky swampland. I heard my people say that thousands of elk, moose, and deer had been caught up in the fiery death the fire carried in its arms. Now, over ten years later, Whiteman could see into the areas that had been burnt to better select areas suited for farming. Everywhere the footprint of the fire had touched, nature was busy refilling with trees. Where trees were growing back so were the fur bearing animals and the game birds and animals that provided the main courses for my people and the white man.

A constant tension existed between those that needed to use the land to grow grain and those that had owned all the land and had used it only to survive. As we stepped off the train, Capono was huffing and puffing in the cold air of the railway station. He was struggling to manage his two heavy suitcases; in comparison my kit bag was a very light load. I suspected that Capono had been briefed to try to keep the lid on any of my plans that might impact on the Residential School mandate. I, on the other hand, was nearly floored by the enormity of the undertaking that lay ahead. How was a simple, half breed man going to make any difference to the way my people were being forced to assimilate into a world that was even more foreign to them than Lac La Biche was to the steadily growing stream of immigrants following the train tracks north to find land and freedom for their families.

I had quickly realized that neither the Bishop nor his priest had any intention of straying from the larger policies and plans of their religious or political masters in Eastern Canada. They, all of them, saw the indigenous people as sullen and primitive heathen children. They would hold firmly to their stated goals of changing us, one child at a time, into Christian Canadian citizens. The voice and legend of Askuwheteau meant absolutely nothing within the context of the Bible. Instead, Indian children were forced to suffer the strap of the priests and the discipline of nuns and teachers who held it as their God given duty to convert our people for our own good.

'Please Manitou', I thought, 'Where are you now that I need your strength and wisdom'.

During the week that I had been waiting in Edmonton for the Bishop and Capono to make up their minds and write their letters to describe the function and purpose of our visits to the Mission and Saddle Lake, I had used a lot of my time visiting with and speaking to men in Edmonton that knew the politics of the area. These were people who understood the Residential School system and the state of development of the area in and around Lac La Biche. I had met with Mr. McArthur the owner of the Alberta and Great Waterways Railway. I had sent him a note saying that I was a returning war hero from the Lac La Biche area and that I would very much appreciate meeting with him to discuss how I might work with him to better the cause of my people in the area. McArthur had just completed the only building in Lac La Biche that really stood out as modern and progressive. He owned the Lac La Biche Inn, which had just opened on the 1st of July 1916. It truly was a 'wonder' on the Lac La Biche skyline. Townspeople would just stand and shake their heads at the near palace-like hotel.

I had sat in the McDonald Hotel in Edmonton with him for two hours. I told him that I would make no excuse for telling him my whole story. I started with Cold Dawn and I ended with the rudeness of the Edmonton journalist. I really believed McArthur understood what I was trying to do for the children of the Cree from Lac La Biche. I repeatedly told him that removing the children from getting an education would be a huge mistake. I told him about how neglected were the Métis children that lived in the north and around Lac La Biche. He clearly understood children needed a sound and modern education and he, like most white people, thought that is what the Residential Schools were doing. It took some time for me to explain the difference of receiving an education within their language and from the arms of their own culture.

I explained to him some of the horrors native children had to go through when completely separated from their parents, their village, and their tribal culture. I asked him to consider his own good fortune of coming to Canada as someone who completely understood the strengths of his own European background and his own religion. I asked him to consider how difficult it would be for a First Nation child to understand and then adjust to being ripped completely out of the safety of their language and culture. How would these thousands of Indian kids emerge as citizens with a future in Canada? When our long and friendly meeting had ended, McArthur extended an invitation for me to stay at his Inn in Lac La Biche for the News Year's holidays. I gratefully accepted. I left our meeting smiling to myself. First and foremost, I believed I had found an understanding ear in McArthur and secondly, Capono would have to spin hard to convince the Bishop to allow him to follow suit because I was a free guest; in the end Capono would have to pay for his own room.

The other ace in the hole that Mr. McArthur gave me to play was, following our meeting, he drafted and signed a short letter to Alexander Hamilton that provided me with an introduction to a man that really held the wheel of power in the town at that moment. Hamilton, a man from Lebanon, was certainly one of the real powerhouses in the local area and in Alberta too I suppose. Not only did he own the largest store in town but also he worked with and for the new railroads as a major contractor. In fact, he hired and fired other contractors and men to provide materials and labour for the newly arrived railways that were active between Edmonton, Lac La Biche, and Cold Lake. Not being of the Christian faith, he was a sound and strong ear for my plea for changing the education system away from church based organizations into cultural based institutions.

With only those cards to play I stepped off the train station platform in Lac La Biche still convinced that Manitou had a greater plan for me before he let me rest again.

* * *

All during Christmas and almost into the New Year a soft and quieting snow fell and slowly covered the ground and the rough edges left over from those gentler days of the autumn. Lac La Biche was pretending to be a busy little village living inside a small huddle of buildings. Many voices using many different languages filled the streets with Christmas greetings. The church bells spoke to everyone and everyone, more or less, was thoughtful of the importance of these holy days of Christianity.

Only a handful of First Nations families remained in Lac La Biche. Most of the Métis and First Nations families were clustered around the Mission and most of them were employed by and lived as part of the convent staff. The Mission no longer had a regular school function and the order of nuns and priests that remained were primary engaged in agriculture. Their lives were consumed by the annual rotation of preparing fields and gardens to produce enough food, meat, and grains to sustain their own requirements and for the families that had attached themselves to the Mission. The majority of people that still spoke Cree were of Métis descent and again the vast majority of them were employed locally, either in food, fish, or fur gathering. They struggled but managed to feed themselves and their families and sold or traded their catch for money or goods from the local white population.

These were the people that I spent the majority of my time with for the period that we were in Lac La Biche. I worked hard to get introductions to the men that I met. Having met the men sometimes led to invitations to meet with their families and that included the children they had at home.

Lac La Biche had no school at all for either their white children or for the local Métis children. The treaty First Nations children were all at Saddle Lake or else were hidden away by families, mostly deep in the back country woods where Whiteman would not know of their whereabouts. I wanted to know what the Métis population thought about the culture they were part of. Frankly, with only a few exceptions, I found they cared not at all.

The life style of the Lac La Biche Métis was, generally speaking, one of the harshest lessons of survival. They worked hard to get enough food to feed themselves. The majority of their day was consumed by the daily requirement to keep body and soul together. Everyone, the men, the women and the children had their roles to play and they played them hard and straight or else they did not make it through the long cold winters. School or going to school was not one of their concerns. Language and maintaining a language equally did not concern them. They spoke whatever language their parents had taught them. They learned to speak whatever language their employment required and they sang their hearts out in French every Friday and Saturday night when the fiddles and drums came out for the dance that was bound to be held somewhere come rain or come frost. As far as they were concerned they had a strong culture. It was built around hard hands; their work ethic had been passed on through their fathers' blood and influence. Dark brown eyes and the acceptance of their lot came piecemeal from their First Nations mothers. They were the real halfway point between the white immigrants and my indigenous culture. They had, over the years, developed a compromise between the need to survive and the desire to progress. They had learned to work in order to survive and they survived in order to progress in a world that was changing from frontier to Western Canada.

The Great War, as it was now being called, continued to retch and vomit pain and destruction across large swaths of Europe. Whomever I spoke to and wherever I went I was told that everyone was sick of reading the casualty notices in the daily newspapers. The war had laid a heavy hand on the people and the resources of Canada. Everyone had a brother or a relative either serving or who had been killed or wounded in action overseas. The war was a constant strain on every newspaper and on everything that people planned to do. On the other hand, people seemed to have money to spend on liquor and Christmas post cards. One of the priests told me that very few of my people had volunteered to join the Army but almost everyone seeking a job could find work.

It was my first Christmas at home in Alberta since I had joined the Army. It was my first Christmas in Alberta without having Cold Dawn to share it with. I tried to forget the last two Christmas periods that I had spent in the trenches of France. But try as I did, the cold and wet and fear of those days still caused me to pull my jacket closer around my one remaining shoulder as I walked the streets of Lac La Biche. The cold clear air of northern Alberta tried hard to convince me that 1917 would fade away just as the other war years had faded. It seemed to me the real concern, for the townsfolk, was not nearly as serious as worrying about the occasional arrival of an artillery shell in your trench line. In many parts of France and Belgium, townsfolk would be praying for their lives. Here, everyone seemed driven by the necessity to ensure the dinner table would have enough turkey to feed all the faces that sat around their holiday table.

Lac La Biche was a 'train town'; each day's highlight was the arrival of the daily train from Edmonton in the south. The big 'iron horse' brought clouds of steam to blanket the station. It arrived with timely precision and a mechanical chorus that no one could mistake. It brought a few people, most returning white family members wanting to spend the holiday season in the arms and homes of people close to their hearts. It brought the mail and it brought liquor. There seemed to be more people waiting for the booze than there were waiting for the mail. The train was like a magnet. Its arrival attracted horses and buggies, a few Ford trucks, people just gawking, most people walking, and then there were those getting off the train and searching for faces they recognized.

The train also brought new wonders, which the town's merchants could display in their windows and on their shelves. Apples and oranges that I saw being unloaded on Monday appeared in boxes at the Mission on Tuesday. Boxes clearly marked, T.E. Eaton, or Hudson's Bay Catalogue Sales, produced smiles and warmth as expectant mothers, and fathers, picked them up at the Station Master's Office. They meant that some lucky child was going to be given new gloves and a woollen hat.

Father Capono gave gifts of printed religious pictures by French artists to the staff at the Mission. For me there was a leather bound copy of the Catholic Latin Vulgate Bible in the French language. Both he and the Bishop had signed it, wishing me a Merry Christmas and a happy conclusion to my quest. I guess I must have forgotten to tell them that I had long since ceased being a Christian. Some time ago, somewhere deep inside of me a realization had grown; if Manitou was ever going to hear my voice describe my travels to the far away lands then my heart and mind had only room for one Great Spirit at a time.

But the daily train did not only carry people that seemed to disappear into the cold, brittle air filled with church bells and voices. It also carried entire boxcars filled with boxes, crates, and large items that railroad men struggled to move, unload, and reposition. It carried more than just mail, newspapers, and packages from the T. Eaton Company carefully packed by workers at the Catalogue Department. Sometimes the train carried caskets and the saddest of messages for someone that had never done a single thing in their lives to deserve such pain and abandonment.

The day before Christmas, Capono and had I walked through the doors of Saint Catherine's Church with the agreed intention of attending early evening mass. I can only imagine that habit and his desire to fulfill his vows had been the overriding force that brought Capono to Saint Catherine's. I came to observe with my own eyes the number and the faces of First Nations people that came to celebrate the anniversary night of the Redeemer's birth. The church was full, not crowded, but most pews had people sitting on the long rows of rich brown wood. Hand made wreaths of pine boughs added beauty and solemnity to the altar. On the left, the wreaths carried the names of local soldiers overseas with the Canadian Expeditionary Force. On the right side, wreaths with black cloth centers, carried the names of twelve local men, killed in action since 1914. These wreaths held a prominent position filling not only the eyes of the beholders but also giving purposeful room for thought on the sacrifices made by resident men in the long and continuing conflict against Germany and Her allies.

Capono and I had just sat down in the front right pew. There was warmth from the additional bodies as well as a swelling of warm air coming up from the basement heater through large grates in the floor on both sides of the nave near the altar itself. We had removed our outer coats, hats and gloves, the organ was being played, music and the awe of Christmas hung heavily on the pine scented atmosphere of the beautiful wooden building.

Of a sudden, Father De Wilde, the parish priest of St Catherine's, came in through the outside door. He approached Capono directly and motioned us to the side of the church near the front of the nave. In hushed tones he said that the stationmaster had requested to see him about an hour earlier. It seems that the recent train had carried a casket and body that had been forwarded from Edmonton. The body was being returned to a family from Saddle Lake and the Station Master wondered if it would be possible, if he supplied the transport vehicle, for Capono and me to take the casket with us on our road trip to Saddle Lake in the week following. Since Capono was assured the deceased was a Catholic and that living descendants were attending the residential school he thought it would be possible to meet the request. Escorting a body was not unknown to the priesthood and this arrangement meant that the church could save money on transport. I thought little more about it until we actually got on the truck to depart Lac La Biche.

* * *

A Rodeo at Saddle Lake.

It had been a long and miserable drive from Lac La Biche to Saddle Lake. The truck that the Railroad provided for us had chains on the tires but nothing could account for the conditions of the roads and tracks that passed as roads that we followed. The January wind blew straight through the truck at almost every possible crack and opening into the crowded little cab that all three of us shared. Even a buffalo skin thrown over our legs was little comfort in a space that large and windy that did not have a heater in it. But we survived somehow, just knowing that behind the cab of the truck, strapped down in his casket, there lay the body of man that someone had loved and had counted on for everyday of their life. We were carrying a very tragic and sad message to someone at the Residential School and neither they nor we yet knew for whom the message was meant. All Father Capono and I knew for certain was that there was a Royal Canadian Mounted Police report and a letter from the Edmonton Chief of Police that accompanied the casket. The letters, the shipping box, and the body were to be delivered to the Indian Agent of the Saddle Lake Reserve.

The Bishop's letter had preceded us by three weeks. The Staff at the School had provided accommodation for us; we insisted that we eat with the students. A heavy sense of suspicion and ill boding hung on every word of our introductions. What possible value could such an encounter provide to the students themselves was a softly spoken comment from one the staff?

"Surely we all must concentrate our interests on the development of citizenship and understanding that our wards and students acquire from their education received at our School. We trust that you will keep this in mind, Askuwheteau, and that you approach our children with the purpose of furthering our approved and mandated curriculum".

One of the Priests, a large and dominating man of French Canadian-Irish heritage and very strong opinions on the virtues of the work they, the teachers and administrators of the school were achieving, took me aside and hissed through his teeth about how much of an inconvenience was my entire visit.

"I understand you were a student here only a short time ago Askuwheteau"? He said, nearly pinning me against the wall in order to attempt to dominate the conversation. "You of all people should know that you Indians must be made to be good and decent neighbours. We can not have your so called warriors and hunters running around scaring and annoying our new settlers". He was nearly foaming at the mouth at the thought that I was here to question their right to completely eradicate any and all of these children's sense of family, culture, and language.

"We Priests and Sisters expect our students to accept our education, our religion, the laws of our land and learn our civilized customs and industrial methods. We will only allow these children to progress and stay at our school if they freely and completely conform to becoming civilized Canadian citizens".

I pushed him back from the space that he had occupied. He had been nearly standing in the same place where I had been forcibly stopped to listen to his rant. "Father", I said, "It is clear to me that you know nothing of the First Nations culture and tribal structure. We indigenous people were living here with our own sense of religion, inside functioning villages, with a strong sense of Nationhood long before Ireland and France were even imagined as countries by our Great Spirit Manitou. Your Bible tells you that your God will judge you when your time comes to return to His heaven. I hope that He can forgive you for what you have demanded these children do in His name".

Now it was time for me to push my finger under his nose, with a discreet amount of venom in my voice I pushed my mouth closer to his ear so that I speaking directly to him. "You and your Sisters should ask these children themselves, as I intend to do, if what you are doing here at this school is the correct thing to do for these Frist Nations children".

With that, and as much strength as I could muster from my one good arm, I pushed my way out of the face of the angry priest of Saddle Lake.

Suffice to say that my entire first encounter with the Principal of the School and his staff was one of being lectured on how much the children learned and benefited from being civilized in a caring school where practical physical skills, religion and education were the overriding mandates of all the staff and. Not one of them had any idea, nor had they ever asked the question about how an Indian child that had been raised with white values would ever be able to speak or live as productive First Nations adults if they were forced to return to and remain on the Reserves as they were today.

A cold and sullen sky lay creased and deeply layered over the Saddle Lake Residential School. The first strong winds of winter had already blown mounds of snow wherever trees could catch the snowflakes and hold them from their seemingly endless eddying. Our feet made crisp crunching sounds as we walked in silence from the dormitory rooms we occupied through the same old school door that still marked the very line on which all children's voices must stop their outside chatter and each child was to become a silent, thoughtful and respectful, Christian student.

The classroom we were to visit was much as I remembered. From the moment I had entered through the front main doors of the school it was as if I was participating in a recurring dream that I had lived for nearly ten years during my own life as an Indian student, here in this Catholic school. There were eight rows of desks; each row contained four single desks. Girl's rows were separate from the rows for boys. Across the room behind all of the other desks there were four single desks for the extra girls in a smaller line. This arrangement allowed for a lot of space for the teacher in the front of the classroom. Behind the area occupied by the students a large amount of the entire area of the room was given up to a large, heavy, wood burning heater that centred the back of the room. Its stovepipe towered up and into the ceiling, disappearing into the ceiling above the classroom.

There were thirty two children, a few more girls than boys, all of them huddled at their individual desks. In front, just a short step from the well worn blackboards, behind a large and imposing wooden desk, sat the center of authority for all of these grade four students, a woman by the name of Sister Mary Rachael.

Like many of the current teaching staff, Mary Rachael was a postmenstrual middle aged nun. She had been a teacher at this school for over thirty years. She had known me as a child and I knew of her from stories told by many of the children that had attended her classrooms. She was known as loving and caring, strict to a fault and not a stranger to using a strap on the hand of any child that offended some rule that few could any longer remember.

From the moment of our reintroduction Sister Mary Rachael's expression was one of extreme annoyance that Father Capono and I had been given permission to sit in during two hours of her precious day.

Sister Mary Rachael introduced her class to her guests by commenting, in French, that they were privileged today to have such important visitors from Edmonton. After many more words in which she reminded them to be polite and to remember that they were to be on their very best behaviour, she asked Father Capono if he wanted to address the class. I cannot remember much of what he said but he did introduce me as a returning soldier of the Great War and asked me if I wanted to say a few words. For the next two hours the classroom belonged to us; by us I mean the children and I. I had every intention to fill their minds with imagination and their Indian culture.

I went to every single desk and offered my hand to the occupant. Some children were so shy that I almost had to pry their little hands from places they had chosen to hide them. Others, the boys mainly, held out their left hands for the coin they had seen offered; their right hands were neither firm nor friendly. I stood my ground until they responded. I introduced myself in Cree, telling them my name was Askuwheteau and that I too was a boy from this village and from this school.

I told them where my house had stood before I had moved away from my grandmother Cold Dawn. I asked them to remember Cold Dawn; I told them, each of them, I was one of them.

With every handshake I gave the child a shiny new Canadian penny. I said it was theirs to keep; I used the Cree word 'kikike', which means forever or always. Each child held the coin in their hands and turned it over and over as if it were some very special thing that they now owned. I believed that many of them had never even seen, let alone owned a penny. I told them we would use these pennies later to play a little game.

Up and down the rows I went; at each desk I asked the child, in Cree, to tell me their names. I asked them who their parents were and where they came from. Slowly, but surely, their mouths and eyes started to open wide in wonder. They wondered why I was so different from all of the other teachers and visitors that they had in their classroom. If I was different from the others why did I look so much like they did? They were beginning to understand that I was genuinely interested because I was part of them and because I had once been who they were. I engaged each child and told them in their own language that they were all, each and every one of them, from my family and my Nation. I told them they must not ever forget that my name was Askuwheteau and that I would speak to them about why that name was important to them.

When I was finished introducing myself to every child I stood in front of Sister Mary Rachael and asked her if she would be so kind as to take a chair in the back of the room.

Then, speaking directly to the children I explained, in French, that I wanted to put on a small play and that I would need all of the room in the front in order to conduct my small production. With some reluctance and dark looks over at Father Capono she carried her large, heavy desk chair to a place in the back of the classroom; the Father, decided to take his chair and joined her. For the entire time I spoke to the class they were two sour faces behind the fascinated children that faced me wondering what I was going to do next.

I became the kind of storyteller that Cold Dawn had been. I crouched and I preened; I whispered and I shouted. I stood tall and I made myself as small as the squirrel that Manitou had just created. I became the Askuwheteau that became the eyes of the Great Spirit. I tried to become real to them, part of them, and I hoped they would consider me to be one of them.

"The forests where your people were born were silent. Days and seasons passed without any sounds except the echoes of laughter that the women made as they bathed in the river. The cries of their babies were the only sounds that made your people turn away from picking berries or cleaning fish from the cold and shining lake that was our home".

As I spoke I made the sounds that bathing makes; I became the bubbles in the water, I became the dimension that people live in so that they could hear me as well as see me.

I held them in my hands as I changed my voice from the storyteller to that of the sly fox that watched from the forest's edge as our hunters came home from their days of hunting and harvesting furs.

Furs, I said, that would become fine coats for beautiful young women that smiled from the tents our people lived in. I told them who we were before the white man came. I told them how we lived in peace with nature and that we left no scar upon the ground we lived on. Slowly at first but after twenty minutes every child but one followed my every move. All eyes but hers were lost in my imagination. It was then I realized that one child out of these thirty-two did not speak Cree.

An hour later, I had led them through the Cree Legend of the creation of our world and how we had lived with nature and how pleased our Manitou had been to see the knowledge we had gained from the grand eagle Askuwheteau. Then, I changed to the French language so that the two sullen eyes that had watched for an hour not understanding the language of my people and these children would be included in the remainder of my stories.

Now I told them of the coming of the white man. I told them that the early days, when Whiteman first came to live with us, were days and years of discovery for both of our Nations, theirs, and ours. I spoke of and held before them the very books that they had learned to read from and of the maps that their classroom walls held which proved to show them how they lived in a world much larger than Lac La Biche.

Then I became the storyteller again. I spoke to them in many voices. I spoke to them in many languages. I pointed to the map upon their classroom wall and read aloud the names of nations that people in Canada came from. I told them a little about the early ships that brought the English and the Irish and the Scottish and the French and Germans, and many others to live with us, on our lands, in our Canada.

In our language, the Cree language, I showed them how large our Cree Nation had been and I spoke to them of many of our dialects like the Plains, the Swampy, the Woods, the Moose, and Saskapi Innu. I showed them on the map the huge territory where the Ojibwa language, the Odawa, Chippewa, and Algonquian were spoken. They were very surprised to learn that there were more than two hundred different First Nations languages and dialects. But more importantly, I said in French, in English and in Cree, that languages are doors that would allow them to enter into many different worlds than just here in Saddle Lake and Alberta. I closely watched the faces of Sister Mary Rachael and Father Capono as I spoke. I could see they were beginning to get caught up in my presentation, every now and then one of them might even nod or allow just the slightest smile to grip and turn up the corner of their bottom lip.

I had worked hard to carry each and every child's eyes across the room and into the sky with me as I spoke. If some misunderstanding clouded a child's face I would immediately turn and speak directly to its owner until I reconnected them to where my story had taken us. Within an hour and a half, I had managed to nearly hypnotize these wonderfully receptive minds. All that is to say expect for the tiny and very timid little girl that sat in the far back corner of the classroom occupying one of the special row of four desks.

I held my hands up, signalling each and all to be very quiet and to listen. Holding my finger to my lips I said in Cree,
"Tell me if you can understand the next language that I use. I am going to speak directly to you all but I want you to raise your hand if you can understand what I say next"!

I spoke over the heads of everyone else, my eyes fastened on and holding that little girl like a wolf might stare out at a motionless rabbit. I spoke to her in her own dialect of Chipewyan. After just a few words I saw her eyes open wide in amazement, her mouth fell open, and then, as if a wave had crashed in over the side of her canoe, her eyes filled with tears and she started to cry. She held her hands over her mouth and she continued to stare at me as if it was the first time she had actually seen me. I went to her and I said in her language,

"Your name here is Emily isn't it"?

In a very small voice, still filled with tears she responded, "Yes".

"And in your own language, the one I just spoke to you, what are you called by your family"?

Her beautiful dark brown eyes sought mine for just an instant before she said in Chipewyan, "My father called me Rainbow. How did you know to speak my language"?

"I knew that of all the children here your eyes and ears did not follow me when I spoke in Cree. I thought that somehow you reminded me of a beautiful woman that used to live in our village when I was a child here. She was from the Chipewyan Nation, which is miles to the west from here. Was your mother or your Grandmother a lady that was called 'Tsiaze', Songbird"?

"Yes", she said, starting to cry again while staring out at me as if I was from a completely different world.

"Why are you crying"? I said while gently taking her by her hand to try to reassure her it was alright to be speaking in her own language.

Slowly, like a small fawn looking out upon a scene too large to really understand, she put her other hand out to me and took my hands in hers. Then, in a little voice still shaking with emotion she said in Chipewyan,

"I do not speak any other language but my own. No one has ever taught me to speak any other language so I am all alone here. Only one other child speaks my language. Today is the first time I have heard any adult use words I understand and you have said them to me".

I sat down on an empty desktop and stared at her in disbelief. "Rainbow", she had said in her language, probably the first time in a long time that she had heard her Indian name spoken!

"Rainbow, how do you go to school and how do you learn if you do not speak French or Cree? It is impossible to learn things if you do not speak the language of the Sister".

Her head nodded towards a boy, who sat in front, his head cast down and blushing for having been pointed out in this conversation.

"My friend, that boy in the first row, his name is William, he learns everything in school and then after class or when we can he teaches me what he has learned. He also speaks my language".

"And French"? I said, "Why do you not learn French? Everyone here has to speak French."

"I have only just arrived here some weeks ago with my father, this is my first month in school. My mother died in our lodge many miles from here and my father and I walked here because I could stay here and be looked after when he left to walk to Edmonton to find work".

Emily, uncermoniously wiped her eyes and nose on her sleeve, a ragged breath caught between her beautiful little teeth before she continued.

"The woman that is sitting there"! She pointed to Sister Mary Rachael. "She knows that I can not speak so she lets me sit in this room until I can learn how to speak the French language".

I turned my attention to Sister Mary Rachael. "Sister, Emily had told me in Chipewyan that she speaks neither Cree nor French. How will she learn the things that you and the other teachers here are telling her"?

Sister Mary Rachel held me with her eyes for a short period, slowly nodding her head as if she was thinking of how she would reply to the discovery of her little secret.

"I am impressed, Askuwheteau. You were able to observe that one child amongst many was not able to speak either your language or mine. You are not only a very good storyteller; you also listen for words that are not yet spoken. Maybe someday you should become a teacher like I am. We need people that can hold the imagination of young minds for as long as you have held this class".

With that the Sister changed to speak French. At first it surprised me that she knew I would understand her, then I remembered that Capono and she would have already discussed their common adversary.

"She will learn to be a student first then she will learn the language that all children here must learn. She is not special nor is she the first child to come to us without being able to speak the French language. She will learn French because God wants her to be a good citizen of Canada. All good citizens of Canada speak French Mr. Askuwheteau"!

I felt the heat building beneath my collar; I knew she was simply turning the cultural knife in my side to see how I would react. She knew how to take the pressure off what her church was doing to the First Nations by placing it on the well publicized and known differences existing in Canada between the two founding European nations, England and France.

I took another shiny new penny from my pocket, carried it over, and placed it beside her on a desk.

In English, knowing that she must speak English, I replied,
"Sister Mary Rachael, here is a coin you can put in the collection box or else you will have to say three Hail Marys' and four Our Fathers tonight before you go to sleep. You are trying to transfer your prejudices concerning the Church of England education standards to me".

My brazen response brought a sly smile to her face, which she held down as she too admired the shiny penny. I moved over to her side and spoke directly to her trying to keep my voice soft and measured. I wanted desperately to maintain the moral high ground.

"I was a soldier that fought for the freedom of all Europeans. I saw no difference in the manner in which the French suffered as Catholics or the English suffered as Anglicans during their experiences of that terrible war. My Great Spirit Manitou has told us all men are equal until they prove they are not. My people speak over 200 languages in the lodges of our First Nation tribes. Not once have I ever heard a man say one language or another makes a man or a woman a better person. Languages are a door that opens and permits us access to a culture. Little wordless Emily must never forget her First Nations culture. It is who she is and neither you nor Father Capono decided that. Her culture is not the same as the culture of William Sharp Ax or any of the other children that are here under your care. Emily is of the Chipewyan culture, it is her language that makes her see and hear and describe her world differently then the other children here that are from the Cree culture".

I paused to gauge her reaction. Her eyes reminded locked on the brightness of the copper penny.

I continued,

"Your Jesus was born into a Middle Eastern culture and he died with the beliefs that his culture surrounded him with. You and all of you here at this Mission and at all of the Residential Schools should acknowledge and celebrate that First Nations children under your care will be better Canadians because they can speak another language. If you do not change your ways at these Residential Schools, then you must know that these children will have lost who they are. They will forget the culture they came from if your teaching takes away the language of their nation".

I turned my attention to the children in the classroom. I could see that my conversation with Emily and then with the Sister in two different languages had filled their expectant eyes with natural curiosity. Smiling at them and their youthful interest I said loudly,
"Emily wants me to thank you all for being patient with her until she can also speak with you in French. The Sister has reminded me that I have yet a few minutes left to complete my performance so let us continue with our lesson".

I was very much aware that I was starting to push the good humour and acceptance of Sister Mary Rachel as I continued to interact with these children.

"So", continuing in French, "All of you, each of you, yes you too Emily, please put your penny on your desk in front of you". Each child stirred until they had placed the coin I had given them in the place on their desk that gave them the greatest satisfaction.

I became the storyteller again. This time I told the whole story in French. I wanted the Sister and Father Capono to understand what I was doing. With my one arm flapping and my story soaring on the edges of my voice I was an eagle flying high above the land of these children from many different families. I spoke to them as if I were Askuwheteau and I spoke to each of them as if they were the main warrior and hunter from their ancient families. I went hunting with them along a riverbank that held within its banks the deep, cold, and clear waters that would soon be joining the beauty of Lac La Biche. I made them see the fish that swam within the water. I introduced them to a beaver that shared the water and Askuwheteau spoke to the beaver to inquire where the best place was to catch the biggest fish.

"I have lived all my life within two hundred yards of my family's lodge", said the beaver in a deep and beautiful Cree dialect. "If I were going to catch a fish today I would look into the deep dark pool that is beside my lodge. That pool is filled with shadows. The long green weeds that love the shadows grow the strongest and the tallest in that part of this river. It is there Askuwheteau that you would find the largest fish that I know of in this part of the river".

Askuwheteau thanked the beaver for his honesty and his help and he wished the beaver and his family a long and happy life. Then, in the voice of Askuwheteau, I dove deep into the river. The cool deep water flowed through my feathers and I worked hard to achieve the bottom but when I reached the surface of the water again, I, the great and strong and very wise Askuwheteau, held the biggest and the best pike fish that the village people had ever seen. Then, with my words and my actions I carried that large and beautiful fish to the center of their village. I truly believe that every child in the classroom could see that fish as clearly as if it were really there with us at that exact moment.

I asked every child to gather around me in the front of the classroom and I said I would sell each brave young hunter a piece of this huge fish so they could take it home and feed it to their families. Every child began to speak at once; each wanted to give me their penny for a piece of the fish. There was some pushing, the larger boys demanded to be first to buy the fish and the girls begged for a larger piece because they had brothers and sisters that were hungry.

It was at that moment I held my hands above my head and told them all, in a stern and authoritative voice to sit down immediately and be very, very, quite.

In just an instant I had a circle of excited but soundless children hanging on my next instruction. These children were no longer in a classroom; in their minds, their beautiful, uncomplicated, youthful minds, they were in the meeting place of their very own village and they were bargaining for a piece of fish.

"You warriors are from the wood lands of our Nation. You are the hunters and the bravest of all of the peoples that sleep in your lodges. You are admired by the men and women and loved by your parents and your husbands and wives and now you all are acting like you are Whiteman. You are not Whiteman you are Cree! A Cree warrior does not buy fish from the Great Askuwheteau! You would hunt and bring home meat and fish and you would share it with all the people of your village. If there is enough food for everyone you would sleep warmly in your beds that night but if anyone in your village remained hungry you would return to the forest and find more food".

I stared at them and to the tallest and the strongest of the boys I said,

"You Robert Knife Edge, you go to that corner and find a fine young deer and bring it back to this village. You, William Short Axe, you return to the river and catch more fish so your friend Emily can sleep with a full stomach tonight".

For at least a minute I stared at them, speaking softly and directly to all of them; I said over and over and over again, "You are Cree children! You are Cree children! You are part of a strong and caring Nation of people".

Then I spoke directly to each of them, one after the other, using the names that they had told me they were called. I asked them to return to their desks and to remember who they were and who I was.

Then and only then did I thank Sister Mary Rachael for letting me speak to her class of Indian children for two hours.

* * *

A Heart is Broken, A Heart is Made Whole

Capono and I ate with the children in their common dinning room. On an average day most of the children only attended classes for two or at maximum three hours a day. The remainder of their time, week after week and month after month, was a harsh and demanding routine of child labour.

Children were hustled out of bed long before daylight. Many of their beds had to be stripped on a weekly basis and that meant that every day twenty or thirty children were busy hauling water from the well to fill the laundry tubs. Boys hauled water and wood, girls washed and scrubbed and pressed and remade beds. The same routine was followed daily for clothes, table linens and washroom towels and linens. The school staff also had all of their laundry done, daily, weekly, and monthly by the same rotating work parties. The Staff, the all important Staff, always supervised this labour.

The preparation and cooking of food, cleaning up the mountain of dishes and kitchen ware were huge tasks, autumn though to summer, requiring another large work force, all working under the supervision of the staff, and performed by the children.

Then there were the gardens. The work of planting, weeding, and picking, washing and peeling was performed by children's hands and was considered a child's contribution and responsibility. The older students carried the team's leadership, the younger children, according to age and ability provided the labour.

Going to school at a Residential School was hard, constant, unrelenting labour for the entire ten months that children were in the school year. And remember, some children had come from villages so far away and through such difficult terrain that many children never got home during the entire school term of ten months.

Many of the children lost parents and other family members during the school year. Most First Nations families could not and would not write a letter and the Indian Agents often did not seem to care about such trivial matters as a death in a student's family. Some children might not even know of their loss until someone came from their village or Reserve and told them not to go home because their home no longer existed.

Sadly, and it sounds equally strange for me to write this, but not knowing was the case for Emily Rainbow. The Indian Agent had received the casket Capono and I had delivered and had read the RCMP report and a letter from the Station Master at Edmonton. After the Agent had read the papers he had dressed and walked over to hold a meeting with the School Superintendent. The last name of the male whose body was certified to be inside the railroad provided casket was Ferguson. There was a child attending the Saddle Lake Residential School with that last name. She was Emily Rainbow Ferguson.

Both Father Capono and I were present when the Agent told the Superintendent that Emily's father had died of hypothermia in a boxcar that had come from Lac La Biche. The investigation of death had determined that:

"Someone, probably Ferguson, had broken a seal on the boxcar door and had made entry into the car. The door had closed and parts of the broken seal and door had jammed the door closed. The total time that the car had travelled from its point of loading until reopened for unloading was four days. The night temperatures had reached minus twenty. Ferguson had been drinking and two empty bottles of whiskey were found with the frozen remains".

The conclusion of the investigation was short and to the point.

"Drunken Indian had frozen to death after illegal entrance of a moving and working freight train. Body was being returned to the only known address that was associated with the remains. The name of a student at Saddle Lake Residential School was found amongst the contents of the backpack carried by the victim".

The Agent had already accepted that he would arrange for burial in the graveyard of the village. The only question remaining was what to do with and who, if anyone would accept custody of the child name Emily. If no one would accept custody for the child should she be returned to her own Reserve because ordinarily children from that area would not attend the Residential School at Saddle Lake? And last but not least who would break the news to her and when?

* * *

The Great and Mighty Manitou had spoken. A life had been lost, the spirit of a warrior would now return to the power that is our great creator. A very sad and innocent girl child of seven or eight years of age was now an orphan.

We Cree believe that everything that occurs in our lives has a reason and a purpose. The weight and timing of Ferguson's death crushed my chest, took my breath away as if I had been facing an artillery shell that exploded at Vimy Ridge. I could not stand so weak were my legs, my reason spun until I was sure I would collapse on the hard wooden floor of the Residential School building I was in.

I had come to Saddle Lake with only the dimmest of visions of how I could act and what I could do in order to influence the Catholic Residential School to rethink their institutional practice of destroying the cultural base of every indigenous child under their care. My recent days and experiences both at Lac La Biche and here at Saddle Lake had clearly shown me how futile my efforts had been and would be in the future.

Manitou had clearly known of this outcome long before I had made it my quest to return to my childhood home to bathe again in the dream that Cold Dawn had shared with me. Manitou spoke to me through the Spirit of George Ferguson. Manitou was not finished with me. Manitou had spoken with infinite wisdom; if my journey could not save every child within my culture then I should try to change the destruction of our culture one child at a time. Emily Rainbow Ferguson was a tear that I could comfort. I swear to you what happened next is as clear to me today as it was at the moment it happened.

We were all gathered in the school Principal's office when the Agent had entered and had given his briefing on what he knew about the accidental death of George Ferguson. I had turned away, almost in shock, as the story had unfolded. I had faced towards the window in an attempt to put some natural element of reality into what was going on in my mind at that moment.

I heard a door open and close. I turned to see who had entered the room but there was no one new or different than when I had entered with Father Capono some twenty minutes before. The Indian Agent remained sitting in a chair just to one side of center on the school Principal's desk. Capono was standing, his back towards me on the left side of the Agent. I had stood a few paces behind them, listening to their discussions concerning who was responsible for the burial, who would inform Emily? The Superintendent was talking about procedures which were customary to notify other Ferguson Family members though there did not seem to be any other close family members listed in any of Emily's records.

I looked around the room again; sure that someone must have entered. I remember sort of shrugging my one remaining shoulder when I realized that I must have been mistaken. Then, in an instant, directly in front of me, only a pace or so away from the others stood George Ferguson. He was dressed in normal winter clothing, he appeared healthy though his eyes were tired and his face drawn. He reached out, two handed, and closed his grip on my right hand. With complete powerful concentration his eyes bored a hole in mine.

"Askuwheteau", he said in Chipewyan, "I am no longer of this earth but I cannot leave until I have spoken for the future of my daughter Rainbow".

His hands left mine and they now hung down by his side, the fire was slowly being extinguished in his soul. "You know because Cold Dawn taught you, our children embrace a special place in Cree and Chipewyan cultures. You know our children, especially our very young children are gifts to us from the Spirit Manitou and that it is our sacred duty to protect them and to keep them from harm".

With those words going through my mind I am certain it was he who pushed me forward into the circle of the other men around the table. I could feel him there with me even though it seemed the others could not see him there in that room with them. To me, I was certain; he stood behind me with one hand on my shoulder and one hand on my back. He seemed to will me to raise my hand to attract their attention. With just the slightest push on my back I stepped forward to stand before them. I maintain, without understanding how it happened, his voice became my voice and as he spoke his words came from my mouth.

I spoke his words slowly but with conviction,

"Emily Rainbow Ferguson will be my daughter from this moment forward". All three turned their eyes on me in surprised silence. "My culture has had, for a longer period than England or France have been nations, a traditional practice of protecting our children at such times when their own families can no longer provide support and love to them. Emily Rainbow Ferguson is not an orphan child, she is a Frist Nations Child, and she will never be an orphan while she is in the protection of someone that will adopt her. I do here and now adopt her. She will then be a member of my family as if she had been born within my house and under the warmth of my blanket".

The Agent's eyes grew larger as I spoke but when I stopped he nodded his head. With just the slightest of hesitations he added, "I know of this practice and I know of families right here in Saddle Lake that have customary adoption relationships with children from other families from the Cree community. I am not sure how your culture makes these commitments or the arrangements necessary to do so but we must be willing to listen to your proposal".

His words seemed to provide a bit of calm from the initial shock that my words had caused. The Principal leaned back in his chair; the Agent scratched a matchstick on the side edge of the desk he sat at and sucked hungrily at a cigarette until he had filled his lungs with the pungent smells of Virginia tobacco.

I could no longer feel the pressure of Ferguson's hands on my shoulder and back. I looked quickly behind me; it seems that Ferguson had only waited to hear my spoken commitment and then, as I had always stood before, I was alone in front of the only group that mattered at that moment.

"The love of children in our First Nations families is not any different from your white families. Our love for our children is as deep and meaningful and sincere as any family that every one of you has ever known".

I had their attention; all three were slowly nodding.

"Look deep into the eyes of a new Cree mother that lies with her newly born child at her breast for the first time. Look deeply into your hearts and try to tell me that our women, our mothers, do not love with the same natural intensity that the women from European cultures do".

I walked around the table and stood at the side of the Principal. I leaned forward, my hand on his desk.

"All children have the basic and inalienable right to be protected from those things they cannot yet make true or fight on their own. All parents of this world have it in their hearts to protect, love and cherish the children they bring into this world no matter when or where that birth might occur. That is one of the great things all mankind shares with one another. We all share a natural love and the common sense of protection for our children and for children in general. When I was at war in Europe the guns would not stop for homes or horses or for churches or trains. But soldiers would not knowingly kill children. That is one thing that the armies of the allies and of the enemy all shared. We all shared the great care and love we have for babies and helpless children".

I knew I had to appeal to their common values and reason in order to win custody of Emily. I only prayed that my words would resonate with equal value within each of their varied breasts.

"Father", I said, "You, of all of us, have a duty and a vow to hold safe from harm each and every child that comes under your hand. You do this because Jesus said, 'suffer unto me the little children' ". I turned quickly to the Agent.
"Mr. Stowell, your many years of hard work and responsibly as an Indian Agent have shown you countless examples of families that have been torn apart by death, sickness and neglect and yet you also know that some other person or family from the reserve or local Nation has always come forward to protect and provide for the children so affected".
"And you Father", I said facing the Principal responsible for the Residential School, "I am sure that you have known of other such cases where a child under your care has lost his or her parents and yet that child was returned to their Reserve so that they could spend their summer months with their new adopted family"?

I looked into the eyes of each of them in turn as I spoke. "Many families in France and England today no longer have fathers either alive or able to contribute to the life and livelihood of their children. I have walked through cities and towns in many places in Europe where mothers on their own can no longer find or afford food to feed their starving children. Here in Canada I am willing to bet that each of you personally know one or more families where there are children living inside of homes that do not belong by birth to the caring family who provides the roof over their heads. Many of our native and white people face sickness, accidents, drunkenness, men away at war".

I could see that each of them in the room was finding some considerable sense with my logic. "But sometimes love and caring is not enough to protect a child. Sometimes even white children are left with living parents or parents that are not capable to look after them, provide for their needs and basic support".

I stopped and nodded my head until they all nodded theirs in return.

"Native families, Indian families, indigenous families have the same problems as white families. Many of our men have turned to drink and can not or do not provide a home for their wives and families. You all know that because you work with my people and for my people every day of your lives".

Again, all of them were more comfortable now that I was back into talking about my people and not their people.

"This is not a new thing to your cultures and neither is it new to my culture and all our cultures here in Canada. We Indigenous cultures have for thousands of years had a traditional customary adoption practice, just as many of your towns and cities permit within your own nationalities. We, the First Nations, have an informal and consensual process just as you do in these matters. When one family can no longer provide, for whatever reason, the love and basic necessities for a child or for their children then other families take one or more or all of those children into their homes and raise them to the very best of their abilities".

I stopped there, looking into their eyes as I went from face to face.

"I have the financial means and the love and interest to take this Chipewyan child into my house and into what will be my family and to raise her within her culture and your culture so that she will have the very best opportunity to become what all of you so desperately want for all of the children under your jurisdiction. You want our children to become Canadian citizens capable of adding to and being part of our country. That is exactly what my intentions are for Emily".

The Agent chewed away on what remained of his cigarette. The Principal pretended to search his desk drawer for a piece of paper on which to write notes. Father Capono continued to stare at me like I had just become someone that he no longer knew. Instinctively I knew the longer I waited for their response the greater was the possibility they would find their voices to question some part of my logic.

"Well Gentlemen, thank you very much for your concessive agreement to my immediate adoption of Emily. I intend to depart from here tomorrow's for Edmonton. Emily will accompany me. As you may know I have just recently been released from the Canadian Army, I have accumulated sufficient funds to purchase accommodation in Edmonton. I will enrol Emily immediately in the school closest to wherever I purchase my new home. As soon as I have settled in Edmonton and Emily is registered and accepted in school I will write to each of you and extend an invitation to visit us there".

I went to each of them in turn, extending my hand and shaking theirs as I said,

"It is my goal to attempt acceptance in the University of Alberta Bachelor of Education program. If I can be so bold may I beg that each of you write a letter of recommendation that I may present? I am sure your support will be of immeasurable value to my application. Please be so kind as to send your letters directly to Mr. Tory, who as you all know is the President of the university, I assure you again that I appreciate your cooperation.

I turned on my heel my heart in my mouth; I crossed the floor, firmly closing the door behind me. Like watching a grenade sailing through the air towards you, I walked down the hallway towards the room the Sisters used as their staff office and dining room. The more steps I took away from the Principal's office the greater grew my confidence that I had escaped unharmed from my out of body experience. The longer that the grenade spun and turned through time and space the greater was the chance it would not detonate.

Where in the hell did Ferguson come from and how was I ever going to understand actually feeling his hands on my hands, on my shoulder, on my back? Perhaps, I tell myself, the love of a father for his daughter is made even stronger when Manitou is present.

'Manitou', I thought, 'you and I need to have better coordination on our attack plans if we are going to win this and the next battle'.

It seemed pretty certain my next battle was going to be trying to win over Emily. How would I convince her to accept the fact that the one light remaining in her life had recently been blown out? How would she learn to accept that the last person in her family, the father that she loved and trusted, was no longer on this earth? Even more important though was finding a way to convince her that I could be a trusting, loving, and enduring father to replace the one she had yet to find out she had lost.

* * *

The bell had sounded for the dinner meal. There was a ritual of washing hands, combing hair, making sure that the dress of the day was being worn. Then the senior class gathered and entered the dinning room first. In succession, each class by seniority entered the dinning room and each student stood by their allocated chair. Absolutely no talking or noise was permitted, it was not until an attendance check was completed that heads were bowed in prayer as thanks were given for the day and grace solemnly recited by a selected student.

Then and only then did the classes, sitting together at their own tables get up and file, table after table, through the food line. From there it was straight back to your seat, eat your meal in relative quiet and then await the call to return to complete after school chores, duties or assignments.

Most of the children worked two to three hours following class dismissal on some labour intensive project such as weeding in the garden, scrubbing the stairs, working in the kitchen or the laundry.

I had explained to Sister Mary Rachael what I intended to do and how I intended to break the news to Emily. I had waited in the dinning room, standing to one side, waiting for little Emily to finish her meal before I went over to her table.

The Sister and I together motioned to Emily to follow us out of the dinning room and together, her hands in ours we went slowly but surely down a short hallway that led into the Residence Chapel. Speaking Chipewyan, I asked Emily to join us as we gave thanks to God and to Manitou for the many blessings that they had provided for us.

Emily very sincerely and sweetly joined us, on her knees, as both the Sister and I intoned special words of thanks for giving each of us life and for providing for our earthly as well as our spiritual needs. When we had finished with our little prayers, I took Emily by the hand and helped her sit up on the bench between us. Both the Sister and I took deep breaths before I started.

"Many years ago the Great and All Present Spirit who created this world and everything in it looked around the beautiful land he called Kanata and saw that one more beautiful girl child was needed in Edmonton".

"Do you know where Edmonton is Emily"?
"Not really Askuwheteau", she replied very politely, speaking softly in the dialect her mother had taught her when she was still alive. Her life then had seemed to be so simple.
"I know that people from my village talk of Edmonton and my father told me he was going there to find work".

I provided a quick translation for Sister Mary Rachael. I had already explained to her that I considered a move away from the school where Emily was just starting to feel a little bit of comfort, a long trip to Edmonton with someone she did not know well and then the news of the death of her father would be too much for her to handle all at one time. I had decided to do all these things, but to do them one at a time. In this way, I reasoned, the shock of one piece of life changing information would not overly impact on the sum of the entire change that Emily was going to have to be submitted to over the next days and weeks.

The Sister had agreed with my approach, so to some extent we were in 'cahoots'.

"So Emily, I have some really good news for you. Tomorrow morning you and I are going to take a long ride on the Iron Horse all the way to Edmonton". Her eyes widened in surprise as the words sank into her bright and inquisitive mind.

"The Sister and I have decided that you are such a good student here and that you have done so well at Saddle Lake that we are going to put you in another school, in Edmonton, and there you will learn how to speak both your language and the French and the English languages. You will have new clothes and a new home and you will live with me in a house where you will have your very own room to sleep in"!

Her eyes were wide with bewilderment, so many words and so many promises, so much for a small mind to understand all at one time.

"Will the Sister go with us Askuwheteau"?

"No, Emily, you and I will go alone. You will be my child and I will be just like I am your Father and together we will travel on the train. Together we will learn to speak languages and every day I will tell you wonderful stories about our people and about the ways we used to live in this beautiful country called Kanata".

Emily looked at me for a few seconds, her beautiful black eyes filled with wonder and questions. Then, like a small bird would feel if it landed on your arm, she reached out and put her hand in my hand.

"Can I say good bye to William before I go with you Askuwheteau"?

Sister Mary Rachael helped Emily pack her few meagre items of clothing. The school gave her a copy of the Bible and a level one reading book in French.

Following breakfast with all of the students, Rainbow shyly stood beside William. It was clear to me that he had been the one beacon of light that she could count on to show her the way through each and every day that she had been a student here. She had depended on his being there for her; they had established a bond that only lonely children could ever understand. They did not really speak, words were not important, but when their hands touched as they parted, their eyes shone with the light that Manitou only gives to special people to use at special times when their hearts are exposed and the truth is bare for everyone to see.

After William had turned to go to his classroom, I said to her,
"Rainbow, William will always be a special friend to you and you have enough room in your heart to remember him like he is today until you see him sometime in the future".

That seemed to be enough for her to take away as we walked out and got into the truck that would take us to the railroad station and the long steam filled ride into the main Edmonton station.

The Indian Agent had delivered a large package just as we prepared to drive away from the Residential School that had held so many memories for both myself and for Rainbow. As we bounced and slid along the track leading to the far away siding where the train would stop and pick us up, she helped me to open all the strings and layers of brown paper that had hidden countless little treasures that Mr. Stowel's wife thought Rainbow would need when she was living with me in Edmonton.

She also helped me open all of the Government of Canada envelopes that contained the monthly allotments I had given to Cold Dawn. I tried to make each opening into a mathematics lesson but in the end she seemed more interested in listening to my story about a wonderful women called Cold Dawn.

Everything we saw and did that day was new to her. With every word we spoke about the future and how we would work to make our lives together as good as we could make them.

That night, in a hotel room near the Bishop's residence, Emily slept her first night as my daughter. The length of the day, the strain of the truck ride and the train had exhausted her. The experience of walking into a hotel, dining in a dining room that was not filled with children, the shock, I would suppose of being with me in a room with two beds, all that might have crushed her into an emotional ball. But no, she lay there, without a care on her brow as I wondered out loud where the world and Askuwheteau would take Emily and me.

* * *

The Box Remains Open

My story does not have an end, it will not end until the Great Mystery calls Askuwheteau to become part of and therefore with the Great Spirit.

My life with Emily is just beginning and even in the beginning I am starting to see her through the eyes that her father would have used. Rainbow, for that is the name we call her now, is a beautiful and caring child. It did not take her very long to learn to speak the same Cree dialect that Cold Dawn had spoken with me. And having Master Barton Andrew Middleton the Third, here with us in our new home in Edmonton has certainly helped her to master the English language much quicker then if I had had to do it all on my own.

And as for me well, slowly, I have learned to speak less and listen more to the professors at the University of Alberta. I am a student at the Faculty of Education and I do believe that somewhere there will be a classroom waiting for me to fill with wolves and beavers that can talk.

We, that is, Sarah and I, have finally stopped staring at one another across the kitchen table. I stare because I can not believe how much courage it took to walk away from her family home in England. I can not believe, that as she left the station in London, her mother had given her a substantial money order which has and will ensure our well being as we become a couple together in Edmonton.

Neither can I comprehend how much courage it took for her to contact a Canadian Officer that she really did not know and to beg for help to locate the father of her child. And then she had to make a war time voyage across the ocean to Halifax and a train ride to Ottawa.

It did take some time for both of us to understand how much work it was for Robert Johnson as he traced me through Canadian Army records and then he took official leave from his office in Ottawa to escort Sarah from Ontario to Alberta. He even agreed to be my best man so that we could be married on the day we were reunited.

Sarah stares at me because she cannot believe I did not know how much she loved me ever since the night that I had cried when I saw paper lanterns on the Serpentine.

No, Askuwheteau's story has not ended. The Box of Tears remains, both in my mind and in the Legend; and somewhere, someday, Askuwheteau may return there to spend a million seasons remembering the joy that filled his eyes when Sarah and my son stepped off the train at the Edmonton railroad station.

* * *

Vimy Ridge A Box Full of Tears is a work of fiction. Any references to historical events; to real people, living, or dead; or to real military units and Bases are intended only to give the fiction a setting in historical reality. Other names, characters, and incidents either are the product of the author's imagination or are used fictionally, and their resemblance, if any, to real-life counterparts is entirely coincidental.

A Note About the Editor.

Major General (Ret'd) David Wightman, CMM, CD. Dave entered the Canadian Services College Royal Roads in Victoria BC as an officer cadet in September 1950. He graduated from RMC Kingston in May of 1954. Dave underwent RCAF pilot training in the summer months, earning his wings at RCAF Station Centralia in August 1952. Following graduation from RMC he converted to the T33 jet at Portage La Prairie and then attended McGill University, obtaining his BSc in Electrical Engineering in 1955. He spent three years instructing on Harvard aircraft at RCAF Station Claresholm, Alberta. He then flew the Lancaster, the Neptune, and the Argus on Maritime Patrol and on developmental testing for five years from both Greenwood Nova Scotia and Summerside PEI.

In 1963 he was selected to attend the United States Air Force Test Pilot School at Edwards Air Force Base in California. He served as an Engineering Test Pilot at the Central Experimental and Proving Establishment in Ottawa and on promotion to Wing Commander in December of 1965 was appointed Senior Test Pilot for the remainder of his tour there. One of the many highlights of this tour was flying the Canadian Aviation Museum's Sopwith Snipe World War I biplane for several weeks leading up to the Rockcliffe Centennial Airshow on 10 June 1967. He also flew the Neptune, the Argus, the T33, and the CF104 out of Uplands during the same period.

In the fall of 1967 he attended the newly integrated Canadian Forces Staff College in Toronto. Upon graduation he flew the F86 Sabre and the CF104 Starfighter and in 1969 became Commanding Officer of 422 Strike Attack Squadron at 4 Wing Baden Sollingen Germany.

Posted back to Ottawa in 1971 he was appointed Director of LRPA Requirements in the Long Range Patrol Aircraft Project Office. This culminated in the procurement of the Lockheed P3 Aurora to replace the Argus as Canada's maritime patrol aircraft. A year in Quebec City followed, then a posting back to Germany as Commander of 4 Fighter Wing at Baden Sollingen. Returning to Canada in 1977, he assumed command of the Aerospace Engineering Test Establishment at Cold Lake AB where he supervised all flight test activities for the Canadian Forces. In 1979, on promotion to Brigadier General, he was posted to Holland to join the NATO Airborne Early Warning Program Management Agency as Chief of the Military Factors Division, responsible for setting up the multinational force and the bases from which the NATO E3A would operate.

From 1981 to 1983 he served as the DND representative in the Privy Council Office, which proved to be a fascinating education in how the Canadian Parliamentary system works. In 1983 he was promoted to Major General and served three years as Commander, Canadian Forces Europe (CFE) in Lahr, Germany. CFE was the only truly integrated formation in the Canadian Forces having both operational and supporting air and land force units as well as a large civilian component under command. MGen Wightman retired from the forces in 1986 at the conclusion of what he still considers the most rewarding and satisfying appointment of his entire career. He returned to Ottawa where he became Senior Vice President of European Helicopter Industries Canada. In 1988 EHI successfully sold the Government of Canada the EH101 helicopter as the replacement for the Sea King helicopter. (Twenty-five years later we're still waiting!)

In 1989 MGen Wightman was appointed Assistant Deputy Minister Aviation in the Department of Transport, where he served 6 years until his retirement. He was responsible for the safety regulation of all commercial and private aviation, the operation of the Air Navigation System, the Air Traffic Control System, and the promotion and monitoring of aviation safety in Canada. While at Transport Canada he convinced nine public service unions, the aviation industry and the Government of Canada to privatize the Air Navigation System and create NAV CANADA. He also sought and obtained the agreement of the hundred or so countries of the International Civil Aviation Organization that smoking be banned completely on all international flights.

MGen Wightman retired in 1995 and moved to the British Columbia in 1997. He now lives in Victoria BC with his wife Tannis. They celebrated their 60th wedding anniversary on June 5, 2014. He was and he remains a source of inspiration to everyone he has touched.

About the Author

Fredrick Keith LaForge was born in Edmonton, Alberta, and was raised by loving parents on a farm near Sandholm. He attended Sandholm School, Thorsby Junior, and High Schools, and has many teachers to thank for their dedication to learning and discipline, of those; Stan Zurek and Frank Kozar were head of their class.

On graduation from high school Fredrick joined the Royal Canadian Artillery in 1962; he graduated from the Royal Canadian School of Artillery, Officer Candidate Program, and went on to command at every level from Second Lieutenant to Colonel in his 35 years of service with the Canadian Army and the Canadian Armed Forces. Fredrick married Vivian van Aggelen in Aug of 1967, Vivian is an understanding army wife, and together they proudly raised three successful children, all of who have produced grandchildren; the light and love of their families continues through their eyes.

During his career Fredrick served with the First Regiment, Royal Canadian Horse Artillery, Canadian Forces Base Gagetown, New Brunswick, and Delinghofen, Germany, 1963-1970. HQ, Second Canadian Brigade Mechanized Group, CFB Petawawa, Ontario, 1970-72. The Second Regiment Royal Canadian Horse Artillery, 1972-74; HQ Canadian Forces Europe, Lahr, West Germany, 1974-77.

National Defence HQ, Ottawa, On, 1978-79, The Third Regiment Royal Canadian Horse Artillery, CFB Shilo, Manitoba, 1979-83. Attended a French language course in CFB Winnipeg and St Jean sur Richelieu, Quebec, 1983-84. HQ Canadian Forces Europe, Executive Assistant to the Commander Canadian Forces Europe, Lahr, West Germany, 1984-85. NATO Defence College, Rome, Italy, 1984-85. Base Administrative Officer, CFB Lahr, West Germany, 1985-89. NDHQ Ottawa, Directorate of Industrial Relations, Ottawa, Ontario, 1989-90. He then served as a Canadian Forces Attaché, 1991-97 and was accredited to Italy, Greece, The Netherlands, Belgium, and Luxembourg.

Fredrick attended and greatly enjoyed the learning experiences acquired at Brandon University, The University of Manitoba (BA), the Canadian Army Staff Course, Kingston, Ontario, The Australian Army Staff College, Queenscliff, Victoria, and NATO Defence College, Rome, and the University of Rome.

On retirement, Fredrick founded and managed a successful consulting company, Quadrant Defence Consultants International, enjoying nearly sixteen years of working with international defence industries and the Canadian Armed Forces in their pursuit of equipping and supporting defence activities on a global scale.

Vimy Ridge A Box Full of Tears is Fredrick's third Novel; ***An Abundance Not Worth Sharing***, and, ***Unintentional Innocence*** are available in both print and e-book formats through Amazon.ca.

A man of all seasons, Fredrick will soon publish a book of poetry with Amazon.ca; **A Song For a Soldier** is a collection of military themed poetry written and crafted with the Canadian Armed Forces, Navy, Army and Air Force, their wives and sweethearts in mind and in rhyme.

CPSIA information can be obtained at www.ICGtesting.com
Printed in the USA
LVOW10s1105220516

489438LV00021B/1082/P